LYNN VROMAN

I0687552

BOOK 4 OF THE ENERGY SERIES

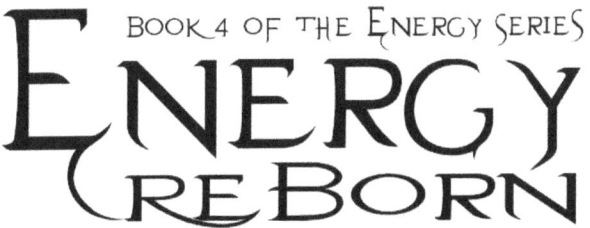

ENERGY
REBORN

Untold
Press

www.untoldpress.com

Energy Reborn

Published by Untold Press LLC
114 NE Estia Lane
Port St Lucie, FL 34983

ISBN: 978-0692622643

PRODUCED IN THE UNITED STATES OF AMERICA

10 9 8 7 6 5 4 3 2 1

DEDICATION

For Tori, Katie, Olivia, and Rhys. Always, everything is for you.

"Where love reigns the impossible may be attained."

~Native American Proverb

CHAPTER 1

TAREK

Target Practice

Crying didn't bother him anymore.

Muffled sobs used to feel like weevils burrowing into his brain. He had wanted the cries to disappear, find a way to silence them so he'd have peace while killing. He hated it, yet understood where the despair came from. He didn't take the truth that well either.

This world, his world, was full of people who weren't real people.

That revelation caused a collective shock to infiltrate every home, every secret corner. Memories of families were manufactured lies. Parents had never existed for most. Childhood thoughts were a farce before the age of six, the median age for bodies the Creation Lab produced before implanting energy pilfered from other worlds. Most would never be able to have children. They were all biobots, synthetic carriers for strong souls.

Tarek learned how to tune out the grief a while ago, and the truth. Issues he only dwelled on when alone–when killing didn't save him from his mind.

He adjusted his scope.

Yes, he could ignore the crying now. A perfect shot had that power.

Tarek lay on his stomach. Rooftop debris–broken syringes and jagged edges of crushed alcohol containers–dug through his sweatshirt. Sweat dribbled off his forehead to sting his eyes.

He ignored his discomfort as easily as the crying and flipped off the safety. Lights, never-ending strobes, bounced off buildings. Staring too long at the changing colors coming from billboard holograms and storefronts threatened a headache, but he managed to keep the jackasses in his sights.

Synod authority harassed a group of men on the street, demanding signed pardons most wouldn't have. The elders considered everyone a traitor.

They were right.

People in this sector *were* guilty of blowing up the capital building and crashing the satellite feeds. Heterodox citizens fought when Oren asked eight months ago, with a promise of truth. Truth, most had come to realize, wasn't such a great prize. Ignorance really was a gift.

Tarek had warned Oren not to tell them, not to reveal the true nature of how most citizens came to be. No Exemplian he had ever met wanted to find out their whole existence was a lie. But Oren believed differently. The man's belief cost them an army. Stupid to tell a mass of people who already dreaded life– beaten down by having too many lives–that what they struggled with wasn't even real.

Get it together.

None of that mattered. What mattered was getting a clear shot between the eyes. His finger hovered over the trigger, the sniper rifle firm in his grip. Zander's rifle. His aim wasn't as precise as Zander's, but he did all right. Tarek had adopted the gun seven months ago when the Guide decided to go back to Earth.

No, don't go there.

He couldn't handle that part of his life–the part who went to Earth with Zander.

Lena.

No.

He peered into the scope.

The second an authority Protector pulled out his gallium cuffs, about to cinch them around the wrists of a man begging on his knees, Tarek shot. Before the other Protector could pull out his weapon, Tarek took him out too.

The deaths didn't create a frenzy, not even when two energy orbs released from the Protectors' bodies and sailed to the sky, ultimately finding their way into the apartment building where Tarek hid. The would-be victims dragged the useless bodies into the shadows, to the garbage incinerators hidden there. Exemplians in this sector had their turmoil to deal with, and what was left of the Synod against them. They weren't cowards, though.

They refused to fight outright since the initial attack on the Creation Lab. But no one had ever complained when a mysterious bullet punctured the skull of an authority Protector. His shots seemed to wake up some of the citizens from a stupor, bringing them to action for a few minutes to get rid of the bodies. Tarek would take that; it'd be enough.

He refused to move from his spot. Where there were two, there were ten more. He searched the crowd through his scope, sweat turning his hoodie to soggy cotton against his back. There, right below the blank screens, were three more Protectors picking through the crowd to inspect the source of the commotion. They plowed through braver citizens willing to stand in their path, tasing them. People dropped to the dirty pavement, their bodies spasming from the high voltages.

Tarek remained steady.

Three...

Two...

11

One...
Pop! Pop! Pop!

The crowd swallowed up the bodies as the Protectors' energies raced into the building. For once, the noise quieted. All that echoed up to his spot was the distant hum of the incinerators, gobbling up bone and blood and flesh. Tarek squinted into his scope, his even breathing rhythmic, relaxing. No other authority assholes rushed the crowd.

A minute passed by.

Fifteen more followed.

No more targets were willing to meet his bullets.

Shame.

Five dead authority Protectors wasn't even a dent in the grand scheme of things. Plus side, those he'd killed wouldn't be coming back for another go at life. Their little army made sure of it eight months ago.

Tarek gave one more cursory search of the crowd in case any Protectors stepped from the shadows to scout the rooftops.

Nothing.

As he lowered his gun, a familiar dark blond mop coming toward this building caught his eye. He looked through his scope one more time.

Sonofabitch.

Not again.

Groaning, so he wouldn't give in and shoot the boy in the leg for being a pain in the ass, Tarek pushed to his feet and stalked to the rusted metal door. Eight flights of stairs separated him from the boy who refused to keep his scrawny butt on Earth, where it was safe.

Peter. Dumb boy.

Dumb, brave, anger-filled boy.

Peter wouldn't be able to get into the building without a code, and the only people he knew who had one wouldn't share it. But that hadn't stopped him from coming here every time something new stuck in his craw. Maybe it was a girl this time.

Or maybe he had another fight with a kid in school. Who knew?

Tarek made it to the lobby in under five minutes, the trek up and down the stairs a workout he'd performed about every day for the past seven months. The kid had already hit the stoop, waiting for some clueless resident to punch in their code so he could sneak in behind.

Usually when Tarek caught Peter here, he'd wait until the boy succeeded. The game amused him some days. Most days it irritated him. Drea, the boy's mother and former overseer of the Creation Lab, had been significant in the plan to destroy Cynosure. Now, she was crucial in the mission to take out the Synod elders who survived the attack, a feat not as easy as blowing up an entire compound and erasing centuries–millennia–of thievery and deceit. Not that destroying it had been easy.

Her only stipulation for helping was that Peter wasn't involved in *any* way with *any* plan they might come up with. Not an unreasonable demand–unless that kid happened to be a stubborn little prick who refused to accept the gift she gave him. Freedom.

Today, Tarek didn't wait for Peter to gain false hope on entry. He flung the door open with one hand–the other wrapped around his rifle–and dragged him in by his collar. Peter fought against the hold. Tarek gripped the boy's shirt tighter, cinching it around his skinny throat. As Peter groped for oxygen, no longer flailing around like an idiot, Tarek loosened his hold and flung the boy's lanky body to the ground.

Slinging the rifle strap over his shoulder, Tarek crossed his arms. "Give me one reason why I shouldn't cripple your legs."

The threat wasn't idle. Tarek had given the boy more than a few bumps and bruises in the last couple of months. That hadn't deterred the kid. Nothing had worked. Not even promises Tarek had no intention of keeping–promises of someday.

Someday, you can help the fight.

Someday, I'll come for you, and we can fight together.

Peter scooted until his back rested against a dingy wall with graffiti covering every inch. Mostly words. Two words, to be exact. NOT REAL. "I have every right to be here."

This argument turned old the first time the boy had given it to him. "No, you don't. If you stay, your mom is out. You can't do anything to help, unlike her." Tarek squatted until they were eye level. "So, again, for the hundredth time, stay away from here."

Peter wrapped his arms around his muddy knees and lifted his chin, his bottom lip trembling. "I don't belong anywhere else."

Tarek closed his eyes. *No.* The tears would soften him. "That's not true."

"Yeah? Do you have to live around a bunch of people who…who're like aliens? People with no fucking clue how the universe really is?"

Tarek smirked, despite the hurt lacing Peter's voice. Being around Lena had dirtied his language up well enough. He opened his eyes. "Be happy you don't have to put up with this mess."

"Don't. Don't tell me what I'm supposed to feel when you're hiding here." Peter's voice cracked, going high and again dipping low. "I'm not like them. I'm not even a real person!"

"I'm done." Tarek rose to his feet, pulling Peter up with him. "We're not doing this again. We're not."

"Fine. Whatever. Take me back. I'll just leave again."

Tarek yanked him up the stairs. Peter's sneakers smacked against the corroded metal as he stumbled. "Go ahead, come back here," Tarek said. "Next time I won't make sure you have a safe trip home. I'll throw your ass in the hanger and let the rats have their way with you."

That threat worked. But from experience dealing with the boy, it wouldn't work for long. Any threat–*anything*–fluttered right out of Peter's brain immediately after he went back to Earth. Another problem would arise–another issue the boy would refuse to deal with.

They trudged up the stairs, passing the third level where Tarek squatted in an abandoned apartment. Far enough away from Celeste to not feel her static but close enough to help when the occasional authority raid would infiltrate the building. The only things he kept in the place were a mattress, a few changes of clothes, weapons, and a computer system to communicate with Oren and Drea.

They hit the fourth floor, and Tarek let the scanner in the stairwell read his eye. Peter struggled in his grip, but Tarek held firm, giving him a shake. "Knock it off."

When the door clicked, Tarek shouldered it open and walked the few feet to home base. Celeste's place had been main headquarters since the rebellion started. Fuzz clogged his brain and drooped his eyelids once they reached the door. Peter became less combative, the static like a drug.

Celeste's pull grew stronger after the attack on Cynosure. Energy from dead Exemplians found its way to her. Oren believed Celeste was some sort of god. Drea believed she was like Winston: a more advanced manufactured being with massive power.

Knowing what it was to be a Warden, Tarek thought differently. To him, the answer was obvious. Celeste had to be an ancient like Belva. Unfortunately, while they all debated the issue, the woman suffered.

Oren swore Celeste was the key, though. The key to what, Tarek had no clue. But Drea had been holed-up in her private quarters in Shalen doing research to try to figure it out. Until she did, Tarek would spend his time playing target practice with the authority terrorizing Heterodox.

When the door opened, Tarek didn't bother with niceties. He tossed Peter through the entryway, ignoring his protest when he fell over the arm of a sofa. "Take him home."

Oren didn't even acknowledge the boy. He saved his scowl all for Tarek, not budging from the door. How the guy could stay in this apartment all day and not crumble under Celeste's power was a phenomenon. A few minutes and Tarek wanted a hammer to shatter his brain.

"Not this time," Oren said.

Impatience blackened Tarek's already crap mood. "Wrong answer."

Oren peered behind him when Celeste came from a back room. The first time they'd met her, Celeste helped Peter find his mother. Now, she helped keep him away from her. The greater good and all that. As she drew closer to Peter, he shrieked and clapped his hands over his ears.

Celeste backed up, the tattoo on her cheek changing colors. "I cannot even console this child."

Oren sighed and hung his head for a moment before lifting his gaze to her. "The boy doesn't need coddling, Cel. He needs a kick in the ass." He moved closer to her.

The static must've been killing the guy. Tarek clenched his fists and dug his nails into his flesh to prevent giving in to the urge to run–and he was twenty feet away from her.

Oren kissed the top of her head. "Go rest. I'll be there soon, and we can practice some more. You're so close, Cel. Almost there."

Tears brimmed in her violet eyes. Before Celeste left the room, she faced Tarek. "I thank you for your aid, Warden."

Celeste had called him Warden since he'd first met her. He hated it but never said anything. Tarek bowed to her, the action almost a compulsion. "Of course," he said.

When she left, Oren hauled Peter up from his fetal position on the floor. "You can't keep coming here. It's not safe."

"But I want to stay…with you. F-fight."

"Someday, maybe. But not now."

Tarek didn't miss the compassion softening Oren's scowl. He loved the boy, an obvious fact after Oren took Peter under his wing in Arcus.

Oren hugged him for all of two seconds before heaving him toward Tarek, the man's usual scowl back and on full blast. "You take him. Last time I went, I couldn't open a portal for weeks."

The Synod elders had some strong Protectors in their ranks. At least one was able to lock the lines for a while, trapping everyone in and barring everyone else out.

Because of that situation, Oren had a valid argument. He was the only one able to be near Celeste without collapsing. The contact had taken a toll; the dark circles under the guy's eyes and his pale face resembled those walking shells in Heterodox–those who had been reborn too many times. But Oren stayed, his willpower obviously as strong as granite.

"Damn it." Tarek snatched up Peter, who now had a mean dose of static and couldn't fight a dung beetle. "Fine."

Oren grinned. His too-pretty face, regardless of its zombie hue, lit up with challenge. "What? You're still avoiding a certain skinny, loud-mouthed woman?"

"Conversation's over." His voice grew quiet, almost a whisper.

"Maybe it's time you faced your green-eyed demon." Oren sighed. "Not that I don't appreciate you being here, but–"

"I'll be back." Tarek pushed the kid into the hall.

"Well, then tell Winston hello for me, will you? I mean, that's what you'll do, right? Ask him to take Peter back so you won't have to?"

No more. He wouldn't talk about it anymore. Tarek turned into the hall. "See you soon, asshole."

"Wait," Oren said, his voice almost desperate. "Do one thing for me?"

The irritation scratching his brain lifted some. "I'll let Grace know you're still alive, still an asshole."

"Yes, but..." Oren paused. "Tell her I'm–she's in my heart." Grace, Oren's Guide in the past. The only person, besides Celeste and Peter, who could breach the shield Oren constructed around himself.

"I'll tell her."

"And maybe try going to Earth, after."

"No. I'll see you soon." Tarek shoved Peter farther into the hallway and closed the door on Oren's face.

The last place where he'd ever step foot was Earth. The last. Which meant a detour and a possible unwanted vacation in Arcus if the lines locked up. Seeing as how the kid was here, Exemplar was obviously open, but not for long. It usually only took hours, and the lines would have their no-trespassing sign up again.

Tarek scanned the hallway before raising his hand in the air. As the atmosphere crackled, he tightened his hold on Peter's sweatshirt in case the boy tried to fight him as they went through the portal.

Oren was wrong.

He wasn't trying to *avoid* Lena.

He was trying to save her.

CHAPTER 2

TAREK

Homebound

This place stirred up too much in his head. Colors here were so vivid the cheerfulness mocked anyone who desired pain.

Lena had told him she loved him the first time in these symmetrical woods.

He also lost her here–twice. The day he had killed Casimir, and again, right after he died.

Depression from rebirth was typical. He knew that. Every Exemplian knew it. Problems followed from previous lives, no matter how infinitesimal. They festered and grew into an exaggerated mountain when life was forced back into the body. No one understood why, but sorrow came with the deal until it faded. For Tarek, this death and rebirth were…different.

Not real.

He couldn't give Lena a future–children, a family. She deserved someone who could. Someone normal. Someone not produced with machines, lab-grown organs, and scientists as creators.

His grip on Peter's sweatshirt tensed until the fabric tore.

"Hey, let go. I know how to walk by myself." With Celeste's effect evaporated from his brain, Peter reverted to his usual pissed-off self.

Which helped bring Tarek out of his head. Good. "Don't do anything dumb," he said.

He released Peter, tossing him in black soil. Squid complained from treetops but didn't come down to investigate. The animals knew who the enemy was, and who wasn't, after all these years. Hell, Tarek had been their Warden for almost three of them.

The boy jumped up and raised his lanky arm in the air. Nothing. Exemplian lines buttoned up tight already. Perfect. Of course they'd leave right before lockdown.

"Now what, boy?" Tarek kicked at some snake-like animals with legs crawling up his boots. "Wait, I got it. How about you take yourself back to Earth without an escort? Save everyone the hassle."

"Why don't you take me? *Wait, I got it.* You're a pussy."

Tarek rammed Peter against a tree, his rage instant. "You want to test that assumption?"

Fear tightened Peter's face. "Go ahead. End it. I don't care."

Shit. Tarek set the boy down and smoothed the wrinkles he'd put in the Penn State hoodie Lena had always worn. "I liked you better before you went to Earth."

Peter's bottom lip trembled. "Me too."

Poor kid. "Let's go. I'm sure Belva knows we're here by now."

Not saying another word, Tarek headed for the path leading to the village. Belva managed to control the weather so much better than he ever could. The tropical temperature that usually plagued the forest saturated the atmosphere still, but the humidity had turned down a few notches. Belva loved it here; his past burdens her joy. Her child, she swore was a girl, would rule Arcus. A True Warden, with the natural power to heal a broken world.

"Why do you all make me stay there?"

Peter's tortured voice slapped at Tarek's ears. No matter how many times he had told the boy why, he'd repeat it. Repeat it until it sank in. "Because your mother asked us to keep you safe."

"She's not my mother. She's a DNA donor."

Tarek stopped and bowed his head. The same answer Peter gave every time. He didn't have any more energy to argue about it. Not today. Since he was stuck here, all he felt like doing was dropping Peter off on Winston's doorstep and escaping to his cabin by the river until Exemplar's lines opened up. "Whether you want to accept her or not, what she wants, we'll give." He met the boy's sneer. "I don't care what your issues are outside of that."

"You're a bastard." The boy's face scrunched as though Tarek had punched him in the gut.

"I know." Tarek continued forward.

They were almost to the clearing when a clicking gun interrupted the forest's normal chatter. Tarek became a statue, and Peter's tromping feet silenced. Even if the boy was a pain in the ass, he was also a trained fighter. A clicking weapon called for instant alertness. With steady hands, Tarek shrugged his rifle off his shoulder. Extra fuzz in his head indicated the perpetrator was a Protector.

Tarek scouted the terrain with his rifle butted against the inside of his shoulder. He couldn't see anything. *Where are you?*

Laughing filled the trees. "Well, holy hell, brother. I barely recognized you." Farren's bright red hair, even brighter from living on Arcus, appeared from the shadows. "You finally cut off all that purdy hair. The ladies aren't going to like it."

Tarek fingered his shorter hair. "It got in the way."

"We can't have that, can we?" Farren holstered his gun and clapped Tarek on the shoulder. "It's good to see you.

21

Everybody's going to flip their shit. Hey, Winston managed to scavenge some scotch during his last trip to Earth. Looks like we now have an excuse to break open the bottle."

Farren's personality infected everyone around him. Now that he was about to be a father, his positivity, which glowed before, was magnified by a thousand.

Tarek slung his rifle over his shoulder. "Sounds like a plan." He eyed Peter, who had a slight grin on his tear-stained face. "First I need to convince Winston to haul him back home."

Farren nodded to the boy. "Nah, let him stay the night, have a drink with us."

"He's barely fifteen."

Peter's grin disappeared on his way past both men. "Seriously…bastard."

As Peter trekked down the hill to the village, Farren whistled. "You upset him good this time."

"Nothing new."

Farren palmed Tarek's shoulder again. "He'll get over it. But let him stay for a minute. If the boy's old enough to fight with us, he's old enough for a shot."

Tarek shook his head, starting for the village. "He doesn't fight with us anymore, and no, he can't stay. Lena's probably a good mix of pissed and worried about now."

Farren fell into step beside him with a chuckle. "Yeah, I'd hate to be him when he gets home."

People swarmed them as they made it down the hill. Jake and Jacie, who decided they liked living on Arcus better than Earth, rushed to greet him. Belva waddled after. She glowed. Literally. An ethereal light glimmered around her, and her golden eyes glittered like jewels. She was beautiful before, but devastatingly so now.

Once Tarek hugged Jacie and shook Jake's hand, he folded the future Warden's mother into his arms, lifting her off the ground. If it weren't for Belva, if fate had never sent her here,

Tarek would be chained to this world, chained to responsibility too important for him to handle properly. She wasn't a god, but she was his savior.

"Welcome home." She wrapped her arms around his neck, her tinkling laughter a salve against his ear.

He set her down. "It's good to be here."

Tarek caught Winston standing behind the crowd with his arms crossed over his chest. He gave him a half salute and waved at Shaina, who'd already attached herself to Peter. She jabbed her finger into his skinny chest then hugged him, those two actions on repeat. In the middle of her tirade, she took her attention off Peter long enough to smile at Tarek before shuffling the boy inside her cabin.

"Hey, brother, careful with my lady." Farren pulled Belva close, caressing her swollen stomach. "My little girl is itching to get out."

The love shining on Belva's face when she looked up at Farren tore at Tarek's heart. Jealousy wasn't a fun emotion. Not. At. All.

He pasted on a smile. "Your daughter is lucky to have such incredible parents."

"Parents." Farren let out a nervous laugh. "Scary as hell."

"You'll be here, right? When she's born?" Belva raised an eyebrow, daring him to say no.

How could he say no? He wanted to say no. "Looks like I'm here for a few weeks." He winked, even as his lungs constricted and his feet demanded to head back into the woods to wallow. "Think she'll show up before I go?"

Belva beamed and reached up to kiss his cheek. "You might have to stay longer. Six more weeks to go, according to Shaina's calculations."

No, he wouldn't be staying, but he needn't tell her that. "Her calculations are usually spot on," Tarek said.

Shaina wasn't only Winston's woman. She was also Arcus's official medical staff. And she was usually right, except for when she had tried to get him to take medication after he recycled. She swore the capsules would help the depression. Tarek assured her they wouldn't. Nothing but time would siphon out the poison from rebirth.

Belva squeezed his hand. He glanced down to sympathy in her eyes.

Tarek cleared his throat and grinned at her before giving everyone else his attention. They all used to think of him as their leader, and by the uncertainty on their faces, some appeared to see him in that light still. "It's good to be home, everyone."

Relief flooded eyes and created smiles. They'd all want news on the happenings in Exemplar. Mostly, everyone would want to know how Oren held up, if he lived…if he would ever come back.

"Oren is alive and well, and cranky as ever. He sends his love."

Grace pushed through the crowd and hugged him. "Thank you."

Her fragile body trembled, and her tears bled through his sweatshirt. Tarek held her a moment longer before pulling away. "He wanted me to tell you his heart is with you."

Grace's tears poured then, following the creases on her aged face. "When you return, tell him that…" Her voice hitched. "Tell him that I'm always here."

"I will." He then focused on the crowd. "I need to talk with Winston, make sure Peter arrives home safely. I promise to fill you in on the details after."

Tarek signaled to Winston, tipping his head toward the tree line. He didn't wait for acknowledgment; Winston would follow. Even if he could be an ass at times, the stronger Protector–the strongest–had enough respect to let Tarek do his groveling in private.

Once they made it close to the river, to where his cabin was in view, Tarek turned. Winston stood behind him. "Will you take him home?"

Winston, always cool, crossed his dark arms, showing off all the tattoos riding up the length of them. "When do you think you're gonna have the balls to take him yourself?"

"It's not about balls, Winston." His voice was quiet, almost nonexistent. Fury tended to swallow it.

Winston, unfazed, smirked. "Looks that way to me." He sauntered closer, his arms still crossed as if daring Tarek to take a swing. "You seem all right. Like you're back to normal and shit. Why not go? Claim what's waiting for you there?"

"I can't." Tarek backed up a few steps as Winston moved forward. "I…I'm not good enough for her."

"She don't seem to agree with you." Winston cocked his head to the side. "Can't say I agree with you, either."

"I'm not what she needs. I can't give her what she deserves." He jammed his fingers through his short hair, gripping the tips hard. "I'm not real."

Winston laughed–more like snarled.

"You need to realize, I–"

Winston waved his hand and sent Tarek flying into a tree. His head bounced against the bark, slicing his temple.

"You breathing, ain't you? Your heart beating? You bleed like any *real* person I ever met." He swiped a finger across Tarek's temple, and blood smeared his fingertip. "See?"

Tarek didn't struggle against Winston's hold; there wasn't a point. He was frozen on that tree with a fresh gash on his head and pain in his chest. "You don't understand."

"You serious?" Winston flung his hand in the air, and Tarek dropped to the ground. "Last time I checked, you and I come from the same biotechnology cloth. *I'm real*, and I don't care how I got that way."

Tarek wobbled to his feet, ignoring the wet soil saturating his pants. "No matter what you say, *I* can't feel different."

"Fine, I'm done talking about it. But this…this is the last time I go there for you."

He'd take that. "Thank you."

"Man…" Winston sighed, his shoulders almost reaching his ears. All his wrath from moments ago transformed to concern, his dark eyes swimming in it. "Lena's waiting. Don't make her wait forever–because she will. And that, you whiny sonofabitch, is the cruelest thing you could do to her."

CHAPTER 3
LENA

Waiting

He'd be back soon. He would.

I had to believe it, play it on repeat inside my brain, or panic would force me to throw stuff against walls. Starting with all the science fiction action figures Peter had collected over the last eight months, the only hobby he found here that calmed him.

Yeah, he'd come back, like always. Usually with an escort, Oren or Winston, but he'd return. We'd talk. Well, I'd talk, and he'd stand there, not even pretending to listen anymore. Everything would get worked out; a Band-Aid slapped nice and tight over the real issues neither of us was brave enough to talk about.

Peter couldn't hack it here, but I'd be damned if I stopped forcing him to keep trying. The kid deserved to be happy, and I'd beat the shit out of him with words, and fists if necessary, until he was.

But again, for at least the ninth time, Peter had left. It would've been nice if he did me a favor and sneaked out like a normal fifteen-year-old. Maybe climb out the window to drink a pilfered six-pack with buddies. That'd be awesome. No, he could open lines to other worlds, places I didn't have the ability to follow.

Soon as the wind had blown hours before, I ran to his room. Again, too late. Always too late with that kid, and like every time I was late, I had plopped down on the old recliner in his room and waited for him to come home–be dragged home, actually.

I lifted my phone: 3:00 a.m.

Tomorrow was gonna be a long day. Longer if Peter managed to go undetected. That didn't happen often. He usually went to the same place: to talk to Oren. Peter spent more time pleading with Oren lately, especially after school started.

Didn't young kids like school? With girls and shit?

Naïve of me to think so. I'd hated school when I went.

My phone dinged, interrupting both my thoughts and the finger tapping against the arm of the chair. *He back yet?*

Zander. He and Erin lived in Jake's old place, right below mine. The four of us were a sort of family. A screwed up family who had more issues than even Freud would've wanted to pick apart.

I answered: *Not yet.*

Let us know when he does.

Me: *Will do.*

Erin went to Exemplar once for Peter the second time he had escaped through the lines. Zander went with her, the best at convincing Peter to do anything. She swore after she came back that she'd never go there again.

I had never gone.

The nightmares were enough for me. Every time I closed my eyes, flashes of the last three and a half years hit replay.

Whatever. Came with the package, I guess.

I sat in that chair for four long hours, staring at the unmade bed with action figures lined up on the headboard. Peter thought they were funny, Earth's idea of future evolution, and all the science fiction paraphernalia that came with it. He had when we arrived anyway, during the first month. Everything went to hell after that, when the shock wore off and reality set in.

Shit.

Shit.

Shit.

Another hour passed before a hole split the atmosphere. Like a child being born, Winston plummeted through the crack with Peter under his arm, struggling against the hold.

I jumped off the chair, my legs wobbly from inactivity. When the hole closed and both Protectors had feet on the ground, Winston tossed Peter on the rumpled sheets. "Past your bedtime, Pete."

Peter stayed there a minute, looking from me to Winston, then pushed off the mattress and stormed to the door.

Well, hell no. I blocked his path. His face, bright with Arcus color, so young and sad—I wrestled between slapping some sense into him and hugging him. I settled for talking. "You can't keep doing this."

Tears brightened his light eyes, and his bottom lip trembled. "Why won't you let me go?" He held up his hands. "*Please*, just let me go."

"Never."

He put his head down, his thin shoulders shaking.

Hugging won. It won every time. I pulled his lanky body in and stood on my toes to kiss his cheek. Who cared about what Drea wanted? Even if she hadn't stipulated Peter stay away from Exemplar in exchange for her help, I'd still have a hard time letting him go. He deserved to be happy.

Why the hell couldn't I make him happy?

I wouldn't explain things to him again. Besides, I'm sure he got an earful before his forced trip home–to a safe room with nothing but school to worry about.

Unless you spent your entire life training, fighting another world, and then finding out you were a lab creation.

If only I could take his pain away…

Once his sobs died down to sniffles, I released him and pasted on my most believable smile. "Go. Take a shower, and clean yourself up. You have school in…oh…about three hours." I held up my phone to show him the time.

"They suspended me, remember?"

I peeked over my shoulder at Winston. "We'll fix it."

He didn't react. No anger, no sorrow. Just a blank face and empty eyes. "Okay." He scooted around me and went to the bathroom.

I didn't acknowledge Winston until I was sure no portals were opening. Peter had only pulled that once, but that one time was bad. Really bad. It took Zander hours to calm him down when Erin dragged him back, their first and last trip to Exemplar.

When the shower turned on, I faced Winston, who lounged on the bed, the television already on. As he clicked through channels, only infomercials and sitcom reruns from the eighties, I flopped down beside him. The strong urge to cuddle next to him washed through me. But I abstained.

I missed him, all of them. Unfortunately, being around them meant danger always hid in the corners. I'd had enough danger to last me lifetimes.

"Tarek brought him to you, didn't he?"

"Bingo."

I already knew the answer. Of course I did. When Oren found Peter, he'd bring him back and leave right after, in case the lines closed to Exemplar. The last time Oren came, he wasn't quick enough and had to stay here for almost a month. I loved the guy, but he was a pain in the ass when his anxiety acted up.

When Winston came, it was because Oren refused to bring Peter home. Same routine, all the time. Tarek would go to Arcus and hand Peter off so he wouldn't have to face me.

If he'd come through the portal, one time…

Winston tapped the remote against his thigh, his eyes on the screen. "You gonna stare at me or talk?"

I fidgeted with the bedspread, trying to find something to say. "So, how's everyone? Belva and Farren? Mom and Jake?"

Winston finally tilted his head my way. "Everyone's fine. Belva's gonna pop any second, and your mom chases her like a shadow. She always that…ah…motherly?"

"Yeah, always." I slid closer to his side. "And…you and Shaina, everything okay?"

The right side of his mouth curved up. "Yeah."

"Well, good. That's good."

He kept looking at me with that smirk, waiting for the inevitable.

I gave in, my face on fire. "And Tarek? Is he doing…good?"

"He's getting there, Tainted. Has to stay in Arcus a while 'cause the lines closed up on him. Hopefully that doesn't set him back. He don't like staying there for long." Winston focused on the television. "Told you he needs time."

"It's been eight months." If I had the nerve, I'd have Winston take me to Arcus so I could confront my giant, but Tarek's sanity wasn't something I was willing to gamble with. Seeing me might set his recovery back, too.

Winston shifted his weight, causing the bed to dip. "Eight months in Exemplian time is like five minutes."

"Well, he's not running on Exemplian time anymore. He only has normal time now, and eight months is a long time in normal time!" I hadn't meant to yell, and sure as hell hadn't meant for tears to fall.

I wipe the wetness from my cheeks with a sleeve, trying to pull it together. Winston didn't respond to my outburst. He was used to them by now.

I gave in and snuggled against him. He didn't pull me close, but he didn't prod me away. A plus. I needed his strength. As much as I hated to admit it, the past eight months sucked. A twenty-year-old, no doubt with a healthy dose of PTSD raised a fifteen-year-old boy with two other semi-unstable people. A boy who also had a mind full of all-fucked-up. Yeah, not how I had envisioned my life at this point.

We watched TV in silence, the distant tinkling sounds of the shower in tandem with the boxed laughter coming from the screen. I concentrated on the steady beat of his heart. It soothed my nerves enough to realize I had succumbed to snuggling with Winston, the badass who underneath was one of the noblest people I'd ever known. His silent strength gave me back mine.

I could do this: raise Peter and make him happy. Live here and run the movie theater with Zander and Erin, too, as we had been doing for eight months. I'd try to live a normal life, try to cope with the nightmares swirling in my head.

Winston was the first to break the silence. "What triggered it this time?"

"A fight at school. Some kid called him a retard or something."

"That it?"

Normally, kids wouldn't get all riled up by a bit of name-calling. Peter, a trained fighter who'd been through more than any kid had a right to, reacted sensitively to any provocation.

Anything.

"Peter blackened the kid's eye and slammed his head inside a toilet." I sat up. "Since you're here, you think you could...fix it for him?"

He shook his head, his famous smirk in place. "How many times you want me to mess with that principal's mind?"

I shrugged. "As many as it takes."

"Dude's gonna be a drooling idiot if I do it too much more."

"He's already an idiot."

Winston chuckled and clicked on another channel. "All right, but tell the kid I'm taking his bed."

I left his side to stand, stretching my arms and legs. "Deal. He can have mine; I'll take the couch."

"Whatever."

"Yeah, okay, whatever right back at you." I went to the door and hesitated. "Winston? Thank you. For everything."

He gave me his attention long enough to say, "Like I always tell you, Tainted. I'm with you."

Thank God, he was.

I left the room, closing the door behind me.

Lynn Vroman

CHAPTER 4

LENA

Back to Reality

One sound in the morning annoyed me more than any alarm clock: someone pounding on the door. At least the irritating *beep beep beep* of an alarm went away after a few hard thwacks against the snooze button. But knowing who thumped on my door–thanks to the fuzz blanket in my brain–that grating noise wouldn't go away as easily.

"Come in already! You have a goddamn key, for Christ's sake." I rolled over and slammed a pillow over my head, the couch not as comfortable as my bed. It also didn't help that I had barely slept.

A few clicks and the door breezed open and shut. Without having to come out of hiding from under the pillow, I heard Zander flop his ass in the chair next to the couch. He said nothing at all, just sat there, spreading his static all over the place.

After what had to have been two minutes of zilch, I pushed up my sun shield to find his phone in my face. I squinted, taking a good look at it. "What?"

He pushed it closer. "Do you see anything there?"

I scooted up to rest my back against the arm of the couch and shrugged, clinging to my pillow and my patience. "No? Should I?"

"Why, yes, Lena, yes you should see something there." He flipped it to view the screen himself, glowering. "But you're right, there's nothing, nada, not one message."

Oh... Oh, right. Forgot to text him. "Shit, sorry. But damn, Erin probably felt Winston and Peter."

"It's called being courteous. Google it." He stood and crammed the phone in the back pocket of his jeans. "And you owe like five bucks to the jar."

Since we'd come back, we all decided to become decent role models for Peter. Erin suggested a swear jar. Needless to say, I put a healthy chunk of my paycheck in it every week.

"Not fair. You woke me up." I got up and snatched my wallet off the kitchen counter.

"That don't matter. You couldn't stop swearing if someone held you at gunpoint."

I laughed, with no humor in it at all, and stuffed a five in the jar next to the fridge. "I've had people hold me at gunpoint, remember? That made the swearing worse."

"Aren't you funny." Zander rested his elbows on the counter while I fumbled around to make coffee. Hated it black, but with enough French vanilla creamer in it, I could down the sludge for the caffeine buzz.

"Nope, it's not funny at all, unfortunately." I turned on the pot and leaned against the sink, arms crossed over my chest. After a deep breath, I said, "I don't know how much longer we're gonna be able to keep him here."

I didn't want to admit that aloud, but this was Zander. We'd been through so much together, and I could tell him anything, knowing he'd get it. And I did tell him everything. All the time, like my own weird therapy. The favor went both ways, though. I was his soundboard as much as he was mine.

Zander tapped the old laminate countertop. "I guess we'll have to come up with a better incentive for him to want to stay."

"Like what?" I made sure to whisper, not wanting Peter to hear. "What can we offer him that will take his pain away? We're as fucked up as he is." Without Zander having to say anything, I dug into my wallet again and added another dollar to the jar.

He grinned, saying nothing about the swearing. "We'll think of something. But around that age, the chance of getting some ass was enough to make me do almost anything." He pulled a dollar from his pocket and handed it over. "Put that in there, will you?"

I slipped it in and rolled my eyes. "So, what are you saying? We become his matchmakers? And I know you're not talking about *getting ass* from me, Alexander Kline. That'll win you a throat punch."

He laughed and held up his hands. "Hey, play nice. I didn't mean you. I had a life before I came here, believe it or not. Not much of one, but I did stuff."

So crazy, all those years ago, like a dream. Both of us teenagers, hanging out in school, dating for like three days…him trying to get me killed. *Ah, simpler times.*

"Congratulations," I said. "But let's hold off on pimping the kid out. Winston's gonna clean up the school mess this morning before he heads back to Arcus. That'll help some."

"All right, your call." Zander plucked an apple from the bowl sitting next to his elbow. "But my vote is finding him some ass."

"Ugh, you're an idiot." I threw a dishrag at his face as he bit into his apple. "Any little whores I find near him—"

"Hey."

We both spun to Peter standing in the hallway, ready for school with his backpack hung over his shoulder.

"Hey, yourself." I pushed from the sink and gave him a hug, wishing the contact could erase the emptiness on his face. Maybe we *should* find him a girl. "You sleep okay? Well, for the three hours you had to sleep?"

He pulled away and nodded to Zander. "Hey, man." After Zander's wave, Peter gave his attention back to me. "Yeah, sure. Um, Winston said he'd take me. I'll see you at work after school, okay?"

So much I wanted to say, words he'd heard a thousand times before. We needed someone to blame, someone all of us could throw our anger at, clean it from our bodies so we could move on.

I forced a smile. "Yeah, sounds good. You have kitchen duty tonight, so be on time."

Peter smiled, too, a smile that didn't quite make it to his eyes. "I'll be there."

I wished for magic words to funnel from my lips. Nope. Nothing. Wilma would've known what to say. Her way of making things right only sounded biting coming from my mouth. I hadn't perfected the dumbass pep talk yet. "We're gonna figure this shit out. I promise."

That smile on his face so obviously struggled to stay there. "Don't forget to add a dollar." He then went to the front door and grabbed keys off the hook. "Tell Winston I'll be in the car."

"Yeah, ok–"

He shut the door on my voice.

Damn.

I stared, willing for Peter to walk back in and miraculously be cured. Have him revert to that innocent boy I first met. When I almost killed him.

No wonder he couldn't get over the muck clogging his mind.

"Tainted." Fingers snapped. "Hey, how many times do I got to say your name?"

I turned to Winston pouring coffee into a Styrofoam cup, not looking at me, just pouring and snapping his fingers. "Oh, um…sorry."

He mumbled a greeting to Zander and finally gave me his attention as he blew on the top of his drink. If I hadn't known better, I would've sworn concern clouded his dark eyes. "He'll be fine. Don't worry."

"No, he won't." I massaged my temples. "I need to fix this."

"Told you, get him laid."

"He's fifteen! Stop saying that." I punched Zander in the shoulder. "Sex doesn't cure everything."

Winston snorted. "It helps."

Zander laughed, holding up his fist to Winston, who gave it a bump.

I scowled at both of them. "Men are dumbasses." I pointed to Winston. "Get him to school before he's late. And…tell everyone I miss them when you get back home."

Winston ambled to the door. "Will do. See y'all next time."

I rushed forward. "Winston? Tell *everyone*. Okay?"

He opened the door, and said, "I got you, Tainted, no worries. I'll tell him even if I have to beat it into his stubborn head."

My shoulders relaxed. That'd be enough.

For now.

∞ ∞ ∞

By the time I got ready for work and made it outside, Jake's Range Rover had returned to the driveway. Since I hadn't gotten any calls from the school, I assumed Winston had taken care of everything and headed home.

A sting zapped my heart. I missed Arcus. Maybe… *No*. I had to give this whole staying in one world and living a normal

39

life a shot. Not only for me, but also for Peter. I had to show him it could be done, lead by example.

I trudged to the car. God, I hated being an example.

Erin came out from her apartment to follow. "Hey, lady," she said. "Long night, huh?"

"Yeah, you could say that."

Erin was a dichotomy I appreciated. A badass fighter who could throw together a gourmet meal and talk poetry like no one's business, the latter talents I hadn't discovered until we came back to Earth. Most of the time, Zander, Peter, and I would listen to her with blank faces. But even though none of us understood a thing she'd say, when she recited poetry, it'd bring tears to my eyes. The saddest music I'd ever heard.

I opened the driver door as Zander shuffled out of their apartment. "Look, ah, sorry…for not texting you. It gets crazy, you know?"

She smiled over the roof of the car and thumbed for Zander to take the backseat. "I get it, trust me. I knew he was home. Zander…he worries."

"Yeah. Just so many dumb things going on at once." I picked at the chipped paint on the top of the door. "I'm not good at the parenting gig, much less co-parenting."

"Stop making excuses. Even *if* Erin feels static, I want to be sure it's from one of ours." Zander pulled Erin in and kissed her. "And I'll let you have shotgun today, only because of this morning."

Erin's face flamed as Zander's smug ass jumped in the back.

"Really, Zander? You have to include me in those conversations?" I hopped in the car, Erin doing the same. Winston was kind enough to leave the keys in the ignition.

"Let's call it payback," he said.

Right. I used to say cringe-worthy, uncomfortable things after Tarek and I–damn. I wanted to have the gift to say those things again.

"I guess that's fair." I zoomed out of the driveway without looking in my rearview mirror. A truck behind us squealed his breaks, and a horn pierced our ears. When I did manage to glance in the mirror, I caught a pretty little birdie, just for me, hanging out in dude's windshield. I gave the guy a wave and sped off to the first stoplight.

"I hate when you do that." Zander clicked on his seatbelt then smacked the back of my seat.

Yeah, a little payback of my own. "Sorry. Forgot to check."

Erin laughed, snapping her seatbelt in place. "You two are seriously five years old."

"No, she's working to get us killed. I, on the other hand, was expressing appreciation for my woman."

I snorted. "I think you have it wrong. You're hers, not the other way around."

Another look in the rearview mirror showed Zander leaning back with his hands behind his head and a huge grin on his face. "I'm all right with that. She knows I'm hers."

"Aren't I the luckiest girl in the world?" Erin reached behind to squeeze Zander's knee, and with all sarcasm gone, she added, "I am, though."

"You and me both–the guy version of that," Zander said, his voice soft.

Even as I smiled, my heart ached. Jealousy sucked.

We drove the rest of the way in silence. I made sure not to pull out in front of anyone, and Zander made sure not to rub his sex life in my face. Win-win as far as I was concerned.

But soon after we parked behind the theater, Zander interrupted the quiet. "Do you guys miss it? I mean, this life we have here, it's easy, but all the action, the unknown, do either of you ever want it again?"

I shook my head and glimpsed at Erin.

She clamped her fists on her lap. "Don't start this now, Zander. Don't."

Before I could ask anything, she threw open her door and stormed out. Zander and I watched her fumble through her purse until she pulled out the keys and opened the door.

I turned to Zander. "Touchy subject?"

"Yeah. Don't get me wrong, this is great, all the domestic bliss, but we're sitting on the sidelines while Oren's fighting almost all by himself."

"That was Oren's choice. He could've walked away like we did." A heavy cocktail of anger, anxiety, and regret teemed through my body. "They're finally leaving us alone, and...we can't keep fighting. *I* can't keep doing it. We lost so much, Zander. Too much." Stupid tears. I hated how they showed up every time we took the lid off the past.

"Hey, no, don't cry." Zander rubbed his face with a yell and punched the roof. After a few seconds, he rested his elbows on the back of the front seats. "Sorry. You're right. Dumb of me to bring it up."

"I wish...I wish we could just be happy. I want to be happy so bad it's eating my insides."

"I know. Sorry, Lena."

"So you miss it? You want to go to Exemplar? Fight?"

He thumbed a tear off my cheek. "I'm supposed to say no, aren't I?"

"Yes." My voice came out like strangled air.

"Well, then no, I don't miss it."

"Liar."

CHAPTER 5

LENA

Desperate Decisions

Tuesdays weren't busy, which none of us minded. The downtime gave Zander the chance to catch up on bookwork while Erin and I cleaned until opening.

Weekdays, we did one matinee without opening the kitchen until four. By 1:20, the back showroom filled up for the current romantic film geared toward housewives. We got that crowd often when some romance movie played. A ton of women came alone to be swept off their feet. A couple hours of fantasy before going home to husbands who fell asleep right after dinner.

Housewives weren't the only guilty love-seekers. I had watched the present movie like twenty times already.

I might not have been in the Lonely Ladies club, but I was human, and I loved watching love. Tarek, though...he knew romance. With only a look, a touch, he made me feel like the only person in a room.

His absence was like a missing limb, the phantom pain sharp enough to keep me awake at night.

Toward the ending of the movie, a happy one that always made me cry, my phone dinged. Erin's picture sat next to the message, ***Peter's here***.

I stood from the back row and stretched my legs. What happened in this very showroom never failed to jump on my psyche. The first time I realized things weren't so black and white in the world. Casimir tried to pull me into Arcus in this room. I remembered the terror–and the fear that I was going crazy at seventeen.

A real smile curved my lips. That memory made me happy. Never said I wasn't messed up.

The quick flash of light caused a few women to grumble when I left the room. *I feel you, ladies.* Nothing worse than someone getting in between a woman and her heart.

Peter stood in the lobby, his backpack hiked on his shoulder. He gripped the strap like a shield. "You watched that movie again?"

No anger or frustration marred his face. Even the emptiness lifted some. Relief forced me to hug him. I wished it were as much a comfort to him as it was for me.

I found myself wishing for so many things these days.

"What can I say? I'm a romantic. School go okay?"

He laughed. The sound like music. Like the sad poetry Erin recited for us. "No, you're not. And yeah, it went fine. Winston washed Darren's mind, too. The dick thinks he got his black eye from falling off his bed, beating off."

Darren was to Peter what Belva was to me in high school.

"Yuck. You owe a dollar, and–what's wrong with you guys? Not funny at all." I laughed, though. Whatever made Peter happy, even if temporary, made me happy.

"Nah, it was funny. And 'dick' isn't a swearword." Peter pulled away, holding that strap tighter. "Darren refused to look up all day. People asked him how he got it, and his face turned so red it looked like it might explode."

"Hmm, sounds like Winston hit close to Darren's extracurricular activities. The kid must spend a lot of time with…ah…himself." I gestured to the kitchen. "Enough of that. Go on, get ready. Slow night, so do homework during the lulls."

"Yeah, sure, whatever." He waved to Erin as she came up to us. "Um, Lena? I'm sorry. I…"

He didn't finish, and I wouldn't make him. "I know. Go, I'll be in once the showings start, help you clean up."

"Okay."

Erin intercepted him for a hug. She whispered in his ear, and he nodded with a weak smile before disappearing through the kitchen door. Concern creased Erin's brow as she watched him walk in. She came over and rested an arm on my shoulders as we kept vigil on the kitchen door. "Have any ideas?"

We continued to stare. Peter escaping through lines always weighed on our minds, especially when he was able to be alone for more than thirty seconds. My brain checked off all the possible ideas that would give our boy an incentive to stay. None sounded at all plausible–except Zander's idea.

Peter was fifteen, and every fifteen-year-old kid I had ever met thought about one thing the majority of the time. A sigh lifted my shoulders, a sort of push from my mind to get my lips moving. "I guess Zander isn't such a dipshit, after all."

Erin tapped her temple with a smirk. "I tell myself that every day. But, want to explain?"

I headed to the registers. "Looks like we find Peter a girl."

∞ ∞ ∞

Mom swore I needed therapy. She had even insisted I promise to find some before I came back to Earth.

No person should ever have to go through what you've been through.

45

Her logic, not mine. I agreed with her to a point, but I'd gotten used to what I had to carry. Running was one of two therapies that worked for me. Endorphins flowed through my brain with as much potency as any prescribed pill after a ten-mile sprint. Plus, the only side effects from running were stronger legs.

The other therapy required a lighter and Peter's absence.

Anyway, every morning I'd follow my old route unless I had to pull an all-nighter when Peter took off. Erin ran with me, leaving Zander to hang out at my place with Peter. He usually drove Peter to school, made sure he finished homework, mundane things like that. Zander gave us the time to run, and we said nothing when he'd go to the range and obliterate a few paper targets. Our little family had a system, and it worked for us.

Erin managed to pick up her pace over the last few months, proving it this morning. I hated to admit her newfound speed irritated me. I mean, the woman could kill me twenty different ways, make a roasted duck, and recite E.E. Cummings from memory. Talent was an unfair whore sometimes.

We broke loose in the backfield of the high school in time to see teachers leaving their cars and slogging to the doors with gallon-sized mugs and heavy bags.

I ignored the teachers' "enthusiasm," though. Only one thought ricocheted through my head this morning: *dumb idea, dumb idea, dumb idea...*

For the last week and a half, Zander, Erin, and I had been planning a "coincidental" meeting with some random girl Peter's age. We had a pool to pick from, seeing as a ton of hyperactive, too-loud teens hung out at the theater every weekend. But trying to play matchmaker with a despondent Exemplian had the positive outlook akin to surviving a beheading.

Once we hit the woods, Erin slowed, nudging my side to do the same. I brought it down a few paces and took the time to enjoy the woods in fall. Best time of the year. Wilma's favorite. My heart pinched at the thought of her. The ache was there, but knowing her energy was safe in Empyrean and she'd have another chance at life dulled the torment to a livable ache.

"Hey, space cadet, why so quiet this morning?" Erin's labored breathing interrupted the serene woods.

I had no trouble pushing air in and out of my lungs. But I did have trouble with what we had planned. I couldn't do subtle. Hated it. Getting to the point was much more efficient. "You think it's wrong? Maybe we should leave him alone, let him find what he needs organically?"

Erin stopped at the wood's edge–right across the road from the trailer park. "He's never going to look for happiness, Lena." She shrugged. "So, we need to guide him to it."

"Yeah, it just sounds…" I swiped damp hair from my eyes. "I haven't been in high school for a while. And I didn't do stuff like this when I *was* in school."

"I get it, but we're dealing with something different. Think of it as a life or death situation." Erin stretched her arms over her head, never taking her eyes off the dump across the road. "If we can't figure out what will keep him here, he'll book it again. One of these times, he's going to get smarter, and we won't find him. Not until it's too late."

I laughed because wailing against the truth would've made me look as crazy on the outside as I was on the inside. "Life or death? You think that's a tad extreme?"

"No, Lena, I don't. Exemplar…it's in shambles right now. Authority is arresting anyone in Heterodox who doesn't have a pardon, and Cynosure citizens are armed and shooting at anyone who seems even remotely suspicious. Abrogation folks are doing the same thing. And it doesn't help that Peter looks as guilty as he actually is. They'll catch him, and there's no doubt in my mind what the outcome of that will be."

Erin and Zander shared this story with me already after the trip they took there to find Peter. Her warning–then and now–was enough to solidify my decision.

Get Peter to meet a girl. Hell, meet anybody his age. Find a friend who didn't have the kind of baggage we all labored under.

I went to cross the road but hesitated, glancing back at Erin, who always stayed behind while I checked on Dad. "To think not even a year ago we were hunting…killing people." Shame forced my gaze downward. "Now we're playing matchmakers, like none of it ever happened."

"We had no choice, Lena. They gave zero other options."

I kicked at the dirt as faces flashed through my memory. Faces that haunted me all the time. "Farren once told me the people he killed working for the authority kept him up at night. I have those faces now. Peter's is the most prominent." I finally met Erin's concerned stare. "How am I supposed to convince him to forget the past when I can't? I almost killed him, and that what-if thought races through my head like fire."

Erin clasped my shoulder. "But you didn't. He's here, with us, safe even if he's confused and upset. And we owe it to him to move on from the past, give him some normal that he deserves." She dropped her hand. "Go, check on your father. But know what we're trying to do here, with *all* our lives, is the right thing. The *only* thing we can do."

"I sure as hell hope you're right." I crossed the road.

∞ ∞ ∞

By the time school let out, my nerves had eaten at my skin. In a half hour, Peter would walk through the front doors as usual, ready to cook for the Friday rush. We made sure nothing special was on the menu, a few deep fried things and other processed garbage. Not too hard to cook, but keeping up with orders from the young crowd caused stress levels to accelerate.

For Peter, though he bitched and complained, those quick rushes were the only time he escaped his head. The stress of trying to keep up was enough to block out the depression. Taking that small reprieve from him was just part of the crap we'd planned to put him through tonight.

"Let me handle him. The kid won't relax if you start talking girls." Zander leaned against the concession stand, devouring a box of overpriced candy.

"Yeah? Because you're such an expert?" I forced his arms off the glass and wiped it with a snort. The smell of artificial butter filled the air and turned my stomach. To think I used to like the stuff–until I had to smell it six days a week. We closed on Mondays, our "family" days. Days when we ate Erin's gourmet food and listened to her sing poetry.

"Well…" He threw a few more candies in his mouth and wriggled his eyebrows. "I did land Erin. I'd say I got some skills."

"Right, why don't you let Erin in on how you 'landed' her? Bet she'd have something to say to that." I snatched the box from his hands. "And stop eating the profit."

Zander stole another box from the display, leaving behind more fingerprints. "We can afford it. So…how's your dad?"

I shrugged. "Alive."

"That's…good?"

"As good as can be expected." I took the box before he could open the lid and put it back. "You sure this is gonna work?"

"No, but we gotta cross it off the list."

"Oh, you're full of right words, aren't you?" I tossed the rag in a bucket behind the counter as the lobby filled up with the afterschool crowd.

"I'm a pillar of honesty, that's all."

I grinned. "You're a pillar of something, all right."

"Love you, too." On his way up to the front counter, he winked at Erin, who peeked from the kitchen door.

Erin had volunteered for kitchen duty so Peter could sell tickets with Zander. All I could say was better her than me. I hated cooking as much as I hated what we were about to put Peter through. "Is he here?" She came out as the tables filled. "You two find any targets yet?"

"No, not yet–for both questions." Oh, God. This night had disaster blaring at us. I scouted for potential Peter girlfriends anyway.

We were so incredibly stupid.

Erin searched the tables, stopping at one with three girls around Peter's age. They were taking selfies and showing each other, laughing like drunken hyenas. "What about one of them?"

"You serious?" I shook my head. "Hell, no. No friggin' way. I'm one giggle away from going over there and smashing phones. Give the kid some credit, will you? He needs someone not…that."

She laughed, smoothing her hands over her shirt already stained with grease. "Fine, mama bear, someone else…" Her eyes stopped at a table with two more girls. "How 'bout them? They're pretty and aren't smiling or anything." Erin punched my shoulder. "Right up your alley."

"Haha, so funny." Nerves danced in my stomach as I rubbed where her fist landed, the same nerves that jumped when I had someone in my crosshairs. Jesus, the two scenarios should not have been synonymous with each other. "Yeah, fine, they'll do." I texted Zander the targets.

"Hmm, sure you don't want to check their teeth? Maybe have them walk around the lobby once, see if their trot is smooth?"

I smirked, waiting for Zander to check his message. "Maybe later."

"You're impossible, woman. But I love ya, anyway."

"Right back at you."

Zander put a hand up in some faces as people tried paying to read his phone. None of us had great people skills. He looked at me after a second, mouthing, *Where?*

When I pointed to the two girls, he nodded with a grin and turned back to some annoyed jocks shoving their bank cards in his face. Man, if those idiots knew how precise Zander's aim was, his bullet always hitting the mark, they'd drop the attitude.

Sometimes, I thought of us as four mutants, trapped in a bizarre, real-life comic book. None of us stood out in a crowd, not really. Zander's dark, handsome face attracted a fair amount of attention from the opposite sex, but nothing out of the ordinary. At times, though…we were living in a surreal alternate reality, a reality that would never understand the universe's true nature. To be oblivious…that state of mind…these people had no clue how good they had it.

Peter walked in, head down and refusing to acknowledge any of the kids he'd spent seven hours with. His mopey ass effectively curbed the budding pity party brewing in my head.

"Here he comes." I shooed Erin into the kitchen. "Go on, I'll intercept him."

Her tense face matched my uneasiness. "All right, just…if he doesn't take the bait, don't push him."

"Gotcha." She didn't have to say it. I'd abort as soon as Peter showed any signs of get-me-the-hell-out-of-here.

When she disappeared into the kitchen, I went around the counter, ignoring a couple people walking up to give an order. They could wait.

"Hey, you. How was school?"

Peter frowned. "It was school."

"Ah…yeah, so good, then?" I sounded like an idiot.

"Sure, why not? Awesome. Even better than yesterday."

I put my hands on my hips and peered up at his surly face. "Sarcasm isn't necessary." As he shrugged and headed to the kitchen, I forgot to act mad and grabbed his elbow. "Wait. Um…no cooking today."

"Huh?" He studied the kitchen door as if the barrier were his only shield against people in the lobby.

"Erin's gonna cook tonight. We figured it was time for you to…you know…learn other stuff." *Ugh, so, so lame.*

His body went rigid. "Yeah, don't think so." He'd consistently began to hate being around other people as the months progressed, and my dumbass enabled him to do it. Not today, though. Not anymore.

"Well, *I* think so." My hold tightened when he made a move toward the kitchen. "You're an owner here, too, and that comes with responsibility."

Jake had come back to Earth long enough to sign his house and theater over to me. I insisted he put all four of us on the deeds. On his eighteenth birthday, Peter shares would be his.

"But I always assum–"

"Nope. What do I say about assuming things?"

He sighed, looking around the chaotic lobby. "This is fucking stupid."

"No, it's not." Video games and teenage white noise stomped on my eardrums, making it hard for me to think. But I didn't back down. I held out my hand. "Dollar."

He reached into his pocket and slapped money in my palm. "Fine. What do I need to do?"

"Help Zander. You can give me a hand after." I pointed at the office. "Put your bag away and get to it."

"For the record, this sucks."

"For the record, I don't give a damn." I jammed the dollar back in his hands. "Hurry up."

For the next twenty minutes or so, I had a hard time listening to people spout off their desire for popcorn and soda. Lucky for Erin, most of the kitchen orders were forgotten chicken scratches left in the notepad on the counter. I had to fight the urge to drag our targets over to Peter and force them, at gunpoint, if necessary, to talk to him. But I had gotten better at self-control these past months.

Nope, I passed out junk food, never taking my eyes off the anxiety-filled Peter and too-chipper Zander. Seriously, Zander's obvious fake smile would've gotten my suspicions up. No wonder Peter inched away from him, checking his phone, probably wishing time would speed up.

Finally–*finally*–Zander gave a not-too-subtle nod in the direction of the girls. I held my breath as Peter glanced over at the table after Zander's lips moved with what I hoped was a convincing lie. My heart sank when Peter shook his head and turned back around.

Zander persisted, gesturing over at the unsuspecting targets with that pasted smile I was positive came with a fake, sugary voice. The more Zander threw at the kid, the more Peter shook his head, his skinny body now stiff and looking ready to snap.

All right, enough.

The whole idea was as stupid as I expected, and it only got worse. I cashed out the last customer in line and headed up front in time to hear, "Shut up! Shut up! Shut up! I'm not going over there, so close your mouth!"

"Hey!" I raced over and forced Peter out of Zander's face, not caring that we had an audience. "What the hell's wrong with you?"

I grimaced at Zander, who returned it with defeat on his face. "I screwed up," he said.

"What…?" Peter's eyes widened. "You two–you guys planned this?"

Oh. No.

I groped for Peter's hand and hoped my remorse poured from my skin to infiltrate his. "Peter–"

"Get off me." He yanked his hand away, searching the now-quiet theater. All eyes were on us, including the girls at the table. "You think a girl is going to…*fix me*?"

"Well–"

"You're unbelievable." Peter backed up, going to the front door. "All of you are *unbelievable*."

He threw the door open, and the glass vibrated. I swore it wanted to shatter. Zander moved to go after him, but I held up my hand, already on the way. "I got this."

Peter was halfway down the block by the time I caught up with him, dodging people as I sprinted. "Will you stop? Wait, dammit!"

He didn't answer, and he didn't stop. He stormed toward our house as if marching into battle.

I snatched up his arm, practically dragging his lanky body to a halt. "Will you listen for a second?"

His legs finally quit eating the pavement when he stood in front of our porch. He faced me. Tears streaming from his eyes almost stopped my heart. "Why?"

All I wanted to do was pull him down and hold him until the pain melted from his face. "I'm sorry but–I didn't think you'd be so mad. All you had to do was say no."

"I *did* say no. A hundred times. You think some baby shit like trying to hook me up with a girl–a girl, I might add, who would never give me the time of day–wouldn't piss me off?" His voice hitched and dipped, reminding me of exactly how young he was.

I held his arm tighter. "You're right. We shouldn't have tried, but you need to open your eyes! See what's around you. Right here."

He jerked his arm from my grasp for the second time. "Open my eyes?" With every syllable, his voice cracked more. "My eyes are open. Wide open! I *see* everything. You think I could even try to have a relationship with some girl knowing what I know? Knowing *what I am*? You guys want me to live my entire life as a lie." His voice broke into sobbing and tears turned his light eyes to drowning sapphires. "I wish I could live here. You have no clue how much I want to be part of something…*anything*."

His tears prompted mine. "All I want is for you to be happy."

"Like you? Crying at night over some coward too scared to come around? That kind of happy? I hear you–*every night*. Don't push your idea of happy on me, Lena. I don't want it."

I flinched as if he'd slapped me across the face. "That's not fair, Peter."

"No, no, it's not." He wiped his cheeks and walked up the porch steps. "None of it's fair."

∞ ∞ ∞

That night, the wind kicked up and the atmosphere tore open. By the time I made it to Peter's room, he was gone.

I was too late.

Again.

Lynn Vroman

CHAPTER 6

OREN

For Love

Oren stared at the injector. Cravings attacked every cell in his body and made his mouth water. The chemicals in the tube didn't give a high, per se. It gave silence. The maelstrom Celeste's aura caused disappeared completely for about three hours as soon as the drug hit his veins. Three hours of blessed peace—with side effects worse than any drug he had ever run into on Earth. It corrupted the very soul if taken for too long, not just the carcass it borrowed for a lifetime. But he wouldn't have to take it much longer. Celeste almost had the power under control when they were alone.

Almost.

Oren lifted the injector, the brilliant green fluid as compelling as the woman who waited for him outside the bathroom door. He focused on the mirror, pretending to overlook his pale complexion and sunken eyes, and guided the only solace he had to his carotid artery. One shot and ecstasy rushed through him.

Silence, so deafening it forced his ass to the floor, eased the ache in his brain. A few more minutes on the cold tile, letting Celeste's addicting cinnamon smell wash over him, and he'd go back out there, give her everything he had. More.

A soft knock invaded the quiet. "Are you all right?"

Oren sighed and closed his eyes. Her voice gave him strength. Made him think he could handle the task of saving the world.

After a grunt, he pushed from the floor and disposed of the injector into the portable incinerator, then opened the door to Celeste's concerned face. Her beautiful, angelic face. Love punched him in the chest as it always did.

During his stolen time with Grace on Earth, he would lay awake at night, missing Celeste's arms, her laughter, the way she could make him feel whole with a look. Yes, he had chosen Celeste over Grace eight months ago. Celeste and the rest of Exemplar. Just as he chose Celeste when Grace decided she was done with Exemplar and desired a new life. Given a choice, he never hesitated to follow his heart.

He pulled his mind from the past and glided a finger down her cheek, tracing the tattoo she despised. A brand. Exemplar's mark of a whore. She was no whore. A slave, rather. A slave he had freed long ago, setting her up in this apartment after he finally realized that he couldn't share her with anyone. Then because of Avery and her deceit, he left Celeste alone in this apartment for nineteen years. Nineteen years he'd spend the rest of his life making up for.

He loved her, and maybe she loved him, too. Unfortunately, what they were up against…whatever they used to have needed to come second. But times like this, when he felt the first effects of silence, his guard came down. He wanted to kiss her, touch her lips for the first time in over twenty years.

"Oren?"

His name on her tongue played like a song, demanding he taste it, but he wouldn't. "I'm fine. No worries, Cel." His touch lingered on her chin for a moment too long.

"You've taken another injection, haven't you?" Celeste's eyes, like Arcus's sky, searched his face, distress causing her tattoo to rapidly change color. *Green, red, blue, gold... Green, red, blue, gold...*

She worried about him too much, a problem that hindered her ability to control the power circulating through her. Sometimes he thought himself a liability, a hazardous distraction to her safety.

"Don't. Don't worry about me." He tried for his best smile. "I'm a big boy."

Her full lips pressed together, refusing to reciprocate. She relaxed, though, as he knew she would. "Your looks can only get you so far." She held his cheek, shooting sparks to every nerve ending. "But you cannot keep putting that waste into your body. Perhaps you should leave for a while."

"No." His hand covered hers. "Never."

"You are destroying your body for me. I am not worthy of it."

"You're worth everything." *Everything.* "I can handle it. Besides, you're getting better. Pretty soon, I won't need it." He brushed past her. "Come on, time for practice."

She scuffed her feet behind him, and he could almost feel her irritation hitting him in the back. "It is hard to concentrate with all of them inside me," she said.

"We'll get them to shut up." He set up two floating chairs opposite of each other. "We've made progress, Cel. It's possible."

He turned to find tears in her eyes, and it took everything in him not to pull her close. "I do not want to shut them up," she said. "I want to help them, make them whole again."

This. This was why the people needed her.

"You will, one day," he said. "Right now we need the energy to help us fight."

The energy. All the emotions of the deceased, from anger to love, rippled through her. She claimed it never stopped, the screaming, she called it. Unless they practiced, for hours at times. The minute it silenced so too did the loud static surrounding her. When that happened, she had powers, powers that went beyond his scope of imagination. No matter what Drea or Tarek believed, to him, Celeste was a god. The savior of everyone in this forsaken world. All they had to do was figure out how to quiet the screaming for good, something they worked on every day.

She sat. "Fine, we will practice, practice, and practice again, but you will stop injecting that foul liquid into your veins. If being near me is difficult, you must leave until you can handle it again."

No, not happening, and he wouldn't lie to appease her. He'd pretend she hadn't demanded it. For the thousandth time in eight months. She'd let him. Celeste didn't want him to leave any more than he desired to go.

He sat across from her and gathered her hands in his. "Okay, beautiful, time to close your eyes."

Her cheeks flushed as her tattoo undulated under her skin. *Blue, gold, blue, gold.* "Your honeyed words…"

Oren's heart thumped faster. When her tattoo swayed like that, lust filled her, just like–*stop.*

Stop.

"It's truth, nothing more. Close them."

She bit her bottom lip–killing him–and did as he asked. "I'm ready."

Someone help him, he was ready too, and probably not for the same thing she was referring to. "Ah, right, good. Now…" He pressed the middle of her palms with his thumbs. "Find your shell."

Her eyelids shuddered while her eyes moved behind them as if she literally searched her mind to find her center. A smile softened her pursed lips after a few minutes, her hands going limp in his. "I'm there."

"Good. What do you see? What's in your shell?" He now regretted succumbing to the need for silence with an injection. When she grasped control of the power inside her, the succor she gave intoxicated him.

Her tattoo surged *blue, gold, blue, gold.* "I see you...and me. We are–" She bit her bottom lip again, undoing him.

He wanted her to finish what she started, say what he needed to hear.

Oren cleared his throat. "All right, excellent. Ready to show me something?"

Her smile deepened as his chair bounced up and down in quick, sharp motions. "I can move things easier," she said.

His chair halted about a foot higher than it was. "See? It's not weakness; it's a weapon."

"I...I see it. I *do*." Her eyes remained closed, her tattoo now solid gold with concentration.

"Show me something else. Something new." He bent from his perch as if his body demanded it stay in contact with hers, and clasped her upper arm.

Her brow furrowed. "What do you suggest?"

"Manipulation."

"I do not understand."

"I want you to reach my mind, force me to do something, anything."

Celeste lifted the right corner of her mouth. "Like kiss me?"

Hell, she didn't need to control his mind for that, but what a perfect excuse to bring her lips to his. "Sure, beautiful. Let's see what you got."

She nodded, her eyes shutting tighter until the skin crinkled at her temples. Sweat beaded on her upper lip as she focused, her tattoo still a vibrant, glittering gold.

Oren could feel her aura reaching his brain, tugging, and after a second heard her whispered, "Kiss me," lap against his mind. But no force drove him to her lips, not anything new outside of his own yearnings. He always wanted to kiss her. More than kiss her.

Finally, her cheeks puffed out with a heavy breath. "I cannot."

He was half-tempted to kiss her anyway. No good would come of it–except for the obvious. He grinned, shifting in his chair at the awkward height above hers. "I shouldn't be so disappointed. Maybe, once you get control, try that out on Yosef. The mind control, not the kissing."

She laughed. "It would be my pleasure to control that buffoon for a spell."

Yosef. The only person Oren allowed near Celeste, besides Tarek, Drea, and Peter. He wasn't exactly trustworthy to a fault, seeing as he tried to kill Celeste when Oren stole her from his brothel years ago. The image was one Oren could never erase: Yosef's bullet ricocheting off Celeste's head, never penetrating her skull.

He would have killed the man then, except getting her away from the life she led deemed more important. Oren even tried to take her from this world, but her body refused to leave through the portal. After Cynosure's explosion, bygones had to be bygones, especially since over a century had passed since that incident. Yosef had connections Oren depended on.

Celeste trusted the man fully, though, which had to be enough. Guilt almost knocked him from his elevated chair. She'd had to return to Yosef when Oren left, revise her role as his high-end whore, servicing the Synod. People like Cassondra…

She spoke, releasing him from his guilt-ridden mind. "What shall we try now?"

"Well, you managed to get into my head."

"I've always been able to do that with anyone," Celeste said. She could give and receive messages telepathically, a gift she hated to use before Exemplar imploded.

"Yes, but have you ever seen what a person thought beyond the answer to a question?"

She tilted her head. "I have not."

"Well, then…"

She went silent again. Seconds later, her now-glowing palm touched his forehead. Her mouth formed an *O* as that tattoo fluttered. *Blue, gold, blue, gold…*

"Cel? Tell me what you see."

She opened her eyes, the color piercing him right in the heart. "I see…me. In you, I always see me, whether searching your mind or watching you sleep. It is where I belong."

He brought her knuckles to his lips, kissing each one. Something akin to omnipotent power saturated him, making him invincible. This woman, this amazing woman, chose him–forgave him for leaving. For whatever reason she did, he'd live up to the challenge. And he'd make sure this fight would end.

So they could finally begin.

Lynn Vroman

CHAPTER 7
LENA

Begging

Peter didn't come back the next day.

Or the day after that.

His room, with the figurines and perpetually unmade bed, turned claustrophobic. I refused to leave it, only to use the bathroom and eat when my stomach begged for food. For two days I sat in that chair, staring up at the ceiling, willing him to come back so I could apologize, yell at him...hug him and promise to try harder.

Nothing.

Erin swore the lines to Exemplar were sealed off. That assurance was the only thing keeping me sane. Yeah, there were a ton of worlds to choose from, worlds I had never been to or will ever have the desire to go, but I wasn't worried about them. Exemplar only had one certain outcome.

If we were to lose him there, we'd lose him forever.

Not one doubt lingered in my head about what Peter planned to do: hide out wherever he was until the lines opened back up.

No way would I let him go.

By day three, I'd had enough. Forget this. I hated the waiting game, and I had always refused to play in the past. Eight months of absolutely no danger hadn't quite erased the urge to get up and do something about it.

Without stopping to brush my teeth or take a piss, I flew down the stairs and barged into Erin and Zander's place.

Knocking had its merits.

"Put some clothes on!" I shielded my eyes with a forearm and backed up until I slammed into the wall.

Gasps, shuffling, and a door shutting followed. Jesus, right there, on Jake's old brown couch...

"They make bedrooms for that type of activity!" My face burned as if I dunked my head into a kiln.

"And they have mechanisms to prevent walking in on that type of activity, too." Zander's voice hit me in the ear as he pulled down my arm. "The door was locked."

I held up the key. "Not locked from me."

"Knock next time." He rubbed his face and gestured toward the couch. "What's going on?"

Opting for the chair, I sat on the edge, and he took up the middle cushion of the sofa. "Okay...here it is. I can't keep sitting around, waiting for him to come back." I wiped at the tears forming, lack of sleep making me way more emotional than normal. "He's never–this is the longest he's ever been gone."

Zander leaned over and squeezed my knee. "What do you have planned? Whatever it is, I'm right behind you."

God, I loved him. If he knew how dependent I was on his presence...

I closed my eyes for a second.

Stop crying.

As Erin came out from the bedroom, I opened my eyes and pleaded with her. "Could you to take me to Arcus?"

Erin sat next to Zander, never taking her gaze off me. "I… Are you sure? Maybe give him another day? He always comes back."

"No, he always gets *dragged* back." I stood. "Look, I have to find him before the lines open. This time, his leaving…it's different. And you said so yourself, if he goes back to Exemplar, if they find him, he's dead."

Erin stood, too, holding out her hands. "Yes, but–"

"Please, Erin. *Please*. I have to know if anybody heard from him. Maybe he's there, and Winston decided to let him stay." My voice rose the more desperate I became. "If he's there–"

"You know Winston wouldn't let him stay." Zander tapped his temple. "Even if he did, you'd get a message."

"I have to try." I faced the window, not wanting to see his logic. "I don't expect you guys to…get involved again." I found Erin over my shoulder, her face now pale. "And I'm not asking you guys to leave here. *I* don't want to leave here, but I can't do *nothing*."

She now wrung her hands, no words coming from her gaping mouth.

"I'm asking for a ride." I tried for a smile and failed. "Please."

Erin turned to Zander. His worry pegged my face, daring me to crack. I so wanted to crack. "What do you think, Zander?" Her voice was thin, scarcely there.

"I think Lena can make her own decisions." He clasped Erin's hand, bringing her down to sit next to him, and kissed her on the cheek. "Take her and come back." He faced me again. "We'll hold down the fort while you get your answers. Don't do anything stupid."

I laughed, even as the tears kept coming. "Can't make any promises."

"Well try real hard." He got up and hugged me. "You have all your gear?"

My gear: 9mm, ammo, sustenance injections, an uncomfortable contego suit I wouldn't put on to go to Arcus, and a whole other paragraph of stuff I never wanted to use again. "Yes."

"Good. Take it with you."

"I'm just going to Arcus, Zander."

"Take. It. With. You. Or you're staying here. Deal?"

"Erin's decision, not yours."

"I can be pretty persuasive." He nodded toward Erin. "Ain't that right, baby?"

"You have your moments," Erin said, her face stoic.

Zander held me closer. "Well? Yes or no, Lena?"

I sighed, done fighting. Instead, I sank into his arms for a few more seconds, allowing his natural confidence to give me some comfort. "Fine."

∞ ∞ ∞

Home.

I ran away from it so fast, swearing I'd never step foot out of Earth again. But when Erin's portal closed and we stood at the edge of the village those I loved worked hard to build, security washed over me like warm rainwater.

And clarity ripped open my heart. I ran because my home stopped being my home after Tarek pushed me away. I gave him my heart *and* my favorite place.

I gave him everything.

Squid chirped, and Arcus's earthy scent filled my nose, welcoming me. I exhaled, truly at peace for the first time in months.

Maybe it was time I take something of mine back.

I turned to Erin. Her face showed none of what tumbled through my body. Earth was her home. She'd made that clear plenty of times.

"Thank you." At that moment, I thanked her for more than the portal jump to Arcus. Finally, after so long, I remembered who I was. The dormant person living inside me clawed to the surface, ready to reclaim what I had refused to let in.

"Sure, of course. So..." She scanned the trees, cabins, wildlife...everything, all with a frown marring her pretty face. "I'd stick around, but..."

I hugged her. "No, it's okay. Go. I'll be home soon."

She held me tighter before letting go. "I hope you will, Lena. I really do." She lifted her hand in the air. "Do you want me to return in a bit, in case you can't find a way back?"

I had a feeling she meant that in the most metaphorical way possible. "No, I'll find my way." I waved her off. "Don't worry. See you soon."

As the wind pulled her up, she said, "Promise?"

The nod and grin, a sign we all used to give that meant "no" under a camouflaged "yes."

Doors opened, and people yelled my name as she disappeared through the portal. Her last comment rebounded against the wind: "I don't believe you."

I turned to the village in time to see a throng of people running up the hill. Mom, Jake–oh, my God–a very pregnant and beautiful Belva, Grace, and Shaina. But the person who rushed the crowd to take the lead sent my emotions over the edge. A cry ripped from my lips as I dropped my bag and lunged down the hill.

My brother.

Farren.

I jumped into his open arms, bawling, laughing, yelling, so many crazy incoherent sounds tumbling from my mouth at once. He hooted, swirling me around, burying his face in my neck. Tears wet my skin, his and mine. I missed him. I had no idea how much until his ginger ass hugged the life out of me.

Why had I waited so long? Why did I think I could live without these people and this place? So many whys…so many.

Farren finally set me down and took one hand from my waist to tuck sweaty hair behind my ear. With his voice cracking and tears flowing, he said, "Welcome home, kid."

My smile grew so wide it hurt, even as I cried. I tried to form a sentence, but every time I opened my mouth, sobs flew out. My sobs encouraged a few from him.

Everyone made it to us, bombarding me with love I sorely missed. I managed to squeak out five words: "It's good to be home."

∞ ∞ ∞

Nothing had changed in the mess hall. Long, splintered tables in two even rows of five with the fire pit in the middle. Flames always burned in it and always had some animal rotating on a spit. The same platform in the front where Tarek used to stand, and now Winston. Wooden benches Tarek carved extended down the length of every table. Slivers were a given, something I had always hated. Now, as the rough wood dug into my yoga pants, the tiny stings made me miss this place even more. Wood smoke wafted like a lazy river, and quiet chatter filled every crevice from the eighty or so Arcus residents. Sensory overload of the best possible kind. Nothing beat the familiar.

I sat in between Mom and Jake, their arms like a cocoon, laced together behind my back. I didn't mind their body heat giving an extra layer to the sauna that always came with being in Arcus's forest. They could've kept their arms around me for the next hundred years, and I would've begged for a while longer.

Belva sat up front on the platform next to Winston, her hands folded protectively over the future Warden. Farren stood beside her chair–his hand never leaving her shoulder.

The only time Belva's voice flowed through my brain in the last eight months was to say, *It's a girl, Lena! Don't ask me how I know, but I do. You had to be the first I told, seeing as being your friend gave me everything. Thank you. Have I ever said that to you? I hope so, and you'll get to meet her...one day, when you're ready to come back. Love you.*

I cried that entire night, not sure if I was happy or miserable. I wanted to be around for the birth. Unfortunately, my desire not to leave Earth was stronger. Maybe not anymore...

While we waited for the commotion to die down, everyone talking as if they didn't spend all their time together, Shaina sat across from us and folded my hands in hers. "We missed you, *chica*."

"And I missed you." I looked at Mom and Jake before squeezing Shaina's hand. "All of you, so very much."

"I'm so happy you're here," Mom said, tears brimming in her eyes, like Jake's. Like mine. "I hate the circumstances that brought you, but..."

I wouldn't ask her to come back to Earth with me. I tried to get her and Jake to stay when he signed the deeds over, but they loved it here. They thrived here, actually. To want them home was selfish.

"Maybe after I kick Peter's ass, we'll come back more often," I said. "I think he'd like that."

"No maybe. Do, young lady." Jake patted my side. "It'll be good for both of you. No need to worry about Tarek, either. He only comes back to dump Peter off on Winston." He winced as the last word left his mouth.

It felt like he stabbed me in the chest. *Tarek*... "Is he here?"

Jake's pinched face reddened. "I sound like an asshole."

I took a hand from Shaina's grasp to cover his. "No, you don't. I'm okay, really." No, I wasn't. "But…is he?"

"Yeah, don't worry, though. He never leaves his cabin. It's an event every time he decides to grace us with his presence. Exemplar's lines open, and he'll be gone."

Lumps in my throat *and* chest made it difficult to do anything but nod. Once those lines opened, Tarek wouldn't be the only one going to Exemplar. I turned back to Shaina, whose dark eyes were full of both concern and the dare to lie. I knew that look. She used to give it to me all the time. I smiled. "I'm okay, Dr. Doom."

She peered right into my eyes and through my bullshit. "When's the last time you had an attack?"

Panic attacks. A weakness I acquired after Wilma's death. The natural remedy I stashed in my bedroom closet kept them at bay, along with the running. "Not since… Not since that day."

The day Tarek turned his back on me.

She rubbed my hand. "Good to hear. Have you seen anybody?"

I snorted. "You mean like a shrink?"

Her eyes narrowed and her lips pursed.

Oh, no. Here it comes…

"I mean like someone who can help you, and if a *therapist* is the answer, then yes."

I shook my head, pulling my hands from hers to fold them on my lap. She caught a lie by checking pulses–swear to Christ. My wrist wasn't gonna give away anything. "I got it under control."

"Lena–"

I held up a hand, so not wanting to argue with one of my favorite people. "Honest. And if I need more help, I'll find it. Promise."

She let it drop. Winston spoke, so she had to.

Thank you, Winston.

"So, looks like we have ourselves an issue, people." Winston, always calm and never ruffled, searched the crowd. "Seems Peter hasn't been home for a few days."

Gasps reverberated through the hall. The whole village in the room at once tended to get crowded, some people blocking the entrance. I wasn't the only one who loved Peter. His ridiculously innocent face, masking his recent piss-poor attitude, managed to hit everyone where it counted.

Once the noise died down, Winston gestured to me. "Tell your story, Tainted. Make it quick."

I stood, straightening my sweater. *Right.* "So…this is what happened." Once I rehashed all the gory details, including Zander's stupid idea, I sat.

Being the center of attention wasn't my bag, and after revealing our asinine plan to find Peter a girl, the last thing I wanted to see was the head shaking and eye rolls. I wouldn't feel guilty, though. I'd have tried anything. That thing, unfortunately, didn't work.

"What do we do?" Grace spoke up. She sat beside a man I recognized, the husband of a Protector who died here during Exemplar's initial attack on Arcus when they blew up the castle. As far as I knew, icy stone remnants, like a shrine, still rested where they landed almost a year ago.

I looked around, waiting for someone to answer. Actually, I waited for *the* answer because I had no clue.

Farren was the first to speak. "There isn't much we can do right now. He's got at least fifty worlds to hide in waiting for the lines to open. Only thing I can think of is sending a few people to Exemplar to find him once they do. Try to be where he usually goes and wait for him."

"Not you, though. You can't go." Belva's petrified voice filled the room, her fear upsetting the wildlife. Squid wailed, and the sound of their shaking tree limbs cascaded around us like rain.

Farren bent to kiss her, covering the hand she held to her stomach. "No, of course not." He stood again. "Tarek will go, obviously, but I doubt he'd be willing to bring Peter back again. We need a volunteer."

No. No way. I jumped off the bench when the chatter grew louder, hysteria shading everyone's voice. "No. that won't work." I thought of Erin and Zander. Thought of how Erin hated leaving Earth. I promised not to involve her this time. Looked like I had to break a promise. "I'll go–without Tarek. We'll not involve him. He can give us the coordinates we need and wash his hands of it. Erin and Zander will come with me."

Sighs imitated each other, and I could almost hear shoulders sagging as the tension fell from everyone. Peter was my responsibility. Whether Erin admitted it or not, he was hers, too.

Winston cocked his head to the side, tapping a finger on his elbow. "So, what do you want from us, Tainted. Anything, you got it."

Going back to Exemplar…my nightmares filled with that idea. "For one thing, I need a lift back home."

"Done. Next?"

I looked around, trying to be brave even as cowardice ate at my stomach. "I don't want to fight anymore, either. And I definitely don't want to go to Exemplar, but I will." I hesitated. "All I ask is…if I need you, any of you…if I get into trouble there…"

Everyone stayed silent, most looking at their hands.

Tears poured down my face, fear howling louder than even the desire to find Peter. "Please…don't leave me there. I–I don't want to die in Exemplar."

Mom sobbed and pushed from the table. She hugged me, and I clung to her. *Why?* Just…why?

As I soaked Mom's neck with tears, trying my hardest to get it together, Winston answered my plea. "I'm with you, Tainted. I vowed to protect Arcus and its new Warden, but your life is as important in my book. And my book is the only one worth reading. We'll figure out a way. If you need us, we'll be there."

My relief almost sent me to my knees. Instead, I let go of Mom and stood taller. "Thank you."

Winston then addressed everyone. "We ain't cowards. And our motto has always been never leave one of our own behind. Lena is ours as much as we're hers, you heard?"

As people nodded, I wanted to hug each and everyone one of them. After all they'd been through, they'd help if I needed it, even if going against Exemplar again scared the hell out of them.

I pressed against my aching heart, trying to find the right words. "I–"

"What's going on?"

His voice. I hadn't heard it for eight months. But the deep sound had seared into my brain a long time ago. I'd hear it in a horde of a thousand.

I turned, hoping my ears hadn't mistaken the voice–and dreaded it at the same time. The crowd parted like the Red Sea in those bible stories, as if Moses came to Arcus and commanded it again.

There he stood. His hair shorter and body thinner, but so perfect. I swear the purple light surrounding all of us glowed brighter around him.

My knees gave, and I slumped to the bench.

Tarek.

Lynn Vroman

CHAPTER 8

TAREK

Ghosts

N<small>o</small>.

No!

Cement trapped his feet, preventing him from moving any farther into the hall. Wait, not cement. The kid was right: *pussy.*

Fear caged him.

Why are you here?

His legs needed to work again so he could run back to the woods.

Why?

Lena stared at him, eons of agony marring her beautiful face as tears fell one by one. Those eyes haunted his dreams.

Her heartache, he did that to her.

He couldn't look away, or run for the cowardly shield of symmetrical trees. Her torment was like a beacon waving him home, pleading with him to erase all the wrongs.

"Welcome to the party, big man." Winston's blasé voice projected through the fog in his brain.

Tarek forced his attention from Lena, the loss of her face like death all over again, to find Winston up front. "What's happened?"

"Take a seat, and I'll fill you in."

Tarek didn't miss the challenge under Winston's calm façade, but he did choose to ignore it. "I'm good."

"All right, then." Winston's signature smirk was out and on full volume. "We got another issue with the kid. A bigger one than usual."

Sweat poured down Tarek's face with the effort to stare forward. Through numb lips, he said, "And…?"

"Kid's been gone for days, and he ain't here." Winston ticked away on his fingers. "He ain't on Earth, and we all know Exemplar's lines aren't open yet."

Bad. So, very bad. "Get to the point."

"Best thing we came up with is intercepting him early. Camp at the places he frequents the most in Exemplar once they open back up for business." Winston paused. "But don't worry, we ain't gonna bother you with it this time."

Dread slinked from his tingling scalp to his watery knees. "Who do you plan to bother, then?" He already knew the answer.

"No one. I'm going," Lena said. "With Erin and Zander."

Her voice hit him with as much force as a gut punch. His favorite sound. A sound he swore never to listen to again.

He slammed his eyes shut and counted to ten. Everything went dark, and the atmosphere grew thick as wood, suffocating him. Inside, he yelled until his throat grew hoarse. Every time he tried to speak, anger bit off his words.

After about five rounds of counting, concentrating on the silence overtaking the hall, Tarek opened his eyes and confronted his everything. "You're not going."

Battles traveled between them–his eyes pleading with her, her eyes setting him on fire.

Lena stood. "Eight months." Her words were whispers powerful enough to knock down buildings and destroy worlds.

He said nothing. He couldn't.

Lena glided to him as if she were stalking prey, slow and lethal. Once she stood in front of him, she slapped his face, hard. Blood filled his mouth as his head whipped to the left, the inside of his cheek gaping.

"*Eight months, Tarek!*" Her faux calm evaporated, her thin body shaking.

He moved back a step. "Lena–"

"I haven't heard from you in almost a year, and the first thing you say to me is *you're not going*?" She slapped him again. This time, no force behind it. But he felt all her pain, her desolation exponentially worse than any physical hurt. "You gave up the right to demand *anything* from me."

"Please, don't go there. Please. I'll bring him back. I'll do whatever it takes, just…don't go."

She shook her head and stumbled backward toward the platform. "*You gave me up.*" She turned away from him. "I don't need you. Neither does Peter."

Finally, too late, he reached out to her. His palm touched her shoulder, and fire zipped through his skin. "*Please.*"

Lena stiffened. "Don't touch me, Tarek." Her voice broke. "Don't."

He'd forgotten where they were–in the hall with an audience of eighty. His hand dropped from her shoulder as he scanned the room, a sort of shock filtering through his veins. Some cried, others glared at him, but most turned their heads, acting as if the world hadn't collapsed. Maybe it hadn't for them. For him, he wished his lungs would stop working and the atmosphere would suck him in. He clenched the hand that had touched her into a fist, hoping the electricity wouldn't dissolve. But with all good things…

Lena stepped onto the platform and went to Farren. "Please take me home."

Farren threw Tarek a pitying look over her head. "Yeah, sure, kid."

No. Tarek couldn't let her go. Not like this. He rushed forward. "I promise, if you stay on Earth, I'll bring him to you." She didn't turn around, heightening the desperation vibrating under his skin. "Please don't do this. I'm begging you." His voice pitched to the point where he didn't even recognize it.

She faced him then, straightening her spine. He recognized the look she gave. She had given it before, only never to him. Cold. Blank. "You've made promises before...and you've broken every one of them."

He had nothing to say. Not one damn thing.

Lena bent to hug Belva, whispering in her ear. Belva touched Lena's cheek, smiling even as tears illuminated her golden eyes. When Lena stood, she nodded to everyone, never setting her gaze on him. "Thank you all...for being there."

Her words hit the right target, cutting him deep. She then walked by him as if he were not standing in the middle of the tables to hug her parents. Before picking up her bag, she also said goodbye to Grace and Shaina. The chill her body gave off as she again stepped onto the platform caused him to shiver.

Without saying another word, she wrapped her arms around Farren's waist and waited.

Farren mouthed *Sorry* to him and lifted his arm in the air.

In seconds, she was gone.

CHAPTER 9

TAREK

Last Resorts

You gave me up.

Tarek pummeled his cabin door, methodical blow after blow until his knuckles bled. Wood snapped and splintered with each hit, the next harder than the last. Still, as solid as his fist slammed into the unforgiving target, Lena's words refused to leave his head.

"*Sonofabitch!*" Blood splattered an abstract pattern on the door and traced a warm path down his wrist.

The door had enough.

His mangled hand was finished too.

Tarek stumbled until the back of his legs hit the bedframe. Not even physical pain could erase her accusation. Her truth.

Why the hell couldn't she see he was protecting her? She had a normal life now, one without war and pain and death.

He didn't give her up. He gave her an out, a way to be free from the tumult. Now she planned to throw away all the normal to put herself in danger again. And he couldn't do anything about it.

Tarek slumped on the bed when static entered his mind. Stupid to believe everyone would leave him alone after what went down.

Stupid.

The knock came.

He didn't bother to answer.

Another thump resounded off his punching bag.

No, no more. What could Winston say that'd change the outcome? If the guy had some kind of magic words, Tarek would've liked to hear them a long time ago.

One more deceivingly polite tap hit the wood.

Tarek sighed. "Not interested in company right now."

This time, the door flew from its hinges, landing in shattered pieces, something ten minutes of fist pounding couldn't accomplish. Winston stepped over the mess, acting as if he hadn't destroyed Tarek's place.

"Thanks for having me." Winston's sarcasm was as irritating as his superior abilities.

"Leave."

Winston took another step into the cabin. "Nah, Imma stay."

"Then talk and get out."

"I'll do you a favor and ignore the attitude." Winston came over and sat next to Tarek. Leaning forward, he rested his arms on his knees. "Lena beat you up pretty good already."

Tarek closed his eyes and clenched the edge of the mattress. If Winston wanted a response, he'd be waiting a while.

"Anyway, Farren's back. Dude don't like leaving his lady too long. She got, what? About four weeks to go before the Warden's born?"

Tarek met Winston's eyes. "Shaina's the expert. You tell me."

Winston chuckled, rubbing his hands together. "I suppose she is."

Tarek didn't do small talk, and he had no plans to change today. "So, what now? Are we all going to get into it with Exemplar again over the kid? That'd be stupid, seeing as those elders left aren't worried about anything but reining in their own people. If a bunch of us go there making waves, we'll be on the radar again." He stared at his hands, bloody, scarred, and useless at that moment. "I'm helping Oren. No one else needs to go starting another war."

Winston said nothing for a few seconds, and then, "You're right. That's why no one volunteered. Everybody's too afraid. Farren would've, but…obvious reasons. And with the birth so close, I can't go off and find unwanted attention, you feel me?"

"That's why Lena stepped up? No one else–not any other Protector–offered to go?"

"That'd be why. She don't wanna go, but that kid means more to her than–" Winston shook his head. "If I could go and know nothing would happen here, I'd be on it."

Tarek understood. Exemplians knew who Belva was now and that she carried the next Warden. Even if there hadn't been any direct attacks on Arcus since Exemplar fell, no one here dared to take chances. Arcus's new Warden was the event of the millennia. No one in centuries had lived to see a new Warden born, and a few people existed who would probably jump at the chance to kill the newborn for her power. Winston happened to be the strongest shield Arcus had.

"I can find the boy, but it'd be better if someone else transports him back. I can't chance getting locked out again. You have the power to force one of the Protectors to go, Winston. Oren needs me there like Belva needs you here." When Tarek did find Peter, maybe he'd break his spine. The little shit couldn't get into trouble if he couldn't walk.

"This ain't a dictatorship, big man."

Tarek rubbed his face, stubble on his cheeks scratching his skin. "If anyone catches wind that Lena's in Exemplar it'll cause chaos. They think she's dead, and we need to keep it that way." He paused. "Someone jus–"

"We're trying to create something here, something special. If Belva or I start demanding people to do dangerous shit, we're gonna lose them." Winston got up to stare out the window. "Without people, this place'll fall back into obscurity, regardless of all the energy we got stored here. Energy ain't flowing no more from world to world. What we got is it."

The man had a point. Shit.

He'd have to do it alone. Oren would understand, and maybe Tarek could find the kid, take him home, and get back to Exemplar before the lines closed again. Peter wasn't that smart. There were only so many places to go.

"I'll do it myself." Tarek pushed off the bed. "Can't you convince her to stay away? Please, Winston. She'll listen to you."

Winston's smooth laugh filled the humid cabin. "Will she, now? News to me 'cause that girl ain't never listened to a word I've ever said."

"That's not true. Listen–"

Winston held up a hand. "How 'bout you listen for a minute." When Tarek stared like a dimwit, Winston continued. "The only way I see it is you gotta go with her, not *instead* of her."

Terror sent shocks to his fingertips. "But–"

"She's going, whether you or I want her to or not."

"There has to be another way."

Winston went on as if Tarek hadn't said a word. "You can bring her and the boy back." He shrugged. "Maybe some more time away from the fight will be good for you."

"She said Erin and Zander are going. Maybe Erin and I could handle this, let Lena stay home."

"Erin don't want no part of going, and you're an asshole for wanting her to, especially since you can ensure she doesn't have to."

He raked a hand through his hair. "This is bullshit."

"Maybe, but it's our bullshit." Winston went to the door. "You know, Zander will go too, even if his lady don't want him to—even if he'd rather keep living the life he earned. He'd do anything for your girl." He threw one last dagger into Tarek's chest before leaving. "Maybe it's about time you do the same."

Lynn Vroman

CHAPTER 10

LENA

Disappointments

Pain never had an expiration date. Sure, it ebbed with time. But everyone had weaknesses, those little reminders that invited pain to stand in front of the line again, demanding an audience. I only had to hear Tarek's name or let my mind wander to the past for the despair to niggle at the barricade and desperately fight for the spotlight. Most of the time, I'd curse it away with a promise it'd have another turn later on.

Not this time.

After seeing him, my pain hadn't been this excited for almost a year.

The hardest part was keeping it bottled inside, not letting it escape until after I begged Erin and Zander to again put their lives at risk.

Peter was worth it, though. He was to me. All we had to do was get in and get out. Farren told me where to look. Celeste's apartment building. We'd need coordinates so Erin could open a portal at Celeste's front door, and not in the middle of Heterodox like she had to do last time–or in the abandoned underground hanger. I didn't want to deal with those rats again.

No, we needed a surprise attack–be there before him, so he didn't have a chance to spot us and run. But seeing as how I left before we could hash out the logistics, Farren promised to have Winston invade my head with more info.

Winston's voice dropped into my mind shortly after Farren's portal took him back home. *Coordinates...ah, coming soon. And, Tainted? Don't get dead.*

Right. Great advice, and no coordinates meant Tarek was either not giving up the info we needed, or he already escaped from Arcus.

You're not going.

That was all he decided to say. After eight months. No, "I missed you," or "My life's been shit without you." Only demands as if he had any right to tell me to do anything.

No, not now.

The last person I needed to think about was my weakness. *You'll get your turn, pain. Give me more time, and you can have front-row seats.*

I stood taller, wiped a few tears away, texted Zander, and made coffee. A couple hours, that was it, some time to get myself together before Erin and Zander came home from work. Erin might not agree, and if she didn't...

Hopefully she'd give me a ride to Exemplar.

After changing into sweats, dousing coffee in a bunch of creamer, and smoking a fat joint in front of the TV blaring *Cops* reruns, my mind was where I needed it to be. I slouched on the sofa, taking advantage of the high, and barely heard the doorknob rattle before Zander and Erin walked in.

"Open a window or something." Zander went straight to the living room window and lifted it to the chilly autumn evening before sitting next to me–and taking the joint from my hands. Without looking in Erin's direction, because she gave sneers when we lit up, Zander torched the end and inhaled deeply. He blew out the smoke and handed it back. "If Peter came home and smelled your habit, you'd have a lot of explaining to do."

One thing we never did was partake in our favorite stress reliever around Peter. Do as I say, not as I do and so on and so forth.

I snorted. "Not just my habit." I took one last inhale and tapped out the butt. "And if he came through that door right now, I'd be pretty happy. I might even let him have a hit."

"No, you wouldn't," Erin said. She turned off the TV and sat in the chair beside the matching flowered couch, waving away our secondhand high. "What's the verdict? They hear from him?"

I sipped my coffee, stalling. "Ah, no. No, they haven't."

"So…who's going after him?" Erin sneaked a look at Zander. I didn't miss the warning on her face.

Zander stiffened next to me, and Erin refused to meet my eyes. They knew damn well what I was about to say.

My stomach twisted into a thousand knots. Obviously, they had "no" loaded and ready to discharge from their mouths. "You don't need me to say it," I said.

Erin jumped from the chair and stalked my living room. "Why? Why does it have to be us? Not one person volunteered to go?"

Just one. Tarek would've said anything to get me to stay away, but that didn't mean he'd follow through on his promise. "They're all afraid."

She stopped in front of me, incredulity smeared across her face. "*I'm afraid!*"

Man, I probably shouldn't have taken that last hit. Where the hell had I gotten the idea that a blurry mind was a safer one? I stood on wobbly legs, wanting to be on the same level while I begged. "I understand, believe me, but…this is Peter we're talking about. A terrified kid with no clue what he's getting himself into."

"He's old enough to know exactly what he's doing. When are you going to stop making excuses for him?"

Zander shifted forward. "Erin, plea–"

"No, Zander." A tear escaped down her cheek. "No. I won't do it. I won't go. I told you the last time *was* the very last time."

I shook my head, stunned. "What are you saying? We should leave him there?"

"No. He's our family, our responsibility," Zander whispered.

Erin held up her shaking hands. "I can't do this. Don't ask me to do it."

"He's just a boy." I captured her hands. "Please, Erin. He's *our* boy."

Erin shrugged from my grip and pointed to Zander. "You're my family." She then focused on me. "No one else."

She should've stabbed me in the chest. It would've hurt less. I closed my eyes, trying not to turn into a blubbering fool– and trying to curb the animosity building for Peter. Why did he do this shit?

Why did Erin have to say that?

I stood straighter and opened my eyes, done with this conversation. I wouldn't convince her, and I sure as hell didn't want Erin to spit out any more venom. "All right, fine." *Push out the bad. Bring the good back in.* Weed wasn't helping anymore, a sign to call it quits. "Can I ask one favor?"

"No," Erin said.

Zander jumped up. "Stop! Stop it now." He held Erin's shoulders and stooped to meet her gaze. "You don't mean it. I know you don't."

Erin's tears fell like rain. "She promised us, Zander. She said she wouldn't involve us this time. We've already been to Exemplar to go after a boy who doesn't want to be found, and we almost didn't make it back." She wrapped her arms around his waist and buried her face in his chest. "I can't fight. Not anymore."

Enough. We'd all had enough. I skirted around them, not wanting to comfort her, but not wanting to poke the flames. Before I went into my room, I turned to Zander, to the defeat on his face. "I'm going to bed. Lock the door on your way out."

∞ ∞ ∞

My bedtime routine hadn't changed much in the last few years. Clothes fell in a fabric puddle on the floor, Wilma's shirt slipped over my shoulders, and Tarek's shirt-pillow was clutched in my arms. As I lay in bed, listening to Zander soothe Erin, I wanted to explode. Demand they get the hell out, plead with them to stay, but most of all, sob until I fell asleep. Peter was right. I cried every night. I wanted to burn the pillow, but I'd had it for almost four years. It was as much security as a reminder.

After a while, the front door clicked shut. Alone never felt so…*lonely*. The apartment was too quiet, leaving enough outer peace to flame the inner storm. Too much thinking.

Too much.

Only one option remained. The one thing I didn't want to do.

In the morning, after tempers calmed, I'd ask Erin to take me back to Arcus.

I'd have to trust Tarek. But...

He won't bring Peter back.

He won't bring Peter back.

I smacked my temple, willing the anxiety to shut up. Stupid thought because Tarek had delivered Peter in the past, but this time was different. Peter wouldn't come back without a fight, and Tarek might not care enough to give him one.

I'd sleep on it. Yeah, find some clarity when my mind wasn't full of pot, doubt, and Erin's bitter words. Definitely time to reconsider going cold turkey, especially if my mind wouldn't shut up after smoking.

Sleep...

I just wanted to sleep.

My mind finally shut off and my eyelids drooped. Right before exhaustion won over the repetitive crap in my brain, Winston entered my head again:

Coordinates are on their way. Be ready, Tainted.

More tears. Coordinates were no good now.

I had no way to get there.

CHAPTER 11

OREN

Escalation

Oren willed his communicator to blink, trying to block out the stagnant air carrying the smell of dirty bodies and excrement that covered the sector. The smell latched inside pores, sticking to the skin.

Yosef was late. As usual.

Oren scanned the area, absorbing the distant wails that came from poverty and hunger. Spending most of his time in Celeste's apartment should have turned him mad with claustrophobia. But no, the exact opposite. Being in there insulated him from his shortcomings. He wanted to protect these people as much as she did, but their pleas made him helpless. He couldn't save them singlehandedly, as much as he wanted to.

He kicked at trash on the pavement, sending it into the street. Stupid bastard. Why did he have to be late all the time? Leaving Celeste alone left her vulnerable. Raids happened all the time, in every dilapidated apartment building polluting Heterodox.

Tarek's rooftop shooting helped keep the invasions to a minimum, and his help when any authority came into their building was priceless. As much as Oren loathed admitting it, he needed the man. Selfish to be glad Tarek stayed, seeing as he hid here instead of claiming happiness on Earth, a safe world. Lena could irritate a pacifist on his calmest day, but she was strong, brave. And exactly what Tarek needed to wake his stubborn ass up.

A crowd thickened near his building, pulling him from his mind. Authority Protectors were herding innocents again, the mob growing denser by the second. A common occurrence lately. The anxious huffs of breath would soon turn into wheezing terror as the shooting worsened, the death toll rising and more energy pushing into the apartment walls, finding Celeste. He'd have to go to the rooftop soon, take Tarek's place until the lines opened.

He secretly wished the authority still had soul-stealing bullets. It'd give Celeste a small reprieve from the pain of absorbing all that energy. But Oren and everyone had destroyed the majority of Exemplar's weapon supply after they brought down Cynosure. Most weapons authority now used were stolen from other worlds.

And if he and Celeste didn't require those sustenance injections Yosef had always somehow managed to get his hands on–and the papaverdilutus, PD, Oren needed–he'd be on his way up to the roof now.

The drug was Yosef's idea. At first, Oren refused, afraid it'd kill him and leave Celeste alone. But PD enabled him to do what needed to be done–like killing a few Protectors to ensure Celeste only had to deal with minimal energies instead of sometimes the thirty or forty they took out.

He closed his eyes and thought of Celeste, sending her a message: *Soon, beautiful. Holding up?*

I am, yes. Pause. *Is it odd I miss you after only minutes?*

He smiled, even as Heterodox stench filled his nose and people drew closer. *Not at all. I'm told my company is pleasant.* A total lie.

And she knew it. *I do believe pleasant is not how people describe you.*

No?

No. Annoying, perhaps.

A laugh escaped his throat while people bumped against him in their haste to escape a threat he couldn't quite pinpoint yet. *Perhaps,* he thought to her.

For certain. Another pause. *Come back to me soon.*

The lightness of her tone eased his nerves, even as people continued to rush down the sidewalks.

Grace had believed in a god of some sort and would talk about her faith most days, especially when he had first told her the truth. He wanted to believe in it with her but knew better. Yet, Celeste's ability to reach his mind was a divine gift, one of those miracles Grace spoke of.

Taking a deep breath to clear his head–yet again–he kept watching the crowd. The people rushing past usually hid in abandoned hangers, willing to deal with the *arratoi* than face the authority's bullets. A few of those huge rats scuttled with the masses, not even bothering to bite and scratch. Fear was contagious across species, it seemed.

If they would pick up a gun! Most knew they could get in contact with him through Yosef, come to him for weapons. Whatever he needed, Drea had in her cabin. One call and he'd have it on his doorstep. But they had all forgotten their bravery from months ago, acted as though it never happened. Tarek believed it was because Oren gave them truth, but no, to look into those empty faces…like they all suffered in a trance.

He glanced at his communicator again. Don't know why he trusted the guy. Trust cultivated by desperation, mostly.

Finally, the machine *bleeped* in his hand. Oren tapped on the auditory cell wrapped around an ear. "You're late."

"Sorry, old chap. People forget streets are for driving, not for fleeing the bad guys on foot."

He rolled his eyes. "A little compassion goes a long way. How close are you?"

"No, please, no need to thank me for smuggling illegal contraband," Yosef said, his droll tone not lost on Oren.

"How far?"

A black hovercraft pulled in front of him, the engine as quiet as a breath. The passenger window evaporated to reveal Yosef wearing a smug grin on his smooth face. "I'd say not very."

The man looked more like a politician, the kind Oren saw when he would watch television with Grace. Nothing like the usual flesh-peddlers populating Heterodox, but Yosef was the most popular.

Oren clicked off his device and went to the curb, shuffling around the hustling bodies. He held out his hand, itching to get back upstairs, grab his rifle, and head to the roof. "Thank you."

Yosef made no move to hand over the bag on the passenger seat. "So…how is our Celeste?"

"Fine." Oren kept his mind blank, a habit he picked up a long time ago. He might trust the guy to smuggle things to him, but who knew if he or anyone else in this place could read thoughts like Celeste.

Yosef lifted the bag to Oren's waiting hand. "Have you or– who did you say was helping you figure out our mysterious beauty?"

"I didn't." Oren took the bag and backed up. "Again, thank you."

Yosef shook his head and pushed a button on the console. "Stay well, my friend. Perhaps someday you will allow me the honor of knowing the truth." The passenger window reappeared and tinted to opaque.

Oren gave a half salute as Yosef finessed his ride through the mayhem on the streets. He'd never give up Drea or Tarek, not even to Yosef. Speaking of which…

He punched Drea's code into his device. Her face, so much like Peter's, popped up on the screen.

"How is everything?" She didn't waste time with niceties, something he wholly appreciated about her.

"Celeste is getting stronger, able to control the power for longer periods. But…we can't stay here forever."

"I am aware," Drea said. "Give me more time. Denzel and I will find a way to bring you both here."

Taking Celeste out of the apartment and having people feel her aura would be a disaster. If the authority–the elders–found out the energy went to her, they'd kill her the only way possible–by lopping her head clean off her shoulders.

Oren clenched the communicator until it creaked in his hand. "And then after? What happens?"

"I do not know, Oren. I wish I did."

The woman was the smartest person he knew. They all depended on her to crack the mystical code that would give them answers to stop this madness.

"Right." What else could he say? Work faster? Harder? Drea and Denzel, Peter's Guide, worked nonstop as it was. "Contact me when you have something." He clicked off and headed inside.

A heavy sigh lifted his shoulders as he pressed a palm to the access panel.

Time to get his rifle–and attempt to save a few more lives.

Lynn Vroman

CHAPTER 12

LENA

Giant Surprises

Mornings were supposed to erase the night before. That used to be Mom's shtick after a night dealing with one of Dad's binges. She'd lay beside me on that obnoxious waterbed, sometimes with a new black eye, and repeat it over and over: *It'll be better tomorrow, baby. You'll see.*

Well, I never forgot then, and I sure as hell didn't forget now. It would've been nice to wake up with amnesia, just once. Pretend everything was normal and the only thing I had to worry about was getting Peter up and ready for school.

I stretched until the stress tightening my muscles relaxed some. Everything was always a struggle. We fought for the right to live our lives, but those lives were a constant battle in quicksand.

Whatever.

Time to get up and start struggling to the surface all over again. I schlepped to the bathroom to prepare for another go at the mire.

Once I cleaned up, I—well, I didn't do anything but sit on the couch and stare at the blank TV screen. *What now?* The first step would be talking to Erin again. I needed her. Sucked, but I did. A lift to Arcus. That was it. No Exemplar trip. Didn't blame her for not wanting to go there while all the craziness brewed. Who would want to land in the middle of a rebellion? *I* didn't want to go. But her words hurt.

She hadn't meant them. I kept telling myself that as I zoned out in the living room.

Okay, time to go downstairs.

Okay.

Okay...

I went to the window. Gray fog, like surging, cold-ass waves, pushed me back down. Last thing I wanted to do was open the front door to the draft in the stairwell, only to meet another frigid gust when Erin answered her door.

But choices were limited–like down to one.

Goddamn Peter.

The scattered mess on the coffee table held my attention: wrinkled papers from failed attempts to roll a joint, tiny green buds neglected once I had managed to get the papers to work, pink lighter, dirty ashtray with blackened residue.

My face burned. What had I become? My father? A bona fide member of the trailer trash mafia?

"Fuck you!" I swiped an arm across the table's surface, throwing all my shame to the floor, cursing at life. Cursing at Peter.

At truth.

Fuck. You. I flipped the dilapidated piece-of-shit table, one of its legs splintering with the force. Next went the remote. Batteries exploded from the plastic rectangle as it smashed against the wall.

"Sonofabitch!" More cursing, which didn't make me feel any better. But breaking things did. I heaved, my lungs working overtime. If I had to destroy everything in the fu–

A soft knock skipped through the room.

I watched the door, adrenaline pumping through my body. *Go away!* Destruction therapy called my name, and an audience would mess up my groove.

Another knock.

No fuzz clogging my head meant no Zander. So that left Erin, and now I'd have to beg her in a trashed house…looking like a psychopath.

She knocked again, which would have irritated me under different circumstances. Why did I give people keys if they weren't gonna use them? Hell, I was glad she didn't, and as much as breaking stuff released the tension, playtime had to be over.

The real world knocked on that door, and even if I didn't want to, I had to answer it.

I smoothed tangled hair from my face before reaching down to right the table, which now balanced on three legs. "Uh, just a minute!"

She didn't respond, and she didn't come in, either. At least she stopped knocking.

I ran to the kitchen, pulled the trash can from beneath the sink, and shoved all my paraphernalia into it, along with the shattered table leg. There. Not so bad, just tiny bits of crap I'd have to vacuum…probably never.

I tugged down my sweatshirt and headed to the front door, hesitating. *Push the bad out. Bring the good in.* A forced smile plastered my face as I flung open the door. "Sor–"

Words lodged in my throat, and the fake smile evaporated. I stumbled backward until I tripped over the chair. But I didn't fall.

Tarek caught me.

His arms sent the fire booming in my chest into hyper-drive. Emotions swirled into a kaleidoscope as the room blurred: love, relief, the familiar, and so many others I couldn't grasp onto and hold.

"What're you doing here?" Words tumbled out, but I had no idea if they made sense. With so many other questions fighting to escape, it was possible they collided to form word vomit.

Tarek's arms tightened around my waist as he steadied me. His eyes...tormented silver. He looked so different. His short hair and thinner body resembled a soldier who had just returned from a year-long tour. Arcus color made him look like a glowing angel. But he was *Him*. My giant.

It took a minute to realize he hadn't answered me–and that he hadn't let me go. God, I never wanted him to let me go.

A part of me–the part that tried to remind my heart I was pissed–wanted to slap him again and push his hands away. But the larger part that remembered what it felt like to be alive bulldozed it into the corner. I ran my hands over his arms, memorizing the dips and planes. Remembering them while I kept my gaze on his.

His eyes closed, breaking the fragile bond. He tried to release me, but I clutched his biceps. "No. *No*, Tarek. Stay."

Tears flowed when his arms didn't move. I had forgotten what alive felt like. Alive with Tarek. It was lightning and fire and comfort...everything. He opened his eyes. "Lena..."

I caressed the cheek I slapped yesterday, soothing phantoms. "Wait. I don't care why or how. Let me be happy. For a second, let me believe you're here for me."

He let go long enough to wipe away my tears. His gesture was useless because they kept coming, the dam busted. "I *am* here for you. I know you don't believe it, but everything I do..."

His presence erased all the anger–*him being here*. He came when I needed him most, despite the depression brewing inside his head. The first step.

The only step that mattered.

Stomping broke our moment, severing it into dust. Tarek's arms released my waist, and he thrust me behind him, confronting the door with gun drawn. My poor giant was always in warrior mode.

Zander met Tarek's gun with his own. "Holy shit," Zander said, lowering his Glock with a smile sneaking to his lips. "*Holy shit*."

Tarek hid his gun again in the lip of his jeans, its grip disappearing under the edge of his stained and ripped-up hoodie. He held his hand out to Zander. "Good to see you, man."

"Yeah, ah, likewise..." Zander took his hand as Erin stormed into my apartment.

The four of us stood in the middle of my living room, no one saying a word. I had a good excuse, seeing as sobs clogging my throat prevented me from starting a conversation. We all used to be as close as family. Closer. Never, *never*, had we stood in the same room weighted under awkward silence. So much water gushed under broken bridges, and not one of us thought to bring a life preserver.

Not smart.

Finally, Erin stepped in front of Zander and met Tarek's gaze. "You should have come sooner."

Tarek lowered his head. "I know."

Erin moved around him and pulled me into a hug. "I'm sorry, for everything."

I held on to her. "Me too."

She pulled away, moisture turning her blue eyes to oceans. "Lena, I–"

"No. It's okay."

"It isn't, but I can't do it." She headed for the door, and without turning around, she said, "I'm going to work."

She disappeared down the stairwell with Zander watching her leave. He sighed after the bottom door closed, and then faced Tarek. "I know you got a plan, so let's hear it."

Tarek ran a hand through his short hair and sat on the couch. He didn't say anything, just rested his elbows on his knees and clasped his hands together. His habit, contemplation in the guise of silence, was nothing new. I missed it, that faraway look he'd get as his brain worked.

Zander came to my side, flinging an arm over my shoulders. "She didn't mean what she said, you know. She's scared."

"I'm scared, too." I turned to Tarek.

His eyes were on me. "You should be, Lena. You should be terrified."

Not wanting to crush the delicate, unspoken truce, I took a deep breath and sat next to him. After a hesitation, I covered his laced fingers. "I'm not blind to the risks." I pressed into his skin. "But Peter is worth it." How many times had I said that? And who was I trying to convince, me or everyone else?

I had to bite back a relieved sob when he turned his hands to hold mine. More sobs threatened as he massaged my fingers, something he used to do all the time. But I refused to make a sound, bring his attention to it.

Again, silence filled the room. Zander sat in the chair and propped his feet on the coffee table. After it toppled under his legs, he smirked at me.

I shrugged. "It broke."

"I noticed."

Tarek sighed and went to stare out the window.

Damn. Talking always had a way of interrupting the calm before the inevitable.

"I'll ask you one last time to let me go without you." Tarek's voice was an ice bucket.

He came. I had to remember that. "And if I say yes?"

"I'll make sure he arrives here, safe and sound, with a new black eye or two."

No. Not the answer I wanted. "How will you 'make sure'?"

His shoulders slumped. "Lena, if yo–"

"Stop. Stop talking." I stood because sitting made panic bubble with desperation. "I'll stay–on one condition."

He said nothing for a few moments, something I completely expected. Then, "I'm listening."

I looked at Zander, searching for…what? Courage, maybe? He tilted his head, and mouthed, *Go ahead.*

Right.

I squared off with Tarek's back. "I'll not go if *you* bring him home…and stay here."

Lynn Vroman

CHAPTER 13

TAREK

Thirty Days

Wood creaked under his fingertips, the windowsill flaking beneath his grip. Lena hadn't acted how he expected her to when he pulled some nerve out of his ass to come here. She was supposed to shout at him, call him all those colorful words she liked to use, and maybe take another swing at his face.

She wasn't supposed to…love him, make him feel like a man again. No, she went against the plan.

She never bargained.

But he couldn't stay; Oren needed him.

And Lena needed someone else.

"I can't."

Again, he expected yelling, maybe a fair amount of said colorful words to tumble from her lips. Her muffled sobs were so much harder to fight. His eyes slammed shut, and his hold on the sill tightened. *Don't turn around.*

Don't.

She spoke, her broken voice turning his restraint to ash. "I'm not asking for forever, Tarek. I'm asking for one month, thirty days."

He turned. "What is it you want from me, exactly?"

Even though tears wet her cheeks and her bottom lip trembled, she held her chin up, always brave. Unlike him. "You're asking me to trust you, and I will...if you give me thirty days."

Zander patted her hand. The guy said nothing, but his slight touch obviously gave Lena comfort. Zander then pegged him with a stare as he fell back into his chair, challenge all over his dark face.

Standing taller, Tarek pulled his hands behind his back, mostly to keep from reaching for her, but partly to hide how much his fingers shook. "Nothing will change, Lena. Thirty days or thirty years, it won't change anything."

She smiled, even as she cried. "You see, that's where you're wrong. I know you love me."

"*Of course* I do." He took a step forward and stopped.

"Then if you're willing to throw us away for good, the least you could do is give me thirty days. If you do"–she held out her hands–"I guess all I got is my word that I'll stay away. I'll stay here, live without you." A sob escaped. "Move on."

He wanted that. Exactly that. So why in the hell did jealousy demand that he destroy the room?

"Tarek? Answer me."

Thirty days.

Only thirty days.

Only thirty more days.

"If I stay...for a month..." He saw it then. Her hope. *What are you doing?* "You'll never leave Earth again? You'll stay, live your life?"

"Yes...with an occasional trip to Arcus to see *our* family."

Tarek didn't miss how she stressed her words. Another dig, one he deserved. "All right, then." He nodded. "Deal."

Her mouth fell open, and surprise brightened her eyes. "Deal?"

He swallowed. "Yes."

"Really?" Lena looked behind her to Zander.

The Guide grinned. "Right on."

"Well…okay." She turned back to him, her hands fidgeting with the lip of her sweater. "So…um…"

"Only thirty days." He clenched his hands tighter behind his back. "That's all I can give."

She threaded her fingers through his weeks' worth of scruff, miraculously healing bits of him. "That's all I need."

∞ ∞ ∞

The shower fogged up the mirror, but he still saw a coward staring back at him. He shouldn't have agreed.

She had so much hope, and he'd have to crush her–again–when he left.

Again.

But he'd give her a month. He'd give her anything.

Almost anything.

A soft knock interrupted his self-loathing.

He cleared his throat. "Yes?"

The door creaked open, and he had to yank his hoodie around his waist, the thin fabric not hiding much. Lena had never let a door block her before, and she obviously wasn't about to let one now.

She stood there with towels bunched in her hands, acting as if she'd never seen him naked, while he shuffled, his face burning–as if she'd never seen him naked.

"Um…here." She handed the pile over. "Razors are in the top drawer, by the way."

He grinned. "You don't like the beard?"

"It's not that." She traced a thumb across his bottom lip, sending heat through his system. "I just love your face more."

Awkward silence.

Tarek set the towels on the sink and covered the hand she rested on his cheek–and released it before backing away. This couldn't happen. He'd stay, but at a distance. Closure was all he could give her. He smiled as regret filled him. *Not real* was a hard mantra to get out of the head, something his brain wouldn't let him forget. "Thanks for the towels."

"Yeah, sure." She pointed to the hoodie. "If you want, I can wash your clothes. I don't have anything here that would fit you, but…"

"I brought more." He nodded toward his bag. "And you don't have to wash my clothes."

"Well, I want to, so throw them in the hall once you're…ah…whatever." She twisted the doorknob and hesitated. "I'm glad you're here." She didn't look at him, her focus on the door.

He held the sweatshirt snugger around his waist. "Me too."

"Good."

Once the door closed, he dropped his shirt and sank to the lip of the tub.

What are you doing?

∞ ∞ ∞

Tarek stayed under the spray until the water turned to ice.

Not real. He was tired of thinking it. Zander, Winston, Erin…none of them had an issue, so why couldn't he get over it?

Because getting over it meant Lena would spend the rest of this life with a person created in a lab.

There. Easy. Inner-battle fixed.

He turned off the shower and yanked on some clothes.

When he made it out to the kitchen, bacon reminded him he hadn't eaten in a few months. Living off sustenance injections wasn't pleasurable, but they did the job. Actual food, though, he wouldn't turn it down.

Lena stood with her back to him at the stove, swearing when grease splattered up. He missed her mouth. In more ways than one.

Grinning, Tarek leaned against the fridge. "So you cook?"

She looked over her shoulder for a second and succeeded in burning her hand again. "Sonofabitch!"

Tarek rushed over and led her to the sink, dunking her wound under water. The smell of her shampoo drifted to his nose as he adjusted the temperature. Apples. It made him think *home.*

"Ah...I have some ointment...in my bag." He didn't let go of her hand, and he didn't back away when she rested her head against his chest.

Thirty days would kill him.

After a few seconds, she said, "Then get it so we can eat."

Tarek left her to procure his bag from the bathroom. His shaking hands made it hard to dig out the tube of Exemplian medicine and walk at the same time. When he pulled the medicine free, Tarek lifted his head to find Lena still at the sink.

"Here," he said to her back. No more touching.

She snatched the tube and squeezed, slathering medicine on her hand. Relief colored her eyes almost instantly. "I missed this shit."

"I never leave home without it." Tarek's gaze landed on a jar on the counter marked, SWEAR JAR. He pointed. "For you?"

She shrugged. "Mostly."

"Is it working?"

The corner of her mouth lifted. "Mostly." She directed him to one of the stools at the kitchen counter. "Sit. Time to eat."

They ate in silence, forks scraping against plates the only sound filling the apartment. Real food glowed like heaven on his tongue. Once the last bits of eggs and bacon left his plate, he forced himself not to lick the grease smeared on its surface.

"You want more?"

Tarek glanced up to Lena watching him, her plate half full. He wanted to kiss her, that simple. Just capture her lips and refuse to give them back. "I'm good," he said.

She pushed the rest of her breakfast to him anyway and moved to gather the dirty dishes. As she filled the sink with soapy water, she said, "Tell me what's going on there."

He finished the last bite, cleaning her plate as spotless as his own. "Where?"

"Where do you think?" Even though her back was to him, he could almost hear her eyes rolling. Ah, yes, he missed her.

"It's chaos."

She stopped washing the dishes and spun, resting a hip against the sink. "Elaborate, please? I figured that much."

"Right, sorry." He studied his hands, cataloging scars, trying to find the right words. "You–*we*–started something there, Lena. And it's the best thing and the worst for Exemplians at the moment."

"I understand, I do, but we destroyed everything. The Synod has no lab, no satellite feed, nothing. Half their authority defected to other worlds, and we managed to kill a hell of a lot more during the explosion. I just…I don't get why citizens aren't pouncing on the old-ass elders and ending this already."

"For one, no one can find where the elders are hiding. There is enough of the authority left to keep them guarded, plus terrorize Heterodox. And two…the people are broken." Tarek shook his head. "I told Oren not to tell them."

"Tell them what?"

Not real. "Once he spread the truth through Heterodox, people shut down. They–finding out you were manufactured in a lab isn't easy news to swallow."

Her body stiffened. "Does it matter how you got here? Regardless if you traveled through a vagina or test tube, you're real. *You're real*, Tarek."

Anger shaded the moment, both his and hers. No matter how he tried to explain, she'd believe what she wanted. Believe until she wanted children. "You won't change my mind." His voice was soft, barely a whisper.

A coffee mug flew from the sink, shattering against the cupboards beside the stove. Another followed. As Lena hurled all the dishes from the water to the wall, Tarek's shock kept him in his seat. He stayed quiet until the last dish met the linoleum floor in pieces.

She heaved, staring at the ground, her silence louder than an Arcus storm.

Tarek left his stool and went to her, brushing hair away so he could see her face. Her smile stunned him. "Feel better?" he asked.

"Not really." Lena's smile didn't reach her eyes. "But we'll get into this later. Trust me." She pushed away from the sink and headed into the living room. Once she sat on the couch, she gestured to the chair. "Join me?"

If he were in a field naked during a blizzard, the frost would've been warmer. But not talking about "the truth" was fine with him. It'd be a conversation inevitably invading the thirty days, but it didn't have to be one of the first ones. He sat on the edge of the chair, waiting.

She didn't make him wait long. "So, what's Oren's plan?"

"Save the world, mostly." On its own accord, his leg bounced.

Lena snorted. "Okay, and how? All by himself?"

"Almost. He has me picking off the authority terrorizing Heterodox. Ah, Drea is cracking through systems, trying to figure out how to get to the elders." His leg bounced faster.

"She's also trying to figure out what Celeste is. Oren thinks she's the key to solving the puzzle."

"Why?" She placed a hand on his knee, stopping its rapid movement.

When her hand stayed, he focused on it like an anchor. "Do you remember how you felt being around her? How we all felt it?"

"Yeah?"

"Well, now it's even more so." He paused. How to articulate something he barely understood?

Lena rubbed his knee, saying nothing.

"After the lab was destroyed, all those…souls, they never left Exemplar. They were absorbed, by Celeste."

"No." Her voice whispered into the room, the fingers gripping his knee now shaking.

"Yes, those people, and any other Exemplians who have died after that. We think the elders are looking for her, but thankfully, they don't know who they're looking for. Oren never leaves her side."

"Except when he's had to bring Peter home. No wonder he went apeshit when the lines blocked him for almost a month."

Shame burned Tarek's face. "Ah, yes, yeah, I'd imagine that would've been the reason. I don't know how he manages it, but he protects her. The static has to be debilitating."

"Oren. The universe's most irritating hero." Lena let go of his leg. "So, when do you think the lines will open?"

"Who's to say? It's been about three weeks, so…two days, maybe three."

"You know where Peter usually goes, then, right? There and back, easy."

"I hope so. Lines stay open for a few hours. Whichever elder has the power to close them seems to need that much time to recuperate. If the kid sticks to his usual routine, it shouldn't be too hard."

"And if he doesn't?"

Tarek sighed. "There are only so many places for him to go. He decided to hate his mother, he's smart enough to stay out of Cynosure, and people in Abrogation shoot at anyone who isn't familiar. He doesn't have a death wish. He wants to fight."

Her shoulders drooped. "He's an idiot."

"He is, yes." Tarek grinned and tilted her chin to meet his eyes. "I'll find him. Don't worry."

"And then you'll be here? You find him and stay."

He released her chin. "Yes…for thirty days."

"So you've said." She took his hand and guided him to the door, unhooking her keys off a nail pounded into the wall. "The next day or two, until the lines open, are free days, though."

"Ah…"

She whipped her head around, drilling holes into his face with her glare. "They're free days."

He hesitated on the way downstairs. "Okay, okay. Free days. But, Lena, we're going to have to…talk."

"I know." She opened the door to the frigid midmorning air. "Tonight, when we're on our date."

"Date?"

She went to her car, unlocking the doors. "Yup. You and I are gonna go on our very first date, even if I have to taser you and stuff you in the trunk to do it."

Tarek stayed on the porch and crossed his arms. Heat trailed through his veins, healing him. *Maybe…* "I get no say, then?"

She pursed her lips as if actually thinking about it. "Hmm, yeah, not this time." She pointed to the passenger door. "Get in. I'm late for work."

He grinned. "Yes, ma'am."

After he slammed the door shut, she snapped on her seatbelt and turned on the engine. When she caught him staring, her face reddened, but her smile shone so brilliantly it became his life support. "You might want to buckle up."

Tarek raised an eyebrow. "Bad driver, are you?"

"Nope, the best. Everyone else sucks."

"Of course." He clicked on his belt as she sped from the driveway.

Maybe...

CHAPTER 14

LENA

Fragile Ceilings

My whole life up to this point had been a fight. Not a struggle, but a knockdown, drag-out brawl. I kept my fists up, though. Tough, but I had done it.

This battle for Tarek wouldn't get any less of my attention. More, actually. The second he agreed, something inside sparked, like I'd been in a fugue for eight months and his answer plugged the cord back in.

Mission Make-Tarek-Stay started now.

We pulled into the parking lot next to Zander's car. Tarek's eyes hadn't left my face the entire ride. Without looking, I felt his stare burn my skin. A burn way more pleasurable than bacon grease. I had him. He just didn't know it yet.

I turned his way. "You ready to work?"

"Work?" His slight grin showed a hint of dimples.

"Yeah, as in mopping floors and cleaning toilets. You up for it?"

"Ah…no?"

"Look, it's not as fun as picking off authority asshats, but there's free food." I opened the door. "And movies." I hesitated before getting out. "You know, this place...this is where my life changed." I jumped from the car and headed inside.

Tarek followed. "How so?"

"How so, what?" I unlocked the door to loud music and Zander's off-key voice blaring from the open office door. I gave Erin a wave, who was busy cleaning the concession counter. She waved back and dropped her rag to go inside the office, shutting the door behind her.

Tarek touched my upper arm. "How did this place change your life?"

"I'll show you." I captured the hand he had on my arm and led him to the back. I flung the door open to the darkened showroom. "Right there, in the last row, is where Casimir tried to pull me to Arcus for the first time." Memories flooded in, as they always did. "And when you became Warden? I used to sit in here, waiting for you to try the same thing."

"I'm so sorry, Lena. For your entire life–all your lives." Guilt filled his eyes. False guilt. I understood it, and I hated it.

"Sorry? No. I'm not." I guided him from the room, back to bright lights and loud music. "You might find this crazy, but I don't regret one minute of my life, not one second. You know why?"

He shook his head.

"Because everything that has ever happened, good or bad, brought me to this moment, with you."

Tarek said nothing, his attention now darting everywhere but on my face.

Okay, enough of this. He'd spent that last eight months avoiding reality; the reminders of the past had to come in small doses.

"Yeah, okay, so...mop's in the utility closet, along with the toilet brush." I pointed to the door beside the office. "Time to get busy, big guy."

A smile cracked through his sadness. "Are you asking me to clean the bathroom?"

"Nope." I beat feet to the office. "I'm *telling* you to clean it."

His laugh followed me into the room.

∞ ∞ ∞

No, I wasn't gonna feel bad. If Zander and Erin couldn't handle a Wednesday night by themselves, we had problems. Since Peter left, we closed down the kitchen, a big "Under Construction" sign posted on the door. A few more days without that revenue wouldn't hurt. They understood, thankfully.

Once the afternoon showing was over–the same chick film that had been playing for a while–I snagged my keys from the office. Did I force Tarek to sit through the movie?

Well, hell yes, I did.

Cleaning toilets and listening to a room of women sigh and sob were enough penance for one day. I wanted him back, yes, but I wanted to hit him, too. Already hit him, and it didn't make me feel any better. Watching him deal with manual labor and crying women had so many better rewards, like his scowl after returning the dripping toilet brush and his heavy, loud sighs when the housewife brigade oohed and aahed over the leading man. At one point, he had whispered, "Do you like this stuff?"

I smiled and tossed more popcorn in my mouth. I had good intentions, besides making him suffer. The more his mind stayed off his fears to focus on something else, the better chance I had to convince him to stay.

Once we were on the way back to my place, he growled under his breath. Sweat stains from beneath his arms peeked out as he rubbed his face. "I'll need a shower before whatever other tortures you have planned for tonight."

119

I flicked on my turning signal and hit the driveway. "No more torture and I get the shower first."

"Fine, just tell me there isn't toilet cleaning on tonight's agenda."

I slammed the door and ran up the porch steps. "Can't make any promises."

He trudged behind me with a chuckle. "Great."

An hour later, I stood in front of my closet, trying to find clothes while Tarek showered. As I scanned what I had, nerves hit my body–and shame. Here I was, happier than I'd been in forever, and Peter was hurting, hiding out in some world until he could go fight a war that wasn't his. I had pushed him away, gave him the desire to leave, and now I worried about clothes. I never worried about clothes. Crazy how the fight for Tarek superseded the battle for Peter.

But hadn't Tarek always won over everything else? Ugh, more guilt, but old stuff, like I had to dust the memory off to remember it. After Wilma had died, I blamed myself–using Tarek as a punching bag.

Not this time. We'd get Peter home, and *I'd* get Tarek back. And I'd use everything in my arsenal to do it.

I yanked out the nicest thing I had in my closet, a red miniskirt Erin gave me for my birthday and a form-fitting black sweater. I didn't have much in the way of curves, but I wasn't beneath using what I did possess. I even dried my hair and straightened it.

After a deep breath, I shuffled to the living room–in black pumps Erin had also given me. I'd break an ankle by the time the night ended.

But it was all worth it when Tarek's jaw dropped. "Wow."

Shy now because even though love always settled on his face when he looked at me, something more appeared at that moment. Like if I had the courage to kiss him, he'd be powerless to stop me. Man, I wished I had the courage. I could've been wrong, though, and his rejection would have ruined everything. So, baby steps.

I twirled, trying not to look like a moron. "What do you think? Too much?"

He wiped the corners of his mouth. "You–I've never seen you wear a…a–*wow*."

"So yes?" I laughed, loving every minute.

"Y-yes." Tarek shook his head. "I mean no, not too much. You're perfect." He stalked the few feet separating us and almost–almost–touched me. His hand came up only to fall back down just as fast. "But you're always beautiful, even after a month in Arcus's woods. Even after a hunt, you're always the most beautiful woman I've ever seen."

See? Those romance movies had nothing on my giant.

"You clean up pretty good yourself. Um…it looks like we did this on purpose." I guided my hand across his chest, the red T-shirt that hugged every muscle and black jeans he wore matched my clothes. "Maybe I should change."

"No. Don't change. Don't." He backed away and plucked his jacket off the couch. "So, where to?"

I snatched my wallet from the counter, really wanting to stand there and find out how far I could get. A kiss? More? "A surprise."

"I don't like surprises." He grinned as he repeated what I'd said to him the day he showed me our home in Exemplar. But that hint of sadness that hadn't left since this morning lingered.

I caressed his chest one more time, loving how the muscles rippled under my touch. As his breathing quickened, I said to him the same thing he told me that day. "You'll like this one."

After a forty-five-minute drive, we parked at Winston's house, a pizza box steaming on Tarek's lap. One thing Winston gave me after I came home was the key to his place. I kept it private from everyone else. It was my paradise, my escape. Winston even finished the ceiling paintings a few months ago–

after I begged for an hour. Now, I had my own personal universe, showing only the good parts. The best parts.

When I killed the engine, I gestured to our dinner. "You got that?"

"Ah, yes, but–are we going to tour a dilapidated house?"

I laughed and got out. "Not exactly."

On the outside, the huge gothic-looking house appeared in danger of falling in on itself. A few spots had new green siding, but that was about it. The structure was sturdy, though. And inside…heaven lived in there.

Tarek followed me in. I switched on the lights to reveal a huge room with stairs leading to nowhere but the ceiling. I made sure the power stayed on. It would've been a shame to hide Winston's masterpiece in shadows.

Tarek looked around, clearly not impressed as his gaze landed on the only piece of furniture, a mattress. Next to it, an easel stood with a painting of Wilma and me, another present from Winston. "Nice picture."

I took the pizza from him and tipped his chin until his gaze found the ceiling. "It's more than nice."

Slack-jawed, Tarek kept his face turned upward as he moved to the middle of the room. No way would I ever interrupt someone's first experience with the four worlds I loved, forever imprinted on the plaster. So, I sat on the mattress and opened dinner. While I ate, trying to sit so I didn't look like a hooker, Tarek kept staring until his eyes landed on Exemplar–on the cabin I only saw as a pile of ash. Winston had remembered the cabin and surprised me with it, along with the orchard, after his very last painting session. Its red shutters, thatched roof, and stone chimney always reminded me of the Seven Dwarves' cottage. I cried for days, loving it and hating it all at the same time.

He looked down at me. "How did…?"

"Winston."

"Brilliant." He examined the paintings again, taking in Arcus's forest surrounding the village we built, Empyrean's floating homes, and the theater here. "This is amazing, just...*amazing*."

I wiped grease from my fingers. "Come, sit." I kept my voice low, afraid of spooking him. The cabin had stunned him. Hopefully the memory wasn't too much.

A relieved breath escaped when he sat beside me, his attention on the ceiling.

I dropped my pizza in the box and set it out of the way. Taking a huge chance, I guided him to lay beside me. Tears burned my eyes when he didn't fight against it. We both lay there in silence, staring at the ceiling, me trying to rein in the emotional flood while wonder and awe colored his handsome face.

After a few minutes, he pulled his gaze from the paintings and focused on me. He wiped a tear from my cheek. "Thank you, for bringing me here."

I captured his hand against my face. "Tell me something."

His thumb slid across my bottom lip. "What do you want to hear?"

"Anything. Just give me your voice."

"Are you happy?"

"I am at this moment." I took our contact further and curled against his side.

His hand gravitated to the small of my back. "Do you want to know what makes me happy?"

"More than anything." My voice broke on the last word.

"Knowing you don't live fighting, and knowing you'll die of old age, not from a bullet."

I wanted to roar, *You could have that too!* But I refused to break the spell.

"I don't plan to die here."

His body stiffened. "What do you mean?"

I moved closer to him, wanting to burrow inside, become one person for a few seconds. Crazy–but I'd been okay with crazy for a long time. "Erin promised to take me to Empyrean when I'm old. When I live again, I want to live with Wilma." I leaned up enough to look in his eyes. "And with you…like how we planned it all those years ago."

He tucked hair behind my ear. "I'd like that."

"So, you'd give me your next life?"

His gaze searched mine, his mouth opening and closing. After another of his famous pauses, he said, "Yes."

"But not this one?"

"Lena…" He moved to get up, but my hand stilled him.

"Sorry, no. Don't get up."

An eternity later, he lay back down. But he wouldn't look at me, opting to explore the ceiling some more.

Okay, one battle conquered. Now, on to the next. I knew how to fight, and everything I did had to be slow and strategic. Time to tread the ground softer to avoid the landmines. Winston had said to be patient. Rebirth always resulted in a weird depression full of regret.

Eight months was long enough to live in pain. I'd heal him. I would.

The silence became too much. I pushed from his chest, instantly feeling his absence. I shook off the emptiness and nabbed the pizza box. "Dinner's cold, but it's the best pizza outside of New York City."

"Pizza? Never had it." He propped himself up on his elbows, watching me with those gray eyes. I'd drown in them one day, and I'd do it with a smile.

"Well, then let me introduce you to one of Earth's wonders." I guided a slice to his lips. When he didn't open his mouth, I said, "You won't regret it."

"I've eaten more today than I have in months." He bit into the lukewarm dough, and his eyes closed as he moaned. "Oh, damn."

Laughing, I handed him the pizza and picked up another piece for myself. "Told you."

Tarek stuffed half his slice in his mouth as he sat up. "All right, every day I'm here we eat this." He ate the rest in about twenty seconds flat.

"That can be arranged." I cleaned up our mess as he finished another slice. We did silence well–when it was the comfortable kind.

"Lena?" A smile hinted at the corners of his mouth.

I stuffed the pizza box in a garbage bag and tried not to stare at his dimples. I missed them. "Yeah?"

"Thank you…again."

I had to swallow a sob before answering him. "Always."

Lynn Vroman

CHAPTER 15

LENA

Back to the Beginning

I watched him sleep as I would a sunset. He was my perfect moment, waiting for the right time to escape into the dark.

Even unconscious, Tarek's sadness followed him. Lines nonexistent eight months ago marred his brow, and in his hand, a pistol rested. Always the soldier before the man, especially now.

Last night was only a start. Love would beat him over the head until his eyes opened and his mind cleared, until the stress erased from his face. I'd never quit on anything, and I sure as hell wouldn't give up now. My life slept on that couch.

His lips curved into a soft smile when my fingers brushed his cheek.

"Please come back to me."

A soft knock bounced off the door, and his eyes snapped open, gun aimed toward the sound. As much as his penchant for always being in warrior mode frustrated me, one thing made my heart soar. When I spoke to him, touched him, he never woke up.

Why?

For the same reason I had never flinched from his touch, awake or asleep.

I was his safety, his home. Just as he was mine.

"It's okay." I lowered his shooting arm.

"I feel static."

"Erin's."

Clarity returned to his eyes, sadness with it.

I held his cheeks, forcing him to give me his attention. "Don't worry. I'll protect you." I meant it as a joke. It came out as a plea.

He covered my hands. "Thanks?"

"You're welcome." Another knock. "I better get that."

"All right. I'm going to…" He pointed to the bathroom.

I opened the door when he disappeared down the hall to Erin sneaking downstairs. "Um, aren't we a little old for the knock-and-run game?"

She turned. "Have to keep you on your toes." On her way back up, her expression gave way to concern. "Listen, about what I said. I–"

"Stop explaining. We're good, seriously."

"Yeah, but…you have to know, I love you–and Peter. You *are* my family, Lena." She tucked hair behind her ear. "I'm a coward, I guess. But what's happening there, it's dehumanizing. I can't go back."

"Hey, no, I understand. Let's forget it, okay?" I grinned when she brought her head up. "Forget I asked you to do something stupid, and forget you were a bitch about it."

"Your way with words…" She hugged me. "Don't ever change."

"Now that I can promise, unfortunately for you guys." I pulled away and noticed her running gear. "About our run…"

The bathroom door opened.

Erin looked over my shoulder. "Raincheck. See ya at work later?"

I followed her gaze to find my giant, all beautiful and serious. "Um…"

Her laugh trailed down the stairs. "Yeah, how about you take the day off."

Tarek nodded to the door once I closed it. "Is everything all right?"

I leaned against the wall and crossed my arms over my chest. "Yeah…yeah, everything's exactly how it should be."

He looked out the window, his fingers tapping against his thigh. "So, what's it going to be today? More toilets?" He focused on me with a soft smile. "I have to say I enjoyed the paintings more, but…?"

"No toilets, ace." I walked by him to my room. Before shutting the door, I said, "I hope you brought more than those boots and jeans."

"Why…?"

"We're going for a run." And a trip back to the past.

∞ ∞ ∞

Unlike Erin, Tarek had no problem with keeping pace. Tables turned when I ran with him. I liked the challenge, though not as much as I loved the competitor. Being with him injected life into my veins. But guilt followed the rush every time Tarek encouraged me to run faster. Peter…I almost wanted to thank him for leaving this time.

Wow. What the hell did that make me?

"You still come here?" Tarek's deep voice interrupted my unfortunate self-reflection.

"Well, yeah. Why not?" I barely noticed we'd hit the woods, my running path as routine as brushing my teeth.

"Bad memories, maybe?" He slowed down, allowing me to catch my breath. My giant could outrun a cougar.

"I've been through worse than what I ever had to deal with here," I said. Funny, but only good memories enveloped me when I thought about that part of my life. The "normal" part.

He was silent for a minute, switching to a walk, for which I was grateful. He moved a low-hanging branch before it swatted him in the face. "I wish I could erase the last three and a half years."

"Huh, weird, because I'd fight you to keep them." I switched directions, heading toward the creek. Leaves crunched under our sneakers, and the breeze carried the earthy scent that only belonged to fall. "Come on, I wanna show you something."

Immediately after we made it to the burn pit, flashbacks hit me in the heart. I was so young when Tarek came into my life. Almost four years felt like centuries. Chairs circled the pit, and garbage littered the ground: yellow grocery bags, empty beer and soda cans, and fast food wrappers. This place hadn't changed much, as if people I grew up with passed it to the younger generations with a promise to keep the fire burning. A haven from the turmoil at home.

Without looking in Tarek's direction, I set two chairs close together, almost on top of each other, near the creek bank–in the exact spot we sat when he first revealed the truth. When I realized *Him*–literally the man of my dreams–was real.

"Sit." I slumped in a chair and dared a peek in Tarek's direction. His face was pale, and his hand shook as he scratched at his short hair. "Hey, I won't bite, promise. Sit down. Please."

He hesitated a moment, searching the woods with a frown on his face. I wanted to pound on his chest and demand he snap out of whatever raced through his brain. Before I gave in and did exactly that, he sat, bent over, and rested his elbows on his knees. He rubbed his hands together, keeping his attention on them. It took everything I had not to lace my fingers through his scarred ones.

God, I missed him, who he was before death broke him.

I straightened my spine. Nope. No wallowing. I'd guide my giant back home, just as he did for me after Wilma's death.

"So…" My breath came out in vapors, the chill sneaking through my sweaty clothes. "Do you remember this spot?"

"Of course."

"Look at me." I wouldn't touch him, force him to see me. *Baby steps.* "*Please*, Tarek."

He refused, still concentrating on those scarred fingers I missed so much.

"I'll bet I know exactly what you're thinking." *Breathe. Push the bad out. Bring the good back in.* "You wish you never came here, all those years ago."

He said nothing, answering me loud and clear.

"You do realize I would've probably died if you hadn't. Or"–I swallowed–"Wilma would've probably died sooner protecting me."

"Lena–"

"Do you love me?"

His gaze finally found mine. "With everything I have, everything I am."

"Then why are you doing this to us?"

"I can't give you what you deserve. I can't."

"*What I deserve?*" My voice rose above the woods' music. "What you're giving me is suffering. Is that what I deserve?"

"You–*I* can't give you a future. A family…children."

"*Children?*" I stood. "What the–I don't want–children. Tarek? You're abandoning me for future kids I don't want?"

"Maybe not now, but you will." He stood too, meeting me chest to chest. Anger radiated off him. Good. Finally something besides sadness. "Why can't you see? *I'm not real.* I'm…I'm a lab creation, Lena. Nothing more."

"That's where you're wrong." I palmed his beating heart. "You're as real as I am, as Zander, Winston, Erin…so many others."

"I can't–every time I think I've overcome it…"

I wanted to kiss him more than I needed to continue breathing. But I wouldn't. "When you died that day, it wasn't your body I followed." I had to stop for a second, the memory as potent and raw as the day itself. "Not your body, Tarek, because your body isn't you." I pressed my hand tighter against his chest, his rapid heart enough to undo me. "I followed your soul–you."

"Why do you love me?" His heart pounded faster. "*Why?*"

Simple answer: "Because without you, I'm not me."

"Lena…I–" His big body trembled under my touch, as if one more word, one more confession would cause him to explode into millions of pieces.

I backed away, instantly feeling the autumn cold. Forcing him into believing me wouldn't work. Tarek had never allowed himself to be forced into anything.

"Okay, ah…I have to–" I shifted sweaty hair away from my face. "I need to check on the old man. He's probably freaking out about now, seeing as I haven't been here in like a week."

"You take care of your father?" Surprise eased some of the pain off his face.

Baby steps, for sure. If the subject needed to be changed, I'd do it. But not forever. "Yeah. Even moved him into Wilma's old place. He's different now, like a child."

"He's lucky to have you."

I smiled even though I wanted to do anything but. "You're goddamn right he is." I walked backward, toward the path to the trailer park. "So, you wait here, try not to scare anybody who might stumble this way, and I'll be back in a bit."

His huge body remained tense, but he smiled. I'd have bet my entire bank account he wanted to smile as much as I did. "I scare people?"

"Only the ones smaller than you." Which was everyone.

His laughter was an even better ointment than Exemplian medicine.

"I'd bring you with me, but you might...ah..." I faltered over a tree root. In my defense, I had a hard time taking my eyes off the big, gorgeous man in front of me. We made progress today. I felt it.

"Understood." He cupped his hands over a frustrated groan. "Tell him I said hello."

"Yeah, right." I turned and jogged down the path, back to the past. Dad would only be getting few minutes of my time today. Staying away from my giant caused separation anxiety.

∞ ∞ ∞

Twenty minutes later, I ran back to the fire pit to find Tarek pacing. Twigs and leaves crunched under my shoes, and his head popped up. He stood dead still. "We have to go. Now."

My lips went numb. "What happened?"

Tarek raised his hand in the air, and an electric current crackled around his fingertips. "Exemplar's lines are open."

CHAPTER 16

TAREK

Aftershocks

The minute he felt the lines release, dread and excitement vibrated through his body.

The quicker he acquired his gear and left, the easier it would be to track down Peter, beat the shit out of him, and bring him home.

Neither of them spoke during the run back to town. No doubt they were thinking along the same lines. Forty-five minutes had gone by, maybe an hour, which meant Peter already had a good head start–and Tarek only had a little time left to find him.

They ran up the empty driveway, and Tarek stormed to the porch, his head already in Exemplar. But once his shoe hit the first step, fuzz slammed into his brain.

Tarek turned to Lena with a finger to his lips. She nodded, no stranger to trouble, her silent footsteps bringing her to his side. He leaned down to her ear. "Is Erin at work?"

Lena peered in the darkened window of the lower apartment. "Yes."

Not good. As he moved closer to the door leading up to Lena's place, the noise in his head grew thicker, not overwhelming, but definitely belonging to more than one person.

Strung tight, he tilted Lena's chin to meet his gaze, and mouthed, *Stay here.*

To Tarek's surprise, she didn't give any argument. No, she just went to her car, popped the trunk, and pulled out a couple guns, handing one with a silencer to him.

Of course Lena would always have some handy.

Of course.

He pointed at her, then to the spot by the door, before pointing to himself and motioning his plan to go up. Lena acknowledged him, mouthing *Be careful* while engaging her weapon.

Tarek tried the knob. Locked. Which meant their visitors knew the coordinates inside Lena's home and waited to ambush her.

Without having to direct her, Lena quietly unlocked the stairwell door, and then singled out the key to the apartment, placing it in his free hand. Her grip was steady on the hilt of her gun, no fear on her face. A warrior, through and through. He gave her a quick grin, not at all feeling it, and went inside.

His shoes made no sound as he trekked up the stairs, slow and steady. More than likely, the invaders felt his static, but he wouldn't assume it and rush in. As much as he struggled with life, he didn't have a death wish.

Thumps and grunts drummed through the closed door, causing the back of his neck to tingle. A fight?

Oh no.

Peter.

Tarek now stomped up the stairs and twisted the key in the lock. The door burst open, and Tarek had enough time to dodge a bullet whizzing past his head. The bullet's muffled *ting* hit next to his ear and lodged into the doorframe. Before the

Protector could get off another round, Tarek tackled him. The move startled the guy long enough to allow Tarek to snap his neck. Energy escaped from the dead man's body and zinged through the open door.

Two more came at Tarek as a third engaged Peter, winning. Tarek tried to bypass them and get to the boy, but the two Protectors gunning for him were quick. His closest attacker got a bullet in the neck. The other managed to swing low, tripping Tarek. He hit the ground, his gun flying into the kitchen.

Fortunately, the Protector lost his gun in the struggle, too, and he was nowhere near a physical match. But the guy wasn't going down easy, squirming from every hold Tarek tried to get around his neck.

Tarek fought with one eye on Peter, who was now on the ground, his attacker pummeling him in the face. If Tarek couldn't get his guy under control...

A loud shot ripped through the apartment, and the Protector holding Tarek went limp. He looked up as a blue orb burst from the guy's open mouth, the energy fleeing through the ceiling.

"I told you to stay downstairs." Tarek kicked the body off his legs and went for Peter.

"You're welcome." Lena pointed her gun at Peter's attacker, shot–and missed.

Shock filled the Protector's gaze when it landed on Lena, but then a smile flashed, showing uneven teeth. "You."

That one word stunned both Lena and Tarek for seconds. But it only took a moment for the guy to push away from Peter, raise his hand, and escape through a portal.

All three of them stood in silence. Peter leaned against the wall, and Lena stared at the dead bodies. Tarek didn't care about the bodies; he wanted to kill Peter.

Whatever happened in the almost-hour Peter spent in Exemplar, he brought the authority back with him. The escaped Protector would fill the right heads with lies, telling them Lena was alive and attacking again.

They'd come for her now.

And they'd make her pay.

Tarek straightened, murder blinding his vision. He had one target: the boy with the deceptively innocent face. "Do you realize what you've done?"

Peter's terrified gaze bounced from him to Lena, who continued to stare at the three dead bodies in her living room. "I–they–I panicked."

He jacked Peter against the wall, holding him two feet from the ground. "*You panicked*? Big, tough boy wanting to play soldier and you got caught, didn't you?"

Tears Tarek gave zero shits about poured from the boy's eyes. "They tried to put gallium c-cuffs on me. I…I didn't know what else to do."

"So you raised your hand–*like a pussy*–and brought them here?" Tarek slammed Peter harder against the wall, and the boy's head smacked against a picture. "You stupid, fuc–"

"Tarek!" Lena was at his side, yanking on his arm. "Put him down. *Please*."

She was strong, but her tug on his arm hardly registered, the violence churning inside too thick to feel anything else. But Tarek did as she asked, planning to kill the boy in private later. He released Peter, who fell to the floor in a heap of bruises and tears. It took every ounce of willpower Tarek had not to ram his foot into Peter's solar plexus.

He turned away from the temptation as Lena bent to coddle the sniveling twit. "Do you realize what he's done to you, Lena?" Tarek said. "Do you have a clue?" Spit flew from his mouth, his voice like thunder in his ears.

"Stop yelling. Chances are the cops'll be here in a minute, without you giving them any more reason." She then returned her attention to Peter, whispering, "It'll be okay. Let's get you to your room."

Peter stumbled to his feet, sobbing and broken. "I'm so sorry. I-I didn't mean to."

She smoothed back his hair, tucking sweaty strands behind his ear, as a mother would. "I know. Shh, it's okay. Everything will be fine now." Lena faced Tarek. "Give me a minute." She then disappeared down the hall.

Once they were in the back room, Tarek closed his eyes and breathed deep until the rage died down to tolerable levels. This was so not good. Battles contained on Exemplian soil would now leak into Earth. He knew it, almost tasted it. He opened his eyes and studied the bodies. Concentrating on them helped ease the desire to rip out Peter's throat.

The evidence needed to leave. Lena was right; the cops would be here soon. Things were harder in a world with strict rules against killing people.

Okay, time to take stock. One bullet lodged in the hallway doorframe, another by the front door. Easy enough. Tarek found a knife in the kitchen, popped them out, and stuffed the flattened lead into his pocket. Next… One broken neck, no mess. Good. Lena got her guy in the back of the skull. Clean, minimal blood. His wasn't so neat, a neck shot messy and leaking onto the floor.

Where to start?

Peter's crying softened. Crying. The kid wanted to fight, but he couldn't stop sobbing like the child he was. Tarek blocked it out and went to work.

Using the area rug his target so politely landed on, Tarek rolled up the body, happy that most of the blood came with it. All three bodies made it into a pile by the front door with a few grunts and a little muscle. Tarek then searched the apartment until he found a length of rope in a hall closet with what looked like a heap of survival gear. He sighed. Even in this huge amount of normal, Lena prepared for the worst case. At that moment, he was thankful.

He looped the stiff yellow cord around all three men and cinched it tight. With one hand gripping the end of the rope, Tarek raised the other to the roof. He gave the hallway another look.

Peter's crying hit his ears again.

Damn it.

He dropped the rope and followed the sound. After a sharp knock, he opened the door to find Lena bent over the boy contorted in the fetal position, sobbing into a pillow. Tarek still wanted to twist Peter's head from his scrawny neck.

"Lena," he whispered. She turned to him with a defeated look on her face, and he had to grip the doorknob to force himself not to wrap her up in his arms. "I have to take care of the bodies."

"How long will you be gone?" Her eyes widened and her breaths came out in gasps. He recognized her symptoms, the symptoms she had right before spiraling into a full-on panic attack.

Screw it.

He went to her, rubbing her back until her breathing leveled out, ignoring the kid, who kept crying silently. When she calmed enough, he said, "A few hours at most. Don't worry."

She wheezed before answering. "Yeah, sure."

"Trust me." He traced a path across her jawline. "Be back in no time."

"Promise me."

"Absolutely." He placed a soft kiss on her temple and left the room.

As distant sirens leaped through the afternoon fog, Tarek and the evidence disappeared.

CHAPTER 17

LENA

Cleanliness

Sirens wailed through Peter's open window.

I freaked, escape plans automatically running in my head. But once the wind from Tarek's portal swirled in the living room, relief weakened my bones. If the cops came in here, the bodies would be gone. And Tarek would be back in hours.

I tried not to show anything while I calmed Peter, even tucking him in bed with another empty promise that everything would be fine. This was bad. Really bad.

I could still hear the Protector's voice after he saw me: *You...*

Tarek didn't need to tell me what I already knew. The authority would be coming to get me. Nothing new about this situation. They'd chased me before, even as we hunted them. Never wanted to be in this position again, but there you go. Elders would think I sent Peter to start an uprising, elders I had never laid eyes on. Mysterious people who had been controlling my lives since I started having them.

I'd be fighting again.

But not alone. Tarek would always fight with me.

He wouldn't abandon me. He wouldn't.

I didn't leave Peter until he fell asleep, his pale face even thinner. His fingers stayed twined with mine, painfully at first, but then they relaxed as the sleeping pills I gave him took hold. Using some of the salve left in Tarek's bag, I smoothed it over Peter's bloodied face, the deep cuts dissolving. I watched him heal, his face ingrained in my heart. The anger Tarek had for him didn't reach my brain. Yes, he had made life extremely difficult with one foolish act, but he was just a boy. A boy who had as hard a time with the truth as Tarek.

When I trudged back into the living room, everything was silent. The cops roamed the streets but thankfully didn't stop in my driveway. Whoever called Mount Pocono's finest obviously hadn't known where the shots came from. Silver linings.

First things first. I pulled out my cell and scrolled to Zander's name: *Peter's home.*

His response was instant: *You need me?*

Not yet. Protectors followed him. All dead but one. Keep your eyes open.

Shit…

Exactly.

It's happening again, isn't it?

I stared at my phone. What to say? I decided to go with the truth. *Yes.*

We're coming home.

No, don't. Tarek and I got it covered. See u tomorrow.

After that, I tossed the phone on the kitchen bar and went to my bedroom. Erin and Zander were strong, capable—and safer at the theater tonight than here with me.

I ripped off all my bloodstained clothing and threw it in a trash bag. None of the blood was mine, all of it belonging to Peter. I pulled out some clothes from my dresser and yanked them on. Then after finding a bucket from under the kitchen sink and filling it with bleach water, I scrubbed the leftover drops of blood off the carpet.

I cleaned until my fingers were raw. Even after the blood disappeared, I kept attacking the carpet with my cloth. Back and forth, side to side, the rhythm keeping the tears in check as my heart turned to dust. I couldn't do it again. Fight. Put myself in death's crosshairs. I didn't want it anymore.

Back and forth...
Side to side...
He left me...
He'd be back.
He promised...

Hours, days–centuries–went by. I wiped that carpet as if it were a genie's lamp. I didn't need three wishes, just one. *No more death, no more killing.*

When day turned to evening, I shut the window then locked the door–deadbolt and all–knowing that wouldn't keep the enemy out.

With the chair turned toward the door, I sat, checked the safety on my gun, and waited.

He'd be back.

∞ ∞ ∞

Was I dreaming? Dying, maybe?
No, sleeping.

I flopped up, only to have numb limbs knock me back down.

Sonofabitch!

Sleeping while people could be here to kill us. Dumb. I managed to keep hold of my gun, a talent I perfected a long time ago.

Instead of forcing my still-sleeping body to move again, I opened my ears. Nothing. Not one sound. Dawn sneaked through the window, its foggy glow causing phantom chills to tingle up my spine.

Maybe they wouldn't come.

Maybe I wasn't on their radar anymore.

Maybe I should wake up and stop wishing.

I tucked my gun in the chair between the cushion and the arm. Coffee. I needed fuel before I allowed my mind to work–before I worried over Tarek's prolonged absence. *Why aren't you back yet?*

I checked on Peter, who was thankfully sound asleep, then texted Zander to let him know all was well and went to the bathroom. Everything ached, every tiny muscle. But I wouldn't give in to the desire to crawl into bed. Nope. I had some planning to do–another battle I didn't want to fight.

As I dumped coffee into the filter, lack of sleep making my hands shaky, the wind kicked up behind me.

What'd I do?

Freeze.

I just…froze.

No gun and no other weapon but a measuring spoon. I peered to my left, finding a paring knife in the sink. *Good enough.*

Before I could reach it, strong arms pulled me against a solid chest. I knew that chest.

My chest.

I turned and pounded on Tarek, no force backing up my fists. Relief sapped all my strength. "You left me, you left, you left…" All logic escaped–leaving only the feeling of desertion.

"No. Never." He held me so close I had a hard time breathing. No worries. He was better than oxygen. "The bodies…"

The dam didn't break this time. It collapsed. I sobbed, burrowing my face into his chest, letting my hands roam his body, convincing myself he held me. I didn't have to handle anything alone.

I had my giant.

"Why did it take you so long? *Why were you gone so long?*"

Tarek lifted my face to meet his gaze. My eyes stung and snot covered my lips and clogged my nose, but I didn't care. He was there. "I had to bury the bodies." He closed his eyes for a second. "I'm sorry. So, so sorry…"

"Don't leave me again." I rested my cheek against his chest, absorbing his heat.

"I won't." He weaved his fingers through my hair, massaging my scalp.

His hands traveled from my head to the small of my back, and I cried harder. I'd have been content to die–or disappear inside him.

Get a grip! I had to stop with the crying, damsel-in-distress shit. I'd fought armies before. Now, I had to reach down in that buried place in my brain and remember how to do it.

I pushed away from Tarek to grab the dishtowel hanging from the oven door. I wiped all the evidence of weakness from my face, stealing time so my voice wouldn't sound frail. After one last swallow, I threw the towel in the empty sink, and said, "What next?"

"Are you okay?" Tarek clasped my shoulders, hunching until eye level with me.

"No, but that's beside the point." I shrugged from his grasp to dump water into the coffee pot. "Want some?"

"You have to trust me." His voice was quiet, haunted.

"I'm trying." I poured more water into the pot and added a few extra spoonfuls of coffee. My chest hiccupped, residual crap leftover from hysteria pissing me off. No more crying. None. Without facing him, because that would open the gates, I went to the front door and opened it when I heard Zander's slam. "We're okay, just Tarek."

Zander stood at the bottom of the steps with his gun out. "You're seriously going to give me a heart attack."

I shook my head, already closing the door. "Sorry. We'll be down in a few hours." I then turned to Tarek. "We'll figure stuff out after I get dressed."

A half hour later, I went back into the living room, showered, dressed, and minus swollen eyes. Peter still slept, his soft snores echoing through his closed door out to the hall. He probably hadn't slept in days.

Tarek sat on the couch, the same couch where I fell in love with him. I hadn't known it was love then, but the memory cemented in my mind a long time ago. Every time I sat on the end cushion, my heart beat faster, and now he sat there, two mugs on the floor beside him.

My gaze darted to the coffee table in the corner on its top, useless after my throwing therapy.

Tarek cleared his throat. "It's...ah...no longer working."

My cheeks heated. "I guess I lost it a little the other day."

Wow. Was that just a couple days ago?

Straightening, I sat next to him and held out my hand. "Coffee?"

"It's cold now." He plucked one of the chipped mugs off the floor.

The coffee was almost as white as milk, how I liked. I accepted it with a grateful smile and sipped. "Ah, heaven." I nudged his shoulder and pointed at my cup's contents. "How'd you know?"

A grin lit his face, showing those dimples that always swelled my heart and flayed it at the same time. "You dumped half the bottle in the last couple mornings." He shrugged. "I learned to put two and two together a long time ago."

"Well, I'm grateful for it." I guzzled my caffeine hit in three gulps. A ton of creamer and sitting for a while meant lukewarm coffee, and as easy to shoot as whiskey. Exactly what I needed.

My empty stomach complained about the acerbic jolt, but it helped wake me up. I set my cup on the floor and got down to business. "I expect they'll be coming soon, probably try for sneak attacks. We need a plan."

"Yes…lines are still open, odd under normal circumstances."

"Leave it to us to change the status quo."

He grimaced. "We're good at it."

Tarek scooped up our mugs and went into the kitchen. Again, his quiet contemplation swept over me. He returned to the couch, and folded his scarred fingers over mine. Tears I thought under control blurred my vision. I said nothing as he focused on our joined hands, afraid to break another moment. Another tiny moment that would help guide him back to me.

"You have no idea how important you are to Exemplian citizens." As with his silence, his long way of explaining things came with the package.

"Why? I was sort of an asshole in my past lives, and *we all* took down Exemplar. Hell, the only thing I did was get caught."

After Protectors had killed Tarek, they captured Zander and me. The way they used that mind shit on us, I almost lost Zander *and* Tarek for good, seeing as I cracked under the pressure and Zander carried Tarek's soul inside him. But yeah, I didn't do much, except–

"You killed Cassondra," he said.

Right. To save Wilma's energy, I blew a hole in Cassondra's head. "Yeah, yeah, I did." No remorse twisted my heart.

A sad smile skated across his face. "And you were not an asshole. Ever."

"If you don't count a year and a half ago."

"Ever, Lena. Even then."

His understanding was a gift I hadn't deserved. I still woke up in the middle of the night when shame invaded my nightmares. I treated him so badly, and he stuck around. Well, it was time to return the favor. I'd stick with him, even if I had to superglue our arms together.

But until then, "So, because I killed that bitch, they…what?" I shrugged. "What exactly am I to them?"

His attention went back to our hands. His callused touch sent electricity from my arm to my chest…to other places. "You're a beacon. Hope." He hesitated. "Because of Cassondra."

"How so?"

More flames zinged through my body as he massaged each finger, making it hard to concentrate on our conversation–making it hard to remember we were in trouble.

"From the way she used Wilma, and how she called you out as a traitor. People saw how you got to her, and they loved it. Oren convinced them to storm the capital…using your name to pump everyone up."

Well, holy shit. "But…they can't possibly feel the same way now. I left them to fight alone." I abandoned them, people I didn't know or care about. They suffered because of my bloodlust. Shame weighed a ton, asleep or awake.

"Rumor has it you died in the explosion." He looked up long enough to grin at me. "Someone spread that lie."

"Someone…like you, maybe?"

He nodded. "Oren, too. We didn't want anyone to come looking for you." He paused. "But all that's ruined now."

I stayed silent, waiting for the rest of the story.

He finally gave it. "They will come here, and they'll try to end you, make sure you're dead this time."

Hibernation here on Earth was over, something I had to come to terms with. "I have an idea."

Weariness dulled his gray eyes. "Whatever you're thinking, I'll find an easier solution."

"Not this time." I jumped from the couch, my arm wrenching at the shoulder joint.

"No."

I yanked against his hold to no avail. "It'll be fine. Just…let go."

He clasped my hand tighter. "You aren't going there. You promised."

Ah, my giant knew me as well as I knew myself. "Well, yeah, yes, I did. But Peter changed the rules."

Tarek stood. "For which I will blacken his eyes. But there are other options. We–"

No more.

I kissed him, partly to stop his argument, mostly to ease the pressure in my chest.

Love rushed through my entire body, melding my soul with his, as it was supposed to be. As it always had been. His lips were as soft as I remembered, and it only took a second for them to relax under my assault.

He moaned, and his tongue pushed past my lips.

I melted.

No, I became whole again.

This.

His lips left mine to glide along my throat. Greedy hands claimed every spot on my body until they rested on my ribcage, right under my chest.

"Please…" I have no idea what I begged for, but my plea brought his lips back up to mine, demanding as much from me as I took from him.

After an eternity, a moment, he lifted his mouth, our lips still touching. "I missed you."

I had a strong urge to rip away the clothes preventing our skin from touching. "You feel it, right? *That's real*, Tarek."

"Yes…"

"And after we finish all this, *together*, you come back to me." I bunched his sweatshirt in my fists and pulled him closer. "You hear me? *Come back to me*."

Instantly, his body stiffened, and he stumbled backward.

No.

No, no, no, no!

Despair cleaned the desire from his face. "I...I can't."

I wanted to yell, punch him in the head until he saw reason. Kiss him until he forgot his unfounded fears. But I did none of those things.

I touched a shaky hand to my swollen lips, straightened my shirt, and gave him the only option he had. "We're going to Exemplar."

I turned to my bedroom, not willing to let him answer.

That wasn't the only thing we'd be doing, but I wouldn't push. Baby steps.

After this was over, and if we lived through it, he'd come back here with me–for good–or I'd be where he was. His choice, but that was the only choice I was willing to give him. Wherever he lived was home, whether he wanted it or not.

CHAPTER 18

TAREK

Surprise Attacks

They were coming.

He sat on the couch in silence, and Peter slumped in the chair across from him. Lena was in danger–again–because that idiot boy couldn't get over his hang-ups. Just as he couldn't, the only reason Tarek refrained from choking Peter out.

He got it, the pain. When Lena kissed him, that pain eased, almost evaporating.

Almost.

Her plea for him to stay awakened him. *What the hell am I doing to her?* Giving her false hope, obviously. He wouldn't stay. Couldn't. She'd resent him being in her life–this life–once danger left and all that remained were the two of them, alone. He'd give her the next life, a life where he'd hopefully be an actual human, be able to give her what she deserved. That was all he could offer.

Not. Real.

Truth bit him harder than it had in a while. A reminder of what he was. The urge to throw the busted table out the window to release some of the rage diminished when Lena

151

walked back into the living room, her lips swollen from his. Rage transformed to regret.

Lena stared at him for a second as if she could read his thoughts. She pursed her lips and shook her head, her eyes telling him she'd never give up.

Why? Why couldn't his brain get beyond it? His heart wanted her more than it desired blood to pump through its valves. But...

His hands again itched to bust that table, finish the destruction Lena had started.

She cleared her throat and confronted Peter. "Go downstairs, fill Zander and Erin in on everything. We'll be right behind you."

Peter gave Tarek a hesitant frown as he stood from the chair and cleared a wide path to the door. The boy was smart to stay away from him.

Before Peter escaped, he hugged Lena, bending his tall, lanky body around hers. "I'll make it up to you, I swear."

"I know you will," she said.

Peter let go and disappeared through the door, the heavy wood slamming in his wake.

Lena's gaze found Tarek's again. "He's coming with us. I've decided–" Her voice hitched, and she closed her eyes for a second before giving all that jeweled green back to him. "I've decided to give him a choice. If we manage to keep Exemplar off our backs, fix all this, I'll...I'll let him go."

Tarek stood, forcing himself to stay a few feet from her, the distance not enough. Too much. "If that's what you want."

"It is." Tears threatened to spill from her eyes. "But, Tarek? I'll never let you go. Not ever again."

∞ ∞ ∞

"So, what're you saying? You're going back to war?" Zander paced the small living room. The same dread that flowed through Lena's eyes with the mention of a fight traveled through his.

"Well, no, not exactly." Lena sat next to Tarek on the brown couch, her body trembling.

"Then, what, *exactly*?" Zander stopped, eyeballing Erin and Peter, who sat at the kitchen table, not touching their mugs in front of them.

"We go to Exemplar to lure them away from here." She sighed but sat up straighter, preparing for Zander's reaction.

"Uh, okay…? Want me to tell you *now* that this is a dumb plan, or…?"

"It's not dumb, just listen."

"What the hell do you think I'm trying to do?" Zander threw his hands in the air, the movement lifting his shirt and showing off the butt of his gun.

Tarek wouldn't involve himself. Lena and Zander had a bond, a strong one that thankfully turned familial instead of romantic. He owed it to Zander to allow him to convince Lena to stay.

It wouldn't work, but he'd give the man a chance.

"Well…" Lena glanced at Tarek. They hashed out all the details when she told him the plan upstairs before Peter woke up. Surprisingly, it wasn't half bad. Matter of fact, it was brilliant. "We're gonna send the elders a message–somehow–let those crotchety prigs know I'm coming for them."

"Are you out of your goddamn mind?"

"Easy, Zander." Tarek refused to involve himself in Zander's pleading, but he had no issue with popping the guy in the lip for being disrespectful.

If Lena didn't beat him to it first.

But she went on, not at all offended. "Actually, yes. I've been *out of my goddamn mind* for years. Why're you so surprised?"

Zander stared at her, slack-jawed.

"As I was saying, we send a message." She got up to hold Zander's hands, lowering her voice after peering toward the kitchen. "And then we help Oren."

"Why? They'll just come after you again." Zander whispered, too, obviously enough in sync with Lena to follow her lead.

"I have to help, Zander. I-I owe it to those people to try– and I owe it to you and Erin to keep Exemplar from here."

Zander wrapped his long arms around her shoulders. "You don't owe us anything, and I'll always trust you. But promise me you won't get killed."

She pulled away–her smile completely unconvincing. "I'll be back here to drive you crazy in no time."

"Yeah, I'm holding you to that." Zander shook his head. "Why is it that every time you two are around each other, there's a life or death situation on the horizon?"

The man had a point. Before Tarek could answer, static filled his head. More of that life-or-death action Zander spoke about.

"We have company." Erin's voice boomed from the kitchen. As much as she hated fighting, her gun was out and ready. Warriors were warriors, even when they didn't want the job.

Good thing.

Because Exemplar took their first shot.

Lena drew her gun, too, as did Zander. Tarek reached for his and moved against the front door. "Peter, get lost. Now."

"But–"

"Now, boy!"

Lena ran to Peter and dragged him by the arm into a bedroom, locking him in there. Before she shut the door, she said, "Do. Not. Leave."

Once she had Peter safe, Lena came to Tarek's side, as much a warrior as everyone else in the room. No one spoke as the static grew stronger in his head. The front door remained clear, and the large bay window showed no one trudging up the sidewalk.

Sweat poured from Tarek's scalp, the wait almost unraveling him. Lena by his side, strong and capable, was the only thing keeping him from storming through the door instead of waiting like willing targets for the ambush. Less than sixteen hours since Peter came home and Exemplar sent the first hunters to kill her.

Sixteen hours.

Fuzz grew louder, and by the intensity, there were about three of them. Not one showed his face. *Where are you?*

"Shit." Lena stalked toward the kitchen. "Back door."

They all followed her lead, slow and quiet. Zander inched up beside her, his gun thankfully equipped with a silencer. He studied the kitchen, and whispered, "They're picking the lock, trying to be stealthy. Dipshits." He checked his gun. "I can tag them. Cover me."

"We have you." Tarek took up the position by Lena, Erin to his right.

Zander then closed his eyes, breathed in deep, and rushed to the back door.

Ping! Ping! Ping!

Zander, a crack shot, took care of the threat in seconds.

Three orbs released from the dead bodies and hightailed it out of the kitchen to the living room, and then on through the enormous window. A few people happened to walk by at that moment. They drank coffee, and one talked on her phone, but none noticed the energy zipping out into the fall morning. Good thing about killing outside of Exemplar: only Exemplians, past and present, could see energy.

Tarek and Zander did a quick recon of Lena's apartment while she and Erin did the same in the fenced-in backyard.

No static, but that wouldn't last forever.

They needed to leave. Now.

After they all met up in the living room, Lena let Peter out from his hiding spot. She then gestured to Erin and Zander. "You guys got body duty?"

Erin lifted her pant leg to holster her gun. "Got it."

"Thanks. Be ready for a few stragglers. They might not get the message right away."

"Will do." Erin hesitated. "Be safe, Lena. Come back to us, okay?"

"Absolutely." Lena hugged her and Zander before grabbing their bags from the couch and coming to Tarek's side. "Time to make an appearance."

He wrapped her in one arm and spoke to Peter. "You have the coordinates to Celeste's building?"

Peter's sweaty hair fell on his pale face as he shook his head. "N-not the exact ones."

Tarek rattled them off and raised a hand in the air. "If you do anything but go where I tell you, when I find you–and I will find you–I'll end you. Understood?"

The boy's face whitened even more. "I-I won't screw up again."

"Good." Tarek turned his attention to the ceiling and let the tear pull them through.

CHAPTER 19
LENA

Static

I fell backward as soon as the portal opened in front of Celeste's door.

Static brought back nightmares. Last time I experienced it this strongly, Farren and I abandoned a woman and her child, leaving them defenseless. On the day Wilma died, too.

This static attacked me as it had during the Empyrean War.

Thankfully, Tarek caught me before I cracked my head against the floor. "We won't stay long," he said.

His hand trembled against my back, sweat from his skin blending with the perspiration soaking through my clothes. Peter slumped against the wall, jaw sagging and chest heaving. We all were about to lose it.

I turned into Tarek's arms, wishing I could comfort Peter, powerless to even try. "Wh-what the hell's happened?"

Tarek punched the button next to the door with his free hand. "Like I said, energy's coming here. She's a magnet for it. Exemplian energy, this concentrated, will turn brains to slush after a while."

"B-but, Oren doesn't leave?" Ugh! No talking. I wanted to crumble to the ground and let the fuzz put me out of my misery.

Tarek's chest rumbled. "His brain has always been mush."

"Funny." The only thing holding me up was his shaky hand.

When the door whooshed open, the static went into overdrive.

All right, that's it. No more. After everything we'd been through, our own brains were gonna kill us.

"What the hell are you doing here?" Ah, that voice. Its melody was as beautiful as the person who owned it. Too bad his personality mismatched his flawless features.

I managed to face the door. "Well, I missed you, too."

Oren's lips twisted into a scowl, doing nothing to diminish his looks. Man, one person should not have so many perfect genes. Even when he frowned, the man resembled a supermodel. "You're supposed to be safe and sound, living a boring, uneventful life." With each word, he jabbed a finger in my face. "Not coming back here, looking for trouble." He elevated his gaze to Tarek, and shock brightened the blue. "Well, sonofabitch. Why is it when dang–"

"Yeah, yeah, we heard it before," I said. Sweat leaked from every pore, and another quick inspection of Peter said we should get out of here. "Can we talk somewhere…less debilitating?"

Oren shook his head–and Tarek guided me to a set of stairs. On our way down, he said to Oren, "Help the boy, will you? We'll talk in the lobby."

"Damn it all!" Oren dragged Peter down the stairs, bitching the entire time. "Not only are you not to be here, you're dead as far as these people are concerned."

Each step dimmed the static until it reduced to a dull throb, but my hands refused to stop shaking. We hit the lobby, and after taking a deep, cleansing breath, I reluctantly left Tarek's arms to face Oren. All the painted despair on the walls–NOT REAL tarnishing almost every inch of space–solidified my resolve. I'd show these people they were real. As soon as I helped saved them.

"Not anymore." My voice came out as thick as glue. "It's time to bring me back to life."

"Why?" Concern replaced his scowl. "What happened?"

Tarek gestured to Peter, who remained silent, head bent. "He happened."

Peter's shoulders fell even lower. Before I could stop myself, I wrapped his skinny body in my arms. "It's okay. We're gonna fix it, remember?" I tilted his chin. Tears. *Poor, poor boy.* "I–"

"He brought Exemplar to you, didn't he?"

I glared at Oren once Peter's waterworks worsened. He pulled away from me and met Oren's gaze. "I screwed up, but"–he wiped his eyes– "I'll do anything to make it right."

The real reason we let him come with us almost escaped my mouth. But hope could break a person or make them whole, depending on the outcome to a problem.

Instead, I stood straighter, not hugging him anymore. The last thing he needed was me treating him like an infant in front of Tarek and Oren. "Yeah, you will. And you can start by staying right beside us when we head out there, understand?"

Peter used the edge of his sweatshirt to clean his face. "I won't leave your side, Lena."

The boy melted my heart to liquid. "I'll hold you to that." I focused on Oren. If I looked at Peter's sad eyes anymore, I'd lose it. "You have any ideas how we could get the word out fast? Otherwise, my plan is to skip down the sidewalks and yell it at the top of my lungs."

Humor lit up those baby blues. "You would, wouldn't you?"

"You bet your ass, I would." I caught Tarek grinning from the corner of my eye. He didn't say a thing, just shook his head.

Oren crossed his arms. "Well, don't do anything Lena-like yet." He stole a glimpse up the stairs. "But I can't go with you." His attention returned to me. "If anyone gets close to Celeste, our future plans–whatever they might be–are blown out of the water."

I punched him in the shoulder. "No shit. Not like I'd let the entire world know our one advantage."

He rubbed where I hit him. "Our?"

"Yeah, it's *ours*." My mood lifted at the smile spreading across his face. His smiles were as rare as spotting a black rhino in my backyard. "I've come to save the day."

"Lucky me." He went to the door and scanned the street through the tiny window. "I know a guy. He runs a"–Oren grimaced after a quick look at Peter–"gentlemen's club."

Unlike my gorgeous, pain-in-the-ass friend, I didn't do subtlety. "A whorehouse?"

He cringed and gestured toward Tarek. "And you love this?"

Tarek shrugged with a grin. "Call it a sickness."

"Har-har, so funny," I said. "But enough. So, what can your pimp do for us?"

"He's not my–you know what?" He waggled a finger in my face. "I didn't miss you at all."

"Yeah, you did." I winked. "What can he do?"

Oren dragged a hand through his hair, his gaze constantly darting up the stairs as if being away from the static was more detrimental to his brain than being near it. "He has skills. The kind that will have every working screen and hologram able to broadcast whatever he wants. You go to him, and he'll have your face smeared across the entire world in minutes."

I headed for the door. "Sounds good to me. Point us in the right direction."

"Ah, not so fast." Oren seized my elbow. "If an authority prick sees you guys on the way, you'll all be dead before you have a chance to break hell loose."

I shrugged from his grip, ready to argue. But the excitement in his eyes–I remembered that excitement. The lust for a fight, once you recognized it, was as familiar as your own face. He wasn't stopping me. He wanted the battle–unlike me.

I sighed. "What's the plan, then?"

"You go to Yosef, do your thing, and head to Shalen."

I rolled my eyes. "Great, how do we do that?"

"In my hovercraft. Yosef's coordinates are programmed into the mainframe."

"And where's your hovercraft?"

He pulled a keycard from his back pocket and dangled it in my face. "You brought weapons, right?"

"Oh… Oh, damn."

CHAPTER 20

TAREK

For Every Action…

Arratoi. They weren't any more pleasant during the second encounter. The trip to Oren's hovercraft counted as twice dealing with the rabid beasts up close–in the six lives he'd lived here. Exemplar's least favorable secret, like a bastard child of a king. No matter how much effort the Synod had thrown at an extermination, the animals bred as zealously as they ate. Now that no one bothered to attempt culling the population, the rats outgrew their hiding spots. Animal attacks on the streets–something unheard of for centuries–were now as common as authority inspections in Heterodox. Tarek spent a good amount of time popping off the vermin while on his rooftop. But to go into their den, the hub of overpopulated rodents? Stupid.

Luckily, he had a few tubes of salve and a mini-flamethrower–after a quick stop at his apartment. By the time they reached the door leading to the hanger, loud screeches and the stench of piss and rot assailed them all. Peter let go of his stomach, as he'd done the first time. So did Lena.

Yes, so did he.

"Sonofabitch." Lena wiped the leftover dribble at the corner of her mouth. A glowing contego suit peeked from under her sweatshirt as her arm lifted. She had two in her apartment for her and Peter. Just in case, she'd said. "Do you think Oren's ride is in one piece?"

Tarek nodded, unable to explain the strength of Exemplian steel. The smell, thick and coating his skin, suffocated him, stealing his desire to talk and let the stench into his mouth. Rats, if they clawed or gnashed at the vehicle, wouldn't even scuff the paint.

Scratching at the door almost had him turning around and risking the chance of an authority capture. Peter actually circled back toward the stairs.

Tarek yanked him to his side. Only taking shallow breaths, he forced himself to speak. "I go first," he said to Lena, "and you bring up the rear."

"Yeah, okay." Her guns were already in her hands. "You make sure to fry as many as possible."

"Will do." His eyes watered, the stench biting into his nose. He engaged the flamethrower, the small barrel lighting up green. He then jerked Peter in between him and Lena. "Shoot at everything."

Fear glimmered in Peter's eyes. "Wh-what about light? How're we supposed to see?"

Tarek held up his weapon. "This'll give us all we need." After Peter nodded, his face almost translucent, Tarek clenched the door handle. Immediately after the latch gave, he blew fire. "Go! Go!"

The flames torched any animal within a six-foot radius. Squealing pierced Tarek's skull as death spread through the hanger; burning rats smelled worse than live ones. He pushed forward, the urge to run almost taking over the need to move steadily and fire into the snarling crowd.

Once Oren's ride came into view, Tarek waved Lena ahead with one hand, never letting up on the fiery assault. She ran to the door as a charred rat toppled from the vehicle's roof and waved the keycard. The door flew up, and Lena gestured for Peter with a frantic hand until the boy jumped in. She signaled to Tarek next.

He gave their attackers one last fire splurge and leaped into the driver seat, with Lena right behind him on the passenger side. When the doors hissed shut, scratching and salivating mouths full of sharp teeth scraped at the windows.

"Did anyone get bit?" Lena was already yanking open her bag and pulling out salve.

"N-no, I'm good." Peter hacked up a lung as he huddled in the back.

"Tarek?"

He flipped on the engine, spat out Yosef's name, and brought them off the ground, steering toward the exit. A hologram of numbers appeared above, and the hovercraft reverted to autopilot. "No extra holes, either," Tarek said.

"Well, all right, then." She returned the medicine into her bag. "You know where we're going?"

The hovercraft broke free from the hanger, and Tarek glanced in her direction. Dirty, smelling like feces, and perfect, not a scratch on her. He pointed to the numbers. "Yes, ma'am."

Tarek knew the name Yosef. Oren's contact, the person who supplied their sustenance injections. He had never met him, though. As with Lena and Drea, he was a secret Oren didn't share with anyone in Exemplar.

Lena grinned, her eyes vivid green behind all that dirt. "Let's go piss off a few elders."

∞ ∞ ∞

No underground hanger gave cover when Tarek landed on a busy street. As much as he hated rats and their stench, the rodents were more pleasant than the Synod's authority. Two strolled by, tasers out and expressionless faces pointed forward. No emotion, no original thoughts, with only the methodical goal to seek and destroy traitors. No one understood their motives, or why they chose to question certain people. But for everyone living in Heterodox, the lifeless authority shells were the enemy.

"Wait." Tarek stayed Lena's hand, preventing her from opening the door. "Let them pass."

Lena said nothing, her attention fixed on the two glowing contego suits that didn't blend at all with a crowd of Heterodox citizens. Clean-cut and sleek clothes never meshed well with brightly colored hair, torn shirts, piercings, and tattoos. The two authority burned like a cancer in this sector's otherwise perfect chaos.

Once they moved farther down the street, Tarek released Lena's hand. "Okay, time to go."

"This city…like a rave party vomited all over the place." Lena flipped her hood up and turned to the backseat. "You stay beside me."

"Yeah, yeah, I will." Peter lifted his hood, too. "You gotta trust me."

Tarek frowned. "Sure, kid, soon as you can prove yourself trustworthy." He didn't miss Lena's scowl in his peripheral. She'd get over it. Perhaps one day he'd get over it, too. After donning his own hood, he grinned. "We look like thieves."

Lena hit the latch. Music, vendors' fried wares, and blurred chatter gusted into the silent vehicle. "We'll blend right in."

"Not likely." Tarek snapped up his bag from the back and popped his door open.

"Ah, shit. This the place, I take it?" She pointed at the holograms of people having sex–in creative ways–along the sidewalks. People walked through them, no longer sensitive to naked flesh and gyrating bodies.

"Yes." Tarek's faced burned. After all his lives, this…ah…display made him feel like a prepubescent teen.

Before she got out, Lena gave Peter one last instruction. "Keep your eyes closed."

"Um…" Peter, completely hypnotized by the holograms, followed her out, eyes wide open.

Right. No way would the kid miss the show. Lena's demand worked about as well as their little swear jar.

"Here we go." Tarek slid from his seat, waving Oren's keycard over the security pad before the door shut.

Lena dodged the grunting, holographic bodies, weaving in and out of the couples as if they were tangible. The shopkeeper spared her sensibilities today. Sometimes real bodies *did* take the place of holograms in front of establishments like this one. Shops like Yosef's were in high demand here. What better way to get a person feeling like a human than having sex?

Peter found the decency to turn combustible red and keep his head down, following Lena's path. Tarek almost felt sorry for him. Almost. The kid wanted to come here, be a grown-up fighter, but he couldn't handle the most grown up act of them all?

When Lena veered too far off target, Tarek gripped her elbow. "Time to walk through it," he said.

"Ugh…just…" She pointed to one particularly talented couple. "Can the human body even to do that?"

So many things he could've said but refrained. "Apparently so. Come on, they don't bite." The moment that promise left his mouth, another couple groaned louder than the thumping music polluting the streets.

"Are you sure?"

"Pretty sure. Keep your head down."

She snatched Peter's arm and moved forward. People, real people, didn't bother to get out of their way. Most walked as if in a trance, the craziness around them camouflaged with familiarity.

Tarek shrugged through the crowd, careful not to piss anyone off lest they take the time to look at his face, and headed straight for the orange door at the center of the hologram show.

Once the darkness inside folded them in, the fried food odors from outside transformed to unwashed bodies and the sting of alcohol. Softer music played, seducing music. The only light in the place came from the glowing tattoos on the workers' faces, multi-colored for the women and flashing blue for the men. Those face tattoos, marks of Exemplar's sullied. Most people Tarek had known in his lives used these people, despite the station in which they lived. Yet, no one ever admitted to it–except Oren.

Celeste came from these people; Oren saved her.

"Oh, my–I don't know if I should be repulsed or… Their faces, like Celeste. Beautiful." Lena stared at the crowd, her gaze darting from tattoo to tattoo. The place resembled the deepest depths of an ocean, dark except for the glowing entities floating in the abyss. Hypnotizing.

"Oren said he took Celeste from one of these places." Tarek clasped Lena's hand, guiding them deeper into the orgy. "Maybe this was the place." He stopped a man a half-foot taller than him. "We're looking for Yosef."

"Are you, now?" The man walked his fingers down Tarek's arm. "You sure you're not here for me, gorgeous?"

Tarek smacked the guy's touch away, ignoring Lena's laugh in the background. "Where is he?"

The man's blue tattoo blinked faster. "Oh, I like them tough. Maybe next time?"

"Where."

The worker's face lost some of its luster, as if he grew tired of the whore act for a moment. "Straight back, glowing rim around the door. You can't miss it."

He sauntered off, looking for a surer payday. The conversation was spoken in Exemplian, but Lena seemed to get the gist, her laughter proof.

Tarek bent to Lena's ear. "Stop laughing."

She tilted her head and kissed him, smiling against his lips. "Staking my claim before any other beautiful people hit on you," she said.

He shook his head, even as his lips burned from her touch. No matter where they were, she made him forget things. "Funny. Let's go."

They bumped against slick bodies on their way to the office. Some were workers, others nameless patrons who had no qualms about a stranger taking their body for a ride in the dark. The tattoos delineating male from female were only a courtesy. Most probably cared little for who made them feel alive, man or woman. Not even the threat of authority kept people from this place.

Tarek cringed when his foot landed on bodies. Outside was a church compared to the happenings in here. Good thing the lights were off. If Peter knew–hell, if Lena knew–they trekked through a room with naked, copulating bodies, the episode with the male whore would be the least exciting thing to happen.

The glowing outline of a door flared amongst the crowd of sweat and music. The tattoos, otherworldly at first, now threatened seizures, the flickering strobes relentless. Tarek banged on the door until a piercing red light zipped out in front of him. The little orb bounced, its pinprick light zooming in on his eyes, waiting.

"Oren sent us."

A few seconds later, the tiny ball blinked off, and the door cracked open.

After a deep breath, Tarek led the way in.

Today, Heterodox would find out their hero lived.

After the message broadcasted, he'd make sure she stayed that way.

CHAPTER 21

LENA

The Art of Public Speaking

Sweat saturated my skin, my contego now an uncomfortable sauna suit. As bizarre and uncomfortable as wading through an orgy was, spending days in that macabre display sounded way more pleasant than outing myself to the elders.

"Don't worry, I have you." Tarek's hand pressed into the small of my back, pushing me forward after the red light zoomed away.

"Right, yeah." I could do this–address an entire world. I could. Hopefully, they'd accept what I had to say. If they didn't, the lines needed to be open so Tarek could get us the hell out of there. Otherwise–no. Who wanted to think about otherwise?

I tugged Peter inside the quieter room, refusing to let go of his hand, too afraid he might want to get lost in the whirling crowd in the main room and catch a disease or two. Funny in an entirely unfunny way, he was pissed when I tried to hook him up with a nice girl, but his eyelids refused to come down in the middle of whorehouse central.

His words came back to me then: *I'm not like these people...I live a lie.*

Here, he didn't have to lie about anything because he was exactly like everyone else in that room, this entire world.

Damn.

The door shut behind us, and the silence screaming in my ears pushed me out of my head. Now wasn't the time–later, after I finished turning myself into a glaring target.

"This place is huge," Peter said, turning in a circle.

I grinned, nudging his shoulder. "And thankfully less populated."

Didn't that create a flame on his narrow cheeks? "Y-yeah, good thing."

He was right. This...office, I guess...was bigger than the theater's lobby. Every piece of furniture to the walls and carpet were glossy white. The color and darkness and brain-screwing music in the main room were obviously too insulting to let bleed into here.

"Okay, sit." I pointed to a row of levitating chairs in the corner. "And if you value your ability to walk, don't go back out there."

Peter's face turned close to purple. "I won't, geez."

Tarek's hand still rested on my back, and the last thing I wanted to do was leave the safety of his touch. But he wasn't the one playing hero today, was he? Time to let him off the hook and try to fake the part myself.

I went to the only other door in the room and pounded. "Hello?"

"Do you think that's a good idea?" Tarek stood behind me, not willing to relinquish his hero role. No worries, I could compromise. He'd be mine while I pretended the capability of being everyone else's.

"Probably not, but I'm all out of good ideas." I faced him. "I just want to get the message out and get out of this city. Shalen's nightlife suits me a hell of a lot better."

Tarek flinched.

Wrong thing for me to say.

He had died at Shalen. He was reborn there, too. Reborn with the notion he wasn't worthy of happiness.

I pressed against his chest, and the sadness on his face eased some. "My turn to say you have me."

"I like the sound of that."

He backed up as the door opened. All tenderness evaporated from his face, replaced with stone. My warrior returned, ready to fight for me. I pulled my gun from the lip of my jeans and turned. I'd fight for him, too.

"Who are you?" I said.

A man, whose smooth face did nothing to hide the age in his endless brown eyes, lifted his hands, a grin playing on his thin lips. "You're in my domain. Perhaps I should ask the questions." He came forward, pushing me back with only his smile. Looking at him was like staring into the eyes of a vulture waiting for its prey to die. "But I already know who you are, little hero. The prodigal daughter has returned from the dead, yes?"

"Ah…"

Fear slinked through my veins as painful as arctic water. This guy shouldn't have intimidated me, this pimp. He did, though. Maybe the static he threw off caused my courage to take a break. He was a Guide–a strong one. I kept moving until I bumped into the solid shield of Tarek's chest. He didn't budge, forcing the man to stop before he climbed on top of me. No one intimidated my giant.

Being free of danger for months softened me up, something I had to rectify soon if life held any future appeal.

"Yosef, I presume," Tarek said. "Oren told us you could help."

Yosef never took his attention from me. "Did he? And what, may I ask, do you need help with?"

Tarek's hand came up to rest on my hip. "We want Exemplar to know Lena lives."

Yosef moved to touch my face, ignoring Tarek's answer. "You look nothing like I imagined. Softer…"

Tarek wasn't having it.

"Don't touch her." He yanked me out of the guy's range, his quiet voice not fooling anyone.

Yosef put his hand down, a grin forever stretching his lips. "She comes with a guard dog, too? The great Warden of Arcus?"

All right, get a grip.

As much as I hated to, I left Tarek's protection and lowered my gun. "This is stupid. We're here for you and everyone else out there. Help us, so we can help you."

He blinked, the intensity in his eyes dimming. "Who's the boy?"

"He's mine. Now, will you help or do we have to find someone else who will?"

Not that we had someone else, and I was positive he knew it.

Yosef folded his arms. "Help our greatest hero? What an honor."

I could ignore assholery–sometimes. "My loyal sidekicks and I would greatly appreciate it."

He glowered. "Cute." He moved to a desk so white I didn't even know it existed in the room until he touched its corner. The entire surface lit up with a hologram of the front room– with the lights on. All those people, rutting like animals.

"Peter–"

"Eyes are already closed." His voice dipped, but a definite smile colored his tone.

Hell, I closed my eyes, too.

"The three of you may open your eyes. Your sensibilities are now quite protected."

Laughter bubbled in the back of my throat, probably from hysteria. Yeah, we were tough-ass fighters who had killed and stood in death's path. We were also hardened warriors who couldn't watch a live porn show without shutting our eyes and giggling like ten-year-olds. The dichotomy didn't go over my head. Whatever. I was fine with it.

When I opened my eyes, a blank screen replaced the party, the hologram's edges barely visible. I covered my mouth to hide the obnoxious cackling. *Shut up, brain!*

Yosef smirked. The laughing almost won out again. Dude enjoyed our awkwardness more than the voyeurism on the screens seconds ago.

I looked at Tarek, who had a grin curving one side of his mouth. He gestured toward the screen. "Are you going to make it?"

"Are you?"

"I sure as hell hope so."

"Good." After a quick look at Peter, who gave a thumbs-up, I turned back to Yosef. His smirk still lit his face. "Oren said you could get me on every hologram and screen working in this world."

"I can, yes, but there are consequences. The probability is high that you and your, ah, sidekicks won't make it ten feet from my establishment before the authority swoops upon you."

"A chance we're willing to take." Tarek spoke for all of us, his voice deep and invasive in the sterile, quiet room.

"We'll see, won't we?" Yosef tapped on the desk's surface, doing some sort of tech shit that escaped my scope of understanding. "Have you thought of this message of hope? What you will say to the downtrodden population who will grasp onto every profound word you spew?"

Yeah…no, I hadn't. And if the jerkoff didn't quit talking to me like I was a moron, he'd get a bullet in the head, and I'd give myself a crash course on how all that computer crap worked. Couldn't be too hard.

"You know what?" Courage settled back onto my shoulders. This guy stood between my family and me. Zander and Erin depended on this plan to make sure Exemplar stayed away, and I had no desire to disappoint them. "Next thing you say better not piss me off, or I'm gonna–"

"What Lena means to say is, 'thank you.'" Tarek held my arm, saving Yosef from a throat punch. "What do you propose she say?"

I gave Tarek as much irritation as I could muster. His eyes pleaded with me, one of our silent conversations we were always great at in full swing.

Yes, I got what his eyes were telling me. Play nice. No hitting the pimp.

Tarek let go of me and stepped forward. "We're open to any suggestions."

"Why, Warden, are you asking for my counsel?"

Tarek's grinding teeth were as conspicuous as the humping bodies in the front room. "I'm no longer Warden."

"Oh, yes, quite right. An ancient is whelping the next Warden. An ancient snogging an Exemplian, no less. Ooh, what some wouldn't give to leap at the chance to–well, neither here nor there, really."

Anyone who tried wouldn't get anywhere near my family or Arcus. Winston and Farren would never allow it.

Swallowing all the threats begging to come out scratched the back of my throat. "Look, I think we've all gotten off on the wrong foot. How about a do-over?"

Yosef leaned a hip against his desk. "A do-over?"

"Yeah, yes, start over. We obviously need you, but you need us, too."

Those must have been the magic smirk-disappearing words. "I need nothing from you, Tainted."

Shit. "Okay, listen. I–"

"You came here–this shining ray of hope–and destroyed the social ecosystem of an entire world. And after? You leave. Wipe your hands clean and play dead, leaving millions to suffer." His hands gripped the edge of his desk, his knuckles as white as its surface. "Now, you drop into my establishment like an avenging angel, promising to make it better with a speech?"

A bonfire flared under my skin. "I-I wasn't the only one who came here."

"No, but you were the only one who mattered. The Tainted hero, come to save her suffering Protector and free the people of Exemplar from years of oppression." He shook his head. "All you accomplished was turning a rather peaceful world into a militant state filled with people who discovered they were nothing but lab projects."

"No, no, you're not *lab projects*." I rushed forward. "None of you are."

"Stop." He held out his hands. "It couldn't have been some altruistic act that brought you here, could it? A raging guilt to right a wrong?" His smirk returned. "What's brought you back from the dead, little hero?"

"I…"

He had me. What the hell could I say? He wasn't wrong. "Please, tell me what I can do. Give me a chance to make it right."

No one spoke, the room as silent as a crypt. If Yosef turned us away, authority would keep going to Earth. But more than that, I did want to try to fix things. Give these people a chance at some normality, like my people handed to me–while they kept fighting. Yeah, shame hurt, and it was heavy, too.

Sounds, like bells above a shop's door, filled the room the same time Tarek's warm hand caressed my shoulder. After a deep breath, I lifted my head to an active screen layered with the different sectors of Exemplar. A tiny blue dot floated in the center of it all. From Cynosure to Shalen, the sectors resembled levels of soil in an Earth Science diagram.

"Say I believe you, little hero. Honestly, what *would* you tell these people if I gave you access to my world?"

I tore my gaze from the screen to find Yosef, no longer smirking or angry. He looked almost…defeated. "The truth," I said. My voice filled the room in stereo, with my words translated to Exemplian. The language wasn't as beautiful as Empyrean, more like efficient, clean.

He watched me for what felt like years. "Good." He pointed to the blue light. "Give us your brightest smile, then. You're on in thirty seconds."

Seconds wasn't enough time to prepare a speech for an entire population. But… *Here goes nothing.* I smoothed back my tangled hair and hoped the filth from the rat hanger wasn't too noticeable. Tarek gave my shoulder one last squeeze before going to Peter, leaving me in the spotlight alone. Nerves jumped on my bladder, and I had to pinch my legs together to keep from pissing myself–or heading back into the ambiguity of the main room.

But these people deserved something more than authority hunting them or fearing what the elders would inflict next. Tears hovered in my eyes, and my lips trembled, but I swiped the wetness away. They deserved a fighter, not a weakling. I might not have all the answers, but I had one.

The light blinked green, and I cleared my throat before giving the tiny dot all I could. "Let me say to you all that I'm sorry. And…" My palms sweat and my throat went dry, but I'd give them the same words Winston always gave me. Three little words that made me strong those times when all I wanted to do was hide from the world. "I'm with you."

CHAPTER 22

LENA

Another Escape

The light flashed back to blue, and I sagged to my knees, trying to remember the importance of breathing.

"Well, you've gone and mucked up your chances of making it out alive, haven't you?"

Yosef might've been a tad pessimistic for my tastes, but I had no desire to argue the point. We'd get out of here. I just had to figure out how my lungs worked first.

Strong hands hooked under my arms, lifting me as if I weighed nothing. "Do you have a back way out?" Tarek held me up when I wobbled, pulling me flush to his side.

Dammit! Get it together. Most of what I had said into that green light dissolved to fog in my brain. Hopefully I hadn't screwed it up too bad.

"I do, Warden, though it will only buy you moments."

"That'll be enough. Our ride's out front, the red hovercraft." Tarek whipped out the keycard. "Help us. Please."

Yosef stared at the card for a few seconds before snatching it from Tarek's hand. "Take the back door. Go to the end of the hall; last door on the left is your exit." He punched a few keys on his desk. "You have access to the locks." Soon as he finished speaking, the door he initially came out of whirred open.

I had enough sense to search for Peter, my head thick with an endorphin rush and Yosef's static. "Time to go," I said after I found him.

"I'm ready." Peter already had his gun drawn. The things the kid had to get used to. He was more comfortable with killing than conversing with the opposite sex.

I nodded to Yosef, who smiled. He almost seemed to enjoy this shit. "Thank you."

After a hesitation, he shrugged. "Performing my Exemplian duty, little hero. Your transport will be waiting. Now go. Hurry."

Tarek yanked me away before I had a chance to say anything else. We sped through the back door as Yosef slipped out the front. No music played in that room now, the orgy silent.

Soft orbs hanging every few feet lit the hall, which went on forever. Once we reached the door, Tarek held up a hand. Peter and I stopped, and Tarek pressed a button on the door. What looked like steel transformed to a transparent window.

"What the hell are you doing?" I shoved Peter from the now-clear door.

"We see out, no one sees in. We can hear, too, don't worry," Tarek said. Sweat drenched his clothes, and his spiky hair glistened with it. He peered out, craning his neck to get a view as far down the sidewalk as possible.

In seconds, Oren's vehicle pulled up, no urgency in how Yosef drove it. When it landed, the engine cut off and Yosef climbed out. He didn't even look our way as he strolled around people so motionless they could have been statues. Every set of eyes focused on a hologram of me and my voice translated into Exemplian on repeat.

"Wh-what am I saying to them?"

Tarek bowed his head, closing his eyes. "I'm with you."

I'm with you, I'm with you, I'm with you...

Peter came up behind me. "We gotta go, Lena. Come on." His voice was a ragged whisper in my ear.

These people... Failure after failure after failure–that was all I had amounted to since my world flipped upside down. *No. Stop it!* Not now. "Yeah, okay." *Deep breath.* I nodded to Tarek. "Ready?"

He gave the streets one last sweep before tilting his head to the sky. "Something...feels wrong."

I moved to his side. "How do you mean?"

"Everyone's on pause, including the authority. As if they're waiting for a signal to act."

Not good at all. "From the elders, maybe?"

"Maybe." He scrubbed at his hair again. "I guess we'll find out in a minute. All right, hoods up."

I pulled mine up with my free hand, my fingers shaking too much to tighten it around my head. "You think we should still go out there?"

"We have no other options, Lena. None."

Of course we didn't. "Okay, so what's the plan, then?"

Tarek stuffed his gun in the lip of his jeans. "Put your weapons away, and make sure your suits are on."

I nodded, my gun now hidden under my sweatshirt. A hint of Peter's glowing suit showed when he did the same. Good. His worked.

"Check your suit." Tarek wrenched up my shirt to find my contego glowed as bright as Peter's.

"See? Calm down." Stupid thing to say, seeing as my nerves were coiled tighter than a spring.

Tarek fussed with his hair yet again, his nervous tic, and sweat flew off the tips, hitting me in the face. "We have three yards to cross, that's it. Keep your heads down, no rushing, and make sure to inspect the holograms once or twice."

Oh…no. The holograms of me–wearing the same clothes I had on now. "Tarek?"

As if he came to the realization at the same time, he swore and spat on the ground, his hands on his hips. Silence occupied the hallway as Tarek stared at the sleek floor. I'd wait out his silence. He'd come up with something.

His head popped up. "Take off your clothes."

I didn't question it, just stripped down to my contego. While I did, Tarek rummaged through his bag and pulled out the red T-shirt and jeans he wore a couple nights ago. Regret strained his face as he tossed them to me. "You'll have to turn off your suit. No one but authority wears them here." He tugged a cap from his bag as he continued. "Tuck your hair inside." The hat resembled the glowing skullcaps I'd noticed a few people wearing outside of Yosef's place.

Turning off my contego sucked ass. One bullet and I'd be erased. For good. But I trusted Tarek. There wasn't much of a choice, even if I didn't. His clothes swam on me, the jeans so big I could pull them up to my boobs and still have a length of denim dragging on the ground. "Please tell me these are Exemplian jeans."

Tarek touched the waistband, and the pants shrank to fit. "Lucky for you."

"Yeah, lucky." I put on the shirt, letting it hang on me without worrying about the fit. With my suit turned off, its black sleeves looked like part of my weird outfit. I blended with the crowd now, glowing head and all.

"Okay, you two ready?" Tarek cracked his neck and jumped in place a couple times.

"Ready," Peter said, his hood tight to his head as if he were about to walk into a blizzard.

"As I'll ever be," I added.

Tarek stopped jumping, and in an instant, his lips were on mine. The kiss was quick, but the connection was enough to ease the fear. "We're going to make it," he said. "Only three yards, then the hovercraft will keep us hidden."

"Three yards, no sweat."

He grazed my hand with a soft touch and turned back to the window. Thankfully, traffic moved, making our escape less obvious. One deep breath shifted Tarek's shoulders as he palmed the keypad next to the door.

The clear window dissolved, leaving us exposed to the outside. God, I loved Heterodox now. With so many people littering the walkways, we could weave in and out unnoticed. Unfortunately, Tarek's height made him more of a target, not to mention his shoulders were wider than the average person. Even with his hood up and head down, power exuded from him. Most of the time, I thought him beautiful, the way his big body glided as graceful as a dancer's. Now? If only he were five feet tall and as unassuming as Peter and me.

Three yards dragged as if it were a mile. No one paid attention to anyone else. All eyes remained on the screens or holograms standing right in front of their faces, listening as if I were talking to them and no one else. Some were pale, their eyes wide. Others cried, tearing my heart to shreds. How could I, a kid from the trailer park, have such an effect on these people? At home, I was a nobody, and damn it, I preferred it that way. But these people…

Guilt and I had been best friends for a long time, and as I witnessed the ranging emotions from anger to awe on the faces of these Exemplians, my best friend tagged along for the ride.

I didn't know!

Once the doors hissed open, I had to refrain from diving into the cab and slamming my hands over my ears against all the silent turmoil outside. Nothing in my entire life gave me more security as when the doors came down to hide the three of us from everyone else. Tarek flicked a few switches, and the engine hummed. We lifted off the street to follow the traffic above.

I tugged off that ridiculous hat, its blinking red lights zinging through the air as I tossed it to the back. My attention stayed on the crowd below, wishing I could talk to all of them. Wishing I could hide from them forever, too.

Tarek's warm hand rested on my thigh, his touch palliative.

I turned to him watching me, autopilot engaged and headed to Shalen. "I… Jesus, Tarek. How could I have left them alone to suffer?"

"This isn't your fight."

Just as he said it, a few authority vehicles whipped behind us, coming close enough I could see their emotionless faces peering into the windows. Tarek resumed control, throwing us into hyper-drive, losing our followers.

When we slowed, no one following us, I answered Tarek's statement. "Well"–I licked my dry lips–"it's my fight now."

CHAPTER 23

LENA

Phantoms

Last time we came here, Peter rushed inside. Not this time. Both he and Tarek stared at the deceptively small cabin after we landed and the engine died–twenty minutes ago.

My boys had nightmares associated with this place. Where I only felt relief, they obviously were having flashbacks that sparked an emotion entirely different.

Nothing came to mind, nothing that would take any of their pain away. I wished words would come, some magic incantation with enough strength to erase all the hurt from their faces.

"So…Drea probably wonders who's in her yard." Small talk definitely wasn't gonna fix things, but it was all I had.

Tarek wiped the corners of his mouth, his long fingers shaking. "I'm sure Oren filled her in." He made no move to open the door–or gave any effort to say anything else.

"Yeah, more than likely." I tapped against my leg, staring out the windshield. *Words!* I needed them.

I searched above ancient trees and shadows of cliffs miles away–cliffs where Tarek lost his life. My heart dipped into my stomach. That day had a concrete spot in my mind, right next to Wilma's death. I lost a piece of me when the dagger plunged into his heart–when life vanished from his eyes.

My eyes slammed shut and I pinched the bridge of my nose, wanting to purge the nightmare from my head. I couldn't think about that day; I needed to concentrate on all the silver shuttles cluttering up the skyway. Authority traversed Exemplar without mercy, stealing away any semblance of privacy. Outing myself to the entire population obviously amped up their patrolling efforts.

Whatever trance Tarek thought most everyone fell under seemingly now lifted. Congested air traffic trapped the afternoon sun. Early morning turned into an illusion of dusk minutes after we left Yosef's place and raced from our authority tails. Those shuttles confined us inside ours, no two ways about it. Good thing we hadn't jumped out.

"Denzel's in there–with *her*." Resentment stained Peter's voice. Denzel–his Guide. His father, technically. Of course Peter knew Denzel was in there. Protectors who were Paired with a Guide always knew where they were. Pairing, once thought of as some sort of miracle, ended up being another scientific manipulation of DNA.

I turned and clasped his hand. "You can do this."

"For you," Peter said. "*Only* for you."

Every muscle in my body went lax. Man, I loved him. I loved him and I ached for him. "Thank you." I squeezed his hand once more and faced Tarek. "Okay…we need to park this thing in the underground hanger, avoid the assholes above."

Tarek's face paled more as sweat dripped from his temples, drawing thin lines down his cheeks. "Lena…"

Underground. The same place that contained Drea's smaller version of a Creation Lab. Tarek had died at the cliffs, but he came back to life in her lab. Honestly, for him, I had no idea what he thought worse.

I covered the shaking hand he clamped around the steering lever. "It'll be okay."

"No, it won't." His gaze found mine; horror laced his gray eyes. That look I understood. Panic attacks lived and thrived behind looks exactly like it. "I'm not the kid, so don't feed me the same garbage."

And with panic, anger always accompanied. I stole another quick glance at Peter. His attention drifted between Tarek and me, his face a white sheet. Yeah, he felt Tarek's imminent eruption bubbling, too, the emotions a slithering fog clogging up the atmosphere. Me losing it was one thing. A six-and-a-half-foot man with biceps like boulders was something else entirely.

"Tarek…please." *Please, what, dumbass?* Another moment I wished I had Wilma's wisdom.

The steering lever creaked under his grip. "I can't be here." *Don't lose it, Tarek. Don't.*

I switched my hand to rest on his back, soothing him as best I could without words. Words, in this case, would've snafued an already shitty situation.

Tarek searched my face, his eyes growing wild. Never had his calm evaporated so fast. Sure, he'd yelled before, but this… He skated on the edge of shattering. He finally spoke. "I'm–do you have any idea? Any clue?"

With every ounce of strength I possessed, I kept my voice even–and told him exactly what he didn't want to hear. "If we get out here, they'll see us. But if we sit here any longer, they'll get curious, maybe come down to investigate. If that happens, we all die. You, Peter, Drea, Denzel…me."

He released his hold on the lever to cup my cheeks. "I won't let anything happen to you."

My jaw throbbed where his fingers dug into my skin, his desperation ready to combust. I ignored the pain and concentrated on keeping my voice calm. "Then we have to get this thing in the hanger." I covered his hands with mine. "*Please.*"

Crackling lights brightened the monitor.

Tarek flinched and let go of my face, his gun out before I could blink my eyes.

"Wait." I lowered his shooting arm. "Look. It's Drea."

Drea's image projected from the console, her eyes wide and mouth open. With Exemplian technology, nothing was ever private.

She saw everything. Tarek losing it…with his gun waving in the air–near her son.

To her credit, she changed her expression to a poker face rivaling Belva's. "Their trackers have you targeted. Forget the hanger and go to the shed. Peter will get you to safety." The image flashed away with the last word she spoke.

Sonofabitch!

I stole one more look above and shaking attacked my arms and legs. "A few are coming down." I closed my eyes for a couple seconds before pinning Tarek with all the fear flooding my body. "We need to move."

Sweat soaked his shirt, the fabric clinging to his chest. But he headed for the shed attached to the back of the cabin. The few yards to the doors took eons. Three shuttles now plummeted to the field. Their engines, like wind chimes on steroids, blared at us even through the protection of our own vehicle.

Tarek didn't stop. That familiar hard edge returned to his face. The shed's doors whirred open to what appeared to be a rundown interior filled with ancient-looking tools easily found on Earth–in the year 3098. But in Exemplar, without a button making them blink or do some other fantastical act, they were just old tools.

As soon he parked on the landing pad, Tarek turned to Peter. "What next?"

"Let me out." Peter slapped the back of my seat until I lifted my door and jumped out. He followed, rushing to the back of the shed. Once he opened a door on the far left wall a crack, which led into a little mudroom, he fell to his knees and pushed a few things from a spot on the floor. He pressed against the dirty ceramic, and a manhole as wide as Tarek's shoulders appeared. "This takes us underground."

Tarek's door shut as I turned to him. If he lost it again, we'd be dead in minutes. But all our bags filled his hands, his face stoic.

Thank you, whoever's listening.

Before Tarek went to Peter, he looked through the open door to the mudroom. "I would never guess what this place is. Your mother's thought of everything, hasn't she?"

"She's not my mo–"

"Save it." Tarek squatted by Peter. "Do you need help with the latch?"

Peter shook his head, his palm already covering a keypad that lit up with the exit's rim. "No. I need to–there!" The hatch popped open without a sound. "You two first. I'll close it on my way down."

Thank God. Tarek was back to being Tarek, and we had an out–until they came knocking on the front door, of course. That tired line about life flashing before your eyes rang with a load of clarity as I rushed down the ladder, my boots clanging against the metal.

Every nerve in my body begged for Peter to close our escape route before the authority stormed our sanctuary. But I kept quiet as I concentrated on the happenings above, my teeth clamped on the insides of my cheeks with the effort. Blood drizzled down my throat as I bit harder when the shed doors

189

burst open–just as the manhole cover quietly sealed shut. Peter then scrambled down the ladder after Tarek.

"Won't they look for an escape hatch?" I dragged hair from my face, hating how my voice shook.

"Sure they will." Peter jumped from the ladder. "But they won't see it. My m–ah, Drea's smart when it comes to security stuff. The keypad out there won't show up without her palm or mine. Or Denzel's, I guess."

Tarek gripped my elbow, dragging me to his side. "They'll assume it's a trap, maybe go around to the front door shooting."

"They can assume all they want," Peter said. "I guarantee they won't get past Denzel. His words are a hell of a lot faster than their bullets." Peter faced me. "And what do you always say about 'assume'?"

"Um…"

"I'm not the ass this time." Peter took off down a long corridor, dim blue lights built into the walls guiding us.

If I hadn't known better, I'd have said Peter was excited to see his mother. Or maybe it was Denzel? Whatever the change from outside until now, I wouldn't complain. This Peter was the Peter I remembered from a year ago: a kid excited to prove something.

I examined Tarek. *Oh no.* His sanity was slipping.

Unlike Peter, who either forgot his anxiety or got over it, Tarek's threatened to erupt in the safety of the tunnel–a tunnel that led to food and weapon caches, the upstairs, and Drea's Creation Lab. I groped for his hand, clasping it tightly. "It's okay."

"I…I'm having trouble with…" He shook his head. "All right. Okay."

We followed Peter in silence, neither of us willing to rehash the past or dig into the crux of Tarek's issues. But midway down the hall, Peter stopped, his back ramrod straight.

Only one person would've had that kind of instantaneous effect on the kid.

Drea. Her static clung to my brain like tar.

I picked up my speed.

Please don't snap.

Please don't snap.

This would be Peter's insanity test, right there in front of him. The woman who gave him life, using machines. The way most Exemplians came to be, except people like Farren, a natural-born.

"Peter." His name left my tongue like air. I let go of Tarek and ran to him, the thumping from my boot soles on the sleek floor interrupting the tension.

If regret were a tangible thing, it'd be Drea's face. I fought the urge to hug her, opting to console Peter instead. His lanky body shook in my arms, but he kept his attention on the woman in front of us. Hate didn't emanate from him, but confusion did in thick waves. Yet, underneath his confusion hid something warmer, giving me hope. Love gleamed in his light eyes, eyes like his mother's. Miracles. He'd spent almost a year despising her from a distance, but maybe seeing her had changed something in him.

Maybe…

As much as I would've liked to play mediator, we had other things to worry about now, like the authority ransacking the shed in search of where we went.

I cleared my throat. "They're behind us."

Drea's tear-filled eyes drifted to me, and her eyelids fluttered as if she only then realized I stood there. The faint blue light illuminated her skin, making her ageless. "All will be well."

She waved a hand, and to her right, a hologram of her cabin lit up. Not the highly advanced cabin with every amenity imaginable that I remembered. No, this time, the cabin looked like a small, cozy shack big enough for one person. A wooden bunk layered with quilts hid in the corner, and a scarred writing desk stacked with actual yellowing paper sat next to it. A fireplace sang with snapping logs. I swear I could even smell the wood smoke filling the cabin in the sterile hallway.

Tarek's hands, his palms moist and hot, pressed onto my shoulders when Denzel stared into the hologram projector's eye, his face set in grim lines. "Be ready, just in case," he said. His voice blared in the hallway as if he spoke through a bullhorn.

The four of us stood dead still, guns drawn and engaged.

Denzel answered the door, his holographic form beside me as if I answered it with him. His robes swayed while he gestured for six authority members to enter with a plastic smile. "Please, do come in, though it may become a tad stuffy in here. Is there something I can assist you with?"

Three Protectors took his offer and the others stayed outside, weapons pointed at Denzel's chest.

The men weaved around us as they searched, their holograms even walking through us in the process. I could almost feel their flesh mixing with mine. One of the men who stayed at the door nodded in the shed's direction. "Is that your aircraft?"

"Why, yes, of course. I've just returned from Cynosure." Denzel lowered his voice, his face a perfect collation of fear and intrigue. "I must say the goings on have me quite dismayed. Is it true Lena Montigue has come back to Exemplar? She is alive, after all?"

Montigue. Tarek's last name and what Old Lena's last name had become during a lifetime before mine.

The man ignored his question. "Do you have documents stating that vehicle is yours, sir?" So professional, so emotionless.

"Is there an issue?" Denzel pulled a thin silver stick from his robe sleeve.

"Our trackers were concerned you might be in need of assistance."

I snorted. Yeah, concerned.

"Well, as you can see, I'm quite all right."

"The documents, sir."

Denzel pressed the tip of whatever he had, and a hologram of documents bounced from it and into the Protector's hand. As he scanned the papers, swooshing through one document after another, Denzel's face remained serene, almost bored.

"What was your business in the capital this morning?" The Protector didn't bother looking away from the hologram.

"I am a recorder of notes and deeds. My office happens to be on the outskirts of our once-beloved capital buildings." Denzel actually sounded heartbroken.

"You've proof of this?"

Denzel pointed at the hologram. "In the documents you scan."

The Protector stopped a moment and looked up with his eyebrow raised.

"I am always prepared, especially in this time of discontent." Denzel swept a hand up to the sky littered with silver shuttles. "Anything I can do to prevent hindering the capture of this traitor and ease your burden."

"I thank you for your cooperation." The Protector clenched his hand into a fist, erasing the hologram from the air. "Please be aware the Tainted and those of her acquaintance have been known to frequent parts of Shalen. If you are in need of assista–"

"I will contact the authority, for certain. And I appreciate your concern."

"Very well." The Protector waved the three roaming asshats from the cabin.

Once they left, Denzel shut the door, his calm vanishing. His pale face came so close to mine, I almost forgot he was a hologram and feared he might kiss me. The image snapped off, leaving the four of us alone in an empty hallway.

I bent over, hoping no vomit escaped. We made it out of another storm. Impossible, but I'd take it. Tarek slumped to the floor, covering his face with trembling hands. This place, it broke him all over again.

Drea took hold of Peter's hands, her eyes declaring an ocean of promises. Promises I hoped she'd keep to herself. Peter needed another empty promise as much as he needed a stake driven into his heart.

Thankfully, she only said two words. "Welcome home."

CHAPTER 24

OREN

No More Planning

Levitating chairs were supposed to be comfortable, the highest form of technology that cushioned the ass like sitting on a cloud. But add uncontrolled static to the mix and the contraptions became conduits for motion sickness.

Celeste's tattoo, constantly rainbows for the last week, fluctuated without any reprieve. Lena being here forced her control out the window and into the middle of the racket outside. A window they had to keep closed to block the heightened pleas and cries from citizens. Lena's message made things worse, something he knew would happen initially.

But as they sat across from each other, Celeste's eyes shut so tightly veins protruded from the delicate skin on her forehead, Oren worried the temporary bedlam would set back her progress.

"Listen to me, Cel. Find your shell. Focus." He gripped her hands, willing any strength he had into her pores.

"Why is she here? She will die; they will not let her live." Her clammy hands trembled, and with each word the static grew louder, more potent.

Oren felt his eyelids droop. His body pleaded with him to fall to the floor, succumb to her power–or shoot another dose of PD into his neck. He had dosed ten times already in the last week, more than his usual.

Not this time. He needed to feel her control–when she finally found it again.

"She won't die, too stubborn." His voice wavered, his words coming out in drunken syllables. "And Tarek won't let her. Don't worry. *Focus, please.*"

"But the boy..." Her voice hitched, those veins on her forehead matching the brightness of her ever-changing tattoo. "Drea will refuse to help. She'll–"

As he explained to her over and over, "I've already contacted her. She knows the story, and she's onboard. Please, beautiful. *Please.*"

His admission eased her tension, her hands relaxing in his grasp. "You do not lie?"

"Look into my mind, and you'll see for yourself."

Her tattoo slowed its change: *green...red...blue...gold...* After a moment, an actual smile softened her lips. "I see now."

"Excellent." The static lifted a fraction. "Now, find your shell. Find it. Remember: this is your weapon, not your weakness."

"My weapon..." Her eyes fluttered behind her lids, searching for her inner peace–him. Just as she was his.

At last, silence.

And there was her power, real power: euphoria drenched in love.

The dissociative fugue capturing his brain dissipated, quiet never so addicting as right after Celeste gained control. "You did it, beautiful." He smiled, the action feeling sloppy and watery.

Forgetting his restraint, he kissed her. Her lips tasted like cinnamon. A moan escaped, his or hers he didn't know, or care. His life resided in this woman. He brought a trembling hand to her long, blond hair, weaving his fingers in its softness, bringing her closer. After twenty years of fasting, he starved for her.

"Oren." His name escaped her lips, still connected to his.

He didn't want to talk anymore; he wanted to feel. Feel her.

She brought her hand up to his chest and gave a gentle push, not breaking contact with his lips. "I must tell you…"

His breath escaped in a whoosh, his self-control ready to snap. He lifted his mouth from hers, and immediately felt shame crawling under his skin, marring the magic she had cast. "I'm sorry. I–"

She tilted his chin with steady, strong fingers until their eyes met. "I am not."

He shook his head, trying to keep calm on the outside as tsunamis flared on the inside. "I'm not helping much, am I?"

She beamed, causing her face to glow. "Oh, I must disagree."

When his humiliation cleared enough to see her gaze, something…happened. Her tattoo, not undulating blue and gold with desire, no. It was solid gold, a sign of focus–absolute focus. "Cel?"

"My weapon. *Our* weapon." She leaned in and touched his mouth to hers again, this time softly. "You are my light, Oren. My strength."

Miracles. They existed, as Grace had promised him years ago. "I–" His communicator dinged in his pocket, vibrating, screaming. "Shit."

He pulled it out and hesitated before punching a button. He had ignored the pimp's incessant calls long enough. Besides, this would be a perfect test for Celeste, see if she could hold her control around others.

Yosef's hologram jumped into the room, the man's face twisted with barely restrained anger. "So she's alive *and* in my world, then?"

Desire and awe that filled his insides argued against Yosef's intrusion. He made an effort to clear his head and shrugged. "Surprise."

"*Surprise*?" Yosef flailed his hands in the air, so unlike the put-together man who had connections to everything. "A little warning would have been appreciated. And Arcus's prior Warden, too? When did he crawl from the gutters? You said he spent his days basking in woe."

"I guess he snapped out of it."

Tarek's apartment below flashed in his mind before he could shut it down. *No thinking.*

Yosef tilted his head to the side, some of the animosity erasing from his face. "Did he? Interesting." His gaze found Celeste sitting serenely, her control well intact. She passed the test. Good. "You look…stronger." Icicles tipped Yosef's politeness. To Yosef, Celeste would always be a whore, something he had told Oren years ago–right before he tried to put a bullet in her head.

Celeste nodded to the man, her countenance regal. "I am, thank you."

Pride burst in Oren's chest. Yes, she did look stronger. She had never been able to control the power for this long–or with another person in the room, even a hologram.

Yosef's image came closer to Celeste. "And here, I believed the energy would do you in." He hesitated. "I'm…happy to see the opposite has happened."

Oren stood in front of Celeste, blocking her from the hologram, and changed the subject. "I should have contacted you sooner. But I thought it better to have Lena arrive unannounced–just in case."

The skin around Yosef's digital eyes tightened. "In case of what?"

Oren shrugged again, forcing his mind to button up and fall in line.

"Perhaps you should trust me with your secrets, Protector, seeing as I'm responsible for enabling you to stay in this quaint apartment with her." Yosef moved closer, searching for…something. "And the boy? Who does he belong to?"

"He's no one," Oren said. "A kid Lena found last year who defected to Earth."

Yosef's gaze seemed to focus beyond Oren's eyes to search his brain. No matter. If the guy actually had the talent, which he never admitted to, there was nothing there to find.

Yosef frowned after a few seconds. "Lena has only made things worse. Elders will make an example of those she claims to want to help." His voice was even, unemotional. "She should never have come back."

"She didn't have much of a choice, Yosef." Oren paused. "The authority found out she was alive. They tried to kill her. She has as much desire to end the elders' reign as anyone here."

A tic developed near Yosef's left eye. "She does not have the means to stop what has been in power for millennia."

"No more, Guide." Celeste's voice, strong and commanding, whispered behind Oren. "We thank you for your assistance. Please…if we need anything else, may we contact you?"

Yosef's eyes dulled. "Of course." Just like that, all the condemnation left the man's tone.

"Again, our appreciation is boundless," Celeste said. "But as you can see, we are in the middle of something."

Oren stared on in shock, speechless. She did it. She kept her control *and* manipulated Yosef's mind–through a hologram, no less.

"Very well. Good day to you both." Yosef's image clicked off.

Oren kneeled in front of Celeste, Yosef already forgotten. He grasped her hands, revering her as a god. "You're amazing."

She freed a hand from his grip to stroke his cheek. "Not so hard when dealing with weak minds."

He laughed, kissing the fingertips he held. "Yosef is far from weak."

"Perhaps. But he is not you. I will never control your mind because..." She pursed her lips and then sighed. "Because you hold me as captive as I hold you. So please, do not ever ask again."

"You have my word." He leaned up to kiss her. "You have my everything."

∞ ∞ ∞

They slept, maybe for the first time in eight months, *really* slept. No static, no fear, no synthetic drug.

Until the static erupted again.

Oren snapped up and rolled from the bed. The noise, the debilitating stupor, screeched louder than ever. He folded into the fetal position, trying to get a grip.

Celeste bolted from the bed, racing for the door.

"Wait!" Oren pushed from the floor and stumbled after her.

"They're here, they're *here*." Celeste's hand came up, and the front door flew from its frame.

He froze. Power like that...he'd only ever witnessed with Winston.

"Cel! Stop!"

She kept going. He managed to capture her arm, only slowing her down. The power radiating from her skin seared him. *What the hell?*

She stopped in the hallway, screaming.

"What is it?" Then through the thick noise, he heard it: the raid downstairs. People's shrieks parroted Celeste's cries as

200

orbs came bursting from the floorboards, slamming into her chest and knocking her down.

Oren clenched his jaw, tried to pick her up, and failed. All he could do was drag her back into the apartment as orbs attacked her, and her aura attacked him.

"The door," he said once they made it inside, "we're exposed."

Even as the light beset her, she lifted a trembling hand and guided the door in place, fixed as good as new. *How?*

No time to contemplate it, Oren crawled to the bathroom–to his injections. He fumbled until he found a needle on the sink and fired it into his carotid. Instantly, the static disappeared. Wasting no more time, he yanked off his clothes in exchange for his contego suit hanging by the shower system. He then pulled two of his many guns from a drawer beneath the sink.

"No, Oren. *Please*. They are killing so many. They…they will kill you, too." Celeste tugged his hand to no avail. Whatever power blew the door off–and then fixed it–didn't transmit through her grasp.

"I'll be fine."

She brought his hand to her chest. "I cannot bear losing you."

When the authority made it to their floor–and they would–they'd feel Celeste's aura thirty feet from the door. Luckily, after he brought her here, he purchased all five apartments on the floor to ensure she had privacy. A decision he was more grateful for now. No one had access, either, except Tarek. But they'd find a way in eventually. They always did, and if elders found her…

Never an option.

"You won't lose me." He kissed her, hard, as if it were the first time. The last time. He broke from her mouth, his lips instantly missing hers. Celeste's tattoo sparkled a dim gold.

Miracles. "If I had known... I would have never stopped kissing you."

"*You* are my power." Tears glistened in her eyes as she clutched his hand. "Come back to me, do you hear me? *Come back.*"

He kissed her again. "Stay inside."

He headed to the third floor. One thing he had always succeeded in was killing. Authority wanted to prey on innocents? Not here, not now.

He hit the stairwell landing that led to the third floor, took a breath, and allowed the access panel to read his eye. The door released, and soft cries from open apartments dribbled into the hallway, the smell of charred flesh and blood teasing his nose. But he couldn't feel any of the intruders, PD working as it always did. He passed door after door, quiet, calm. No sign of any authority caught his attention–until he reached Tarek's apartment. Metal crashing to the floor turned his blood to ice.

Elders knew where to look for Tarek. Which meant it wouldn't be long until they wondered why he chose to live in this building. Another deep breath escaped as he sidled up against the broken entryway.

They wouldn't find out today.

Silent as vapor, Oren stalked into the apartment. Three Protectors ransacked Tarek's meager belongings, and one sat in front of his computer console, hacking into the system. In one fluid motion, Oren aimed at the computer hacker's head and popped off a quick round. Brain matter splattered the screen as the man slumped. It didn't take a second before the others blasted Oren's contego with bullets.

None infiltrated the fabric or fazed Oren. He shot one in the head before giving a kick to another in the throat. A bullet whizzed past his ear, skimming the tip. Too close. Oren confronted the shooter, his aim better, dropping him with a bullet between the eyes. Adrenaline rushing through his veins, Oren stomped to the woman he'd kicked. Before she had the chance to lift her gun, he captured her neck in the crook of his arm, squeezing until she stopped struggling.

Silence filled the apartment as he looked around, making sure all of them stayed as dead as he assumed they were. A small sound, like fingernails scratching wood, came from the doorway. Oren turned, his gun up.

He quickly lowered his weapon. Three young men, tattoos and piercings covering every exposed part of skin, shadowed the door, scared and pale.

Oren went to them, not missing how they flinched. "Think you boys could do me a favor?" Blood from the wound on his ear ran down his neck, hot and wet.

All nodded vigorously, hands up and staring him in the eye.

Oren gestured to the four bodies bleeding all over Tarek's dingy floor. "Feed the rats."

One of the boys stepped up. "Th-thank you."

He thought about eight months ago, when these people fought alongside him. What happened to that bravery? "*Fight back*. You don't need to be targets."

The boy shook, fear evident in his dark eyes. "S-since Lena... Authority has already cut off the food supply. Th-they're killing everyone now. Just...shooting them down. How can we fight against that?"

The boy had a point, and it was time they did something about it. No more planning. Action. Now.

"Get rid of the bodies," Oren said. "And I swear to you, this will end. Soon."

As he headed toward the stairs, the boy brave enough to speak said, "Lena said she was with us, and then disappeared. They slaughter us because we believed her. Why hasn't she come back?"

These poor, wretched people, grasping on to any hope flung at them. "She will, son. Hold on for a while longer, and spread the word. We're ending this."

He left the trio to clean his mess and raced up the stairs, his mind already in motion. Instantly after he touched the keypad, the newly fixed door opened to reveal Celeste waiting at the threshold. Her tattoo again raced through colors.

"You are hurt." She lifted a hand to his ear, and warmth rushed through him.

The wound no longer burned.

She healed him. Even without complete control.

"You're doing it, Celeste. You're ready."

"I cannot control the power well, unless…"

Unless they touched. No, more than that. Love channeled through their connection, giving her strength. So simple.

He kissed her glowing cheek and then went to the chair where he left his communicator.

"What are you doing, Oren?"

He punched in Drea's code. "We're leaving here."

CHAPTER 25

LENA

Broken Giant

After I had lost Wilma, a part of my soul darkened and sizzled away. Nothing, or no one, helped. Not Tarek, Farren, my parents. Without that piece of myself, I withered into an aching mass of cantankerous resentment, pushing everyone out. I was broken then. Lost. But what remained constant during my stint in the black was Tarek's tenacity to stand in the line of my fire and hate until my spirit repaired itself. Tarek's love did that. His stubborn, stubborn will had forced me to accept I was worthy when I felt I didn't deserve him or anyone else. That dark place lingered, a reminder that a slice of my heart was missing, but I had learned to live again.

What Tarek did for me then, I needed to do for him now. Only, how to convince him that he was worthy of love when he refused to acknowledge his own humanity? My missing piece would've had the answers–she always did, even if it ended with "dumbass." Just as I thought he was on the mend, this place enlarged that "not real" tumor eating at his soul as methodically as a surgeon slicing into a patient.

Six days.

Tarek hadn't left his room for six entire days. Not to eat. To bathe. Nothing. I wished the room didn't have the tiny bathroom connected to it. I'd have then been able to intercept him when he needed to take a piss. Force him to talk to me.

Drea assured me his pain would ease. Death always exacerbated issues from the past.

I hated hearing that. Again. That excuse would be engraved on my headstone: *Died waiting for the pain of death to pass.*

Tarek took his stuff in there with him, thankfully. In his bag, a month's worth of sustenance injections sat in an inner pocket. He wouldn't starve himself to death. To make sure, I'd stand in front of his door after I woke up, and before I went to sleep, listening. Any rustling, any movement, I'd breathe, releasing oxygen as if someone held me under water for hours.

Day seven. Nothing, still.

Day eight: "Do you think he'll come out soon?" Peter's voice dipped and cracked, something that only happened now when he was nervous or pissed.

I turned, my face burning as if caught peeping on the boys in the locker room. "When he's ready, I guess."

The sun barely peeked through the huge window on the second floor, authority invading the sky blocking the natural light. An otherwise beautiful day brought the illusion of rain and fog and sadness. Elders even ordered the daylight away.

"Come on." Peter laced his fingers with mine. "Time for breakfast–and more hours listening to them argue theories."

I pulled my hand back and did my best not to snarl. "Wait. I'm not ready." I pressed my ear to the door. *Make a sound!*

"Lena, please."

"Wait. Just…wait."

Sound finally stole through the thin metal. A creak, as if Tarek rolled in bed. A sign of life–the life I needed to sustain my own.

206

"Okay. Let's go." Before following Peter to the lift, I kissed the door, as I had for over a week. Stupid, but that door became the substitute for my giant. Proof he inhabited the same world as me. The sound didn't matter, whether a creaking bed, a muffled yell, glass shattering against the wall.

Peter never commented on my ritual, his face forward and hands fidgeting. He was the sole person I allowed to witness my weakness. Drea and Denzel would never see me crack, especially not now, when Exemplar headed to complete anarchy.

Two hours after my broadcast, elders had cut the food supply to Heterodox. Two days after that, Heterodox infiltrated Cynosure. Hungry people had no inhibitions, and authority needed no other reason than theft to gun down desperate scavengers. Drea made sure we saw everything, so we wouldn't forget, become lazy rebels. Holograms blared nonstop on the cabin's main level. We walked through the devastation to go to the kitchen for food, the bathroom, underground to the storage rooms for supplies. Dead bodies flashed on working screens in the capital and the slums of Heterodox, my words scrolled across their lifeless faces in Desis, the language I understood. *I'm with you.*

I gritted my teeth and clenched my fists. Revenge, an emotion I hadn't felt in a long time, slithered a path under my skin. I'd kill all of those sadistic bastards, and give these people back their lives.

People roamed the fields of Shalen, too. Drea said they were Abrogation citizens, most likely forced from their homes by people from Heterodox who desired the less-resistant older population. Easier to steal food and supplies from those who already decided present life needed to end.

While all of this hysteria erupted, holograms always on and filling the cabin with the riots and slaughter, we stayed safe, hidden like cowards as we contemplated what-ifs. We planned,

Denzel had said, for the greater good. The excuse seemed to make him okay with the decision to watch from afar.

Tarek's isolation prevented me from demanding we do something. Maybe the majority of my reasons landed on the selfish side, but realistically, we needed his help. No way could our tiny lot go up against a mysterious gaggle of elders without Tarek's skills. He'd come around. He was the strongest, most honorable person I knew, even if he struggled with his humanity.

But… Why hadn't he come out of the room yet?

The lift stopped on the main floor. I shook the thoughts from my head and beat feet through the rioting to the control panel, Drea's hub. Tarek would snap out of it. He had to.

This morning, Oren's gorgeous hologram lit up beside the chaos, Celeste sitting beside him. "So, what do you suggest? Take out the elders–if we figure out where they're hiding by some miracle?" Oren's craggy voice rumbled through the room, his hair disheveled and dark circles shading his eyes.

"What's he talking about?" I sat beside Denzel, who had his hands out, pleading with Oren's image. Drea stayed quiet, her concentration on the kitchen where Peter hydrated some food–her attention always on her son.

"*I'm* talking about the crazy ideas Denzel is coming up with." Oren scooted to the edge of his chair as he pointed to me. "Maybe *you* could talk some sense into him, so *I*"–he jammed a finger in his chest– "don't kick his ass after *I* get there."

The man was always strung tighter than a nun on Sunday.

"All right, take it easy, gorgeous," I said. "Wouldn't want that pretty face to develop worry lines."

"You–that's–" Oren stood and paced through the holograms. "Why the hell do I even try to talk to you?"

I shrugged. "Good question."

Easy answer, though. Because he loved me. Like I loved his annoying ass.

I challenged Denzel with a dull stare. "What have you come up with this time?"

"It is a logical assumption, I assure you."

"Hey, Peter?" I never took my eyes off Denzel.

"Yeah?"

"Tell me again what I always say about assuming things?"

His laugh answered.

Denzel didn't find it so funny. He slammed a fist on the console. "I've sat here for over a week, letting you take jabs at me without a word. When will you trust that I'm on the same side as you?"

I shifted my gaze to Oren, who took his seat by Celeste, her tattoo rapidly switching colors. "When all of us make it out of this thing alive." My attention landed on Denzel again. "You do that, maybe I'll stop thinking about ways to torture you if you betray us."

No one jumped to Denzel's aid, not even Drea.

He folded his arms, meeting my scrutiny without flinching. "It will be my pleasure to prove you wrong."

"Great. So, tell me about this 'logical assumption.'"

He straightened his robes and slicked back his light brown hair. "As Tarek has already *assumed*, we do believe Celeste is indeed an Exemplian ancient–or something along those lines. Oren told us she has managed to do things only strong Protectors and Guides are capable of."

"So far, I don't hear a plan," I said.

Oren snorted and mumbled something about growing up.

"You are relentless, aren't you?" Denzel shook his head. "Anyhow, from studying the way in which the lines are opened and closed, I assu–I mean, it appears as though one or all the elders may have similar attributes as our Celeste."

"I am not yours, Guide." Celeste's musical voice tinkled through the room.

"Right, of course. I–bugger it all! I. Am not. The enemy."

209

"What Denzel is trying to say, if you would allow him"–Drea rocked back in her chair, her attention now on the conversation–"is we already know scientists who developed the Creation Lab figured out a way to circumvent the need for a Warden, or natural evolution, rather. And when the energy containment units were destroyed, and the lab and all its files demolished, the organic flow of energy reverted to prior times, ancient times."

"Okay…?" Seriously, no need for any convoluted explanation. I wanted to skip right on over to the solution.

She grinned, not at all irritated by my impatience. "As Denzel explained, the lines have never been controlled like this before. Sure, a strong Protector has had the ability to block one person from crossing the lines, but the entire population? Not one documented case have we found."

"So…another ancient–or whatever? An elder?"

"Precisely," Drea said. "With the energy not…contained for manufacture…it will gravitate to where it feels comfortable, giving those wielding it greater power. It is likely not all energy is flowing to Celeste, as I do believe it would have killed her. So, my conclusion is one or more Exemplian elders are absorbing some, too."

She paused, tapping a finger on her lip, acting as if she hashed out the details as she gave them. All of us waited in silence, giving her the respect we refused to give Denzel.

"So, same as how it works in other worlds," she continued, "I believe that if Celeste is the one to take another ancient's life, she will absorb the energy, become stronger, not weaker." She looked at Oren. "Oren believes she is now able to handle it. And if she were ever to carry a child, we would have our next Warden. We could begin again. Live as we were intended to live."

Celeste's tattoo began to change fiercely. "I am not a breeding cow, Drea."

"Of course not," Drea said. "But if you are the only ancient, you will be able to control the energy flow of this world, even if you never have a child. Make it whole, natural again."

A tear fell from Celeste's eye, her tattoo not stopping its colored assault on her cheek. "I cannot control it fully."

Drea smiled wider. "I'll help you. And Oren has said you are doing better under certain circumstances."

I rubbed the back of my neck. "You guys figured all this out since this morning?"

"Well, no, not all of it. We've been working on this for months, contemplating our options. Now, it seems we must put theory to the test." Drea waved a hand toward a hologram of an authority Protector slaughtering three people who were on their knees in front of him, begging. "They have infiltrated Celeste's building to search Tarek's flat. It will only be a matter of time until they get to her."

I winced, watching the holograms. Each death twisted my heart, hollowing my stomach.

"Our people need us, Lena," Drea said. "*Our* people."

Yes. Time to act. Time to fight. "What's the plan?"

Drea stood to stretch. "First, we must figure out a way to bring Celeste here. The city is not even remotely safe for her anymore. Her survival is paramount to Exemplar's liberation."

Well, finally something that makes sense. "Then let's get her." I was already up and calculating how much ammo I'd need.

"Do you think it's as simple as pulling up in front of the building? Her energy garrotes any brain within a thirty-foot radius." Oren's irritation blared. "Why do you think we've stayed here in the first place?"

Oren's question scratched against my skin like sandpaper. "How about you stop asking questions you know the answers to and be more helpful, then?"

211

He closed his eyes. When he opened them, the dickhead mask disappeared, replaced with concern. "I wish I had the answers, Lena. I really do."

I wanted to hug him then. Fling my arms around his hologram and pull him through. The reluctant hero. If ever anyone fit the cliché, it was Oren. I sat and scooted my seat as close to his image as I could. "What about the hanger? Is there another hovercraft?"

"No," he said. "The only solution I see is a distraction. Something so epic, Celeste's aura goes unnoticed by anyone around her."

This conversation, so familiar in the sense it touted danger–death–for someone. "Okay, say we get Celeste out of harm's way. Then what?"

"We begin to taunt the elders," Drea said.

"Explain." I was in no mood for this beat-around-the-bush shit.

"We let them know we have an ancient, at least, the one who has been pilfering so much energy. I'm sure it irks whoever might share her heritage on the elders' council. They'll need all the power they can get to return Exemplar to its prior dominance."

Wait. "You're gonna offer a trade?"

Drea smiled as her eyes frosted over, causing my skin to prickle. "We will have them think that, yes."

"And then?"

"As soon as we are near them, we ensure Celeste is in the position to end them."

Okay, one major hole in this plan. "Oren told me once that Celeste can't die." I nodded to her. "Isn't that right?"

"Yes–unless I'm with no head." Celeste's throat bobbed. "A few have tried to end my life in the past."

"So, wouldn't the elder or elders have the same…immunity to death?"

212

"More than likely." Oren caught Celeste's hand and brought it to his lips, kissing her knuckles.

Hmm…interesting.

"Which means…what?" I tried to keep my voice gentle. "You'll have to lop off a head or two? Can you even fight?"

Celeste's shoulders slumped. "I cannot."

"A minor bump we'll adjust to." Drea spoke as if we discussed the weather.

I laughed because exploding would've made the tension worse. "You know this plan is as flimsy as it gets, right?"

"Yes."

That was it. All Drea had to say. *Yes.* Well, didn't that suck the confidence out of my body? But we'd work on the last part of the plan later.

I swiveled my chair to view the death and terror. The hunger in empty eyes. Fear in those who valued what life they were given. We had to help them.

Distraction…

"So…who's going to be the diversion?" Peter's voice whispered through the holograms.

Obvious answer. The people needed me, authority searched for me, and the elders no doubt wanted me dead.

I stood and faced Oren. "Looks like I'm gonna come save your ass, princess."

He grinned, some of the stress evaporating from his face. "Aren't I luck–" His eyes drifted behind me. "Ah, hey, man."

I spun. "Tarek?"

He stared at me, through me. "If you go, I go."

His voice, the voice I loved more than breathing, could shatter me with only a few words. I ran to him and wrapped my arms around his waist. His arms stayed at his sides.

I pulled away, and what I saw disintegrated my insides to embers.

Pain seared his face, the haunts of his death attacking him all over again.

No.

I wiped at tears I hadn't realized poured down my cheeks. I wouldn't let him build the walls back up. Not this time.

I stood straighter and let the tears fall without caring. He'd see the hurt. I'd make him. "Well, then, it's you and me, isn't it?"

CHAPTER 26

TAREK

Triggers

This place elicited ghosts not yet far enough in the past. The docile-looking cabin, the cliffs minutes away, the dull throng of blue lights lining the sterile corridor.

The lab where Drea repaired his artificial body and re-implanted his energy.

Not artificial, she'd said. All organic, living body parts, from his heart to the hair growing from his scalp. He accepted the idea of what he was before the knife plunged through his heart at the cliff. Came to terms with the notion he never had parents, memories of his mother's arms a farce. An implant.

But after he died…

Triggers. They ate at him until he almost dissolved.

The moment they had made it into the cabin, after the authority left, muscle memory took him to this room, the room he'd shared with Lena before, when he believed they'd end up together on Earth. If only time would reverse, not to re-experience the horror they'd endured then, but allow him to feel what he had felt. Alive.

215

The second day in the room, Drea made sure the screen on the far wall stayed on, showing him the activity on the main floor: the holograms of pilfering and slaughter; the arguing; desperate plans that turned into decent, if not weak, plans. At first, he ignored the happenings, allowing the triggers free rein over his mind. But on the sixth day, the screen grew more interesting. And the triggers? Instead of letting them spark memory after memory, he faced them.

Death will pass.

It had to, or he'd end up a slave to its decay until this life was over.

Death had no power over Lena's safety, though. None. On the eighth day, when she volunteered herself, the fog he'd lost himself in cleared. As dirty and smelly as he was, with no bath and face itching under a week's worth of hair growth, he stormed from the room and hit the keypad on the lift.

"Ah, hey, man." Oren's usual sour countenance transformed to pity.

The man pitied him.

Yes, time to wake up.

Tarek ignored Oren and gave Lena the demand she'd given to him before they came to Exemplar together the very first time. "If you go, I go."

She ran to him, and his body stiffened. When she wrapped her arms around his waist, guilt turned him into stone. Her tears were barbed reminders on his skin. When would he stop hurting her? Just as he lifted his hands to pull her closer, she backed away.

What to say? He couldn't find the words.

"Well, then, it's you and me, isn't it?" Her chin trembled, but determination turned her eyes to glittering emeralds, made brighter with the tears. Tears that wrecked him–giving him one last kick in the ass. Definitely time to man-up.

"Yes." He was afraid to say too much. Afraid to say the wrong thing.

"All right." She then faced Oren's image, her spine so rigid it looked in danger of snapping. "*Tarek and I* are gonna save you."

Oren shrugged. "My odds of survival plummet by the minute."

"Funny." Lena returned to her seat.

Tarek hesitated, lost for a moment, before following her.

"No." She gestured toward the kitchen after he tried to sit beside her. "Eat something. It looks like you lost ten pounds. We need you strong."

His gut pleaded with him at the mention of food. "You're sure? I coul–"

"You trust me?"

"With everything I have."

She smiled, tears still in her eyes. "Then eat."

Tarek searched Drea's and Denzel's faces, both Guides doing their best to act inconspicuous. He then wiped a stray tear from Lena's cheek. "Okay."

His action caused more tears, but her smile lifted higher, healing parts of him all over again. Before he made a fool of himself and dropped to his knees in front of her, Tarek went into the kitchen as ordered.

Sustenance injections only did so much, and Lena was right. He'd be a liability in the condition he allowed himself to get into the last week. Damn triggers. They wouldn't win anymore.

While he waited for food to hydrate, Peter nudged his arm. "Um…are you okay?"

No. "Sure, never better." His food popped from the hydrator, the smell of roasted pig and gravy causing his stomach to complain.

"Lena waited by your door, morning and night." The anger vibrating from the boy's cracking voice both made Tarek's guilt fester and sparked respect. Peter loved Lena almost as much as he did. "She thought you would kill yourself or something."

Tarek stopped shoveling food into his mouth and faced Peter. "What?"

"Don't do that, okay? Don't kill yourself." His face reddened to the edge of bursting. "I don't give a shit, but that'd kill her."

Tarek downed his mouthful of flesh and fat, the food he craved now threatening to choke him. "I won't."

"Good."

"Are we okay now?"

"Depends."

"On?"

"I'm coming with you. Whatever you guys are doing, I'm doing it, too."

"No."

"You can't stop me." Peter's chin jutted up. Despite how much ass he put behind his words, the scared boy inside lurked below the surface, visible in his trembling bottom lip.

Brave. Stupid as all hell, but brave.

Tarek kept his attention on Peter as he took another bite. He chewed with purpose, slow and methodical, until Peter's eyelids fluttered and he looked away.

"You d-don't intimidate me," said the lying, cracking, high-pitched voice.

"Maybe not." He took a sip of water, his focus never leaving the top of Peter's head. "Drea?"

The boy's head snapped up. "Stop it."

"Yes?" Drea's smooth, sure voice blew into the kitchen.

"Your son would like to join Lena and me. What would you say to that?"

"*Hell, no!*" Of course Lena would have an answer.

Tarek bit the inside of his cheek. The boy didn't need someone laughing in his face. Tarek understood courage,

218

admired it. But Peter wouldn't be tagging along. Not this time. He took another sip of water, and turned toward everyone else.

Fear stole color off Drea's face. From what he witnessed on the screens, everything she had said to the boy was careful and planned. The last thing she'd want to do was deny him anything. Lena had no problem with upsetting Peter–she loved him enough to do it.

"Why? I can fight as well as you can." Peter stumbled to Lena, his hands out and waving. "You can't keep treating me like I'm some teenager on Earth. I'm not. I've trained for this."

Lena stood and palmed his cheek. "You don't have to be from Earth to be a teenager. You're too young. I'm giving you the gift I was never given. Here, you're safe, with your mother and"–she looked at Denzel–"father."

"Stop. Stop calling them that. *Stop it*." Peter backed away, heading toward the stairs to the underground storage rooms. "You told me I was *your* family. *You said I belonged with you*." His tears prompted Drea's. Lena's too. "What happens if you die? What happens if I lose you?"

The boy's pain seeped through the room, his hurt scorching anyone who gave him a piece of their heart.

"You won't lose me." Lena moved forward but stopped when Peter shook his head. "I-I promise you. Please."

"Don't promise me anything." Peter disappeared, the door slamming in Lena's face.

Lena rushed to open the door, but Tarek beat her to it, covering the keypad. "Let him have his time."

"I… What if he leaves?"

"He can't." Drea stood, her hands shaking as she smoothed down her shirt. "I've denied his access to all doors and vehicles. He is trapped here." Her voice broke.

"Thank you." Tears dripped from Lena's chin, creating wet paths down her neck.

"No, thank you," Drea said, her face now void of color. "My son loves you, Lena. I only hope he will love us one day, too."

"He's just a boy. He will come round." Denzel reached for Drea's hands, but she pulled back.

"I do not think he will. Forgive me." She switched off Oren's hologram after giving him a nod. "I believe some time on my own is needed." She went to the lift.

Denzel followed. "Looks like we all could stand to use a break."

Tarek kept rooted to the floor, Lena in front of him, almost touching his chest with hers. Two doors swooshed open and closed above, and still they looked at each other. He had hurt her, again. But before he could make it right, a few more demons needed conquering. Demons he had to face alone.

He grasped her hand. When hope pushed at the sadness in her eyes and a soft moan escaped her lips, he could've taken on the authority alone. But he needed to heal one last part of himself first.

"He'll be fine. Go. Get some rest too." Tarek grinned as he backed away. "And no need to listen at my door anymore. I'll…ah…I'll see you soon."

"I thought I lost you." Sorrow choked her words. "I thought I lost you again."

Her fear demanded more from him. It vibrated through his entire body, daring him to refuse her. He wouldn't. He never would again.

Before he could change his mind, in all his sweat and filth and dirty clothes, he went to her. He leaned down to her parted lips, her breath coming out in gasps. With his mouth touching hers, he gave her the vow he'd uttered years ago, one he now intended to keep. "Wherever you are is where I'll be."

∞ ∞ ∞

The door wouldn't open unless he touched the keypad. He stared at it, afraid some cosmic joke would slide the innocent-looking sheet of lightweight metal to the side before he gathered the nerve to face his last demon, the one he couldn't seem to shake.

Not real.

Dying was never as hard as having to live again. He had died four times before, but never with Exemplar's dark, screwed-up secrets fresh in his brain. A lot to ask a person to accept when rising from the dead. It needed to end, though. This self-imposed prison from his life. From Lena.

Second chances were miracles; he understood that. He and Lena had been lucky enough to have more than one. What was it now? Four second chances? Five? Whatever life had thrown at them, the universe brought them back together. He had to cling to that. He had to allow himself to accept it. But first–

Demons.

"Okay, coward, open the door." His voice reverberated through the blue-lighted corridor, whispering back to him in stereo. A thousand Tareks demanding he dance with ghosts of his past. One more time.

Open the door.

Open the door.

Open the door.

One deep breath.

Another.

Okay.

His palm inched closer to the keypad. Each centimeter caused the food he'd eaten to roil and burble in his stomach. If his gag reflexes won, he'd have to take another shower, find clean clothes–stop.

He had stalled long enough.

His palm flattened against the panel.

"Lights."

Fluorescent beams brought the lab from darkness. Everything looked the same, except one thing: Peter's body double no longer nested in the incubation chamber. The metal womb sat empty, as sterile as the room, a shrine for a boy who would never be. Stringent cleaner assailed his nose, attacking his senses and making his eyes water.

Tarek stood at the entryway, his gaze stuck on the silver glint gleaming from the steel table. So cold, so detached, an object without any remorse. He spent months hating a table that had no capacity to hate him back. An innocent piece of medical equipment. His eyes closed against the flood of emptiness threatening to pull him in. He could feel the biting cold of the steel against his skin, the dried blood crusting his hair. Dried blood that caked his entire body.

With his eyes shut tight, he reached for his hair, remembering how it gnarled and tangled into clumps of matted strands with blood from his past life. He had cut it when the feel of hair against his nape brought back the memory too often.

The sterile room with the body that would've become Peter had he died. A body kept alive with machines, a body that only needed a soul to stimulate the brain. Science. They were all the science experiments of a maniacal government bent on controlling the universe.

Lena's face, the face that was his religion, his salvation, flashed through his mind, blocking the table and blood and hate.

His eyes opened, and he touched the table's cold, impersonal surface, his hand shaking.

What had he expected? Actual demons to manifest from steel, maybe?

No, the demon was a table. A table.

A table.

His hands balled into fists, more to prevent himself from flipping it or throwing the sterile metal into the sterile incubation chamber. All sterile. Lifeless.

Tarek stumbled backward until he hit the wall then slumped to the floor, his focus on the table. The longer he stared at it, the more the table became just a table. Hours must have gone by, days, maybe. His body grew numb, and his stomach growled. But his mind finally became clear.

Yes, he could do this.

He could live.

He had to.

No.

He wanted to.

Right now.

Tarek pushed from the cool floor to his feet–then turned his back on the last ghost.

The doors couldn't close fast enough. Sure, moving on topped his agenda, but that didn't mean he wanted to ever step foot in that room again. He'd be able to if a situation called for it. That'd be enough. As for getting on with living, now was as good a time as any. One destination took over his mind. His home.

He headed toward the stairs, his walk turning into a run. Before he climbed the first step, he looked to the right. Peter slept, his tall, lanky body pinching Tarek's heart.

The kid appeared as innocent as he was, and so alone. Alone when there were three people upstairs who would lay down their lives for him. But their love wouldn't matter. Tarek understood that better than anyone.

The boy had his demons, ones so similar, yet different somehow. Where he had false memories of parents who never were, Peter had parents upstairs. A father who was Peter's Guide, his responsibility in the old order of Exemplar. A mother who became a mother through DNA splicing, to a son who wanted her to be more than that.

Yes, Peter had demons, too.

Tarek crouched by his curled body. Peter's face, even in sleep, scrunched in pain. What could he do? If only the answers were as easy as the questions.

Tarek stood and switched directions to a storage unit he knew had blankets, clothes, pillows, and any other simple amenity one could dream up. He found a soft blanket and a pillow infused with Torporine, a natural component that relieved stress. Once the pillow slipped under the boy's head, the pain left his face, and a soft smile hinted on his lips. Tarek spread the blanket over Peter's skinny body, and he curled even tighter under it, bringing the lip of the soft fabric to his face, sound asleep.

That was all he could do, give the boy one night of peaceful sleep. Tomorrow he'd try harder to help the kid.

But tonight…tonight, he'd fix the part of him that meant everything.

CHAPTER 27

LENA

Thirty Days to Forever

Wherever you are is where I'll be.

I hadn't imagined his promise. He said it.

I hoped he had actually said it.

Maybe my ears picked up what my heart wished he'd say.

Morning turned into afternoon, and faded into night. Everything in me urged my feet to head to Tarek's bedroom door, listen for sound, for life. But he had said not to worry. So, I stayed in this claustrophobic room, its quaint wooden furniture and delicate quilts mocking my anxiety.

Peter and Tarek were broken. Tarek had death to blame. Peter…well, Peter just wanted his mother. Only he hadn't realized it yet. He needed Drea to show him–hell, what did I know? What did I know about anything? Obviously not a whole lot.

"Lights." I yelled the command. If I didn't have my giant to demand answers from, might as well take it out on machines.

The room illuminated with soft yellow light, darkness from outside peeking in from a tiny ceiling window. But the night wasn't opaque. Nope, twinkling lights from shuttles with subtle orange spotlights scouring the ground invaded the solitude. No Synod Guides. The Empyrean War took care of a huge number, and Drea said that Oren had made sure to destroy the nests in Exemplar's capital during the explosion–his priority. No more collecting.

Whatever. Good for us.

Wherever you are is where I'll be.

Huh, funny, because where *I was*, was alone in this too-pretty room, wearing a path in the too-shiny floor, and no giant paced with me.

He said he'd see me soon–twelve hours ago. Not "soon" the way I saw "soon," not at all.

If I had to search for him, I–

Tap, tap, tap.

The sound barely reached over my building anger, but it was there, a knock on the door. Instinct forced me to grab my gun off the desk before answering. In Exemplar, no matter how rigged Drea had this place, I never relaxed at a knock, at any foreign sound. With my gun cocked and ready, I released the door.

When the door opened, I froze. No, that wasn't true. Everything inside turned hot, my blood raging and swelling. Tarek. Not the Tarek from the last week, the last year, but my Tarek, only thinner. His eyes shimmered, the gray like polished swords, blinding me. My gun, loaded and ready to fire, fell from my grasp. Thank God Tarek's reflexes were sharp. He scooped it up before the weapon hit the floor, saving us both from a potentially fatal mistake.

Without taking his eyes from mine, he set it on the table next to the door. He grinned, his dimples making me cry. "Hi."

I sobbed, afraid to touch him, afraid he was an illusion. "Hi." I think I said that. Some kind of noise squeaked through my lips.

"Can I come in?"

I cried harder. Laughed, too. I stood there, laughing, crying, loving him with every cell in my body, every piece of my soul.

Tarek hesitated before gliding his fingers across my neck and weaving them through my hair. Slowly, his eyes never leaving mine, he bent until our mouths touched. A kiss so soft it broke me into shattered glass and repaired me at the same time. His lips lifted, his eyes wide, so wide, luminescent, begging. "I'm so sorry."

"You don't have to be."

"I do." He kissed me again, just as soft, just as exploding. "So, let me do this, please?"

"I–okay." I bunched his shirt in my hands, dragging him in until his chest was flush with mine. "As long as you swear not to leave this room."

He grinned, a dangerous grin, almost feral. "Never again." He pulled away to touch the keypad until the door shut and then carried me to the bed. Instead of sitting next to me, he kneeled at my feet, folding my hands in his.

Silence took over the room as he massaged each of my fingers, his attention focused on the task. I didn't care. I'd stay in this silent room with my silent giant until breath no longer pushed through my lungs.

"I've lived six lives now." His voice whispered into the room. "My first life, I remember my mother's arms. I remember her holding me crying before offering me into the Energy Redistribution Program. My duty, she had said. An honor to train, to…ensure the survival of humanity."

My mind screamed and sobbed, and my fingers itched to wrap him in my arms, protect him from the horrid truth he swam in for almost a year.

He stopped and started a few times and applied gentle pressure to my hands. As much as I wanted to comfort him, give him sugary words, I said nothing to interrupt the quiet. He needed to tell me his story, as much for himself as for me.

"My second life, when I became your Protector, I felt more alive than I ever had. This infant, no parents to speak of, just an old caregiver who called you her natural beauty." He looked up for a second. "Drea knew more of your history than I did, and she...she told me of it a few months ago. You were a natural-born, your parents forced to give you up to the Synod. Long story, one I'll tell you someday."

"I don't care about that." I rested my forehead against his. "It doesn't matter now."

"I know." He breathed in deep. "My point is, during my first life, and until I met you, the one thing keeping me from forgetting I was a person was the memory of my mother's arms. I can even remember her smell, the feel of her robes against my cheek. And when I found out she hadn't existed, that I wasn't...real..."

My heart broke for him. Tarek, the strongest part of me, suffered.

"I came to terms with it after Drea admitted the truth, though. I accepted it because I had you." He finally gave me his gaze. "But death–I know the side effects. Mentally, I understood why I couldn't come to terms. I let it take over anyway. I let it win." He brought our joined hands to his lips, kissing my fingers. "Not anymore. I can't give you everything–children, a family–but everything I have, everything I am, is yours."

I remembered those movies and the women who held on to every word the hero had to say, knowing my giant put all those heroes to shame.

I was right. He melted me with words, with the plea shining in his eyes. He made me whole.

"I have a family–*we* have a family. And I'll take you, Tarek Montigue. Everything that *I am* has been yours since the first time I saw you." Tears mangled my voice, making it airy when I wanted it to ring with conviction.

But he heard, and his smile warmed my soul. "So, we save the world, and then go back home, eat pizza, and stare at Winston's paintings every night, for the rest of this life–not only for the next thirty days. Next life, we spend with Wilma."

In seconds, the world became more colorful, breathing easier. "I kinda love that idea."

"You're sure?"

"I've never been more sure about anything." I pulled my hands from his and brought his mouth to mine, where it belonged.

After that, neither of us wanted to talk, not with words. Tarek stayed on the floor, on his knees, our kiss deepening, healing me from the inside out.

"Lena…" My name touched my lips, his breath scorching me.

My entire body trembled, my heart thrumming to the wild beat of his as he leaned up until he lay on top of me. He supported all his weight with his forearms on either side of my head as he kissed me. His mouth was reverent, worshiping, as it glided across my lips.

It wasn't enough.

I laced my fingers behind his neck and pulled, needing his weight. I wanted to be burned by his skin. His smile brushed my mouth, and an escaping sigh inflated his chest. "Thank you, Lena."

"For what?" My own smile hurt my cheeks.

He touched my chest, right above my pounding heart. "For this."

All the right things. He always said exactly what I needed to hear. "I love you, Tarek."

"I love you, too." He tucked hair behind my ear with a shaky hand.

"Then show me." I slid his shirt over his head, his golden skin taut under my fingertips as I traced the muscles on his back.

That grin–the one that demanded and promised and begged–shaded his mouth. Tarek stripped off my shirt, our skin finally touching. Finally.

His lips drew a path from my collarbone to my chest, his tongue creating a frenzy I couldn't control. I gripped his hair, holding him close, refusing to let him go as electricity rippled through my veins, igniting secret parts of me only he could unlock. His mouth drove me to the brink as he tugged off my pants, just as I yanked down his. My body shook. Like an addict, I missed what brought me to life so many times before. His lips. His hands. His breath moistening my skin.

His mouth trailed up my body until he touched my ear, sending rivulets of white heat coursing through my blood. "I'm yours, Lena, and you are mine. Forever."

∞ ∞ ∞

Perfection, a word created from moments like now. A fight loomed over our heads as raw as a canker sore. Danger–always danger–hid at the edge of everyone's calm, and today could very well end up being my last day. But right now?

Perfection.

Tarek's arm slung around my waist in sleep, his soft snoring a cadence I had missed. Every time I moved, he'd tighten his hold. Even unconscious, he wouldn't let me go. About time, I'd say.

He was mine, and I was his. Something I had always known, something he finally came to accept. We would always find our way back to each other. Across worlds. Across lives. In this ridiculously comfortable bed, with his ridiculously heavy arm securing my waist, that truth sank in completely. I'd never doubt it again, regardless of what happened today–and if we were lucky enough to survive, whatever happened after.

My eyelids grew heavy, the comfort of forever intoxicating. But pounding against the door never relaxed anybody.

Tarek had leaped from the bed, yanked on his pants, and snatched up my gun before I even took a breath to tell whoever invaded our time to fuck off. The man had a gift, and his reaction was more productive than mine.

Before Tarek opened the door, he tossed clothes in my direction. "Put these on."

Wow, we were a fidgety, untrusting couple.

Without a word, I tugged on the sweats and T-shirt I had on yesterday and moved to stand behind him. He kept the gun at his side, neither of us exactly tense. The only danger we had probably avoided was someone catching us naked. At my nod, he touched the keypad.

Peter stood there, wringing his hands, giving his irritated/repentant frown. The same frown he had always given me on the days after Winston or Oren carted him back to Earth. "So…you guys kissed and made up. Cool."

Laughing, more from relief that cranky Peter stood there and not devastated Peter, I bypassed Tarek and reached up to encircle his scrawny neck. "Hey, you."

He gave my back an awkward, I-hate-hugging pat. "Sorry."

"You've got nothing to be sorry about." I pulled away, biting my lip to keep from sobbing. This kid had seen me cry enough. "But you understand, right? You get where I'm coming from?"

His gaze fluttered as he shifted it from me to Tarek, to the back wall. "Yeah, sure, I get it."

I clenched his chin between my pointer finger and thumb, forcing him to look at me. I knew a pile of shit when someone shoveled it at my feet. "Peter. Don't. Whatever you're thinking, it's not a good idea."

He swatted my fingers away. "I'm not thinking anything. I even apologized to Mom and Denzel. We've been talking all morning while you guys wasted time in bed. I won't put myself in danger."

I felt a smirk trace my lips before I could bite it back. I wouldn't say we wasted the time, but whatever. "Well, good. That's really good." I jabbed him in the shoulder, affection he was more comfortable with. "About time you listen to me."

Tarek snorted. "As if the kid listened to anyone."

Man, I loved my boys. "Well, miracles happen every day." I reached on my toes to kiss Tarek's cheek. "Wouldn't you say?"

He smiled. "I would."

"Ugh, no. Gross." Peter made a gagging noise until I punched his shoulder again. "Ouch, quit it."

"You quit it," I said.

"Fine. But, Lena, I–"

I tilted my head, waiting for his darting gaze to land on my face. "Yes?"

His attention settled on his shoes. "Nothing." He raised his head, a tight smile on his face. "It's nothing. Come on. Breakfast is ready."

CHAPTER 28

LENA

Papaverdilutus

"I feel like a coward." We drove with the authority traffic, maneuvering in and out of nameless, faceless assholes all searching for yours truly.

Tarek shook his head. "It's not cowardly; it's smart. We're no good to anybody if we die."

"You say it like it'd be the only outcome."

"It would be if we stood in the middle of a Heterodox street. We want to cause a commotion, not commit suicide." He stroked my leg, my skin tingling under his touch. "I think we'd be happier in our new future if we both continued breathing."

The two-foot gap between us turned into an ocean. I unlatched my harness and flew into his arms, planting kisses all over his face. Good thing for autopilot. "You could say that a million times, and I wouldn't get tired of hearing it," I said.

He laughed, wrapping his arms around my waist. "And what, exactly, did I say? If it causes this kind of reaction, I'll say it after every sentence."

"*Our future.*" I rubbed his nose with mine. "I think it's gonna happen this time."

"As long as we stay alive…for *our future.*"

I kissed him once more before returning to my seat. "As long as we do that, yeah."

"Which is why we need Yosef." He glanced out his window when an authority shuttle hovered next to ours a few seconds longer than what made him comfortable. Drea ensured we were camouflaged, though. If authority ran a scan of our vehicle, they'd see past the tinted windows to find only one person: Denzel. Just a middle-aged-looking man intent on the traffic ahead of him. Thank God for her tech savvy.

"You mean, which is why we need a pimp." I had trouble with trusting outsiders. Denzel still hadn't quite made it in my bubble, much less a guy I met a week ago.

His dimples appeared. "Sure, however you want to see it."

I snorted. "Gee, thanks."

The plan was simple. Meet Yosef at Celeste's. He'd set up some fancy hologram contraption, and I'd taunt the elders with a personal message to rouse the people. Then during the chaos, we'd sneak out with Oren and Celeste. Sounded easy enough. But easy never ended up being easy.

The worst part? Rats. We'd be visiting them again, the poisonous rodents. Thankfully, we'd only be dealing with them going in. Yosef would have a ride waiting for us in front of Celeste's building. An authority shuttle. I looked in the backseat, reassuring myself there were two flamethrowers this time, with more power than the one Tarek had acquired from his place. Our bags hid a large supply of magic medicine, too.

"So…we get as close to the door as possible, okay?"

Tarek brought my hand to his lips. "Are you afraid of a few rodents, love?"

"Um…hell, yeah."

"Good."

I tugged at my fingers. "*Good*? Is this my pep talk? Because it sucks."

He held fast as I gave one last half-hearted jerk, though it didn't take much effort on his part. My hand could stay in his forever, and it wouldn't have been long enough.

"There was a time when nothing scared you, when you put your life at risk every day," he said, voice tightening. "I thought I lost you, even if you stood right beside me."

Jesus, we'd been through hell. So many scars marred our hearts, so many past nightmares that would always niggle at our minds, no matter how happy we became. "Did you ever feel like everything would be better if you disappeared?"

Silence.

Finally, he said, "No." He turned to me. "As skewed as my reasons were, I thought... Every action I took, every decision I made, involved your happiness, including keeping myself alive."

Longing and guilt and fire. Emotions that shouldn't have blended as well as they did. "*You* make me happy."

"Then why are you crying?"

What? I touched my cheek and moisture coated my fingertips. *Would you look at that?* I leaned over again and tasted his lips, my salty tears mingling with our kiss. When I lifted my mouth, I said, "Because you fill up my heart, and sometimes it bursts."

He glided his thumb across my cheekbone. "Have I told you how much I love you?"

"Hmm..." I shrugged, tears still running, mouth still stretching in a smile wide enough to swallow us both. "Not in the last hour or so."

"How neglectful of me."

"If the two of you are done, how about we move on to the task at hand, like...oh, say...not dying." Oren's voice dumped ice water on my head.

I found his pretty face lighting up the console monitor, a smirk coloring his lips.

"You're being extra assholey." I slumped back into my seat to the background of Tarek's chuckle. "Ever try...*oh, say*...not being a dick?"

Oren crossed his arms and batted his lashes. "Not in the last hour or so."

"You're hilarious." My face burned. "And you're still a dick."

He laughed. Of course it sounded like honey. "So you said."

Tarek, not in the least mortified, got down to business. "Yosef make it to your place."

"He's a few minutes out." Oren worried his bottom lip, giving a rare glimpse of nerves. Yes, he had always been a dickhead but a confident one. His nerves gave mine an unneeded jolt. "What's your ETA?"

Tarek checked the screen above Oren's face. "We're coming up to the building now. I'm going to take a lap and circle back around, just in case."

"Good. I'll meet you at the hanger door." Oren's face blipped off the screen.

All warm and fuzzy dissolved. We had forever to be sappy. Now, we had to get to work.

I touched my left shoulder to turn on my contego, the hum vibrating through my body. Thankfully, Drea had a suit in her arsenal for Tarek. I reached over to turn it on as I scanned the airways. "You think someone's following us?" Not that I had been paying attention. Stupid, but come on. When had Tarek and I ever been in a situation where we weren't looking over our shoulder? We stole time from danger. We had to.

"None that I've noticed, but I won't chance it." He switched off autopilot and resumed control, pulling up until we flew vertically.

Once we were above traffic, he headed back toward the main hub in Heterodox, where more debris littered the sidewalks than usual. People were scarce, except for the authority patrolling. A barricade of Protectors lined the boundaries of Cynosure. They gunned down people brave enough to go against them–or hungry enough. No struggle, no fight, just the strong preying on the weak.

"We have to do something." My attention stayed on the barricade, the firing guns, the zombie-like people wanting nothing more than to be treated like the humans they were.

"We are. What we're doing now, it's the next step to ending all of this."

I pressed against the window, my heart shattering for those lifeless bodies scattered in front of Protectors. No one even attempted to remove them, give them some dignity in death. A warning to others. "Coming here…I made it worse for them."

"No. *We* sped up the inevitable by coming here." Tarek flew us toward Celeste's after no other vehicles followed our path around the city.

I tore my gaze from the mayhem and focused on my giant. "Don't you think the plan's flimsy, though? I mean, if Celeste has to kill people–a woman who has barely left her apartment in years, much less sliced off any heads–I don't see the bright side."

He smiled as we descended nearer to the street, now close to the rat hanger. "When I first met *you*, I would have never guessed you'd become the fighter you are now."

"Way different. I had no choice and a few years of training with you guys."

"Agreed." He drove into the opaque hanger, the hovercraft's lights picking out rodents scurrying from our path. "But, she'll have me, you, Oren, and Drea to hold down the cowards, make it easy for her."

Great, another image my future therapist would be hearing about. A milder, less murder-like version. Truth on Earth would only win me a straightjacket and heavy medication.

Tarek stopped as close to the stairs leading into the stairwell as possible. Corroded cement and massive groups of rats prevented us from sitting right on the stairway's platform. Soft bodies thudded against the sides of the vehicle as I reached in the backseat to snatch up our weapons. Even though Tarek torched a shitload of them over a week ago, the population hadn't thinned out.

"All right, love. Time to play with the wildlife–hopefully for the last time." Tarek held out his hand.

"Can't wait." I set one of the flamethrowers in his open palm.

"On three. Ready?" He gripped the door latch, and I did the same with a nod. "One...two...*three!*"

Flames exploded from our guns soon as the doors flew up. Walls of fire singed squealing rats, their burning flesh stinging my eyes and nose. We were methodical, walking back to back until we hit the stairs' landing, a shield of black smoke and flame making bonfires out of the animals. When my boot hit the first step, I torched a wave up the stairs, killing any hissing rats perched on the rusted metal. Beady red eyes glared at me before disintegrating. Tarek strode upstairs backward, fending off any beasts stupid enough to follow us.

I hit the door with my shoulder, my gun firing over the railing to the rat massacre below. They kept coming and coming, climbing over burned bodies, willingly going into the fire.

On the second hit, Tarek was by my side as the door flung open. Surprised, I stumbled into the stairwell, thankfully with enough sense to take my finger off the trigger. I was strong, but no way would that door open with a bit of shoulder-checking on my part. I didn't question how the door opened until Tarek

238

and I slammed it shut against scratching claws and scraping teeth.

I huffed and wheezed, the acidic piss smell seeping under the door mingling with the sweet, bitter smell of frying rats. "Let's have this be the last time we go in there, okay?"

Tarek's sweaty face came into view when I opened eyes I hadn't remembered closing. "You'll not hear an argument from me," he said, and pushed off the door, his breath coming out in ragged gasps, like mine. "Thanks for the help, man."

I turned to Oren's pale face, his hand cupping his nose. "My pleasure, truly." Sarcasm and Oren went together like Exemplian rats and flesh-eating poison, neither combination pleasant.

"Yeah, okay, I'd love to stand here and chat, but if we don't head upstairs, my breakfast will be leaving a cute puddle on the floor." I strapped my gun to my back and hit the first step before turning to Oren. "Oh, and thanks. You're, like, Superman or something."

He grinned at Tarek and shook his head. "Seriously, out of all the women in the entire universe, you've chosen this one?"

"Yup." Tarek came up behind me. "Lead the way, love."

We trudged up flight after long flight, the distant smell of death and rot motivation to keep a steady, quick pace upward.

After about four flights, Oren stomped ahead of me. "Time to stop acting as if you know where you're going."

"Whatever." I learned to pick my battles with him, and arguing over the truth would've taken too much energy.

Once we stopped in front of a door, Oren held up his hands. "Before we go any farther…"

Ah, shit. What now?

I leaned against Tarek, my legs aching from the climb, and waited for whatever Oren was gearing up to say. He continued to stare at us, hesitation straining the corners of his eyes as he patted down air.

"Oren? It's not as if we have a lot of time." Tarek's deep voice vibrated against my back.

"Right, yes." Oren reached into his back pocket and pulled out two injection-like mechanisms that reminded me of miniature plastic water guns. "Have you ever considered how I manage to stay around Celeste?"

"We assumed your lack of brain matter helped," I said.

Oren tilted his head with a bored sneer. "Really...?"

I shrugged as Tarek reached for the tiny guns. "You've been drugging yourself," he said. It wasn't a question. "I should've known."

"Well, now you do." Oren folded his arms across his chest and rocked on his heels.

I snatched one of the things from Tarek's hand. "How do I work it?" I had no other questions. Anything that would combat Celeste's power, I was up for taking.

"Just hold on a minute." Tarek stilled my hand. "This'll kill you, Oren. You take too much, and your brain will shut down."

"I understand the risks." Oren didn't flinch, his voice steady.

I, on the other hand, had zero tolerance for my asshole friend putting himself in danger. Tarek's revelation also stopped my willingness to stick myself with a needle. Dealing with static was one thing. Killing myself to get rid of it was something else entirely. "Whoa, hold on, timeout." I pointed in Oren's face. "What, exactly, have you done to yourself?"

"I'm fine, Lena."

His pale face, circles under his eyes, and hollow cheekbones sank in. No. No way. "You don't look fine."

He gave a weak smile. "Careful. You might let me see how much you care."

"I *do care*, you asshole. How long have you being shooting this...what is it, anyway?" I looked from Oren to Tarek, both men eyeing each other. "Well, goddammit?"

Tarek answered. "It's papaverdilutus. A diluted form of the same chemical in gallium cuffs."

"*What?*" I dropped the injection with a tinny clang on the metal landing and shoved Oren, the push not budging him. "Why're you doing that?"

He caught my hands after I shoved him again, holding them to his chest. "In small doses, it's harmless, and it makes the static disappear. She needs me, Lena."

"No need to lie to her," Tarek said, his voice calm, as if talking to a ledge-jumper. "It isn't harmless, not when used for long periods of time."

"How long?" I flipped my hands and laced my fingers with Oren's. "How long have you been taking it?"

"Lena–"

"How long, Oren?"

He concentrated on our joined hands. "Ah, seven months, give or take."

"*Seven months*? You can't die. *You can't*."

"I won't." He lifted his gaze to mine. "You can't get rid of me so easily."

I shook my head, hating the tears looming. So many tears. These people who fell into my life by chance, circumstance, whatever, had become everything. "Swear to me."

He squeezed my hands. "I swear it."

"If something happens to you–don't let something happen to you." I rubbed my tears and snot on him before letting go.

Oren wiped the front of his shirt, his eyes tender. "Gross."

"You're welcome." My voice broke, but I held my head up. We had to do what was necessary, and if we couldn't think with all the brain fuzz, we wouldn't succeed. I grabbed the injection from the floor. "Will one time hurt me?"

"No," Tarek said. "One time will do nothing but alleviate her effects. The drug, though, it becomes addicting. Peace from static isn't easy to find here." Tarek's soft assurance was all I needed, and becoming addicted didn't concern me. I wouldn't be in this world long enough to develop a habit anyway, even if the effects took me to nirvana.

"Okay, then. Where do I shoot it?"

"Let me." Tarek took it from my grasp, and with one hand cupping the side of my neck, the other shot the papaverdilutus into my carotid artery. Instantly, everything in my brain went quiet. No buzz, no high, just calm with complete awareness–like I sat on my couch at home, on Earth.

"It's all gone. All of it." Tarek's warning invaded the euphoria. If I lived here full-time I'd definitely become addicted.

"Easy." Tarek steadied me before I fell down the stairs.

"I got this." I gripped the railing behind me to make sure. "Your turn."

He injected his neck and pitched the needle over the rail, a distant clank sailing up.

Oren winked in my direction. "Time to stir up trouble, as you do so well."

The door opened after Oren's eye scan, and I took off down the hall. "Looking forward to it."

CHAPTER 29
LENA

Illusions and Reality

"It's quite simple, little hero. You relax, I put circles on your temples and your occipital and frontal lobes, and you just talk away." Yosef sat on a floating chair across from mine, his legs crossed and a glass of something or other in his hand.

Celeste sat next to me, her tattoo flaring color after color. Concern darkened her violet eyes, eyes like Arcus's sky. They made me homesick for a place I hadn't called home in almost a year. "You do not have to do this, Lena," Celeste said. "We will find another way."

The injection was nothing short of magical, her presence even relaxing. Cinnamon sat thick in the air, the scent a part of who she was. Soothing.

"I owe these people. And if that means helping you so you can help them, I'm game." The authority had succeeded in taking over the screen feed after my first message, overriding and tracking any transmissions since then. Yosef said this was the only way, the last way to touch the people.

She folded my hands in her delicate ones. "But the procedure...it will be uncomfortable."

"It's fine, really."

The procedure: Yosef would be tapping into my energy, my soul, to activate my dormant Guide skills with his handheld machine. Not understanding it, but my subconscious would travel through wires and machines and project wherever I thought to walk in Heterodox. A hologram at the most advanced level, he'd said. Science.

Bullshit.

Sorcery, plain and simple. I wasn't too proud to admit my brain had a hard time wrapping around what he spoke about as casually as instructing how to pull on pants. Oh, yeah, and he admitted at the end of his "simple" explanation that it'd hurt like a sonofabitch at first.

"Like a headache?" I asked Yosef. "Not brain-oozing-from-my-ears pain or anything?"

"Absolutely, just like."

"A pimp, huh? You should have gotten a job with the Synod with all this, ah, knowledge."

Yosef gave me an ice-cold smile that frosted his eyes and set his glass on the table beside him. "Well, if that were the case, you'd have killed me. Most Synod Guides died in your little explosion act months ago."

Was I supposed to feel this guilty? I leaned up. "I–"

Tarek kneeled in front of me, ignoring Yosef and interrupting my need to apologize. He stole my hands from Celeste, and said, "We'll see everything you see on the screens." He caressed my cheek. "And I'll be here with you."

"I'm fine. It'll be fine." I found Oren standing behind Yosef's chair. In this light, his complexion resembled freshly fallen snow. "Oren?"

"Yes?" He crossed his arms, trying to look annoyed. But his worry copied Tarek's worry. Celeste's.

"After today, no more of that stuff, got it? We'll figure out something else once we get to Drea's."

His lips twitched. "Since when do you give me orders?"

"Since I decided I liked you better alive–a long time ago."

He watched me, not flinching as a few energy orbs pushed through the walls and absorbed into Celeste's chest, same as how energy had traveled to Tarek when he was Warden and someone died. Then he said, "Doesn't that make me special?"

My favorite asshole friend in the universe.

"I think so," I said, meaning it in the most honest way possible. I brought Tarek's hand to my mouth, letting my lips linger for a few moments. "Okay, I'm ready."

"Sit by your woman, Warden." Celeste went to Oren's side. "She will need you."

Tarek didn't say anything, just took the seat beside me.

"Right, then." Yosef slapped his legs and jumped from his chair. "Do try not to holler too much. It will do us no good if the authority hears your agony through the windows."

One: the one window in the room was shut and covered.

Two: Oren found his rival for the biggest dickhead award.

I bit my lip to keep from letting the pimp know exactly what I thought. Despite his annoying personality, he knew his way around technology, maybe even better than Drea.

He kept his mouth shut while hooking me up to a machine as big as my cell phone. The circles he spoke of were thick, plastic-looking magnets, magnets attracted to skin. He connected five, from my temples to the back of my skull, the electric hum vibrating against my face and scalp.

"Relax, little hero." He moved to the far wall and tapped on the screen, the screen where I saw Wilma's energy trapped for the first time. My heart skipped, the memory not one of the better memories. Heterodox filled it this time. "You'll have approximately five to eight minutes before the authority regains control of the screens. They will be able to shut us down, but they won't be able to track the signal." He paused. "Pity most of their smarter numbers perished in the explosion."

"Yeah, pity." Nerves jumped rope on my bladder.

He lifted a blue rubber mouthpiece to my lips. "You'll want to bite down on this."

Shit, this was gonna hurt. As Tarek's grip tightened around my thigh, I opened my mouth.

Yosef fit it in place, the rubber surprisingly tasting like mint. "If at any time the shock is too much, give this signal"– he tapped his elbow with his pointer finger–"and we will end it."

I grunted, saliva gathering in the back of my throat, gagging me until I swallowed.

Yosef looked around the room. "Everyone ready?"

"Get on with it, man. Press the button so we can leave this hellhole." Oren's cranky voice swam in my ears.

I clenched the arms of the chair, digging into the fabric until a few nails bent backward. My eyes stayed glued to the screen ahead, my lungs constricting to pebbles.

"Close your eyes, love," Tarek whispered in my ear. "Try to relax."

Calmness and humming electrodes coursing through the body didn't mix well. But I closed my eyes, and waited.

Push the bad out.

Bring the good back in.

Dull silence filled the room as if everyone quit breathing. Tarek's hand grew hot and damp, heavy on my leg. I clung to the feeling, fixated on it as if it were the anchor keeping me locked into my own sanity. A grainy click bellowed in the quiet, and Tarek's touch disappeared.

Everything disappeared.

Everything, except the pain.

Daggers attacked my brain, like sharp ice slicing at raw skin. Loud grunts and screams blared inside my head as I chomped down on the mouthpiece until my jaw cracked, until I swore my teeth shattered. Every layer of skin felt like it was struck with concentrated radiation, bubbling, boiling, sizzling like the rats in the hanger.

My yelling mingled with Tarek's and Oren's in a cacophonic blur, cheering on the torture. Hands grappled at my head, the magnets protesting as they held on after a tug. And another. More screams. Yells. Threats.

Finally, nothing.

No more pain, no more noise. A buoyancy took over, a weightlessness akin to what it must've felt like to skip through stars.

I opened my eyes, squinting into the sunlight to find myself on the street. "What the hell?" My voice ricocheted back to me as if I were a hundred miles away from my body. All my senses except hearing became dormant. No smells, nothing. I couldn't even feel the connection between my boots and the cement.

"Time to stir the masses, little hero. You've less than eight minutes." Yosef's voice was as distant as mine, disconcerting me. Terrifying.

Push the bad out...

Bring the good in...

Even my breathing sounded far away.

"Go, Lena. Hurry." Tarek's soft plea held the panic at bay. I imagined his damp palm clutching my thigh. My center.

Memory turned my feet toward the center of Heterodox, near Yosef's brothel. I ran as if in quicksand, a dream. Slow motion took over my psyche, but I think I might have flown, getting blocks away from Celeste's in seconds. I stopped short when people came into view. Small groups huddled together, and individuals rifled through the decay littering the sidewalks, probably in search of food. I surveyed the blank screens.

What if they didn't turn on? What if the authority managed to fi–

"They will turn on after you make contact."

Yosef. As if he read my mind–or watched me from the screen in Celeste's apartment. Who knew, and at that moment, I refused to give it much thought.

After a deep breath, I sidled up to the biggest crowd and settled into the middle of their group. *What to say, what to say?* "I-I'm here." My words, translated into Exemplian on the screens, resounded like the aftershock of cannon fire.

Dirty, pierced faces, some with those blinking tattoos, stared at me in shock, mouths agape. Some contemplated me before their attention skipped to the screens.

I followed their gazes, finding me staring back at myself. *Well, I'll be damned.* I appeared like an omniscient savior, a rat-shit-covered sage. People standing directly behind me were completely visible through my body.

I felt a grin spread across my face, fear leaving, replaced with courage. I turned back to my gathered masses and stood taller. "Do you hear me? I'm here! And I'll fight until the last breath leaves my body."

Shock turned to mumbling turned to shouting. The crowd cinched around me. Hope seeping from the citizens filled me up, making me invincible. What coursed through my veins was nothing short of God-like, the power addicting. Something foul and dark coated my gut for loving it, but guilt cured any budding sense of sapience. No wonder lesser people died in the effort to retain that type of worship.

Another deep breath escaped my lungs, and I imagined myself lifting above the crowd. As I pictured it, I ascended, my view of the people clearer from a higher vantage. When I confronted the screen, I noticed everyone I looked at, anyone I addressed, appeared alongside me. Whomever I saw, the entire crowd saw, too.

Well, then. Let's talk to who needed to listen.

I coasted back to the ground as Protectors rushed the crowd, guns drawn. "Stop." I held up my hand, my translucent body halting four trained authority members. I yelled over my shoulder, my attention on the emotionless Protectors. "People! These are your traitors, your *Tainted*."

Cheers erupted as pandemonium unraveled.

"Your so-called elders are their Tainted puppet masters." I glared at the screen, addressing the faceless people who had ruled long enough. "And we're coming for you. We're coming for all of you."

The crowd overtook the authority, their guns now in the hands of civilians. No matter how many Protectors came in shooting, their monotone voices demanding people to cease and desist, citizens emerged from opening doorways, bombarding the armed authority with numbers and sheer will. Chaos. Complete and utter chaos.

I wished that I were corporeal. I wanted to fight with them, face death at their side, these brave men and women piling on the Protectors, overwhelming them, forcing the enemy to retreat as shuttles hovered ever lower to the ground. Lines, like pulley wires, slinked down from them and snatched the more aggressive rebels with thick clamps. But all that did was make the hesitant bystanders certain, joining the fight, stripping the authority Protectors of their guns, supplies, even their contego suits.

Passion would always win over emotionless duty.

"Time to stop playing now." Yosef's too pleasant voice invaded my brain. "We've a real hero to save."

"Then wake me up, or whatever you have to do." I whispered the words, talking more to myself, not wanting what I said to project from the screen. But my fist itched to pummel enemy faces, my trigger finger searching for a phantom gun.

I took it in, the weak overpowering the strong. One voice– it could've been Tarek, Oren, whoever–all these people needed was one person to believe in them. Someone like Celeste.

It was time to uphold our end of the deal.

I turned, my confidence up and ready to work on phase two. Everything changed once I saw the face in front of me.

Phase two no longer mattered. "No. No!"

Peter stood there, his contego suit glowing under his sweatshirt. He fired his gun, the bullets hitting their marks between the eyes of the enemy. He stopped long enough to nod my way, fight brightening his eyes.

I tried to grasp his arm, but my hand rushed through his flesh. I tried again, desperation blocking rational thought. "Come with me. *Come with me now*." The boom of my voice resounded from the screens, causing war cries to rise all around us.

Peter shook his head. "No."

Before I could say another word, a long, metal pulley-line zipped down from the sky. The claw captured his waist and yanked him upward. Peter's cry for help washed over my brain as hot as lava. I shot up, my hands swiping futilely at his body. Before the hatch closed and he disappeared, I saw the Protector controlling the pulley. He smiled at me. Smiled.

My body floated to the sidewalk like a deflated balloon. "No! No! No!" My voice didn't blast from the screens.

But another voice did. A voice so calm—almost familiar—lulled fighters into obedience, as if it had the power to persuade through the screens. "You are no *sage*, no *savior*."

Shock rippled through my misty body. His words… *He read my mind…*

"I *am* the puppet master, and these…are my puppets." Chuckling, soft, ugly. "I'll be waiting for you."

Once the voice disappeared, fighting continued, though not with the same vengeance. Confusion marred faces of the citizens as they dealt blows, no power behind most of their strikes. As if they forgot why they fought in the first place.

I faced the largest screen. Nothing was there, just an opulent blue room—like the inside of an oyster shell. A room so familiar, it brought me to my vaporous knees. *No.* The same type of room Cassondra used to force me to give up secrets, where I endured the torture of reliving both Wilma's and

Tarek's deaths. They'd torture Peter with nightmares, and then they'd kill him.

A whoosh flushed through my soul like a vacuum, pulling me from the on-going fray, from Peter, and back into my body. In seconds, I again sat in the levitating chair, with Tarek's hand clamped to my leg.

Fear ate at me like rat poison, killing off everything but the image of Peter jutting into the air, disappearing into that shuttle. The smiling Protector as he shut the hatch on Peter's screams. The voice, admitting to toying with these people as if they were dolls…

My panic gave Peter to the enemy. *Why did I talk to him?*

I spat out the mouthpiece and wailed until no more sound left my throat, until it felt bloody and torn. Tarek pulled me onto his lap, his big arms crushing me in the effort to keep my boneless body from crumbling to the floor.

"What's wrong with her? What'd you do?" His voice cracked with rage, fear underlying every syllable.

"I–nothing! I've done nothing! You watched yourself; you all did. The screens went dark, and she came back, as we planned." Yosef's voice, no longer uppity, saved me from losing it, bringing me closer to the surface.

"Then how do you explain this? Is her energy not whole now?" Celeste sounded dangerous, helping to ease the panic even more. She had power. It radiated through the entire room as tangible as the walls, the floors.

"Wait, just…" I forced air into my lungs. Peter needed strength now, not weakness. I tucked my face into the crook of Tarek's neck, finding *my* power there, against his pulse. "They have Peter."

He held me closer. "Are you certain?"

I nodded against his skin, his pulse now thumping hard against my cheek.

"We'll get him, and then I'll break his legs so he can't run off again." Tarek's arms trembled, his voice warm against my ear.

Break Peter's legs… Yeah, I liked that idea.

I stood, using the willpower I stole from Tarek's words. "The fight…it's already waning."

"Why?" Oren pushed Yosef aside to stand directly in front of me. "What happened down there?"

"I-I think an elder–a voice took over a screen," I said. "It… whoever it was could read my mind, and convince people to stop. They're using this battle, *our battle*, as entertainment."

Oren's eyes widened, but he didn't answer. Instead, he stalked to the door with Celeste by his side, his gun out and contego suit already lit up. "Let's get the hell out of here."

I rushed to him. "But the fighting… I screwed up. They'll see us."

He didn't look at me, his focus on the door. "We're wasting time."

"Listen to me! We need to think abo–"

He shook his head and held up a hand as he turned, strain tightening the skin around his eyes. "I'm willing to chance it, for them,"–he pointed to the blackened screen–"for you, for everyone in this room. And for Peter." He opened the door. "Aren't you?"

I stood straighter, and I didn't have to turn to know Tarek stood behind me. "Hell, yes."

Oren opened the door. "Then tighten your big girl pants and turn on your suit. It's time to end things."

"Wait," Yosef said as we all started for the stairs. "You need the keycard…for the shuttle."

Tarek went back to the door and took it from Yosef's offering hand. "Thank you."

"No, thank you." Yosef waved. "Go, now. And…good luck."

CHAPTER 30

LENA

Loss

Different types of quiet existed: the comfortable kind, like soaking in warm bathwater in an empty house; the confident, like the silence in a room while Tarek thought our way out of a bad situation; and the hopeless, when the mind howled, but no words existed to ease the fear.

The last filled our shuttle. My mind replayed my blunders over and over again. I gave him up, handed him to the enemy. We left him there. Alone. The torture he'd endure… By the end of the night, elders would know exactly where we hid and who we all were. Even the strongest person would crack in that oyster room. I had cracked, had broken into thousands of pieces.

No one came up with a solution. After I had mentioned the room shining on that screen a few minutes into our ride, everyone knew what I had described, and everyone knew Peter would dissolve under the weight of his fears. *He was just a boy!*

Buzzing filled the silence every few minutes, the only sound. Every time, Oren released the steering lever, reached into his jacket pocket, and shut it off. Tarek's fingers would clench around mine when the chime interrupted the hopelessness.

Drea couldn't hack the authority shuttle's mainframe, so Oren's private communicator was her only means to reach us. She had probably already realized Peter left. No one wanted to confront her yet, tell her that her son was gone.

A conversation I had never wanted to have. If only they could've taken me instead. If only…

Shuttles polluted the sky, a uniformed search, but an almost lazy one. Exemplar was small, not many places to hide. We weren't going anywhere, and they knew it. Couldn't if we wanted to. Tarek had checked the lines before we left the apartment building. Locked. No one in, no one out.

It had been easier to beat them when the enemy hated me. Cassondra wanted revenge, and it made her actions sloppy. The elders who lived? They wanted something else entirely. Today showed they could control the population, turn most Heterodox citizens into submissive peons if they needed to. Protectors lifted those who didn't seem controllable into hovercrafts, their fate a mystery. This was all a game to them, the only conclusion I came up with.

That voice! So pleasant, as though he enjoyed our feeble attempts at rebellion. Mind reading, too. *Something* about the voice! I'd heard it before, but where?

One thing was certain. *We* weren't the ones flushing *them* out. Elders waited for us like a pride of lionesses hiding in the brush for an unsuspecting zebra. Of course all the death would get to us.

Of course we'd rush to act to end it.

Shut up, brain.

Shut up!

Shut up!

I pulled my hand from Tarek's to cover my ears, wishing that were enough to block the doom and gloom from taking over. I'd been there before, the black an inviting place. Part of me wanted to give in, but I couldn't go there again. I couldn't let it win.

We'd get him back.

I'd die trying.

Static crinkled into my skull, easing the anxiety but constricting my brain. I eyed Tarek, who pinched the bridge of his nose with his eyes shut. Looked like a dose of papaver-whatever had a lifespan of only a few hours.

I cleared my throat. "Oren? How far?"

He checked the monitor. "Five minutes."

"I don't think we're gonna last that long."

Celeste flinched when I moaned, the static getting louder, like waves slapping against a rock wall. The smell of cinnamon went from pleasant to suffocating, causing my stomach to burble.

"I am so sorry. I..." Celeste shook her head, frantically reaching for the door latch, willing to leap from the vehicle.

"Concentrate, Cel. Focus on your center, imagine the shell." Oren's raspy voice turned soothing as he used one hand to rub Celeste's hunched back.

"My nerves, they are too great." She sobbed now, her body shaking while static rolled off her and attacked us.

I huddled in a ball, my head resting on Tarek's lap. All I wanted to do was hop out and take my chances with gravity and the authority. My eyes stayed glued to Oren, whose calm alleviated the urge to escape, even as the white noise in my head thickened.

He clicked on autopilot and cradled Celeste's face in his trembling hands, the only sign that her power had gotten to him, too. "No, look at me." When she shut her eyes, Oren's voice grew desperate. "Cel, *look*."

She let a whimper escape before doing as Oren ordered.

"Good. Now, find your shell. Do you see it?"

After long, agonizing seconds, she nodded.

"Use my voice to help guide all the energy to that shell. Tuck it away, save it, nurture it. It's not weakness; it's a weapon."

Tears flowed from her violet eyes as the debilitating noise lessened. "It is not weakness. Not weakness…"

Love blazed so bright on Oren's face it blinded me. "It's a weapon. Say it, Cel. It's. A. Weapon."

A fragile smile curved Celeste's mouth. "It is…a weapon."

The static dulled, not disappearing, but ebbed enough to where the shuttle quit being a cinnamon-smelling compression chamber. I sat up, nice and slow, afraid of interrupting whatever connection Oren and Celeste shared.

Tarek's hand found mine on the seat, neither of us saying a word.

The quiet now shifted to the best kind. Confident quiet, where everything would find its way back together. No more rabid thoughts attacked my mind. No more.

The monitor blinked, letting us know we made our destination. We all ignored it, our gazes on Celeste, her face nestled between Oren's hands. Buzzing vibrated Oren's pocket again. We ignored that, too. As we landed, going straight back and into the shed without a pause, Oren lifted his hands. "Keep your eyes on mine. We'll be okay. We always are."

"We must find a room where I can stay, protect them from the energy." Celeste's voice matched the calm in Oren's.

"We will. Focus. Almost there."

The engine clicked off, and a metallic voice coming from the main console told us we reached our destination. Still, none of us thought to make a sound. We sat in there staring at Celeste, witnessing a miracle. Oren kept his composure while Celeste held onto his gaze with hers.

Our bliss melted when the hatch flung open. We all gave our attention to the windshield to find Drea storming out into the shed.

Celeste moaned.

Static filled every hole in my body, narrowing every blood vessel in my brain. "Ah!" I bent forward, squeezing my eyes shut against the pain. "Open the door, Oren. Let us out, dammit!"

A thump. Another as Tarek jumped out. Grunts and a hard tug followed.

He had me out in seconds.

Oren shot out and ran over to Celeste's side. "Why the hell did you do that?" He aimed his anger at Drea.

She ignored him to search the shuttle, the fear smothering her face as excruciating as Celeste's aura. "He's not here." She kept searching, even though the cab had barely room enough for the four of us. "*He's not here!*"

Oren didn't wait for the inevitable confrontation. He pulled Celeste to his side and spoke to Tarek, his face grim. "Where can I take her?"

Tarek nodded to the hatch, holding me tight against him. "The lab, last door on the right, two stair flights down."

"I remember." Oren wasted no more time. "Come on, Cel. I'll take care of you." Strained though his face was, his voice stayed unruffled as he spoke to her.

Celeste let him guide her after a pitying look toward Drea's frantic search, the woman still calling for Peter. In seconds, the two disappeared underground. Once they left, the static eased, my brain now sagging in my skull, the relief heady.

Relief didn't last long.

"*Where?*" Drea's agony hit its mark.

"Drea…" I moved toward her but hesitated. *I'm sorry! I'm sorry!*

Tarek pulled her from the shuttle, holding her as she sobbed against his chest. "It's all right. Shh, he'll be fine." He smoothed her disheveled hair as she cried, his eyes staying on me. His words didn't match the doubt I found there.

"Where is he? Where's my son?"

Drea's muffled plea pierced my soul. I remembered that fourteen-year-old face all those months ago, its innocence, its blemished skin. And I led him to slaughter.

I allowed the tears to escape. "We need to get underground."

Tarek nodded and led Drea to the hatch. He then gently brought her to kneel down with him. "We need your palm, Drea. You'll need to close the hatch."

Sobbing, she stayed close to Tarek.

He used his free hand to wave me over. "You first."

I raced down the ladder, my feet not bothering with the rungs. Through the flickering blue light, I watched the opening, holding my breath until Tarek and Drea came down and the hatch closed. Residual static from Celeste added to what emitted off Drea. Nothing incapacitating, just uncomfortable as if dull nail heads scratched my brain.

Drea's shoulders slumped, and wretchedness oozed from her pores, evidence of it all over her face. "They have him, don't they?"

I found Tarek's gaze behind her before answering. "Yes."

"How?"

"I...I screwed up." Tears turned my voice into a soupy, incoherent mess.

"He promised he wouldn't leave. He promised me, and I believed him." She wasn't looking at me anymore. Her attention went to her splayed fingers. "I gave him access again to show him... To prove I trusted his word."

She didn't need to say anything else. Guilt volleyed in the space between us, both of us willing to take the blame.

Tarek rested his hand on her shoulder, his eyes all mine. "This isn't over. Not by half."

Before any of us could say another word, Denzel tore down the hall, his robes flapping behind him. "Do they have him? Is he here?"

Drea shook her head, her eyes remaining on her hands.

The older Guide's face paled, the blue light giving his skin a gray pallor. "Then why are you all here? Go! Bring him back!"

"And how do you propose we do that, Guide?" Tarek stepped forward. "Run outside and flag down a shuttle? Ask them kindly to take us to him?" Tarek's quiet voice didn't fool me. Fury threatened to burst onto the surface and bury Denzel under its rubble.

"Yes, *Protector*. That is exactly what I wish you to do! They'll kill him, if not." With every word Denzel spoke, he took a step closer to Tarek. "Our only demand after this rebellion started was for your people to keep Peter away, and you failed."

When Tarek shifted his hips and clenched his fists, I jumped in front of him.

"Wait. Just wait a minute." Deep breath. "They know he's important to me. They…they saw that today. If we go out there pissed off and desperate, we'll feed into exactly what they want. Then all this will be for nothing."

"All of this *is* for nothing if they kill our son." Denzel's hands fisted at his sides, his face now red.

His anger caused my skin to tingle, and Celeste's warning all those months ago vibrated in my head: *Drea may trust you, but I do not…*

I held up my hands. "We'll get him back, but we have to be smart. One day, two at the most, and we'll figure out the rest of the plan."

Bullshit. I called complete and utter bullshit on myself.

To the rhythm of Drea's sobs, Denzel shook his head. "They will not give him *a day, two at the most*."

"Enough." Tarek took my hand. "You'll listen, or I'll lock your ass in a room until this is over. We have a path, and we're staying on it."

"You do not rule here," Denzel said. "You do not rule anywhere, anymore."

With a lethal calm that turned my legs into rubber, Tarek gave Denzel all of his attention. "If you do anything to jeopardize one of mine for that boy, I'll gut you before the authority lands in the yard."

"Your threats do not scare me."

The gray in Tarek's eyes froze to ice. "Oh, there are no threats here, old man." He then turned his back on Denzel, my hand secured in his.

"Tarek?" I whispered, my hand tightening around his as we walked toward the end of the hall.

He looked down at me before the door leading to upstairs opened. Ice-cold rage didn't mask his face anymore, the dread underneath saying everything I didn't want to hear. "Stay away from him."

"You think he'll try something?"

"Absolutely." Tarek stalked the main floor of the cabin, going through holograms showing death and defeat. Kill after kill.

Elders had no qualms about slaughtering everyone, putting humans on Exemplar's extinction list.

Why?

∞ ∞ ∞

The door to our room shut and Tarek let go of my hand. He wouldn't stand still, wearing a path between the bed and the connected bathroom. Curses flared from his lips.

I collapsed to the floor, my back against the cool metal of the door. We were fucked, just unavoidably fucked. Denzel and Drea wouldn't sit back and let Peter die. Freedom from an oppressed government meant nothing to them without their boy. The boy I most likely had killed.

"Why did I talk to him?"

Tarek stopped, his gaze searching mine. My guilt cascaded through the entire room, showering us both.

"If I would've just ignored him, found a way to snatch him before we left…" Tears trailed down my cheeks, but my voice stayed flat. Too flat.

So fucked.

Tarek crouched in front me. "It's done now. Whatever happened, happened, and we can't change it. We need to focus on a solution."

"A solution? Do you honestly believe there's a solution that doesn't end in our death?"

Silence.

I shrugged, tears draining all my strength. "That's what I thought."

The next time he spoke, his desperation trumped the guilt oscillating between us. "We could leave. As soon as the lines open, we could go. Run. All we'd have to do is lay low until we can cross. We could hide in the caves near the cliffs; no one would find us."

My heart seized. Not because his suggestion sounded as wrong and cowardly as it was, but because I wanted it so badly, I could taste its bitterness on my tongue. "We can't."

He lifted my hands to his lips. "*We can*. Forget everything and leave. Go back to Arcus. No one would be dumb enough to come after us there."

As he spoke, anger darkened my vision. I hated that he gave us an out. Hated that I wanted it more than the blood gushing through my veins. "You would leave them, let Peter and Oren die without even trying?"

"Aren't you tired of fighting? Tired of living your life always wondering if they'll succeed in destroying it?"

"Yes." My voice hitched, a sob swallowing the anger. "So please don't ask me to leave again."

After another pause lasting a lifetime, he said, "I can't lose you."

I wanted to tell him that we'd make it out of this as we always had, scarred but alive. I couldn't.

But one thing *was* certain.

I slipped a hand from his slackened hold to press against his heart. "This life, it isn't the end for us. Whatever happens, my soul will find yours; it always has."

Tarek lifted his head, and his eyes gave me all his love and fear and strength. He gave me everything, as I would always give him. No more words, we didn't need anymore. He brought his lips down on mine, urgent and searching.

I moaned into his mouth, gripping his hair, tugging him closer–never close enough. His kiss filled and emptied me. Taking all and giving everything back.

One second we were on the floor, the next I was in Tarek's arms, flying. He set me on the bed, his lips never parting from my hungry mouth. I arched my back after he unzipped my suit to give his hands better access to roam my skin, his fingers kneading until tingling turned to fire. His shirt was over his head and suit pulled down seconds after. I had no idea if I took his clothes off or he did, our hands fighting to get our bodies closer. God, I needed him.

I'd always need him.

His tongue traveled up my neck, turning my skin to lava. When he reached my ear, his lips captured my earlobe and sucked until I groaned.

"Please…" I pulled him closer.

His moist breath heated my ear. "You need to promise me something."

"Anything." At that moment, I'd have given him the skin from my body.

His touch disappeared, and the emptiness left behind almost killed me. "Open your eyes, love."

I did as he asked, my body begging for his.

"Don't die."

Pain sneaked into our bubble, his fear punching me, seeping into my heart. I leaned up until our mouths touched, wanting to erase it, crush it into nonexistence. "Only if you promise the same."

He brushed a thumb across my chin. "Deal."

Promises, no matter how good intentioned, had a habit of coming up empty for our group. Not this one. I wouldn't let it, and neither would he.

CHAPTER 31

OREN

Searching for Silence

The last door to the right. Not far, a few yards left to go.

Oren pushed forward, his eyes on the target and Celeste's hand secured in his. Fighting her power, the roaring inside his head, made his knees wobble. He stumbled inches from the door.

Celeste gripped him under his shoulder, her strength surprising. But her strength wasn't enough to keep him on his feet. They both fell at the entryway to the stairs. This was it; he wouldn't be able to help.

"I'm killing you," Celeste said, her voice a whisper against the noise attacking his brain.

"N-no, you're not." His denial drifted into the hall as feeble as an infant's pummeling fist.

"I will no longer be your burden, Oren."

He held the nape of her neck and brought her forehead down on his, the blare in his mind now excruciating. "You're. Not. My. Burden."

"I am. But I will no longer be."

Quiet, not complete silence but bearable, stifled the turmoil brewing in his head and his heart decelerated from its rapid pace. He pulled back to find Celeste's determined gaze.

Oren didn't say a word, refusing to interrupt as Celeste grasped control of the energy alone. She focused on his eyes, not her usual way with eyelids firmly slammed shut. Her tattoo shimmered in cadence with the scattering of blue lights in the hall, as if one were in rhythm with the other. It changed slowly now, unlike the hurried way it flashed through colors in the shuttle.

"We must go now," she said before holding up her hand to the closed door. Without needing access to the panel, the door opened.

The power...

He curbed his awe and pushed himself up with Celeste's help. Neither spoke as they passed a few storage rooms, the promise of silence too fragile to destroy with any wrong words. A dull throb thumped in his head as they reached the lower level. Her control wasn't complete, but it was enough to mask the potency of her aura.

As they neared the lab, the lights surrounding them dimmed to almost nothing. He kept Celeste's hand in his as he collected blankets off some shelves on the way. Once they made it to the lab, she waved a hand. The door obeyed, gliding open.

He cleared his throat. "Ligh–"

"No." Celeste pulled him inside the room, and then moved to stand in the middle. "Leave them off. Please."

He smiled in the darkness. "All right." He took deliberate steps toward her, loving how her glittering tattoo now undulated gold and blue.

Her backside bumped into what Oren knew was the metal table. The heavy steel actually budged from her touch, emitting a small screech as it moved.

Oren tossed the blankets on the table and steadied her with a hand at the small of her back. "How, Celeste? How did you…?"

"I do not know, exactly." She left his hold to take the blankets off the table, spreading them on the hard floor. Her tattoo was the only light in the room, its color stopping on gold longer than blue. "But hurting you is like stabbing my own heart." She brought him down to the nest she'd made and rested her head against his shoulder once he gathered her in his arms. "And it is time for me to be strong, save these people, our people."

"You won't have to fight them alone, Cel." He traced a line up her arm, her soft skin making his fingertips vibrate with need.

"You have given up so much for me. Grace, your peaceful life…" Sluggish static heightened in his head with each word she spoke. "What have I given you except torture?"

He tilted her chin and bent to kiss her. When he lifted his mouth from hers, he said, "You're wrong, beautiful." He placed a hand on her pounding heart. "You're *everything*."

And just like that, she gave them complete silence.

"Your honeyed words…" Same thing she said every time he spouted anything remotely romantic, which he was never any good at.

He kissed her again, his trembling hand finding the edge of her top and lifting it up until his palm burned with the feel of her skin. When she moaned, the sound drove him over the edge. He pushed his tongue past her lips, tasting her moans as she matched his urgency. The silence she created poured desire into his soul—just being with her.

He needed more—her skin on his, scorching him. Bringing him to life. He broke the contact long enough to pull his sweaty shirt over his head and unbutton her white gauzy blouse. His eyes never left her face, her tattoo bright, bright gold. "You *are* beautiful, Cel. All of you, every single part."

She threaded her hands through his hair, the glow from her cheek enough to reveal the love in her eyes, so violet. "I love you, Oren."

"And I you, from the first moment I saw you." He lowered his chest against her softness and sought her lips, feeding off her like a madman as his hand dipped underneath her skirt, seeking, devouring.

Again, she moaned, arching into him. "Oren!"

No more. He couldn't hold back anymore. He leaped from the floor and stripped down, only to return to Celeste's writhing body, her mouth a magnet. Before he could rid her of the rest of her clothes, Celeste moved to wrap her arm around his neck–and successfully flung the heavy steel table across the room.

Oren laughed, even as he continued to strip the clothes from her body. Not even flying metal would keep him away. "Who says you can't fight."

A grin lifted the corner of her mouth. "It looks as though I was mistaken."

He laughed again, feeling free for the first time in years. His lips made a wet trail from her lips to her earlobe, and he whispered, "My hero."

CHAPTER 32

LENA

Traitor

Celeste's aura felt like snakes coiled around my brain. The static was loud, yes, but the squeezing had the power to make a person catatonic. Her energy so potent, so concentrated, even the thought of it made my brain twitch with phantom pain. No other feeling came close to that torture.

Except one.

My eyelids snapped open, the hypnotic lure of Guide energy in its raw form demanding my attention. I tried to say something, wake Tarek, but no sounds left my throat. This kind of torture wasn't debilitating in a constricting way as Celeste's; it was addictive, consuming.

A blue orb ghosted above me, stronger than Zander's, but I'd had plenty of practice fighting the temptation. I watched it, trying to will residual sleep from my mind to think clearer. An authority Guide? No. Experience said they always traveled in packs–more than one would've done me in.

The orb silently skipped to the door and back to me, Tarek's soft snore the only sound in the room. *So, it wanted me to follow.*

Denzel or Drea. Which one was brave enough to come in here?

I went to shake my giant, but the light zoomed near my hand as if trying to yank it away from Tarek's shoulder. This wasn't good, not at all. But I'd play the game–for now. I scooted off the bed, naked and not the least bit concerned about it. The light dipped behind the bathroom door, and I shook my head as I threw on Tarek's refitted jeans and a white T-shirt.

Definitely Denzel.

I straightened my shirt and gestured toward the hall. Denzel's light escaped the room as I touched the keypad. Before I went to see what havoc the Guide had probably done, I turned toward Tarek, sound asleep. In my presence, he slept like the dead. Denzel was smart coming up here in energy form. If he had tried to come up here corporeal, Tarek would've had his gun on the older man before the door had the chance to open.

I took the lift, gun in my hand. After what happened this afternoon, I didn't trust any Guides in this house. Denzel fluxed through holograms until the lift stopped on the main floor. After his energy disappeared through the door leading downstairs, gooseflesh trailed up my arms. *Now what?*

I engaged my gun as sweat beaded on my forehead. I'd been through a lot, but following that light down those stairs–*dumbass* blared in my brain with every step forward.

Deep breath.

Sweaty palm to the keypad.

The door opened.

One last look behind me. I should've woken Tarek.

Denzel waited at the base of the stairs, bouncing in the soft blue light that almost cloaked him from sight.

I lifted my gun. "If you try anything, I'll put a bullet between your eyes before your energy has a chance to implant."

Energy Reborn

He could understand me in his celestial form, but that didn't mean he'd listen. We stayed there a few seconds, him blinking at eye level, with me holding my gun to his energy– not that it could hurt him.

Finally, he whisked down the hall, away from the door leading down to the lab, the weapon caches, food supplies, and ended up zipping into a room close to the hatch to the shed. I stopped, holding my gun tighter. An ambush, maybe? *Forget this.* Tarek needed to be there, whether that flashing son of a bitch wanted him to be or not.

I turned back toward the stairs, and the door opened.

"If you wake anyone, Peter is as good as dead."

I clenched my jaw to prevent the sob riding up my throat from escaping. *Push the bad out, Lena.* Without looking at Denzel, I said, "What have you done?"

"What any of you would have done for the person you love."

Oh, no. No, no, no.

I spun, my gun up and ready to decorate his face with a couple more holes. "I should've killed you a year ago."

Sadness, more like defeat, sagged his cheeks. "Yes, perhaps you should have."

Sweat now poured from my skin, my hand slick against my gun's grip. Denzel didn't try to beg for his life. No flinching. No pale sheen dulling his face. He stood there like a man who had nothing to lose. *So, so fucked...*

"If you are going to kill me, do it now," he said. "Otherwise, listen to what I have to say."

My knees wanted to give, but the weakness only made me stand taller. "Where's Drea?" I scanned behind his shoulder, toward the open room.

"She is upstairs, asleep under heavy tranquilizers. Her world has shattered, Lena. She can no longer help the cause."

"So you...what...decided to save the day? Give us up to the elders?"

"Not everyone."

Shoot him! Pull the trigger! "You told them about Celeste."

"Are you truly that naïve? Do you not think they know a good portion of the energy flocks to her? They know she exists, and they don't give a bloody damn about her! If they had, she'd be captured already."

"Bullshit. They'd have tri–"

"*They do not want her.*" His shaking hand wiped his brow.

I opened my mouth, wanting words to fly out, anything to make *his* words disappear. Nothing.

A sharp laugh erupted from Denzel's lips. "So, I do have superpowers. Never thought I'd see the day when your venomous tongue stopped working."

"Who do they want?"

Denzel pointed at me.

"Why?" My throat went dry, and that *venomous tongue* Denzel spoke of felt coated in sand. Obvious reasons entered my mind, but dammit, I wasn't the only person to help bring them down.

"I don't know, nor do I care. They've agreed to a trade–*all* I care about."

So many questions ran through my head, from how he knew where to look for the elders to why we let him stay around, given all our doubts about his loyalty. But only one sentence poured from my lips. "I don't want to die."

I lowered my gun, stumbling backward until I hit the wall. Cowardice, guilt, fear, all of it twisted my heart, so much more convincing than courage.

"Did you honestly expect to come out of this alive?" His delicate voice screamed through the claustrophobic hall.

I ignored him, turning my attention toward the lab. Oren and Celeste were so close; Tarek slept two floors above. I could run to them, let them know what Denzel had done. I could.

"They want you. Alone. If you refuse to come with me, if you alert anyone, I will leave my body this instant to inform the authority circling the skies. No matter how strong Tarek and Oren are, they cannot beat a hundred."

I flopped my head in his direction. His face, regardless of the despair, was resolute. "You'd let them kill Drea?"

"She would give up her life for the life of her child, as would I."

I closed my eyes. So this was it? This was how everything would end? "I could kill you, you know. End you right now."

"You could, yes. But when I do not arrive with you in tow, Peter will die." He paused. "Are you willing to fail him again?"

Tears flowed hotter.

I hated him.

I hated Peter.

No, that wasn't true. I hated that I loved Peter more than my own life.

Disgust filled me, anger as heavy as cement. Rage, so much better than giving up. I opened my eyes and pushed to my feet, faltering on the way up. Denzel's question skipped through my head: *Did you expect to come out of this alive?*

Yes, I had expected to live–and I would. I made a promise to my giant.

Once I faced Denzel again, I smiled, even as fury blazed through my system. "He *will* kill you."

Denzel swallowed, his throat bobbing. "It will not matter if Peter is safe."

"And you think he'll be safe after Tarek finds out what you've done?"

Fear widened his eyes, but he said nothing.

I nodded toward the hatch. "Well, then. I suppose we should let you save the day."

"*He's my son*. What would you have done?" He held out his hands, fingers splayed.

I looked up, refusing to allow him to see any more of my tears. He was right. I would've betrayed every single person in this house to get Tarek back. My giant told me once that I was his flaw. He was mine, too.

And Peter was Denzel's.

Push out the bad.

Bring the good back in.

"I need your word on something, Denzel. The least you could do for me." I wouldn't meet his gaze, afraid I might lift my gun and end it–and effectively kill Peter.

"I'm listening."

Don't lose it... Push out the bad.

I breathed in deep, forcing my lungs to accept the stale oxygen. "Before Tarek kills you–and he will–you need to give him a message."

Silence.

I went on, my voice breaking. "Tell him...tell him that I expect him to keep his promise, and I'll keep mine."

∞ ∞ ∞

"How many are there?" I studied the authority shuttles sharing the sky with us. My gun rested in my hand on my lap, a security blanket that wouldn't protect me from anything anymore.

He cleared his throat. "To whom are you referring?"

"You know who I'm talking about."

"I don't know." His voice barely rose above the quiet engine, but lies screamed, no matter how softly they were spoken.

My finger clicked off the safety without my brain commanding it to. Reflexes were hard to overcome. I switched my attention to Denzel's profile. "I might not kill you, but I'll sure as hell put a bullet in your leg, maybe both your hands."

He slammed his fist against the steering lever, the first sign of anger he'd shown since the hallway. "I don't know! No one knows. There could be a thousand. And they could be anyone."

"But you said—"

"I know what I said." He rubbed the bridge of his nose. "You'll see how people 'speak' to the elders once we arrive."

We flew closer to a nondescript building in Cynosure. "In there?"

Immediately after the question left my mouth, a voice invaded the cab. "You are flying in protected area. Please allow us to guide your craft to its final destination."

The steering lever jerked from Denzel's grip and locks engaged on the doors. Fear filled the vehicle, a mixture of both Denzel's and mine. In minutes, there was a good possibility that'd I'd be fighting for my life. I scrutinized Denzel and felt a smile ghost my lips.

He'd make a decent shield.

But the smile disappeared before it had the chance to form. *I don't want to die!*

Whoever controlled our flight steered us to a lower level of the building, so unlike the sleek buildings we blew up almost a year ago. The closer we flew, the smaller my lungs became. I was gonna lose it before I even had a chance to fight.

I slammed my eyes shut and pictured Tarek. Pictured him as he was a few hours ago, beside me, one finger drawing circles on my arm, love pouring from his eyes and filling me up. *I promise! I promise!*

Breathe, Lena. Just…breathe.

A jolt rattled my body as we landed, but I kept my eyes closed. Panic needed more than one image and a promise. It needed an entire lifetime to focus on. Pictures flashed through my mind: Mom, Jake, Wilma, Farren, Belva, Winston, all the people who meant everything, with Tarek leading them. People who would demand I not give up in this shuttle with a person who had never cared if I lived or died. I wouldn't. Not now. Not ever.

Push out the bad.

Bring the good back in.

The locks clicked and the door opened. Canned air breezed through, cooling the sweat dripping from my scalp and trickling down my temples. My eyes remained shut. Those faces, I needed them. All of them.

A hand touched my shoulder. "It's time to go, Lena."

"Don't." I opened my eyes, expelled all the fear from my body, and dumped it over Denzel. "You touch me again, and I'll break your hand."

"Very well." Denzel pursed his lips and slipped out.

I watched him for a minute, maybe longer, as he walked toward a cluster of authority Protectors. "All right." I engaged the safety on my gun and stuffed it into my waistband. One more breath. "All right."

On legs powered by a surge of adrenaline, I joined Denzel and his circus monkeys. No one spoke as one Protector pulled my gun from my jeans before the rest led us to a lift.

A Guide in energy form zipped across the hanger and through Denzel's vehicle, causing me to buckle. It had to be a more advanced Guide. Only someone strong could bring my brain almost as close to mush as Celeste's power. One of the Protectors slapped a hand to the small of my back, saving my head from splitting against the hard floor.

The Guide disappeared through the hanger ceiling after inspecting the shuttle. Maybe there was only one of the flying balls of shit left? Who knew, and it didn't matter anymore.

The quiet lift took us so far up I felt the lack of oxygen, my head getting lighter with every floor we passed. The air grew frigid, the vents bringing in the chill from the higher elevation. Whoever the elders were, a serious God complex afflicted them all. An image zoomed through my mind of the Greek pantheon sitting on clouds, looking down on the teeny, tiny ants who worshiped them.

When a polite ding tinkled through the lift and the doors opened, a Protector tried to coerce me with the barrel of his gun to get out. I wanted to beg them to take me back down. Whatever they wanted to do to me in the hanger–in the lift–would be better than what would happen in this room.

Another oyster, with pearly walls and spongy floors and nightmares waiting to attack.

Another jab hit my back, the hard bite of the gun stinging my flesh.

"No." I stumbled, shaking my head. "*No.*"

"Yes," Shoving Protector said, his tone void of emotion.

My lips went numb, and my legs finally said enough. I crumbled to my knees, still shaking my head, terrified of the opalescent walls and a floor that would feel as if I stood inside a mouth and hopped on a tongue.

"Please, Lena." Denzel hunched in front of me. "*Please.*"

"I hate you." I fumbled for his robes and bunched fabric into my fists, bringing him closer. "*I hate you!*"

He opened his mouth, but two Protectors pulled me from my knees, lifting me between them as if I weighed nothing.

"Wait! No, wait!" My effort to escape didn't sway them. They tossed me into the oyster without a word. I struggled on the gelatinous surface to reach the perceived safety of the lift, but this oyster was different, the floor suctioning my body to it. I fell, my hands and knees now imprisoned in its soft, fleshy substance. "Help me!"

I had no clue whom I begged, but if the elders planned to torture me with Wilma's death or Tarek's–Peter's–I'd never make it. Not again.

Denzel stepped from the lift, the floor not restraining him as it did me. He viewed a set of screens on the far wall and straightened his robes. "I've brought her to you. Now, please, give the boy to me."

"Who the hell are you talking to?"

The doors to the lift stayed open, and Protectors guarded the entrance. Denzel stood by me as I stayed on my hands and knees. I became his disobedient dog he planned to give back to the shelter. He ignored me, staring at those screens like he would another human being.

Finally, "You will acquire the boy in due time, Guide. Thank you for your loyalty." A voice filled the oyster, pleasant, almost soothing–the same semi-familiar voice from the Heterodox screen.

Denzel didn't find it so relaxing. He fidgeted, his folded hands twisting in the front of his robes. "But, you gave your word–the boy for the Tainted." The familiar soft, ugly chuckling infiltrated our prison, pissing Denzel off, his control snapping. "You–"

"It is not wise to argue. You will lose."

My body relaxed some, and my hands broke free from the floor. I straightened my back, trying to find courage while pinned on my knees.

Denzel stepped forward, his anger now desperation. "Please! I beg you. He's my–" His hand flew to his mouth, catching whatever words he was about to say, holding them in.

"He's your what, Guide?"

Denzel's lips quivered.

"Answer me."

"He's my…son."

Stupid, stupid.

Screw this.

Screw it.

I struggled to my feet, finding strength in Denzel's weakness. They wouldn't break me, not in this oyster.

I stood next to Denzel and took his hand. Sweat leaked from his palm. Mine–finally–was steady and dry. "Let Peter go. You have me; let him leave."

Minutes ticked by. Hours.

"We will release the boy once you've given us assistance." So, so pleasant–so deceivingly accommodating.

"I'm here, aren't I? Whatever you want, you have now."

"We shall see."

Denzel yanked his hand from mine. "You will pay for this."

"Your threats do not concern us."

The voice instantly dropped Denzel's shoulders.

"You remember nothing of your time here. You will leave, return to your *rebels*, and face their wrath. Go. Die by their hands with dignity. Am I clear, Guide?"

"Yes, perfectly clear."

What? I peered down at Denzel's face to find nothing there. Just a blank, drooling slate. "Denzel?"

He didn't acknowledge me. Instead, he turned toward the lift, the right side of his face slack as if he'd had a stroke.

"Denzel!" If he forgot everything, if none of this stayed in his head, Tarek and Oren would never find me. They'd never get the chance to– "*Denzel!*"

Once he stepped into the lift, the doors closed, shutting off any chance of rescue.

I regarded the empty screens. Every nerve in my body roared with the desire to fight while fear pleaded with my mind to give up. I lifted my chin, opting to listen to the former. "Now what?"

The screens dissipated, giving way to a set of doors. This time when the voice answered, the familiar became the certain. "It's time to bargain, little hero."

Lynn Vroman

CHAPTER 33

TAREK

Persuaded Enemy

Thump!

Tarek shot up, his gun in hand and engaged before his feet touched the cold tile. He raced for the door–open.

Another thump.

Odd. He was the only one awake and alert. Lena had the same acute intuition, always knowing whe–

Cold slithered through his veins, dread sinking his stomach. He didn't want to turn back toward the bed.

He closed his eyes. "Lena?"

Silence.

Another thump. Yelling. Drea's.

Oren's: "*What did you do?*"

Please be there. *Please.* "Lena?"

Maybe if he didn't turn around, if he kept his eyes closed, what blared loud in his mind wouldn't be true.

He had to turn. Had to.

He opened his eyes and spun.

Rumpled sheets and two pillows–empty.

Maybe she went downstairs. Maybe. *Please have gone downstairs!*

Tarek rushed into the hall, dressed only in the jeans he grabbed from the floor, barely remembering how to work the hydro-lift as the yelling on the lower level worsened. Once the lift stopped, he searched the faces in the main room.

No! Not here, not here, not here.

He found Oren holding Denzel in the air, the Guide's jaw slack and eyes empty. Drea huddled in the corner, sobbing. No one else. No one.

"Lena's gone," Tarek said. Saying those two words put him over the edge.

Denzel moaned, his puny hands going to Oren's fist, yanking at it, trying to escape.

No. The man would die. Tarek would tear him into bloody, mangled pieces. He took a step toward him, needing the hate to burst from his eyes and burn the Guide to ash. "Where is she?"

Drea moved in front of him. "Tarek–"

He shoved her out of the way. Denzel needed dead, and not a damn person would stop him. "*Where*?" His voice was a quiet ghost. A threat masked with whispers.

Oren nodded to him, the Guide's struggle nothing more than a bothersome fly to the stronger Protector. "Are you sure she's gone?"

Tarek stepped closer. *Murder.* "Yes."

Oren dropped the Guide at Tarek's feet, fury animating his face. "He's all yours, then."

Tarek wasted no time hauling the frail man from the ground, bringing him up until they were eye level. "You don't have much time, old man."

"I do not–I-I can't remember."

"Liar!" He shook him, the Guide's head snapping backward. "Tell me where she is!"

"I swear to you, I don't know! I don't!" The man's lips shook, and his ashen face paled even more. "Please. I–"

Tarek yelled, throwing the man across the room, through the holograms. Helplessness scorched his mind, weakening his legs. He turned to Oren. "Please. Tell me *something*."

Oren tilted his head toward the front door–the door none of them had used since being there. "He landed in front of the cabin. I found him wandering in the field. Tarek"–Oren moved closer holding up his hands, shaking his head–"I think someone scrubbed his mind. Whatever he did, it's gone. All of it."

Tarek faltered backward, tripping over a chair leg. "How's that possible?" Clarity fought against the despair, the answer slamming into his soul. "He went to the elders."

Oren raked a hand through his hair. "Yeah, seems so." He challenged Drea. "Did you know? Are you in on this?"

Tears flowed from her eyes, her face vulnerable–innocent. "No. I would have never agreed." She peered at Denzel. "You betrayed us?" More tears. "How did you know where to look?"

Denzel stayed on the floor, his body bent as if praying. "I-I don't–I remember needing to save him. I remember thinking–"

"You're dead, do you hear me? *You're dead.*" Tarek stomped toward him, fingers itching to pull out his throat.

"Wait!" Oren held Tarek's arm. "We have other options. Just don't kill the asshole. Not yet."

Tarek's vision cleared some to find Denzel whimpering at his feet. "Tell me," he said to Oren.

"Celeste. She–she might be able to read his mind."

"Might?"

Oren let go when Tarek lowered his arm. "She has trouble, but if she can focus…"

Tarek tore his gaze from the Guide to stare at the open door leading to the lowest level. "Go get her."

"Yes, but–she needs calm, a serene atmosphere." Oren's voice softened as if he were already getting himself into the right mood.

"She'll have what she needs." Tarek's anger gave way to desperation. "Please. Help me."

"Give me two minutes." Oren was already on his way downstairs.

Moments later, static slammed into Tarek's brain thick enough to bring him to his knees. As fast as the feeling hit him, he fought through it, forcing himself to his feet. He struggled to a side table, using its edge as a crutch. He wouldn't say a word. Give one indication Celeste's presence weakened him. Her guilt from the effect she had on others only exacerbated her power, made it so much stronger with her pain. Experience these past months proved that.

Drea moaned, her hands trapping her head.

"Go. Upstairs." Tarek spoke through gritted teeth, keeping as much stress as he could from his voice.

Drea didn't acknowledge him with words, just crawled to the lift and slammed her palm on the keypad. The lift stopped on the upper level and a door swooshed shut. After a deep breath in, he kept all his concentration on Celeste and Oren.

Oren had his hands on Celeste's shoulders, and to the sounds of Denzel's wailing, he said, "Remember, it's a weapon. Focus, Cel."

Celeste shut her eyes, cringing every time Denzel released another tortured bellow. "I…I am trying."

"You can do it. Remember what you did in the lab. *Remember*. That was you, your power."

"I–" She looked to Denzel.

Tarek bit down, clenching his jaw against the static. Five steps brought him to the Guide, and his fist planted into Denzel's soft jowls. Instantly, the moans stopped. Without a word, Tarek resumed his spot by the side table.

Oren gave a small grin over Celeste's head. "Thanks."

"Just hurry up." Tarek gripped the table until his knuckles ached.

"Right." Oren bent to meet Celeste's eyes. "Okay, you can do this. It's not weakness."

Minutes ticked by until Celeste relaxed, her shoulders slumping. She turned her attention to Denzel's quiet form as the static disappeared from the room like mist after a storm. "No, it is a weapon. *Our* weapon."

She kneeled by the Guide, her palm glowing. She then placed it on Denzel's forehead and closed her eyes.

Tarek straightened, almost not believing the pain was gone, and went to stand next to Oren. Neither man spoke, both concentrating on the one person who could save Lena. Watching her, Tarek finally became convinced Oren was right. The woman would save them all. Her eyelids fluttered as the tattoo on her cheek flashed solid gold. The longer she touched Denzel's forehead, the less color his face had, as if her hand sucked life from his body. A wheeze escaped from his mouth before it went slack–the same time Celeste opened her eyes.

She stood, coming to them, a tranquil expression softening her features and brightening her violet eyes. "He will no longer be a threat, Warden."

"You killed him."

She shook her head. "No, he betrayed under persuasion not his own." Her chin rose higher. "I know where Lena is."

"Why?" Fear constricted his heart, cut his oxygen. "Why did she go with him?"

"Those who manipulated Denzel's mind gave no choice, Warden. If she had not, all of you, including Peter, would be dead. But we have a chance now. We can fix what has been broken."

Adrenaline poured into his body, overriding everything else. "Well, then let's go get her."

He took off for the lift, his mind already working out details.

"Warden?"

Tarek stopped, using every ounce of patience he had. "Yes?"

"Lena gave Denzel a message for you." She paused. "She has commanded you to keep your promise, as she plans to do the same with hers. You understand this?"

Relief, waves of it, soaked through his bones. "Yes."

She would keep her promise.

And so would he.

CHAPTER 34

LENA

Ultimatums

After everything that had happened, nothing surprised me anymore. Traitors, different worlds, killing–none of it. Yosef's voice was no exception. His betrayal didn't cut as Avery's had. I half expected it. Yet, lack of shock didn't block the hate that boiled and churned in my stomach. If I couldn't make him pay, Oren or Tarek would. An elder, for Christ's sake. An elusive, omniscient being was nothing more than a whoremonger.

I straightened my back, brushed hair from my face, and took my time reaching the doors. Defiance wasn't my goal–stalling was. Tarek and Oren would find me; they had to. I just had to give them enough time to figure it out.

"It will do you no good. No matter how slow you are, your saviors will not find you."

You can read my min–

"Yes. I can."

The urge to rush through the doors, rip out his Adam's apple, and watch it bob with his agony filled me. Instead, I smiled. "Well, aren't you full of surprises? But then again, I hear a whore has to keep his customers guessing."

287

His chuckle fanned into the oyster, no anger coloring its deep rhythm. "We do, indeed."

I moved even slower. "We've wondered where your people have been hiding. Looks like Denzel knew all along."

"Denzel, is it? No, he only knew because I told him."

"What? How–"

"How about I kill you–after I pull that boy's heart from his chest?"

No, not that. I double-timed it to the exit, needing to see Peter, see Yosef, too, and how many other elders waited for me beyond the pearly walls. I crossed into the other room, and the spongy floor transformed into something harder, smoother. My bare feet slid on the shellacked surface of a hollow space. The doors closed. A dim light illuminated the room, and silence, even more deafening than in the oyster, clogged my ears.

I took a moment to allow my eyes to adjust, squinting into the darkened corners. My attention halted on a figure slumped in a chair to the right, disguised in shadows. I stepped closer. "Yosef?"

"No, little hero." His voice tickled the back of my neck, and I recoiled as if kissed by a snake.

I closed my eyes and tried to tamp down the burgeoning terror. "Anyone ever tell you it's impolite to sneak up on people?" I turned to that pleasant face that fooled us all.

"Oh, I'm sure my father may have dispelled similar knowledge once or twice." He led me toward the figure, his hand on my upper arm. "Allow me to introduce you."

A spotlight flashed on in the corner, revealing a withered man with a shock of white hair and vacant face.

"This the grandfather pimp?"

Yosef *tsked* close to my ear, his breath like eels thrashing underneath my skin. "That is no way to speak to Exemplar's Warden." He forced me to my knees, his pleasant voice hardening. "Show respect."

Warden?

Warden?

Shock numbed my lips, making them stick to my teeth. "I-I thought Exemplar had no Warden."

He squatted next to me, staring at his father with absolutely no emotion. "That would be impossible."

"But the Creation Lab…the bodies…all those energies, trapped in tubes."

Yosef stood. "Yes, well, he sacrificed himself, his very essence, for an advanced society, one that could control the entire universe. The selfless act finally drained him of everything but a functioning heart." He shrugged. "A few millennia, a good run, I'd say. But you made sure that ended, didn't you?"

I kept my eyes on Yosef's profile, afraid to get up, afraid to look at the empty human carapace in a chair that resembled a throne. The gilded frame mocked the older man's exhausted power. "I–"

"Enough of this." He reached for me. "I want to show you something else."

I hesitated a second before setting my fingers into his awaiting hand. Yosef lifted me from the ground and led me farther into the shadowy room, my feet slapping the floor next to the clapping of his boot heels. As we walked, I eyed his smooth face. "There are no elders, are there?"

He grinned. "I suppose not. At least, not as one would expect."

"Then…?"

His sharp gaze landed on me. "Well, there is my poor, weary father–and myself, of course." He paused, his grin turning to frost. "And you've met my sister."

Oh, my God. "Celeste."

"Quite right." A door opened, and he gestured for me to go ahead like a deranged gentleman. "Almost all that energy, releasing from those tubes and slamming into her chest instead of mine–not the way I had foreseen it."

"But she–"

"My father's true heir once upon a time." He spat out the words as if they were venom. "She never enjoyed the way Father gave up his power for the greater good. So, he had to take hers away, wipe her memory clean. Smartest decision he ever made."

What? "So she's next in line for Warden?"

"No more questions." Warning tinted his polite tone.

My jaw clamped shut, a thousand questions racing through my head. Why hadn't he killed us that first time? Why did he let me warn Exemplians? And *why the hell hadn't he killed us the first time*? The voice from Heterodox whispered in my mind: ...*these are my puppets.*

I was correct in my assumptions after Peter's capture. This was all a game to him.

My mind raced until static almost as strong as Celeste's slammed into my skull.

"Ah!" I fell, my hands covering my ears.

"No more questions. No more theories. Whether spoken or thought, understand?"

The ringing lightened, now only mildly paralyzing. "You're the energy that zoomed in here from the hanger; I recognize it. What the hell are you?"

He pulled me from the ground. "I am neither Guide nor Protector, and I am both." We stopped in front of an opaque wall. "Here we are."

I stared ahead, my mind reeling from the dose of static. Celeste had more energy than he did. If she could control it like Yosef, we'd–

"No!" The wall turned into a window, and there, in the middle of yet another oyster room, was Peter. I slammed against the cool surface. "Let him go. *Let him go!*"

Peter's terror ate through the barrier, his eyes wild with it. Whatever he saw, whatever nightmare played inside that lustrous room, killed his mind, inch by torturous inch. He screamed, cried, held out his hands to plead with his phantom haunt.

I confronted Yosef, bunching his shirt into my fists. "*Please!* You're killing him."

"That matters little to me. Anyone who I couldn't control received a death sentence. Why should this boy be any different?" His eye twitched. "And then you came back. The hero who led her flock to even more slaughter."

I barely heard him. "Just let him go. Please, please, *please.*"

"No." His pleasant mask disappeared for an instant. "You are no hero, and I've made sure the lambs outside these walls are aware."

Sick, sick animal. I let go and focused again on Peter, wishing my fists had the power to shatter glass. "What do you want?" I faced him, desperation injecting adrenaline through my limbs. "You said you wanted to bargain. I'll do it. Whatever it is, just let him go."

"See, I was hoping you'd be cooperative." He blinked, and the room behind us went dark, swallowing Peter, erasing him from sight. "I want a new world, a fresh start."

Dread sizzled inside my chest. "What? I–what?"

Yosef captured my wrist in a gentle hold. "This is my sister's wretched world; one I'll never be able to win from her. So, you…you are going to give me Arcus." His thumb grazed the sensitive skin, forcing gooseflesh to perforate my arms. "I want that raw, wild passion, and you will make sure I get it."

Without any warning, he jammed a gun-like mechanism into a vein inside my elbow. A sharp pain lanced my arm, and when he released me, a glowing ball flickered underneath my skin.

"What're you doing?" I held my arm, backing up against the wall blocking me from Peter.

"A failsafe, nothing more."

"I'll never, *ever*, help you destroy another world," I said, and spat in his face.

He pulled a cloth from his shirt pocket and wiped his cheek. "It would be a shame if your little refuge in Shalen blew up–as you've done to my beautiful city."

Denzel would have never put Drea in danger. *Never.* "Bullshit."

"Oh, I disagree." Yosef waved a hand, and a hologram of Drea's cabin flared behind him. "It is quite simple to track an authority shuttle." He tapped his temple. "I didn't have to do anything but seek out the weakest mind in the cabin and send a mental demand with coordinates to bring you to me. Your Denzel's mind was the one to obey. Elementary, really."

He tracked the shuttle he gave us when we rescued Celeste…and coerced Denzel under persuasion. *My God!* Denzel would die for bringing me here. Tarek or Oren would make sure of it, and there wouldn't be a damn thing I could do to stop them.

I pressed harder against the wall, my gaze on Drea's cabin. *Tarek and Oren*. The cold from the wall reached my bones. *Peter.*

No.

The image disappeared, replaced with something else. A hologram portal–to Arcus.

"I wish to start over. There. This world is broken." He shrugged. "My sister can have it–it's rightfully hers, anyway– alongside her bleeding-heart Protector and my catatonic father."

This wasn't happening. *This couldn't be happening!*

"You take me to the ancient and make those who live there trust me; that's all you have to do. You do that, and I'll send you back here, to the boy and your insipid love. Win-win."

"You want to kill Belva's child." I lifted my chin. "No way in hell."

"If you don't, then I'll kill you–and everyone here." He pulled out a remote, waving it in my face. "There are two buttons: one to kill you and one to send the order to obliterate that cabin. Want to feel yours?" He pressed a button.

The orb in my arm sent an electric current through my vein, jolting my heart. I fell to my knees, clutching my chest. The shock disappeared as quickly as it came, but the threat remained. He'd kill me–stop my heart without batting an eye.

"Fuck you." The curse wheezed from my mouth.

"Such language." His voice took on an edge, slicing every nerve in my body. "Behave."

"You sonofa–"

Another jolt shut me up.

"Isn't it better to kill one–an infant who has not had the taste of life–to save so many."

"They'll never believe me. Winston...he'll kill us both before he allowed any harm to come to her."

"I have faith in you, little hero. If they love you as blindly as the giant..." He tapped his bottom lip.

My lungs turned to stones. "I'll kill you."

He ignored my threat. "You don't have much time. I do grow bored so easily."

What do I do? What?

Then it came to me.

I cleared my mind, blank, nothingness.

He wouldn't hear anything. *Nothing, you asshole.*

Yosef raised an eyebrow. "Well?"

I pushed to my feet, sweat pouring from my skin, blinding me as residual tremors from the jolts pumped through my vein. "Fine. You win. Take me home."

He pulled me tight to his side and opened a portal. "You've chosen wisely."

Lynn Vroman

CHAPTER 35

LENA

No Thinking

We landed in frost.

Glossy black rock tipped with ice tumbled into the edge of tropical woods. Yosef dragged me through it, the soles of my feet bloody and stinging with cold. Everything in me wanted to fight, break free from his hold, and find my way home. Warn them so Farren or Winston could take care of him, despite the threat of my death and those I left in Exemplar.

But...the cold. Arctic fire drained my will and gouged my skin.

"Why would you open here?" My teeth chattered.

Agony and awe mingled on his face. "I have never been here. I..."

"Not the raw, powerful world you fantasized?"

He staggered forward, a smile creasing the corners of his mouth. "Oh, it's that and more." He gestured toward the rock graveyard. "Are these the ruins of Arcus's legendary castle, the last remnants of a time before? I can hardly remember that first war, so very long ago."

Warm blood coated the bottom of my feet, the contrast with the biting hoarfrost making me dizzy. "Y-yes. The castle your people destroyed. I'll bet you remember that."

"Cassondra's idea." His booted feet had no issues with the angry stone as he hauled us farther into the forest, toward warmth now teasing my aching body. "I lost heart for battles with other worlds long ago–but, who am I to deny those who haven't?"

"Monster."

He laughed. "You are not the first to believe so."

Flashes of the past ripped through my mind: Tarek becoming Arcus's Warden, Wilma's death, the destruction in Teenesee's world…

And he didn't care about any of it. Everything we'd been through, all the loss we suffered, and it was all a game to him. A goddamn reality television show.

I looked up. The squid stayed concealed in their trees, quiet, waiting. Silence never boded well in Arcus's forest. Never.

Yosef tightened his hold on my elbow. "Why not?"

"What're you talking about?" I concentrated on avoiding the sharper rocks, wanting to move faster to get to the soft, black soil.

"The silence? Why isn't it good?"

Mind-reading asshole. "The squid." I pointed up, waiting for his gaze to follow my finger. "They're waiting."

Finally, some fear on his self-righteous face. "For what?"

I freed my arm from his hold, the tropical weather now stronger than the arctic. "I'm sure we'll find out soon."

His attention darted from the animals to me. "Do you know where to go from here?"

Shut up mind, shut up mind, shut up mind… "I don't know the woods that well. Didn't spend much time outside the village."

Shut up.

Shut up.

Shut up.

"How, then, do you expect us to find our way?"

I laughed, laughed so hard I forgot about the pain lancing my feet. "This is your plan, not mine."

He lifted the remote from his pocket.

"They already know we're here. The squid communicate with Belva. We walk long enough, and they'll find us, so put it away."

Yosef lowered his weapon, his face strained. "Do not laugh at me again."

"Don't worry, you're not that funny." I braved a few steps ahead of him, picking a clear path through the symmetrical trees.

We walked in silence, with me veering us farther away from the village. I wouldn't make it easy. Nope. But I wasn't lying. Winston, Farren, or another Protector scouting the woods would find us. Belva's army always let her know every time a person sliced through her world's lines.

My feet throbbed, my steady walk turning into a limp. But I wouldn't show weakness. Limping was one thing, crying about it, bringing verbal attention to it, was something else. I cleared my throat. "So…little old you, playing a panel of elders…?"

His boots crunched twigs, the sound reverberating off the trees. Definitely not skilled at stealth. "For the most part. My father lost his mind some years ago. But"–a pause, more boot-stomping noise–"you appoint power, create an entire governing body. Then make them believe there are old, decrepit figures behind a mystical veil capable of doling out dire consequences. There isn't much that needs to be done after that. Unbelievable how humans can muck up the most advanced sciences, abuse the gifts my father sacrificed."

I snorted, getting closer to the river, its breeze lifting my tangled hair. "Not that surprising at all."

"Right, of course. Silly of me for assuming otherwise."

Assuming. God, I hoped Tarek would get to Peter. "Well, you know what they say about assuming shit."

"I'm afraid I don't."

Whatever. Dumbass.

We trekked farther until the river came into view. I didn't wait for Yosef's permission and skidded down the riverbank to soak my feet. I cupped my hands into the water and brought fresh liquid to my greedy mouth, drinking as much of the fluorescent blue as I could hold.

"The squid, I read they were wretched creatures, killing with little provocation."

I tilted my head to see him inspecting the water. "Like I said, they know we're here. Unlike the way you and yours handle business, Belva won't have her army kill until they know who crossed the lines." I dipped my hands in the cool blue. "Water's safe, not that you have to worry. Aren't you damn near immortal?"

He immersed his hand into the water and brought it to his lips before answering. "Only the heir is privy to a certain immortality, a burden that chains her there…unlike me."

Interesting. "So, yo–"

That was all that left my lips before a force ejected my body from the water and slammed me against a tree. Yosef followed a half-second after. Even with the wind knocked from my lungs, excitement trailed through my limbs.

Now to play *my* game. God, I hoped Winston knew me as well as I believed he did.

"What…is going on?"

I tilted my head to Yosef, both of us against the same tree, his face pale. Before I could answer him, we plummeted to the ground, our shoulders knocking against each other. Yeah, he was stupid to allow humans free rein with science. No one should be as powerful as Winston, but I was sure as hell happy he existed.

"What're you doing, wandering the woods, Tainted?" Winston's voice, calm disguising all the strength, almost brought thankful tears to my eyes.

Shut up, brain!

I stared at him, not speaking, not moving, holding my hands up–and not acting at all like myself.

Winston stood over me and crossed his tattooed arms over his chest. "Who's your friend?"

Still nothing.

Don't think, don't think, don't think.

"I-I'm Yosef. We...we had to leave, escape." Anxiety influenced every syllable he spoke. An act–a good one. "The elders have declared outright war, annihilating cities, killing everyone."

Winston ignored him and looked at me. "Where's Tarek?"

Tears blinded me as I kept my mouth shut and hands up. *Don't think!*

"He's dead–along with everyone else." Yosef even managed to sound devastated. "I was able to steal Lena away. Sh-she said to come here."

Winston's eyes widened, but then he slammed his laid-back façade in place. "That true?"

Don't. Think. "Yes," I whispered, barely able to get the word out.

He raised an eyebrow. *What's wrong with you?*

Winston's concerned question blared in my brain–loud enough for Yosef to hear. I spun to see Yosef reaching in his shirt pocket for the remote.

Instantly, I was on my torn feet and shoving Winston's chest. "Stay out of my head! How many times do we all have to tell you?" I slammed my hands against him again and pleaded with his shocked gaze. "*No talking in anyone's head!*"

"Okay, okay." Winston took my hands from his chest, and his thumbs gently skated over my wrists before letting go. "I tend to forget what…everyone says."

I stumbled backward, putting all my fear into a display of tears and crying, going as far as burrowing my face in Yosef's thin chest. "They're all dead. *All of them.*"

Yosef took his hand away from his pocket and patted my back. The hard metal of the remote smashed against my shirt, digging into my flesh, every time his palm came down. "She's been through much trauma, Protector. We watched everyone die." His voice was the perfect balance of sympathy and exhaustion.

I sniffled and turned back to Winston, hoping he read what I couldn't have rushing through my head. "I'm sorry–for snapping."

His lips pursed, but I saw it–what I hoped for–clear on his face. Understanding. "Yeah, not like you at all."

I wanted to break down, fall at his feet, and thank him for being…him. Of course he knew me. *Don't think.*

"You're a little far from the village," Winston said.

Yosef spoke up, helping without me having to say a thing. "Lena admitted she wasn't familiar with the terrain, so I opened a portal and hoped for the best."

Winston grinned, his eyes ablaze–like they usually were right before he was about to kick some ass. "Yeah, sure." He nodded to me. "Sorry about your man."

It wasn't hard to cry. Just the thought of Tarek dying brought tears–exactly what I kept my mind on.

"Well, all right, then. Let's get to it." Winston raised his hand, and the squid mewled, knowing they were about to get some food. As he pointed those wicked fingers in Yosef's direction, panic made the tears real.

I ran to him and flashed my arm, the orb hopefully bright enough for him to see. "Take me home. Please."

Winston lowered his hand. Tension crinkled the corners of his eyes when he viewed the orb before I hid it again. But like the pro he was, his worry disappeared before Yosef could see it. He then bent to whisper in my ear. "You always getting yourself in trouble, ain't you?"

"Always." *Shut up, shut up, shut up!*

He slung an arm across my shoulders and turned toward the village. "You following...ah...Yosef? Hope you like to walk, 'cause it's a long one."

Yosef caught up, his gaze intense on Winston's face. "How many people live in this village?"

Winston didn't extend a look in Yosef's direction. "Enough."

Perspiration beaded Yosef's brow.

Happiness almost took me to the ground. Yosef couldn't control everyone's mind. Not mine. Not Winston's. I shouted the thoughts inside my head, hoping it'd hurt his.

Yosef smirked, keeping pace with us. *I don't need everyone, little hero.*

Lynn Vroman

CHAPTER 36

TAREK

Escape Plans

It took him minutes to yank on his suit and collect his weapons. His lungs grew tight every time he thought of her, but losing it wouldn't help. She made a promise, and he'd make sure she was able to keep it. This would end. Tonight.

As soon as he left his room, another door down the hall opened. He spun, his gun drawn.

Drea, contego suit glowing and guns holstered on her belt, strode next to him. "I'm going with you."

Tarek didn't move for a second, warring with the notion she might betray them. He lowered his weapon. Her goal mirrored his–to bring home the person she loved more than anyone. "Let's go, then."

She lifted her chin, and the tears that had stained her cheeks were no longer visible. "Thank you, for not killing Denzel."

"I hope we don't end up regretting the decision." Tarek headed toward the lift, fury eating his skin.

"He's Peter's father, and Celeste said he betrayed under persuasion. But…you would have done the same thing. Do not pretend otherwise."

He wanted to deny it, but she was right. He'd do anything for Lena, even give up an entire population to keep her safe. His flaw. "I would have." Tarek continued forward.

Drea added nothing else and followed him to the main floor.

Before the lift hit the ground, Tarek leaped from the platform and stalked to Oren, who had his eyes on one of Drea's monitors. "You ready?"

"I don't think we're going anywhere at the moment." Oren pointed to the screens. Shuttles landed in the front field and the back, near the underground hanger where all their vehicles waited. Once doors lifted, Protectors oozed out like vermin, their weapons raised.

Tarek turned to Drea. "Tell me you have this place secure."

"They will not get in here." She moved to her console and punched a few keys. "And now anyone who tries will die."

Evidence of her words animated the screen seconds later. A current rippled from the cabin's walls and sent the closest Protectors flying through the air. The aftershock carried inside, flickering the lights. Charred, lifeless bodies hissed on the ground, and their energy zipped through the walls and slammed into Celeste's chest.

Static clogged the room, squeezing his brain, until Celeste's face lost that euphoric rush that came from absorbing energy–a feeling Tarek knew all too well. She opened her eyes, her soft smile evaporating after looking at him and Drea. "I am sorry. It's harder to control when…when death hits me."

Tarek nodded, not yet able to use words but grateful she was able to control it as well as she did.

"That's it! That's what we'll do." Oren held her shoulders, his eyes shining. "You can make them leave."

"How?" Celeste smiled, her faith in Oren so obviously absolute.

"Yes, how?" Tarek moved closer to them, stepping over Denzel's motionless body.

Oren ignored him, and said to Celeste, "You can control it; I have faith in you. Use your weapon, Cel. I'll be right behind you."

Celeste's gaze hardened. "I will not harm any of those Protectors."

"Spoken like a true leader." Oren grinned wider before kissing her. "You won't have to. Make them helpless long enough for us to get out of here."

"I do not know if I can shut it off once we are safe."

"You will, like we've practiced." Oren shrugged. "And if you can't, so what. We can handle it." He found Tarek over Celeste's head. "Isn't that right?"

Confidence exploded through Tarek's veins. "Absolutely."

So, Oren was more than Celeste's self-appointed Protector? Good. Exemplar would prosper because of it–after they fought one last time.

"Well, all right." Oren kissed her again before turning to the screen. Protectors now stayed away from the house, their dead friends a clear enough warning. "We'll have to thank Denzel for parking our ride in the front yard."

"What should we do with him?" Drea kneeled by Denzel, resting his head on her lap. "The security will have to be turned off for us to leave. If we keep him exposed, they'll kill him."

Tarek forced himself to keep his booted foot on the floor and not ram it into the traitor's stomach. *Persuasion, remember that.*

"We will make sure he is safe." Celeste's thin body belied the strength underneath. "His coerced betrayal is the sole reason we have an ending in sight."

Tarek's anger deflated.

Yes, Celeste was exactly what Exemplar needed.

To Drea's surprised gasp, Tarek hefted Denzel's limp body over his shoulder. "Where do I put him?"

Drea climbed to her feet, her bottom lip trembling. "The lab. It's the only room hidden from naked eyes."

Tension rode his shoulders on the way to the stairs. Of course it was.

By the time he dumped the guy, rougher than necessary, onto the lab's floor and raced back up to the main room–after a quick stop at one of the weapon caches–everyone was ready to get the show moving. He pulled out his gun and went to stand by Oren.

Celeste, who took the lead, turned to him. "You will not need your weapon, Warden."

"I'll take my chances."

She smiled, and the moment she did, her aura polluted the entire cabin. "If you wish, but I doubt you will be of a mind to use it."

He returned his gun into its holster with a shaky hand, ignoring Oren's strained chuckle. He then offered Celeste the weapon in his other hand–a sword made of the strongest Exemplian metal in its scabbard. "You'll need this."

"Thank you." Celeste's cheeks reddened as she took took it from him, strapping the sword to her waist. "Please, Drea, release the door."

One hand holding her skull, Drea touched the keypad next to the door with the other.

Authority Protectors instantly succumbed to Celeste's power when the door opened, most dropping their weapons as they fell to their knees. Tarek almost felt sorry for them. The first time he experienced Celeste's newly heightened aura, his mind wasn't right for hours after.

But though he, Drea, and Oren were somewhat used to the power, getting to the vehicle felt like climbing the steepest snow-covered mountain on bare feet. The fallen Protectors almost had it lucky. They could give in to the vise-like noise.

Drea released the hovercraft's driver door, and she scrambled inside, unlatching the passenger door. Tarek dove into the backseat. Celeste's aura followed them in as Oren sat next to him and Celeste sat up front. While Drea lifted the aircraft, moaning against closed lips, Oren put his hands on Celeste's shoulders and leaned up. "Okay, breathe in, find your shell. Easy."

Celeste did as he said and closed her eyes, breathing in and out in a slow rhythm until the static bottomed out.

Tarek slumped in his seat and closed his eyes, picturing Lena, hearing her promise on replay. She'd be alive, fighting until he could get to her. Longer.

I'll find you.

∞ ∞ ∞

"How many do you think we're up against?" Tarek leaned forward, eyes on the windshield, as Drea maneuvered the hovercraft through Cynosure. None of the rubble had been cleaned away, authority Protectors the only loyal Exemplians to the elders. They were all too busy killing innocents to worry about a massive pile of debris.

"Your guess is as good as mine." Drea punched a few buttons, and a slight hum filled the cab.

Damn glad they had the woman. With the hum came apparent invisibility. Other aircrafts zooming by didn't give so much as a hint of suspicion.

"But we need to find out quickly because this shield will only last for minutes." She gave a dry laugh. "Surprised it worked now."

"Excuse me?" Oren's crotchety, normal mood returned. "We're betas for one of your programs?"

"Exactly right, Protector," Drea said. "You're welcome."

"Are you crazy?"

"It isn't far, just up ahead," Celeste said, reaching her hand to Oren. He seized it without hesitation. "Do not worry."

"Whatever happens, you stay beside me." Oren glanced out the window to the other hovercrafts. "But you will have to kill today."

Celeste flinched and let go of Oren's hand to grasp her sword.

Palpable tension filled the cab the closer they got to a plain, unassuming building. A building that would blend anywhere else except here, where everything was metallic, sleek, and shining–how everything used to be, rather.

As they reached the building with an open hanger separating the top half from the bottom, hair on the back of Tarek's neck prickled. This was too easy, regardless of the shield, as if whoever had Lena expected them–or maybe believed the attack on the cabin a success.

Tarek freed both his guns from his belt. Fine, let the elders trap them. It wouldn't work; Celeste would make sure of it so they could get to–damn. So they could confront who knows how many others probably as strong as her and more in control of their powers.

He tightened his hold on his guns. No. He wouldn't waver. They asked for a fight, and now they'd get one.

Drea maneuvered the hovercraft into the hanger. Everyone's attention centered on the six or so Protectors guarding the entrance of a hydro-lift. "Once the engine is off, the shield will disintegrate." She let go of the steering lever long enough to pull her weapon. "Be ready."

"Please," Celeste said, "let me try to subdue them first as I did the others."

Oren shook his head. "No."

"They are only acting as they've been told to act for probably centuries."

"We need our minds clear, Celeste," Tarek said as soothingly as possible. "Who knows what's waiting for us beyond those six."

She closed her eyes, breathing deeply before saying, "You are right, Warden."

Oren nodded to him, saying nothing.

Everyone but Celeste checked their guns, waiting for the right moment. Drea unlatched the doors seconds before the engine cut off, and after the hovercraft touched solid ground, they were all out and shooting.

The authority Protectors showed surprise, real emotion, as they ducked from bullet spray, fumbling with their weapons. Oren held Celeste behind him, using the hovercraft as a shield. Tarek and Drea stayed on the driver side, doing the same.

Once the opposing gunfire dwindled, Tarek yelled to Oren over the roof. "Cover me!"

At Oren's nod, Tarek pushed off the metal and targeted the lone Protector. The terrified man's gun fired an erratic pattern as guttural cries escaped his lips.

Deep breath.

A leap.

Tarek had him disarmed and immobile before the authority Protector had a chance to focus. But when he did, Tarek almost loosened his hold.

Shock mingled with awakening consciousness. A scared authority Protector, acting as if he actually understood the danger he was in. So different from the zombie-like army Tarek had been picking off from rooftops the last seven months.

"Please. Please!" The Protector's hands flailed in surrender, his eyes wide.

What the holy hell?

None of them ever spoke, always the perfect silent army. *Too easy, too easy, too easy.*

Boots echoed through the hanger, and Tarek glanced up long enough to assure himself they belonged to Oren and Drea. He then concentrated on the man he held down with an elbow to the throat. "Where are the elders?"

"The elders? I-I don't know."

Tarek pressed harder, his prey now a sickening shade of blue. "Liar."

The Protector wheezed.

"Warden!"

One second he was killing the Protector, the next, he landed on his ass, feet away from the now gasping man.

Tarek's mouth fell open. "How'd you do that?"

Oren offered a hand, pride shadowing his face. "She can do that and more."

"She's stronger than Winston." Tarek clasped his hand.

Oren hauled him up, and said, "I know."

Everyone then surrounded Celeste, who now crouched at the Protector's side, soothing him with soft words and a glowing hand to his forehead.

"We don't have time for this," Tarek said. He tried to keep impatience from staining his voice, but the sniveling Protector barred him from Lena–and the end of this war.

"His mind has been tampered with, Warden, as all those we have fought these past months. Can you not see that now? He remembers nothing of the vileness perpetrated here."

Didn't matter. "Can you make him remember?"

She cast him a smile before returning her attention to the whimpering Protector. "Of course."

CHAPTER 37

TAREK

One Door Closes

Minutes later, they were in the lift, heading to the top floor. While everyone reloaded weapons, Drea confessed what ate at Tarek's mind since leaving the cabin. "This has all been too simple." Her gun shook in her trembling hand. "What if they killed Peter already? Lena, too?"

He wouldn't answer her. Oren and Celeste didn't, either. To give credence to her fear might destroy them.

No one waited in ambush when the lift door opened. No guns blazed. Just a torture chamber greeted them with an exit door wide open on the opposite wall. This innocent-looking room had enough power to tear them all down and steal their minds. One person pulling the strings in some secret room was all it would take to bring them to their knees. Game over.

Oren cleared his throat. "I'll go first. If you see me struggling after a few seconds, find another way in." His boot connected with the soft floor.

Celeste jumped in front of him before he could take another step. "No! Absolutely not. You'll not be a martyr, not for me, not for anyone."

"It'll be okay." He took yet another step into the room. After another, his body froze.

Celeste lifted her hand. "No."

"Let me go, Cel."

"I will not. Not ever."

His body stayed frozen midstride as Celeste's hand shook.

Static snaked into the room, a clear sign Celeste's calm unraveled. It wasn't debilitating, but it would be soon if things kept going this way.

"I'll go." Tarek strode into the room, his temper hot enough to melt glass. These elders had used fears against them far too long. He only had one fear, and the solution to end it existed beyond that open door.

His first few steps on the gelatinous floor spiked his blood pressure, squeezing his temples. When nothing happened, he went a few more tentative feet, keeping his eyes on the door. Slushy footsteps followed him. No one spoke, afraid to wake the room's controller.

He hit the solid floor of the next room and let out a pent-up breath. His mind was still his. He turned.

As were everyone else's.

Sweat drenched Tarek's back and soaked his head. "Everyone okay?"

Drea nodded, her gun up and pointing into the room. Oren and Celeste moved to stand beside him. "We're good," Oren said.

"Great." Tarek swiped his drenched scalp, looking around. "Ah, where to from here?"

"There." Celeste pointed to a darkened corner.

Oren followed her as she made her way to a mystery person.

"Do you think...?" Drea moved to stand beside Tarek, her gun at her side.

"I don't know. Maybe?"

An elder. One lonely elder sitting atop a floating, gilded throne.

"Lights." The computers controlling the room obeyed Tarek's command, surprisingly.

Fluorescent light revealed an aged man and nothing else, just white walls and a whiter floor. The man's slack-jawed gaze remained empty—until he found Celeste. "Daughter?"

What?

Celeste stopped short of the man's now outreached hands. "Who are you?"

Tears flooded his eyes—eyes so purple they glittered like amethysts. "I am so very sorry, child. So very sorry," he said, his voice as thin as paper.

"Wait." Oren held Celeste's arm when she moved forward, a sob escaping her lips.

She struggled against his hold. "I must."

"Don't believe everything you see, Cel." Oren spoke it loud enough for everyone to hear, including the old man.

"I am of no threat to her, as I cannot even stand from this chair, boy." The elder's wheezing voice barely rose above a whisper. His watery eyes fell back to Celeste. "Please, take my hand, and you will see the truth."

Oren pulled Celeste closer. "No," he said.

Celeste, no fear marring her face, covered Oren's hand. "Come with me, then."

"I can't..." Oren buried his face in her hair, his voice desperate.

"You have put your entire faith in me, even when I doubted myself." She pulled back. "So trust me now."

"Okay. I—all right." Oren released her arm.

Celeste kneeled in front of the throne, a placid smile painting her lips. The older man's sobs grew stronger as he held his hand out farther. Once Celeste took it into her swirling palm, a current transferred from his thin, wrinkled hand to her smooth, flawless skin, the light powerful enough to see. Both closed their eyes, the voltage seemingly pleasant, maybe soothing.

As the contact continued, Tarek held Drea's hand and went to stand next to Oren, whose love for Celeste burned hot on his shocked face. The three of them watched as spectators to a marvel of some sort.

When Celeste broke free, she opened her eyes. Tears pooled in those haunting orbs as her smile turned regal. A queen. She was a queen, plain and simple. "Father?"

The old man wept, his sorrow-filled apology after apology filling the room.

Celeste reached to hold him, bringing his head to her chest. "Shh, it's over now," she said. "It's all over."

Oren stepped forward. "Celeste?"

She acknowledged him over the man's head. "Allow me to introduce the Warden of Exemplar, my father."

Oren fell to his knees. "What?"

Tarek's throat froze, his grip on Drea's hand tightening. *Warden?* Impossible. So, she wasn't an ancient as they assumed, but the daughter of a Warden, a Warden said to have long ago died when Exemplar learned to function without one.

How?

Celeste moved to help Oren to his feet. "The elders?" Oren said. "Where are they?"

"There are no elders, only me and my son, who has abandoned our world for another," the old man said, rancor coloring his gruff words.

Fear twisted Tarek's gut. The son. Instinct told him wherever he was Lena was with him. Before he could demand

314

answers, Drea ran to the man, kneeling at his feet as Celeste had done. "*My* son, he was taken. Please, is he alive?"

As the last word left her mouth, a door opened. At the threshold, a glimpse of another torture chamber waited inside– with Peter, shivering and scared.

Drea cried out, running to release him with a few keys punched on an access panel next to the prison wall. The barrier evaporated, and Peter was in her arms before Tarek could register what had happened.

"Are you well?" She held the boy up, his skinny frame now supported by her able shoulder

Peter buried his face against his mother's neck and sobbed. "I-I'm so sorry. I should have never…"

"Hush now, hush. You're safe, all that matters." Drea brought him into the room, keeping him close. "Thank you…Warden," she said.

The Warden nodded, his frail body hardly moving with the effort. "I am only grateful my son's tortured ended once he left. Everything and everyone under his control are now free."

After he said the last word, a hologram of Heterodox lit up the room. Confusion filled so many faces as some authority Protectors sat on sidewalks, rocking back and forth. Others wailed while looking down at dead people scattered at their feet. The most shocking of all were the few citizens with glowing tattoos on their cheeks consoling those devastated Protectors.

"Stupid boy. Never strong. And now his reign is over." The Warden held out his hand to Celeste. When she took it, he continued. "You are the rightful heir, and he cannot kill you. No one can." He raised his eyes to everyone else in the room. "The only reason you all are alive is because of Yosef's fear of her wrath. No matter how convinced he was of her docile state, he'd never chance it, not while in this world."

Yosef.

Yosef!

"That bastard!" Oren jammed a finger in the Warden's face. "You did this–all of this. You and your *son*. Celeste spent centuries suffering." He gestured wildly to the hologram. "*An entire world spent centuries suffering*! He forced her to–"

Oren didn't need to finish. They all knew Celeste's history, what she did before Oren found her–what she again had to do after Oren was forced to leave.

The Warden met Oren's anger with more remorse. "I thought I was doing the right thing all those years ago. Give the population the gifts I had, make them powerful, and hand them the universe." He paused, shame covering his face. "My daughter did not agree, which was why I took her memory centuries ago. My greatest regret. It has cost me everything, and now I have ruined so many lives, including those of my children."

"You turned an entire race into…into monsters made in petri dishes." Oren's fist clenched. No one in the room was willing to interrupt what the Warden deserved to hear. "Your *son*. Where is he?"

"As I said. He gave up his rights here, left Exemplar to rot in an attempt to rule another world." The Warden found Celeste again, Oren's anger putting absolutely no fear on his face or in his voice. "But you are here, my daughter, able to right millennia of wrong. Wrong I had started and your brother has exacerbated."

Celeste shook her head and held out her hands. "How?"

"By killing me."

"I cannot kill you. I cannot." Quiet tears streamed down her cheeks.

"You must, child. I am so very tired." He thumbed a tear from her cheek. "What I saw in your heart tells me you will keep Exemplar safe from threats within and without, allow this world to rebuild anew. Look." He lifted a finger to the hologram. "Our people need someone to lead them back to happiness. They need *you*."

She rested her head in his lap and kept her gaze on the hologram. "I do not–I have trouble controlling the power. *I need you*. I cannot do it on my own."

The Warden covered the top of her head with a shaky hand. "You will kill me, and take your rightful place as Warden of our beautiful world. When you do, you'll have more power than any being ever known."

"How can I rule? These people are so broken."

"You will know what to do; the power I give will guide you. You are the True Warden, and it is time to give our people back what they deserve."

"Where do I start?" Celeste's voice, as if the Warden's tone soothed her, sounded stronger.

"The power will allow you to close Exemplar's lines from the rest of the universe. Forever. You do this, and then find a way to bring healing to our people."

"There was a woman here, only hours ago." Tarek had stayed quiet long enough. Their war was ending; his wasn't.

The Warden acknowledged him, understanding on his aged face. "Yosef took a girl with him to Arcus. He believed she could aid in accomplishing his feat." The Warden hesitated. "He plans to kill the infant Warden."

Fear tasted like vinegar on his tongue. Celeste couldn't close the lines. Not yet. "Celeste? Can you send Lena a message?"

She stood, coming to him, worry in her eyes. "Yes, I–"

"If you send a message, Yosef will hear it inside the girl's head and kill her," the Warden said, his voice a thin whisper.

"Why?" Celeste went back to her father, gathering his hands in hers. "How is that possible?"

"Because he has powers, like you. Only...weaker."

Celeste looked at Tarek, the anxiety in her expression as potent as the burn in his chest.

Everything–*everything*–came down to this moment. "Okay...okay..." Tarek pulled Peter from his mother's arms and dragged him to a corner. "Lena wanted to give you a choice. Stay here... or come back with me." He didn't elaborate; the boy wasn't stupid.

Peter's ashen face fell, and his eyes filled up as he watched his mother. He then looked Tarek right in the eye. "Tell Lena I love her, and I always will."

Tarek looked over Peter's shoulder to Oren. "Maybe you'll be able to tell her yourself. Soon." He gathered Peter in his arms, holding him tight for a second before letting go. "I'll miss you, boy."

Peter snorted. "No, you won't."

"Not true at all." He then nodded to Drea. "Go. Tell your mother the good news."

Tarek waited until Drea had her arms around Peter, her grateful cries giving him peace, and then faced Oren and Celeste. "Keep the lines open, a while longer. Please."

Oren cocked his head to the side. "Why?"

"I'd wager this world could benefit from Yosef's power."

Oren smiled, his eyes cold. "We'll be waiting for him."

"Good. I'll let you know when to come collect the bastard." Tarek raised his hand in the air–and left as Celeste kissed her father's cheek, her sword in hand.

CHAPTER 38

LENA

Death

We made it about ten feet before Farren jumped from a tree to confront us. The squid howled as if his leaving their protection pissed them off. He stayed silent, his dark eyes never leaving Yosef.

He'll kill you before you have the chance to get near his child.

I kept that threat on repeat in my head. Yosef's delicate sneer said he'd heard me loud and clear. Good. The threat wasn't idle.

So, this is the natural-born.

God, I hated his voice in my head.

Farren lowered his gaze to me and stalked the gap between us. "Where're your shoes, kid?"

I inspected my mangled feet, keeping my mind clear. "Forgot them."

He put his index finger under my chin and lifted until our eyes met. "Dumb."

"Yeah..."

War heightened the color in his eyes–he'd heard everything from his perch, not a doubt in my mind. Farren pulled me to his side, his grip on my shoulder so tight, it almost crushed bone. "Want to make sure our guest gets back okay, Winston? Lena and I need some alone time."

"I ain't gotta problem with that."

The faith flowing through my body almost made it impossible to keep my brain empty. They knew me.

Do they, little hero?

Fuck off.

Your friends aren't warming up to me. Try harder.

Fuck. Off.

I clamped my mind shut, forcing devastation onto my face. Tarek was supposed to be dead, and that horror had to show outside.

Laughter filled my head. *He might be.*

I stopped, ripping away from Farren to confront Yosef, who walked alongside Winston. "What did you say?"

Yosef could play possum better than anyone I had ever met, his face a blank sheet. "Excuse me?"

"*What did you say?*" Panic oozed from my pores, mixing with hate. *You said he was alive! You said I could go back to him!*

He shook his head, the barest hint of a smile teasing his lips. "Is everything all right?"

"Yeah, sure, everything's fine, right, Tainted? Just fine." Winston didn't need to speak inside my head for me to hear the warning.

"Yeah, fine. Sorry." *I'm gonna kill you.*

I turned, and Farren grabbed my hand, squeezing.

Tarek was alive.

He promised.

We walked in silence the rest of the way, Farren doing his best to pick the softest path. My yelping feet thanked him. I looked over my shoulder every so often when murmuring interrupted the quiet.

Winston talked to Yosef as if they were long-lost friends. The sentence, "Thanks for bringing her back," even left Winston's mouth.

Once we reached the opening that led to the village, Farren stopped us. Before the other two caught up, he bent to my ear. "It's all good, kid. No worries."

I cried then, just sobbed. "I'm sorry. So, so sorry."

"Don't be." He held my hand a moment longer before releasing it to lead the way, leaving me with Winston and Yosef.

"How utterly quaint." Yosef rubbed his hands together, awe flooding his face. "Like a bustling port town from yesteryear."

I wanted to pull out his throat and watch him drown in his blood.

"Yeah, right, whatever you say, man." Winston nudged me. "Get going. A lot of people wanna see you."

I took a deep breath, hating myself for bringing the enemy into our home. As I climbed down the hill, the squid wailed in their trees. Branches shook and dropped bright green leaves at our feet like a windy summer day on Earth. For the first time in forever, their anger had actual fear pulsating through my system. They knew Yosef was the enemy.

"Why are they so perturbed of a sudden?" Yosef walked backward, his face tilted to the leafy treetops.

"They get like that sometimes, especially with someone new." Winston shrugged, perfectly at ease with deception. "I got something to do. See you in a minute." He took off down the hill, leaving me alone with Yosef.

"My own army of tree squid." His excitement clogged the atmosphere, making me sick.

I stopped. "They won't let you win. *None* of them will let you."

"Right, well"–he continued to walk–"a mind will do as I ask it."

A sharp laugh escaped before I could bite it back. "You think my mind is strong? Winston's?" I narrowed my eyes and gave him all my hate. "You won't be able to persuade anyone here. They've lived through wars, death, sometimes hunger– you're an ant to them, easily squashed with a thick boot."

He turned. "That is where you are wrong." His eyes bulged with fury as he raised two fingers, lifting me an inch from the ground. "You think your friend is the only one with neat parlor tricks?"

An inch? *That's it?*

Before I could emasculate him, my name reverberated through the air.

Yosef set me down and straightened his shirt. Sweat poured from his face, probably from his little levitation trick. "Greet your family, little hero, give them your attention now. They will miss you when you are gone."

I turned to meet Mom and Jake, letting them fold me into their arms. Their soft crying almost brought the truth to my lips. Almost had me confessing it to the squid. But Tarek and Peter–Oren and Celeste–their lives depended on my silence. All I said was, "I love you both, so much."

"Thank God you're here, baby." Mom's sobbing somehow made me stronger. "Your life…it's not fair. It isn't."

"Everything's gonna be okay. It will." I nestled my face in her silky hair. "Be strong."

"But–"

"*Everything*, Mom."

She let another sob escape as Jake pulled me close. He guided the four of us into the middle of the village. "Thank you, for bringing our daughter home," Jake said as Yosef came to his side.

Yosef's face scrunched in mock regret. "I only wish I could have saved everyone."

I glared at him over Jake's shoulder. *I hate you.*

His dull eyes sparkled. He loved this–all of it.

But once Farren came out of his cabin with a very pregnant Belva tucked under his arm, all the smugness vanished from Yosef's face. *Is this your ancient, little hero?*

I wanted to gouge out his eyes and feed them to him as he screamed. So many things I wanted to do to him, and I couldn't lift a finger. *What do you think, asshole?*

He stumbled from Jake's side to grasp Belva's hands. After he touched her, the squids' cries blasted us from the treetops. We all slammed our hands over our ears.

In seconds, complete silence took over as Belva freed her hands from Yosef's to wave in the air. Her poker face, I knew it as well as Winston's false calm. She targeted Yosef with it now.

He didn't seem to notice the frost, obviously too enraptured by her beauty. "You are a vision," he said. Sweat beaded his forehead, and the skin around his eyes crinkled.

Perfect. He tried to read her mind–or persuade her. Belva's shield was one he couldn't crack. *You can't read her mind, can you?*

He scowled but otherwise ignored me.

Maybe after his eyes, I could rip out his tongue…

"Thank you for bringing Lena home, but I'm sure you've heard that a few times," Belva said, all regal and queen-like.

Don't think. Don't think.

She moved away from Yosef to hug me, her trembling arms hard to miss. "Why don't you let Farren take you to your old cabin, Lena?" She went back to Yosef. "Rest. Winston and I will see to our new friend, make sure he's taken care of."

On cue, Winston came from his cabin, unruffled. Deceptively so.

Don't think, goddamn it.

"Go on now, Tainted. Get yourself some sleep. You look like hell." Winston pulled his dreads back into a ponytail as he walked past me to stand by Belva. He tipped his head to Mom and Jake. "Why don't you guys get everyone around. Tell them to meet us in a couple hours, usual spot."

When Winston told us what to do, we listened. We always had, especially because he only told us what to do when in danger.

Mom hugged me one more time, her body shaking. She knew something was wrong. So did Jake, whose face whitened. But if Winston wasn't sharing in front of their new guest, no one would ask. Years of war had trained us all.

"Yeah, sure. We're on it," Jake said. He took Mom's hand after kissing my cheek and headed toward the hall.

Before I could say anything, Farren left Belva's side and gripped my elbow. "Come on, kid."

"Perhaps I should go with you." Yosef's voice held a warning. "I feel quite overprotective of you, after all."

Don't think!

Farren's hold on my arm tightened. He stopped and gave Yosef a cursory glance over his shoulder. "No need, man. I've been protecting her ass for a long time now. Fill Belva and Winston in on what's going on. If ours are dead, we want the bodies." Without waiting for an answer, he rushed me away to the farthest end of the village, to my old place.

He closed us in, a sigh shuddering his entire frame, and then he folded me into his big arms. "What the hell, Lena? Who is that guy?"

"I–" *I can't say! A despicable asshole bent on killing the love of your life–after murdering your child.*

He pulled away and pierced me with his dark gaze. "Tell me."

"He…he saved me." The words stung my lips as I covered my arm. If he saw the glow from Yosef's weapon, he'd never be able to control his thoughts.

Those eyes, deep mahogany, searched my face. He didn't believe me. Thank God. After a long moment, with my body trembling and tears pouring from my eyes, Farren held my face in his hands. "Listen to me, okay?" After I nodded, he continued. "I hear you. When you speak and when you don't, I always hear what you're saying."

I chanced one warning. "Don't…don't think anything."

He smiled, understanding filling his eyes. "I have no problem with that."

"I love you, Ginger."

He kissed my forehead. "Right back at you. Rest. We'll fix whatever's broken soon. I promise you."

∞ ∞ ∞

We sat in the mess hall, Yosef next to me, accepting my mother's praise. Yes, he saved me. Yes, he was just as devastated no one else made it out alive.

Yes, he was a straight-up asshole.

But once everyone quieted, he stopped his theatrics to give his attention to where everyone else focused–at the threshold of the building where Belva and Farren stood. She held her head high, a queen attending her court–and acting nothing like the warm, caring woman I knew her to be. Poker face.

It took everything in my arsenal to keep my mind blank as we all watched them walk to the front of the room. They reached the platform, and Farren stood behind Belva as she scanned Arcus's people. Her eyes barely touched mine.

I loved her.

Brave all the time, no matter what.

Yosef stared at her–more like trying to penetrate her skull with his eyes. Yeah, her mind was Fort Knox.

That's power. Right there in front of you. Remember that when you take your last breath.

Still, he didn't look my way, but he pulled out the remote with the subtlety of a magician and flashed it to me before hiding it in his closed hand on his lap. *I might have misinformed you earlier. There is only one working button on this remote.* He now leered at Belva. *Everyone died before we even left Exemplar.*

My body went numb. *Liar.*

I'm afraid not, little hero.

Despair stabbed my heart. No. *No!*

"We have lost some of our own to Exemplar yet again," Belva said.

Tears flowed down my cheeks as she spoke.

No, no, no!

"But we are fortunate to have such brave allies." She faced Yosef, and my life fell apart. "Thank you, for bringing Lena home safe."

Yosef stood and bowed to her. "It is my honor."

I rocked–*back and forth, back and forth*–as the sobs unleashed with a fury.

Farren jumped from the platform and scooped me close as Mom and Jake looked on through tears. Grace and Shaina came over, too, crying with me, mourning Tarek–oh God. Oren. *Peter!*

I grappled for Grace's hand. "I'm so sorry. It's my fault they're dead. *My fault.*"

She cried harder, shaking her head, squeezing my hand.

"As you can see, our loss is great." Belva's voice rang above the haze in my head. "Again, thank you, Yosef. We'll find a way to repay you."

My life didn't matter, not anymore, and if I had to die to make sure my family lived, so be it. My soul would find Tarek's. *It always has.*

I pushed away from Farren and ran to Belva. "No! He–"

But I was too far away from her. Too far, with an orb stuck in my arm.

Electricity gunned through my veins, bringing me to the ground. Everything inside me sizzled and burned. Hands struggled for my convulsing body as the tremors squeezed my heart. Spit frothed from my mouth. Cries sounded miles away, the mechanism in my arm attacking me.

"She's seizing!" A yell, Shaina's, rose against my ear.

Pain sliced my arm, and hot blood scorched my flesh.

Then I heard his voice, calling for me.

Tarek.

After that, I was weightless, floating as the electricity fizzled away.

My soul could now find his.

Lynn Vroman

CHAPTER 39
TAREK

Last Battle

Tarek landed in the middle of the village. Howling squid shook their tree limbs as they climbed to branches closer to the mess hall–where the sounds of war pitched higher than the animals' cries.

Too late!

He didn't stop to think.

He ran.

A nightmare smacked him in the face once he reached the building's entryway. Farren and Winston, with a few other Arcus Protectors, stood in front of the main platform fighting their own people. So many attacked, including Grace, Jacie, and Jake, with knives or forks, any weapon they could find in the room. None of the Protectors used any kind of deadly force–no one wanting to kill innocent people. People who were so obviously under the same spell Yosef had the Synod authority under. Denzel. Heterodox citizens.

Tarek dove in, punching those he spent years protecting, and winced every time he felt a nose crunch or a jaw crack under his knuckles. About sixty people, all puppets for Yosef.

The man was feet away from Belva, hiding off to the side like the weasel he was to avoid Winston and Farren. Belva stood on the platform, one hand over her swollen stomach, the other holding a gun.

But she didn't have to use her weapon.

Her army ripped the thatched roof from the walls with thick, straining tentacles. They swept innocent attackers away, almost gently, before forming an organic barricade around Belva. Their people, like zombies, rose after the squid moved them and attacked again. They stabbed at the pink flesh blocking Belva–or had another go at Winston and Farren. At him.

Tarek perused the room, frantic as he searched for Lena. People barraged him with makeshift weapons. Some even left the hall and headed in the direction of Arcus's weapon supply. They'd return with guns–and then those hypnotized people would leave them with no choice.

"Lena!" Tarek lashed and kicked, closing his heart off to the wounded cries.

She wasn't anywhere.

Where are you?

"Tarek! Over here!"

He spun to find Shaina–her mind thankfully still her own–protecting Lena's prone body. A gash in Lena's forearm gushed with blood, and her face glowed a sickly gray.

Too late…

He stopped fighting, his body on autopilot, heading to his love. The battle became sludge in his ears. Nothing mattered but her. Nothing.

Shaina's eyes widened. "Look out!"

He pivoted in time to avoid a steak knife in his neck. Jake stood there, his weapon in the air for another strike, no emotion on his blank face.

Tarek grabbed Jake's knife-wielding hand and snapped it backward. The loud crunch of bone followed. Still, Jake's face showed no sign of life. He stumbled back, picked up the knife with his other hand, and staggered toward Tarek again.

Damn it! Yosef would have them all killing each other.

Tarek moved away from Lena and Shaina, making sure not to draw attention to them as Jake kept coming. Sweat glistened on the other man's forehead, his face graying to the same color as Lena's. From the corner of his eye, Tarek noticed the rest of the people forming a wall around Yosef, not moving, just standing there as the coward hid behind them. To get to Yosef, Winston and Farren would have to kill their people.

Tarek darted another feeble stabbing attempt by Jake, and then yelled, "Winston! Tell Oren to have Celeste open the lines, here in the hall."

"You out of your mind?" Winston's face strained under the pressure of what he would have to do. He'd start killing to protect Belva. So would Farren. So would all of Arcus's Protectors.

"Trust me!" Tarek grunted as he elbowed another person behind him, dropping the man with a hit to the nose.

"Watch it!" Winston lifted his hand as Tarek ducked. He slammed someone running back into the hall against a tree outside. The gun the woman carried fell to the ground. "All right, big man. But you better know what you're doing."

Tarek sure as hell hoped Celeste had managed to control her power, or he'd kill these people, too. Their people.

He dodged another blow, and then swept Jake's legs out from under him. The smaller man hit the ground with a thud. Tarek slammed his fist into Jake's jaw, finally knocking him out.

Yosef yelled some garbled command, and the crowd protecting him pushed forward, some surrounding Winston and Farren, others coming at him. Tarek shifted his hips and glanced in Lena's direction. Shaina had a gun in her hand as her small body covered Lena's motionless one.

If Celeste didn't bleed the lines soon…

As if she answered a prayer, the atmosphere broke and crackled at the doorway. Light burst from the struggling bleed in rainbow shards, so much like the tattoo on Celeste's face.

Then she was there, right on the cusp between her world and Arcus, with Oren, Drea, and Peter at her side. She found him in the melee, her tattoo an iridescent gold. All Tarek could do was stare at her, even as the fight escalated. A knife skimmed his shoulder, not penetrating the fabric of his contego. He turned to Jacie, empty-faced and ready to try again.

No. He couldn't hurt her. Never. Moving quickly, he knocked the weapon from her hand and wrapped his arms around her frail body, holding her as she struggled. Protecting her from herself.

"You will stop this now. No more fighting. No more." Celeste's delicate voice, like a symphony, washed through the hall.

The entire room quieted. Jacie stopped struggling in Tarek's hold, except to push at his chest. "Let me go. Lena…"

He released her, and she ran to her daughter. Tarek was right behind her, trusting Celeste would finally tame her brother.

He stooped beside Shaina and touched Lena's clammy forehead. "Is she alive?"

Shaina's dark eyes glistened with tears. "Barely."

No, no, no, no! Not after all of this. After everything, she wouldn't die–she promised. He buried his face in her neck, his tears drenching her skin. "Please, love. Don't leave me. *Don't leave me. Please.*"

"You!"

Tarek snapped his head up to find Yosef running for his sister. She simply held up a hand as Oren pulled his gun. "You are finished, Brother."

Yosef's jaw slackened with every word Celeste uttered.

"You will no longer treat the universe as a spoiled child treats his toys." She closed her hand into a fist. "But I will not kill you. There has been enough of that."

Slobber dribbled from his gaping mouth. "But...I wanted to be...powerful."

All these years of war, all the pain they suffered, for one simple man's need for power.

Celeste waved him closer. "You will only know what it is like to be *powerless* for the rest of your life. Come now. You've wreaked enough havoc."

A tear trickled from Yosef's eye as he obeyed. No longer the terrorist, only the defeated boogie man.

As Drea cuffed Yosef, yanking him farther across the lines and out of sight, Oren and Peter ran forward. Oren to Grace, and Peter to Lena.

Peter sank to his knees beside him. "Is she okay?"

Tears blurred Tarek's vision as he looked at the boy. "I–"

Piercing screams boomed across the atmosphere as squid unraveled their shield around Belva. She bent over, holding her stomach. "Farren!"

Not possible, not now...

Farren leaped to the platform and caught Belva before she fell to the ground. He laid her down gently as a loud groan ripped from her throat. Scream after scream after scream slammed into everyone's ears. The squid squealed with her, mimicking her pain.

Farren looked in Tarek's direction, beyond him, to Arcus's only medical personnel. "Shaina? I-it's time. *It's time*."

Shaina gave Tarek one last frown before running to Belva. "Get everyone out, Winston," she said. "Now!"

As Winston rushed the stunned crowd from the hall, all avoiding the bleeding lines, Belva's cries continued to slice through the air.

Oblivious to everything, Oren whispered in Grace's ear. After he lifted his head, Grace went to kiss Celeste's cheek and left too, tears flowing from her aged eyes.

Oren then found Lena. His eyes widened when they landed on her silent form. He stormed over, and without bothering to explain, scooped her up and rushed her to Celeste.

"Hey!" Tarek jumped to his feet and followed, Jacie and Peter right behind him. "*What are you doing?*"

Oren refused to acknowledge him, and to the laboring cries coming from the platform, he set Lena at Celeste's feet. "Can you heal her?"

"I will try." Celeste kneeled at Lena's side and waved a hand over the gash in her arm. As it healed to a puckered wound, she placed her palm over Lena's heart. Light transferred from her hand to Lena's chest.

Seconds ticked by.

Minutes.

A thousand years.

When her green eyes flew open with a gasp of air, Tarek lost it. He brought Lena to his chest and rocked her as she pulled in deep breaths.

"Is she okay now?" Peter squatted beside them, tears tracing his dirty cheeks. So much crying.

Tarek smiled, and then laughed as he cupped the boy's nape over Lena's heaving body. "She's perfect." Unconscious, but absolutely perfect. Alive.

Peter beamed through his tears, but then frowned "Will you tell her? Tell her I love her, okay?"

"She loves you, too, Peter. Remember that." Tarek held him tighter before letting go.

Celeste cleared her throat. "We must close the lines. I've a world of my own to heal."

Tarek stood, holding Lena in his arms as he stepped from Exemplar, his feet solidly planted on Arcus soil. "Thank you…Warden." After all this time with Celeste addressing him with the title… Fate had a sense of humor.

Celeste tilted her head in his direction, her wraithlike face now forever etched in his heart. "I will miss you," she said, and then went to Oren's side. After Peter found his mother's arms, Celeste lifted her hands. "Be well."

Oren gave him a salute as the lines closed–closed on a life he'd never know again.

Good.

The soft sounds of an infant's first cry tinkled into the room.

As if Arcus's new Warden commanded it, Lena opened her eyes, and whispered, "I was too far away," before closing them again to oblivion.

He kissed her forehead as Farren hooted and Shaina wept with Belva. Happy tears. The best kind. He had no clue what Lena meant, but he did have an answer. "Never."

Lynn Vroman

CHAPTER 40

LENA

New Life

I woke up.

I didn't want to wake up.

Grit stung my eyes as my lids struggled to open. Once I managed, I tilted my head to the side–to find Tarek sitting on the floor, watching me.

"Welcome back." His pale face, with dark circles under his eyes, was the most beautiful face in the universe.

Maybe I died?

"Tarek?"

He pushed up from the ground and came to me. His big hands covered mine. "I'm here, love."

"But–" I tried to sit up, failing. "Am I alive? Are you?"

He brushed a kiss across my cheek. "I promised."

The straw from the bunk scratched any exposed skin, and sharp pain teased where the orb rested inside my arm. But none of that mattered. I closed my eyes against tears, and even though my body felt like lead, everything in me was alive–because Tarek was.

"Yosef said you were dead, all of you." I couldn't stop crying, my limp arms lifting, groping for him. I needed him closer, a connection deeper than bones and skin.

He pulled me up until I leaned against his chest, his strong arms steadying me. "No, everyone's fine–including Peter and Oren. Celeste…she's the new Warden."

"Thank God, thank Go–" Fear stole the relief and replaced it with adrenaline. I pushed myself from the bunk, wobbling on my feet. "We have to go. Belva… We have to get to her."

"Easy. She's safe."

I shook my head, trying to remember how to walk. "No, no, she's–"

He took my wrist and gently lifted my arm–that now had a puffy scar instead of a blinking orb. "Someone cut it out while you were–I thought I lost you, Lena." His voice broke. "I thought I was too late."

"I promised, too."

"Yes." His eyes never left the wound on my arm.

"And Yosef…?"

"Celeste took care of him." He wiped his eyes, a grin shadowing his face. "When you're stronger, I'll tell you everything."

I stood there, staring at him with my mouth hanging open. "Huh?"

Tarek guided me back to the bed. "Rest now." He lay beside me, his hand pressed to the small of my back, the heat from his touch soothing. "You have a little person to meet."

"What?"

His chest rumbled against my cheek. "Rest, Lena."

"How long have I rested already?"

"Two days."

An argument tipped my tongue. He needed to tell me everything.

No, he needed to keep me in his arms. "It's over now, isn't it? All over."

He massaged my back, quiet for a few moments. "Yes."

"Peter…did you give him a choice?"

"He said he loves you." He moved his hand from my back to clasp my hand. "The lines to Exemplar are locked, Lena. For good."

A small cut lacerated my heart. I'd never again experience Oren's cranky affection. And I'd never see my lanky boy. But… "He'll be happier."

He brought our joined hands to his lips and kissed my fingers. "We all will be, from now on."

∞ ∞ ∞

I had never held new life in my hands. But holding Willamina, Arcus's Warden, caused courage, hope, love, and so many other perfect emotions to course through my body.

She was the future, a new, beautiful beginning to a universe that needed it. I needed it.

Belva lay asleep on her bed, exhausted and gorgeous as I sat in the single chair in the room. It took a ton of begging on my part to convince Farren to let me have private time with his little family, but this would be the last time I saw my goddaughter and best friend for a while.

Tarek and I had to go home.

We had a life to live.

A soft knock invaded the cabin before Tarek walked in, clean and fresh from a bath in the river. My heart hurt, it grew so big.

"Hi," he said, his soft voice not waking Belva or Willa.

Every time–every single time–I heard his voice, saw his face, tears filled my eyes. Finally.

Finally.

"Hi, yourself."

Tarek smiled in Belva's direction before his silent footsteps brought him to me. His long finger stroked Willa's cheek. "I can never give this to you."

"I have all I need."

He bent to kiss me. "I hope it's enough."

Farren came in before I had the chance to bring his lips back to mine, missing the touch already. "All right, not in front of my kid." He scooped Willa from my arms, his big body almost engulfing the tiny Warden. He slid a thumb over the infant's cap of red hair, pure love glowing on his face.

I stood, going to my giant. "Farren? It's time."

He lifted his head. "You say all your goodbyes?"

No tears. None. "Ah, yeah, yes. But we'll be back–and with Zander and Erin. They'll want to see our new Warden."

He leaned down to kiss his daughter's cheek. Without looking at me, he said, "Don't think I'm saying goodbye. How about, 'see you soon'?"

I left Tarek and wrapped my arms around my brother and his daughter. "I'll take it."

"You better." Farren nodded to Tarek when I moved away, patting Willa's bottom. "Take care of her, brother."

"And you yours." Tarek clapped Farren's shoulder. "Two women–you have your hands full."

Farren beamed. "Hell, yes, I do."

We made it outside to hear the reverent hums of squid surrounding the village, patiently waiting for another glimpse of their Warden. Beautiful. I'd miss this place, the wildness of it. But I'd be back. My family lived here, after all.

Tarek kissed me, and then he wrapped an arm around my waist. His eyes glittered like silver stars. "I love you."

I smoothed a finger over the coarse hair on his cheek. Mine. Forever. "Love you, too."

He smiled, giving me his dimples. "Good. Let's go home."

E<small>PILOGUE</small>

REBORN

Empyrean, 120 Years Later…

She assessed the wares, running her hands across smooth surfaces and shining jewels. So beautiful, and she could only choose one. Her seventeenth birthday, a day she had anticipated for far too long.

Her mother touched her shoulder. "Have you chosen?"

"Why must I have only one? They're all so beautiful." Lena beamed at the vendor, and his chest puffed with pride. It wasn't every day when the Warden and her daughter shopped in the market.

"Because you will not be greedy. A ruler–"

"Sacrifices for those she rules and does not covet material things." She grinned at her mother, picking a brooch from the table. "Just one."

Her mother held her hand out for the piece, a smile lighting her ethereal face. "Such sass, my love." She winked. "So much like your namesake."

"So you have said, time and again." Lena nodded to the brooch her mother now inspected. "What of that one?"

"It's quite gorgeous. The emerald matches your eyes." She handed the jewelry to the proud vendor. "We'll take this one, please."

He held up his hands, awe on his dark face. "Oh, no, Teenesee, your presence is payment enough."

"Nonsense." She pulled her purse from her belt and handed him a coin. "We thank you."

Lena pinned the brooch to her robes, already in love with the way the sun glinted off the jewels. "Thank you, Mother." She curtsied to the vendor. "And to you, kind sir."

His large body swept into a graceful bow. "The pleasure is mine, mistress."

They walked the market for a spell, admiring robes and ceramic pottery, eating food fresh from ovens. As they sauntered down the cobblestone street, Lena pointed to a couple of men arguing. "Look, by the bridge."

Teenesee sighed with a look a mother would give her dueling toddlers. "Stay here. I'll be back soon."

Lena grinned. Her mother, the great Warden of Empyrean, reduced to separating disgruntled brutes. It was not the first time, nor would it be the last. She drifted to a robes vendor and sorted through hanging fabrics, enjoying the way the silks felt against her fingers.

"I knew I would find you."

Her fingers stilled. She turned–and had to crane her neck only to discover eyes the color of polished steel. "Pardon?"

The boy smiled, dimples indenting his cheeks. "I saw you, last night standing on the balcony of Teenesee's keep." Before she could stop him, he tucked a flying strand of hair behind her ear. "The most beautiful sight I've ever seen, like an angel."

Lena held up her chin, trying to act regal in spite of the swirling dips in her stomach. "Do you always speak so brusquely to ladies you first meet?"

His dimples deepened. "Only you."

"I–"

"Boy! It's time to go. Stop harassing that poor girl."

They both turned to a stout woman with unruly dark curls framing her pudgy face, her hands planted on ample hips.

Lena took the boy's hand, and tingling rode up her arm. "Who is that?"

"My mother." He brought her hand to his lips and brushed them across her knuckles before backing away. "I have to go, but I'll see you again, soon. I promise you."

"Wait!"

The boy left, leaving her with a hand burning from his touch.

Once Teenesee returned, Lena pointed to the robust woman and her tall, lanky son. "Do you know them, Mother?"

Teenesee's gaze followed the path of Lena's finger with a knowing smile. "Why do ask, child?"

"He…he came to me." She rubbed her knuckles. "He said the strangest things."

Her mother's tinkling laughter caused everyone around them to stare in adoration. She laced her arm through Lena's and moved toward the boy with silver eyes and his mother. "Come. I want to introduce you."

THE END

If you enjoyed The Energy Series please leave a review!

Lynn Vroman

GLOSSARY

Arcus- A world depleted of humans, with an evolution that falls behind many others. This world's highest evolved species is giant tree squid. Also, the vivid color permeating the world is "contagious" and transmits to those humans who happen to go there.

Contego suit- An Exemplian uniform that protects from dangers found in all the worlds.

Cycle- Each life a person lives is considered a cycle.

Desis- A common language spoken in many worlds, including Earth.

Dimensions/Worlds- Dimensions are worlds connected to each other with dimension lines. Each dimension is in a different stage of evolution, with some more advanced than others.

Dimension lines- Intangible lines, akin to electrical currents, separating each world. Only Protectors have the ability to open these lines to other worlds. In some cases, when a

Warden is strong enough, the lines can be bled between worlds, or erased, for short periods of time.

Empyrean- A world more evolved than Earth but not as advanced as Exemplar. The villages float over lush fields and streams. This world is as close to utopian as possible.

Energy- The soul

Exemplar- A world that is more evolved than any other world known. Humans from this world are more advanced, as well. Exemplar is responsible for manipulating the energy circulation throughout the entire universe. Only the most "privileged" energy is brought to Exemplar to live a cycle.

Guide- An advanced person from Exemplar who has the ability to read energies and transport them to other worlds. Also, their energies are able to leave their corporeal form and travel to other dimensions. Some are more advanced than others, depending on how many cycles they have lived in Exemplar.

Pairing- The act of one Guide and one Protector being matched together in Exemplar. The Pairing helps Protectors know if their Guides are in danger.

Protector- An advanced person from Exemplar who has the telekinetic ability to open lines between worlds. They are able to travel across world lines in their corporeal form, unlike Guides. Their duty is to protect Guides as they collect energy from other worlds. As with Guides, some Protectors are more advanced than others, depending on how many cycles they have lived in Exemplar.

Synod- Exemplar's governing branch

Synod authority- Exemplar's army

Tainted- 1. (n) An Exemplian traitor

About the Author

Lynn Vroman

Born in Pennsylvania, Lynn spent most of her childhood, especially during math class, daydreaming. The main result that came from honing her imagination skills was brilliantly failing algebra. Today, she still spends an obscene amount of time in her head, only now she writes down all the cool stuff.

With a degree in English Literature, Lynn used college as an excuse to read for four years straight. She lives in the Pocono Mountains with her husband, raising the four most incredible human beings on the planet. She writes young adult novels, both fantasy and contemporary.

OTHER WORKS

BY LYNN VROMAN

Young Adult Contemporary Romance

Macy Diaz has managed childhood friend Jeb Porter's crush for years. However, his infatuation turns to obsession, even putting a kid in the hospital just for hitting on her. In the past, Macy brushed it off, explained his bizarre acts away. But now she harbors a secret. She's in love…with Jeb's sister, Rachel.

By some miracle, Rachel loves Macy back, and despite the small minds polluting their sleepy southern town, they're sticking together. Unfortunately, making sure Jeb never grows suspicious proves harder every day—until everything falls apart.

As a sick, unstable Jeb starts to threaten all Macy values, she is reminded of what has always been perfectly clear. Macy belongs to him, only him, and he won't let her go. Ever.

If only Macy could've loved Jeb, she wouldn't have to worry about surviving him now.